ALSO BY CARRIE BROWN

The Last First Day

The Rope Walk

Confinement

The Hatbox Baby

The House on Belle Isle and Other Stories

Lamb in Love

Rose's Garden

THE
Stargazer's
Sister

THE

Stargazer's
Sister

Carrie Brown

Pantheon Books, New York

All rights reserved. Published in the United States by
Pantheon Books, a division of Penguin Random House LLC,
New York, and distributed in Canada by Random House of Canada,
a division of Penguin Random House Canada Ltd., Toronto.

Pantheon Books and the colophon are registered trademarks
of Penguin Random House LLC.

Library of Congress Cataloging-in-Publication Data
Brown, Carrie, [date]
The stargazer's sister : a novel / Carrie Brown.
pages ;   cm
ISBN 978-0-8041-9793-9 (hardcover : acid-free paper).
ISBN 978-0-8041-9794-6 (eBook).
1. Herschel, Caroline Lucretia, 1750–1848—Fiction. 2. Women
astronomers—Great Britain—Fiction. 3. Herschel, William,
1738–1822—Fiction. 4. Astronomers—Great Britain—Fiction.
5. Brothers and sisters—Fiction. I. Title
PS3552.R68529873 2016   813'.54—dc23   2015014806

www.pantheonbooks.com

Jacket image: *Portrait of a Gentlewoman* by Bonito Giuseppe
(detail). Mondadori Portfolio/Getty Images
Jacket design by Oliver Munday

Printed in the United States of America

First Edition
2 4 6 8 9 7 5 3 1

To Jennifer
And to the Bear Tamers
And to John, as ever, as always

Though my soul may set in darkness,
it will rise in perfect light;
I have loved the stars too fondly
to be fearful of the night.

—SARAH WILLIAMS,
"The Old Astronomer"

Seeing is in some respect an art,
which must be learnt.

—SIR WILLIAM HERSCHEL

Contents

England 1788–1822

Lisbon 1823–1833

Hanover 1833–1848

Let Whatever Shines
Be Noted

The wind is with them, and she watches from the ship's rail as the hard places disappear, fortress and stony beach and the long humped quay at Hellevoetsluis, the church and bell tower reduced in minutes to dark notches on the horizon. It is Saturday, and the church bells were ringing as they came aboard—not the hour, thus either a wedding or a funeral, she thought—but she cannot hear them anymore. It happened quickly, William taking her hand and helping her into the little vessel which took them out to the packet boat some distance away at anchor. She looks back from the ship's deck now and realizes that for the first time in her life she is not standing on solid ground.

The afternoon is cool for August, shadows of clouds drifting over the land behind them, but as the ship moves farther from shore, a slant of sunlight falls from sky to ground, illuminating the row of painted houses facing the water. Glass in the windows flashes, pricks of light glinting along the vanishing quay in the dark afternoon.

She holds tight to the rail. She has dreamed about this departure, longed for it. Now she cannot look away from the glowing scene shrinking on the horizon, retreating from sight as if being tugged backward toward a void.

At last all definition is lost, beach and quay and houses and church and bell tower gone entirely. She no longer can make out the inlets leading into the marshes or the mouth of the river. An egret lifts from somewhere and can be seen for a moment, bright scrap against the tumult of dark clouds. She tries to keep the bird in sight, but finally it, too, disappears. Then there is only a thin black line on the horizon, barely visible, to suggest what they have left behind. When the line vanishes completely, she feels her stomach constrict. She has to remind herself: it is not that the land has slipped off the edge of the planet and into the void, though that is definitely the impression.

Her mind *knows* the land is still there, but what she *feels* is its absence.

Bright shifting patterns wrinkle the sea's surface. Far out, floating patches of darkness, giant cloud shadows, roam over the water.

She turns to find her brother, but William has been absorbed among the passengers gathered at the rail.

Spray from a wave lands on her face and hands, startling with its cold, and Lina laughs even as she wipes her eyes. A woman beside her turns and gives her a questioning look.

ON THE POST WAGON YESTERDAY, the final day of their voyage toward the coast of Holland from the forested slopes surrounding Hanover, her black hat had blown off. The land had been flat and flooded in places with shallow water that reflected the sky, and she'd looked back to see her useless hat floating on a mirrored patch of cloud-strewn blue. A further weight had seemed to leave her.

William had closed his book and glanced behind them at the shimmering field. "Your hat," he'd said. "Shall I ask them to stop?"

"Oh! No," she'd said, trying not to smile.

With every kilometer between herself and the home she had

left behind, she'd felt lighter, as if soon she would float up off her seat.

William had shaken his head, puzzled, a brother amused by his sister's inexplicable amusement.

She had not told him this: sometimes during the years he had been away from home, she'd walked down to the river at the bottom of the orchard. She'd known that if she waded in, perhaps even only as far as her knees, her dress would have become too heavy for her to struggle back up the bank to safety. The current could be powerful, especially with snowmelt in early spring. Illness had weakened her, and she was not strong. She had never learned to swim, as her brothers had. A girl was not taught anything she could use to save herself in the larger world. She had frightened herself, staring at that river.

Finally she'd written to William in England. Two words: *Save me.*

In a postscript, to maintain her dignity, she'd added: *There is no one here with whom to converse anymore except the horse, and he has few opinions and a poor vocabulary with which to express them.*

It had been necessary to make it possible for William to understand her plea as lighthearted. She could not have borne it if he had refused a request made in earnest. Yet he had known. He had understood her. He would not disappoint her. He was sorry it had taken so long, he wrote by reply. He had been making plans. He had not forgotten her.

NOW, LESS THAN A year later, here they are, six days away from Hanover, six days away from her abandoned life. England's invisible shore beckons.

She will never return, she thinks. Nothing could ever make her return.

Waves close over the overlapping road of their wake.

William appears beside her, touches her shoulder. She turns.

They are sailing out from beneath the clouds, and the packet moves as if passing into another realm out of the shadows and into bright sunlight. She can actually watch the sharp edge of the clouds' darkness sliding along the deck from bow to stern, until at last they are free of it entirely.

The heat of the sun falls against her skin.

Again she has to wipe her cheeks. Well, these are tears, after all, and just as salty as the ocean. She knew they were there behind the laughter, tears for how awful it has been, all these years.

Her old life—and the life she always imagined would lie before her—is gone.

She turns away from what they have left behind.

She is twenty-two years old. Her brother William has set her free.

AT NIGHT ON THE COACH from Hanover, William had pointed out constellations: Pegasus rising, Corona Borealis—clearly visible—as well as Cygnus the Swan and Delphinus the Dolphin. She'd noticed that the stars were reflected in the darkness of the watery fields, too.

"Look," she'd said to him, pointing at the moon traveling along with them, sliding beside them from flooded pasture to flooded pasture, and he had smiled. She'd touched the medallion at her neck, a gift from William for their journey. Inscribed on it was the Royal Astronomical Society's motto. *Let whatever shines be noted.*

Now, standing beside her at the ship's rail, her brother glances down at her as if feeling her eyes on him.

"You're not afraid?" he says.

Everywhere she looks: water. She has a wild feeling—part terror, part elation—in her chest.

"Never," she says, lying.

She clings to the rail, makes a vow: nothing William might require of her will be too much. He has emancipated her. He has given her a *life*. She loves him beyond compassing. She would do anything for him.

William smiles. "Never?"

"Never," she repeats.

She will be equal to whatever lies ahead.

BELOWDECKS THAT NIGHT, the evening meal finished, the other passengers have retired or sit at the long table in the galley with Bibles or books or sewing, lamps swaying gently overhead.

It is late, near midnight. William has wanted to wait for the moonrise, which is late now, as the moon is waning and heading toward a crescent phase. She and William have climbed to the deck, and she waits while William bends to the telescope he has set up on its tripod on the deck, making adjustments. The sea is very calm, the water strangely flat, almost as if she could walk out onto its black surface. Around them, the night sky: resplendent, royally decorated, assemblies of stars stepping forth. For all that, though, it is the *darkness* she feels. Head tilted back, she senses it, the darkness somehow hurtling away—why does she feel it *moves?*—beyond the glittering domed ceiling.

She shivers in the cold.

An arm around her, William guides her to the telescope's eye-piece. "It's difficult to hold it steady on board," he says. "We're lucky for such a calm night. Still, this isn't the best circumstance for looking at the stars. You'll see enough, though. Something, anyway. But here you are now, the moon in partial phase, so you can see the detail a bit better."

It takes her a minute to realize what lies before her. The darkness of the night is gone, and the light filling her vision is the moon's immense ballast shifting impossibly near against her eye. It seems as if she could reach out her hand and touch it. She can't believe what she is seeing.

She staggers as a small swell runs beneath the ship. But the water had been so calm. She thinks of sea creatures, a whale moving below them, and the dizziness returns. William catches her, rights her against him. She manages to keep the moon in view, its mottled plain. She feels strangely as if she is being observed in return, seen as well as seeing.

"You have it?" William says.

Tenderness fills her. Here it is, the moon that has followed her everywhere through her childhood—racing between treetops to find her, darting over rooflines, appearing suddenly in the river at her feet or reflected in the barrel in the courtyard when she bent to rinse her face. Here is the *moon*—dear, distant companion—yet now intimately near and patient, kind, as if it has been waiting for her. Since childhood she has always thought of it as William's moon, as if he had invented it. Certainly she has always felt connected to him by it. Wherever they were, no matter how far apart, the same moon looked down on them.

"I have it," she says. "Yes."

She feels, foolishly, close to tears.

It is remarkable, what she can see with the telescope. "Are those . . . *mountains*?" she asks after a moment.

"And valleys. Perhaps forests," William says. "Perhaps other beings like or unlike us."

She looks up at him. *Forests* on that lonely, ashen plateau? Inhabitants on the moon?

"Perhaps they are looking at *you*, Lina," William says, as if he has read her mind. "Even as you are looking at *them*."

· · ·

THE NEXT DAY, a storm breaks out across the Channel. Lina can keep nothing in her stomach but a little water. The voyage lasts for two days of the ship's terrifying pitching and groaning, of horizontal rain and waves carved into chasms. Lina is moved to pity by the plight of a young mother with infant twins. The woman is too ill to care for her children, and with a servant equally ill. Lina fights off her own nausea to bring the babies to their mother for nursing, sees them in dry linens, lurches with them up and down the plunging passageway belowdecks, the babies bawling in her ear.

Finally they arrive in Yarmouth.

The packet has lost a main and one of its masts.

The ship drops anchor in the harbor. Lina stands on deck, holding one of the babies. She scans the green shoreline. A dozen or more ships are moored in the harbor, a forest of tilting masts. The water is calm, the sky a pale, exhausted blue. It feels to her nothing short of a miracle that they have survived.

Men in rowboats advance toward them to ferry them to shore. She kisses the baby she's been holding, returns it to the nurse, and takes the other twin, the little girl, who has fared poorly during the voyage and is listless now. The infants' mother is hollow-eyed, her hair dull, smelling of milk and sick. Lina kisses the little girl. The little boy cried for hours during the worst of the storm, but he kept down what milk he took. Lina wishes his sister had similar strength.

She and William are separated as the passengers are sorted to climb down to the rowboats. The nurse and Lina each hold a baby. The mother, moaning with fear, is installed on another boat. Under her black bonnet, her face is white. Lina watches as her boat moves away, the woman turning to try to keep them in sight.

On the plank seat, Lina sits upright, uses one hand to grip the side of the little boat, with the other holding the baby tight against her chest. A sailor takes up the oars, and their craft threads a path through the ships towering above them.

When they approach a clear section of stony sand, other men wade out from shore to carry the women and children through the final feet of surf. Hands reach out, and she passes the infant over to someone. The baby makes a feeble mewl of protest.

A big man stands thigh deep in the water next to her side of the rowboat. He holds out his arms to her.

"Up we go, darling," he says. "Before the next wave comes in."

And then there is the sensation of being lifted by him, plucked from her seat on the boat. In a minute she is over his shoulder—just as she had held the baby—her breasts and belly pressed against him, his arm cupped under her backside, one hand between her shoulder blades. She gives a little scream, presses her hand to her mouth. She feels him laughing beneath her. Gulls careen over their heads, screaming. A wave rolls in past them; she tastes salt.

When he sets her down some distance up on the shingle, she staggers. The hem of her dress is soaked.

She is aware of their sudden separation, the loss of her body held against his in that way. She has never been that close to a man, never been held like that. She had felt the muscles of his arm beneath her buttocks, her breasts pressed against his shoulder.

"Steady." The man reaches out to catch her arm. "All right?"

His hands hold her.

He is laughing, brown eyes laughing. "You're a tiny thing," he says. "I thought you were a child. I wouldn't have held you so, miss."

He lets go of her, lifts his cap, and wipes his face with an arm.

She thinks: I will never see him again.

He is smiling. "Welcome to England."

And then he turns away, disappearing into the crowd, wading back into the sea that laps the continent islands of the planet. Somewhere is her brother. She stands still, waiting for him to find her.

Hanover
1755–1772

ONE

Victory

•◆•

Bleak November, the intervals of sunlight briefer each day. The season's dwindling light and early darkness, as if something big leans its shadow against the house, oppresses her. She is five years old, happier in summer, with its long days and fleets of yellow butterflies in the tall grass.

Sleet sounds now against the shingles. In the narrow orchard running down to the river, a banked fire of branches broken by the ice has smoldered through the night. The ground is muddy, streaked with snow. From the kitchen window, Lina follows the bright shapes of the copper-colored bantams wandering among the bare trees in the morning light and pecking at the windfall of rotting apples. Clusters of sparks from the bonfire draft upward, a solitary line of smoke against the gray sky. She watches the bantams, heads to the ground, proceed in the cold mist like a line of orange fire down through the orchard toward the river. Flocks of blackbirds contract over the fields on the far shore, looking for gleanings.

It is early, the moon still visible in the morning sky. William, who is almost seventeen and knows everything about the world, says creatures live on the moon and even on the sun. They live on every planet, in fact, he tells her, but they need very big heads to withstand the force of the atmosphere. She has tried to imagine such creatures. The fat priest has a big head, but Lina shrinks from him, towering in his dirty chasuble and his long black linen *messe-shirt* that smells of his sweat. His head is lumpy as a turnip, his nose covered with greasy boils. From the wide opening of his sleeve, like a dark mouth leading toward secret, unpleasant regions of his body, his hand emerges to bless her when she and her family attend church. She tries to resist the impulse to shy away under his palm when it approaches, but she fails and earns a slap from her mother. Still, she does not want that hand to touch her.

The moon people—the Lunarians, William tells her—do not look like the priest.

In the margins of her father's sheet music, she draws pictures of these Lunarians, giants with long slender legs and faces calm as lakes. She gives these pictures to William, folding them into tiny squares and leaving them in his books or the pockets of his coat, waiting and watching for him to find them. In her mind, the moon creatures have shining tonsures and long eyelashes like those of the gentle horse that occupies the stable. They wag their heavy heads in contemplative agreement with all they see. Soothed by the singing of the stars, they are pleased by everything.

"Excellent!" William says, smiling, unfolding one of her drawings. "It is exactly as I imagine them."

Now, kneeling on a stool by the cold window, she watches the moon fade as the day brightens by degrees. The bonfire's smoke rises into the morning light, carrying with it the sour must of rotting apples and the distant voices of the people in the street. She imagines the Lunarians inclining their ponderous heads from their high plane to look down and regard the earth. She imagines one of the bantams' flame-colored feathers rising lazily inside the smoke, the outstretched arm of the creature that slowly opens its hand, fingers unfurling, to receive it.

Snowflakes drift through the roof in the attic where she sleeps.

Sunlight falls through the chinks in summer. This morning the bedclothes wore a layer of frost. She feels the unhappiness of the house around her, her mother's anger and silence like a presence in the room.

She will not be allowed outside to play, she knows.

She leaves her stool to kneel on a chair by the plain deal table closer to the fire and takes up a spoon, dipping it into a cup of water to fill the spoon's bowl. Recently William demonstrated for her the mysterious ability of liquid to exceed its space and yet fail to overflow its banks. She raises the brimming spoon to eye level, just as William did, to regard the miraculously curved surface of the water.

The phenomenon in the spoon, William told her, is convexity.

All her brothers—Jacob, William, and Alexander—are clever. All of them are scholars and musicians, but Lina knows that William is the most advanced of the three boys, though Jacob is older by four years. It is William, Lina understands, on whom their father rests his hopes for the family's glory.

The boys serve as bandsmen in the Hanoverian Foot Guards, where William's mind is wasted, their father frets to Lina, when the others are not around to hear.

William is our genius, he confides.

Lina knows that there is a war, the rulers of England and Prussia and Austria and France in conflict over who will have dominion where. She understands that her family and their neighbors' loyalties are to the King of England, as he is elector of Hanover. They all hate the French and must defend the English crown.

William shows her faraway England on a map. She is surprised that it is only a little island, a hunched-over old woman with a beaked nose.

Not even twenty years old, their father laments, yet surely William will be killed in battle.

"Such a loss to the world," their father says, as if it has already happened. "Our good, *good* William. Struck down too young."

Lina hates it when he speaks in this manner.

WILLIAM TEACHES LINA THINGS. For instance: convexity. Also animalcules.

A drop of water, William had explained—indeed, all matter in the world—his composed of many tiny particles called atoms, invisible to the naked eye. They cling together even without the reinforcement of walls.

"It's true," he'd said, studying her face.

He'd put his cheek beside hers. Together they had gazed at the bulge of water in a spoon.

"That little swell in the water's surface?" he'd said. "That's a heap of atoms, all of them piled on top of each other. Atom is from the Greek *atomos,* meaning indivisible. Everything may be divided *except* an atom."

"It is the smallest thing there is?" she had asked.

"Exactly."

He's told her, too, about Galileo's instruments of magnification—his telescope, his *occhiolino,* his little eye, as he called it—and about the Dutchman Anton van Leeuwenhoek's microscopes, in which were revealed scores of little swimmers. William had given her van Leeuwenhoek's word for them: animalcules. They reside in every drop of pond water, William had said, every human tear, in human spittle and blood and mold on a loaf of bread and in the living green of leaves.

He had showed her pictures of van Leeuwenhoek's drawings.

She'd leaned over the table on her elbows to watch William turn the pages of the book.

Animalcules with little tails! Animalcules with tiny snouts and horns and even hair! How amazing that these creatures perambulate inside the substances that hold them prisoner—even inside her own body—by means of curling and uncurling themselves or twitching their hindquarters or swimming like eels and fish.

Lina had looked at her hand, made a fist, unfolded her fingers.

After this, when she follows the erratic paths of raindrops down the glass with her fingertip, she sees in every drop a city, its minarets and towers, its bustling populace.

It is from William that she understands the central mystery: worlds upon worlds exist in all things.

IT IS JACOB, THOUGH, not William, who is their mother's favorite. She praises the elegance of Jacob's face, his aquiline nose and finely arched eyebrows. But Jacob is hateful, and he likes to direct his malice toward Lina especially. He laughs as he administers secret pinches, fingers gripping her earlobe. She knows that the appearance of pain or fear or anger attracts him, and she has learned to empty her face of all expression when he is near. She has learned, too, to detect his hidden presence behind a door or a tree, waiting to frighten her.

It is William's example that Lina wants to follow, William whom Lina loves. William, their father says, is the philosopher king among them. He is the peacemaker, too, somehow holding himself apart from the unhappiness of their family, their mother's shrill anger, Jacob's cruelty. Only William is capable of creating harmony in the household, engaging her brothers and their father in discussions of science or mathematics. If William picks up the oboe or violin and begins to play, soon their father joins in, and then Alexander and even Jacob, too, who likes to show off.

Lina and Sophia, who is now twelve, are not given instruments, but Lina loves to listen from the stairs when her brothers and father play. From the first, it has been easy for her to hear the harmonic line. William plays familiar songs for her in parallel keys to demonstrate major and minor scales, the reason one song makes her cry while another makes her dance.

She loves music.

She also loves the placid horse with the drooping lower lip in the stable.

She loves the taste of the yellow apples and the scent of the orchard budding in spring.

She loves her father's foolish jesting, loves the sound of William's and Alexander's voices through the bedroom wall at night. They discuss theories of harmonic construction, questions of philosophy.

"These are complicated matters, Lina," William says, when she asks questions, but he teaches her to read, writes down words for her.

Calculus. Fluxion.

She loves William's eyes, which are very dark, almost black, and in which she can see herself reflected when she sits on his lap and holds his face between her hands and stares deep into his eyes. He is not like their father, though, with his ready sympathy, his cooing and tut-tutting and damp gaze and kisses. William does not offer himself to her as her father does. He does not pet her or comfort her. He is elusive in a way that draws her to him. He is always reading or thinking. It seems that with his thoughts alone he can exchange the unpleasantness of the world, the trouble in their household, for something better, finer. She tries to stay near him. If she is at his side, perhaps she, too, will be transported to a better place.

NOW, ON THIS COLD MORNING in the kitchen, Lina kneels on the chair, holding the spoon before her eyes as William has shown her. The light captured in the water's swaying surface sways a little, too.

Then, strangely—the swaying increases. She tries to hold the spoon steady, but it is her hand that is trembling, she realizes, and the arm attached to the hand. No, it is her whole body, and the chair on which she kneels!

A scattered mound of dry peas on the table jumps and dances as if dropped from an opened fist poised a half inch above the table's surface. In her mother's cup with the delicate blue rim, the tea shivers like the surface of the river when the wind blows. On the far wall, the tin plates on the dry sink begin to clatter.

Lina looks up in alarm.

There can be no explanation but this: the unseen particles of the world, the animalcules and atoms, are in revolt!

Drops from her spoon fall onto the table.

She rears back, expecting that from these drops hundreds of animalcules will spring forth, waving centipede legs and wagging their bumblebee heads.

The world as she knows it is about to fly apart, the secret life of all things revealed!

But nothing happens, except that the terrifying trembling intensifies. In the fireplace beside which her mother has bent to tend the kettle, the logs collapse suddenly as if by dark instruction. Sparks roar up the chimney, and a tide of embers erupts onto the hearth by her mother's feet with a dry sound like pebbles shifting. Lina sees her mother jump away from the red coals, groping for the mantel with one hand to steady herself, flattening a palm over her big belly.

She turns toward Lina. From her expression, Lina knows what her mother is thinking: Lina is somehow at fault.

But Lina is all the way across the room, terrified and wide-eyed on her chair.

She grips the table's edge. The rumbling runs from her fingers and up her arms and into her head and teeth. The peas scatter and fall to the floor. With her eyes she follows the teacup as it totters across the tabletop, a precarious half inch to go before it falls and shatters. She knows she should save the cup, but the chair rocks beneath her, and she cannot release her fingers from the table's edge. From the next room comes a violent musical chaos as the instruments tumble from their places against the wall: the violins, flutes, guitar, the little harp. A moment later the cup tilts over the table's edge and shatters with a sound like ice breaking.

From above them comes the crash of something heavy— a wardrobe falling? Pots sway from their iron hooks in the beams across the kitchen ceiling.

Lina cries out and puts her arms over her head.

But then, a moment later, the movement dies away. The peas roll to a stop. There is no further parliament of voices from the cups or the fire or the pots or the plates or the harp. Instead, in the fireplace and on the hearth, the thick carpet of fat red embers rustles quietly as if to say, *nothing here, nothing here, nothing here.* Harmless little new flames begin to raise their blue and white and gold hoods among the disarranged logs.

Lina looks out the window. Through the rippled glass she sees that the iron lid of the November sky remains locked in place. She can't see the moon, though. Perhaps it has been shaken loose from the sky, its collision with the earth the cause of the terrible shaking.

Except for the noise of the fire, there is silence in the room— silence everywhere, she realizes.

There is a taste of sick in her mouth.

Her mother has fallen to her knees on the floor, forehead and palms touching the bricks.

Lina scrambles to stand up on her chair. It seems somehow safer up there.

She suffers from what her father calls excesses of feeling, the

Überangst. He, too, is a fellow sufferer, he confides. Their nerves are too sensitive for this world and its rough treatment. They often have pains in their stomachs.

Now she claps her hands. She wants the world restored, and she wants to shatter the frightening quiet.

"Mama," she says. "Mama!"

Lina understands that when her father says she is a person of passionate feeling, he means it fondly, even admiringly. He is sympathetic. They are united in this weakness that is also somehow a sign of their refinement in the family. But when her brothers are wild, they are simply shooed outside, while if Lina so much as jumps from bench to floor in high spirits, her mother comes after her with a furious face and catches her by the apron strings, wrenching them hard to make her sit down. A girl is not supposed to demonstrate her feelings as a boy can.

When she is scolded, Lina runs outside and hides in the stable. She lies on the horse's back, her face in his mane. Against her cheek she feels the vibrations of his big teeth grinding as he tears at the hay in his stall. Her mind goes into a buzzing state in which she thinks of not her mother, not her mother, not her mother. Nothing.

Now she stands on the chair in the silent house. Her mother remains kneeling, forehead to the floor, her palms flat against the brick.

"Mama!" Lina says again. She claps her hands. *Mama, Mama, Mama!*

Slowly her mother rises, turns a stone face toward Lina.

Lina stops clapping. She sees what is coming, but she cannot prevent it.

In two strides her mother crosses the room and slaps her. Then she collapses on a chair, one hand on her belly, the other across her mouth, eyes closed, moaning.

Lina slips to the floor, her own gaze averted, her cheek burning. On her knees, she collects the scattered peas one by one. Then she crawls under the table and sits there cross-legged, the peas in her lap. These incidents when her mother strikes her fill Lina with anger—she wants to hit back, to claw and scratch, but knows she must not—and also a strange embarrassment and sadness. She does not look at her mother now.

Then voices are raised in the street. From under the table Lina watches her mother wipe her face and gather her bulk and cross the room to the door that leads to the courtyard, opening it a crack. Between her mother's feet, Lina sees the bantams outside rush the doorway and set up a clamor that joins the clamor of human voices. Cold air, bright and sharp with the smell of smoke, slides across the floor. Her mother's skirt disappears. Lina hears her quick footsteps cross the courtyard.

In the fireplace, the flames chuckle and murmur. The room is smoky, Lina realizes. Her eyes tear.

When the church bells begin to ring, bells in steeples all across Hanover, it seems, Lina does not know if the sound is one of celebration or warning. All the bells' voices raised together at once make a mighty noise. *We are here, we are here!* But alone under the table, she feels far away from whatever is taking place in the streets, joyful dancing or preparations to flee. Will someone remember to come get her, if everyone decides to leave? Will William run home from the parade grounds and find her here?

She thinks about the animalcules and atoms. Surely the shaking was the cause—or the result?—of their restlessness. The animalcules are everywhere, trapped in everything. She thinks of what would be left behind—only the empty skins of things?—if the animalcules finally broke their bonds and escaped. She imagines all the objects of the world collapsed, limp as discarded stockings.

William says that through careful investigation every natural mechanism in the world may be understood. On his example, Lina pokes the horse's fresh manure with a stick, observes the trapped steam rise into the cold air. She lies in the hayloft and watches the yellow dog give birth to a litter of pups, each in its wet blue sack. She fogs the window to see the damp flower of her breath bloom and contract against the glass.

She likes it when William takes her down to the river to show her his catch, the action of the trout's gills, its gaping mouth as he clenches the fish in his fist. He admires her collections, picking through the items with her when she takes him by the hand and shows them to him: beechnuts and sticky black walnuts, hawk and pigeon and chicken feathers, pretty pebbles. She keeps her things in the stable, wrapped in an old cloth so her mother will not sweep them up, complaining of Lina's filth. The forests around Hanover are rich with fallen nuts and gigantic ferns, their fronds nippled all over beneath her exploring fingers. The grass beside the river is filled with nests and sometimes eggs. If she could, she would stay out in those places all day.

Could one investigate the behavior of the animalcules now? If she had a microscope like van Leeuwenhoek, could she see what the animalcules are doing, chattering among themselves, perhaps, readying for another siege?

She feels both fear and relief when her mother returns after a few minutes. From under the table she watches her mother's advancing baby stomach and the movement of the broom as her mother sweeps up the shards of broken teacup. She listens as her mother sets the instruments to rights in the next room, as she goes heavily upstairs and then returns. Pieces of the brown bowl and ewer go past in her mother's arms. The door opens, and Lina hears the sound of broken crockery dumped on the rubbish heap in the courtyard.

Then her mother steps inside and closes the door.

"Caroline," her mother says. "Come out from under there."

Lina does not want another slap. She wishes her mother would take her and hold her against the mound of her stomach. Sometimes, if she plays at being a little goat, butting her mother gently, her mother will stroke her head.

She crawls out from under the table and approaches her mother, head down, and leans carefully against her apron. It, too, smells of smoke. Lina holds her breath as she puts her face to her mother's belly and mouths hello to the baby. She imagines its face turning in the darkness of their mother's womb toward her voice. She worries about the baby. She understands that there are too many Herschel children, Lina and Sophia and their three brothers, also a baby who came before Lina and died, and then another who came after her and died, and now this new baby who is almost here. Lina understands that God has put the baby in her mother's stomach. Therefore it is also God who makes her mother retch into a basin in the morning, and walk with a hand at her back, and who swells her mother's feet and ankles. Such suffering, she understands, is part of God's plan for women.

The last time there was a baby, Lina went to the stable, her hands over her ears, but she could still hear her mother's wailing. The last baby died. That was God's plan, too.

Sometimes her mother does the things mothers do. She combs Lina's hair with quiet hands, ties the strings of her apron, and buttons her dress in the back. But often if Lina tries to rest against her, as she does now, longing for her touch, her mother's fingertips push Lina away.

"Don't do that," her mother says now and steps away.

They are burdens. All the Herschel children are burdens to their mother.

"Say your prayers," her mother says. "God has protected us today."

Lina folds her hands and bows her head. But she is not praying.

Of course a tiny animalcule would be no match for God. God is the biggest thing there is. And God made everything, which must mean that he made the animalcules as well, and that therefore they must be under his dominion, just as she and all her brothers and her sister are under his dominion, even horrible Jacob. God sees everything, she understands, but that does not mean he is always available to hear your prayers and help you. He cannot be looking everywhere at once.

Perhaps the animalcules are like the good angels and the bad angels. William has told her about these, reading aloud to her from the poem called *Paradise Lost*. Perhaps there is always a battle raging under the surface of the world, just as the Foot Guards are always marching to and fro at the parade grounds, the men and boys in their red coats, piping and drumming and preparing to die.

A FEW DAYS LATER, William comes home with this news: he has met two vagabonds watering their horses at the post house. The men carried with them reports of the earthquake, an event so great in scale that it traveled over two thousand kilometers, William says, reaching places even as distant as Hanover. Despite everyone's fright that day, Hanover had received actually only the smallest of shocks, the quake's farthest ripple.

Even on the shores of North Africa, William tells their father and Jacob, who is also at home, the earthquake was felt.

An earthquake? Lina, sitting on the stairs, does not know what this is, but she will not say so.

William sits beside the fire to take off his boots.

It began in Portugal, he says, in the city of Lisbon. Because it was All Saints' Day, every candle on every altar had been lit. When the earthquake struck, flames engulfed the altar cloths in the churches and cathedrals, where the Catholic faithful were massed in number as on no other day of the year. Soon the whole city was in flames. People were buried beneath the collapsed buildings, crushed by the weight of timber and stone.

Their father closes his eyes. "It is a picture of hell," he says.

"That's not all," William says. "The earthquake was followed by a giant wave that rushed over the city from the river Tagus."

"I don't believe it," Jacob says. "A giant wave."

Lina sees their father drop his head into his hands.

William puts aside his boots and stares into the fire. He ignores Jacob.

"Despite the flood, the city is still smoking," William says. "Those who survived the devastation live now in tents pitched on the rubble. Flames still flare up in the ruins, the men said."

Lina is unable to be silent any longer.

"It was the animalcules?" she cries finally. "The bad animalcules?"

Her father looks between Lina and William. "What? What is she saying?"

Jacob laughs. "Stupid idiot," he says.

Lina slinks down the stairs, shamefaced. She understands that she is confused about something, that she has revealed her foolishness.

"Lina," William says. He tries to catch her skirt as she goes past him, but she shrugs away his hand and runs to the stable.

She presses her forehead to the horse's flank.

It was not the moon falling from the sky, for she has watched for it every night and seen it rise as usual. And it was not the animalcules, she sees now.

It was *God* who moved the earth, who buried everyone under the fallen churches. She thinks of the people in tents, their dead below them. In her heart is the *Überangst*, her sad state of affairs. *Eine traurige Sache.*

A cart rumbles past the courtyard; she can tell by the sound that its load is heavy, wood or coffins or manure. The stench of the pigs in their neighbor's courtyard is vile, strong in the cold air. The familiar knot of worry forms in her stomach.

When her mother calls her from the house, Lina kisses the horse again and again on its nose, but she leaves the stable. She does not want a whipping.

When she goes inside, she is glad to see that Jacob has gone away. Only William and her father remain in the big room before the fire. Her father says her name and she goes to him, head hanging.

He takes her onto his lap. "Perhaps do not always tell her so much," he says to William over her head.

William gets up and crouches before her. She curls away from him, pressing her face against their father.

"We do not understand what causes an earthquake," William says. "Some great instability within the earth, of course, but it is not the animalcules."

She is silent, listening.

"They are . . . *like* creatures," William says, "but they are forever trapped inside the things that contain them . . . because they *are* the things. Things do not exist without them. Do you understand?"

She does not.

"Can we *see* them?" she says, speaking into her father's chest.

"One day you will," William says. "One day we will have a microscope and a telescope and then everything will be revealed to us."

She keeps her face turned away from his.

"Why would *God* kill all the people?" she asks.

She feels her father's hand, which has been stroking her hair, stop. She knows that William and her father are looking at each other.

"God is not responsible *in that way*," William says. "It is difficult to understand, I know."

No one speaks. Lina listens to the sounds of the fire.

Then William says: "A great philosopher tells us that we live in the best of all possible worlds," he says. "*Beste aller möglichen Welten.* There is suffering, yes, but it does not mean God *intends* us to suffer."

He is silent for a moment. Then he says: "God intends for us to *triumph* over suffering, to come to know his great creation as fully as we can."

"But *why* should there be suffering?" she asks. "Why not only happiness?"

Again William hesitates.

"To teach us to be kind," he says at last. "To teach us to be better than our human instincts might prompt us to be. To bring us into closer knowledge of God."

Her father pats her back, but he says nothing.

She thinks of Jacob. She does not think the earthquake will make Jacob kinder.

"You'll see," William says. "The people of Lisbon will rebuild their city. One day it will be more beautiful than ever."

She closes her eyes and leans against her father. His heartbeat is faint in her ear. She concentrates on it. She does not want to listen to any more of William's explanations.

But he understands her, anyway.

"Think of everything you love, Lina," he says. "God made all of that, too. Don't be afraid."

"I'm not," she says, but she keeps her eyes closed, her ear against her father's heartbeat.

THE NEXT MORNING, William takes her to the esplanade in Hanover to see Winged Victory, who toppled from her perch on her high pedestal during the earthquake.

Wouldn't she like to see Victory's face up close?

In the esplanade, fallen Victory's face is beautiful, Lina thinks, but her eyes are disturbingly empty, like the eyes of the blind knife sharpener, his thumb made of leather, who walks the streets with his cart to collect the knives and hatchets.

Victory's head has been cracked open on one side, her nose chipped. One green wing has broken off and lies severed in the grass. On the ground the wing is so much larger than Lina could have imagined, an angel's massive wing fallen from heaven.

She kneels and puts her hand to it, strokes the cold feathers. She looks up to the top of the empty pedestal. She knows that Victory has only fallen from her high perch. But where *are* the angels? Where *is* God?

She has understood from William that the stars do not go away during the day; they are still up there, burning and burning into eternity, only they cannot be seen when the sun is shining and the sky is bright. It has to do with the rotations of the earth and the sun and moon, William says, everything rolling in the sea of the sky in separate orbits.

He has drawn pictures for her, shown her how the earth revolves around the sun, how each planet itself spins on a fixed path. He's shown her the positions of the moon and the sun, the orbit of the earth, drawing pictures with dotted lines.

He has explained—drawing arrows from the moon to the earth, earth to the sun—that when it is daylight on their side of the world, everyone on the other side of the earth is in darkness.

"Their night is our day," he says.

"Upside down?" Lina says. "Hanging on by their feet?"

"No, it is not like that," he says. "It is difficult to explain. But think. At night, you are just as you are now. You are not upside down."

She shakes her head. It is too confusing.

"How far does the sky go?" she asks him as they gaze down at Victory.

"The universe," William says. He looks up at Victory's empty pedestal. "We don't know," he says. "Far."

Lina takes his hand and makes him stroke Victory's wing with her.

"Where *do* the angels live?" she asks. "And God? Heaven is above the planets?"

About God and the angels William has no immediate reply.

"God is in another . . . realm," he says finally.

Lina looks at Victory's ruined face. Perhaps the angels look like Victory.

"We will see God when we die," she says.

"Yes," William agrees.

Together they look down on Victory's shattered wing.

Lina is not sure she wants to see God. She does not like the priest, and why would God have a servant who is so unpleasant and ugly? All God's angels except Satan are supposed to be very beautiful, like Raphael and Michael in *Paradise Lost*.

But God also made the horse and the orchard and—suddenly she looks up at him, marveling—he made *William*.

And he made her.

"Truly," William says, looking at Victory. "The mystery deepens, the more I know."

• • •

MANY YEARS LATER, when she is an old woman and has returned to Hanover after a long absence, she will see Victory again.

She will stop on the esplanade late on a winter afternoon, leaning on her stick and gazing up at Victory restored to her pedestal, her blind eyes gazing into the distance.

So much about the world will have changed by then—everything, in a way. It will seem strange to Lina that Victory still stands, her great wings flexed as if she is prepared to leap into the sky.

Ageless, heroic Victory will wear a foolish little cap of snow.

Lina will remember her childhood, remember the earthquake, remember when she and William stood at the side of the fallen statue and touched her cold wings.

She will remember her sense that day that mystery had been all around them.

As she stands there, an old woman looking up at old Victory, a pigeon will alight on Victory's shoulder, ruffle its feathers, and settle down as if to sleep.

Though it is cold, Lina will stand with Victory for a long time, until the square has emptied, waiting for darkness and the sight of the night's first stars.

They had dwelt always in that mystery, she and William. He had led her there. That, at least, had never changed.

TWO

Moon

On a cold morning in early spring, the Herschel family gathers in the courtyard with the wooden bucket and the broom and the bantams and the evil Hamburg rooster, who eyes Lina from his perch atop the bench by the door and rushes to peck her feet, if given the chance. The thaw has begun, but the air is bitterly damp. In the courtyard, a shelf of wet brown smoke hovers. That morning, a fat black cinder dropped onto the stones at Lina's feet. When she touched it with the toe of her boot, it fell apart to expose its glowing heart, bright against the gray stones.

It is three years since the earthquake; Lina is eight years old. Sometimes this winter she has been allowed to go by herself to stand bundled up on the wall of the *Stadtgraben* in the early evening dusk, watching the other children dart over the frozen ditches on their skates. The air smells of snow and of the tangle of frozen rushes hanging on at the edge of the *Leinestrom*, of the icy fields beyond, of the cloud breath from the horses pulling sleighs. When she puts her hands over her cheeks to keep them warm, the smell of the courtyard smoke clings to the damp wool of her mittens.

She is often ill, and she is not allowed to skate, as the boys are. She is considered too weak for sport or gaiety, though not for work about the house.

In the courtyard now, as she waits with her father and brothers and Sophia, her feet ache. The cold air stings her nose, and the smoke makes her throat burn and her eyes stream. Inside the stable attached to the courtyard, the horse strikes the wall of his stall with his hoof, making his lonely, prisoner sound, which is what he does when he is bored. He stops for a moment and then begins again, rhythmically knocking. When Lina cleans his stall, she crouches under the roof of his belly with the long hair and puts her ear to the shining pile of his thick coat, listening to the rumbling business inside him. He stands planted as if his feet are made of stone, and she strokes his silky legs. William has taught her the secret way to run her fingers down the horse's fetlock, so that he will lift his heavy hoof for her as if it were magically light as air.

It is rare that all the Herschel siblings are together, but William has organized them for this important occasion. He has dragged a wooden tub into the center of the courtyard and filled it from the well. Sophia, her hair in a long plait wound around her head in a new, adult way, is very pretty. She has been away for several months, helping their uncle at his farm and vineyard, caring for their little cousins since their mother's death. When Sophia has undressed in their old bedroom on the last two nights, Lina has stolen glances at the pear-shaped weights of Sophia's breasts, the speckled vee of wiry hair between her legs, the cello shape of her hips and her waist. It seems impossible to Lina that she will ever grow up to look as Sophia does.

William stands next to their father. Beside their father's aspect of ill health—his sunken cheeks and dull skin and damp hairline—William, at nineteen, seems like a different creature altogether. When he picks her up and lifts her to his shoulders, she feels the strength in his arms. William's heart, she thinks, is big like the horse's heart.

Alexander is beside William, holding little Dietrich by the hand. Alexander, who is twelve, admires William, as Lina and their father do. She feels jealous of Alexander that he can go anywhere with William, while she must stay at home. But Alexander is good to her, at least. He shows her fingerings on his violin. He helps her in the kitchen when their mother does not see.

Bad, dark-faced Jacob prowls the perimeter, scowling and dragging his feet. The day before he had wrenched her arm because of his knife being unclean at dinner, though she could see nothing on it. Her father had intervened, going to his chair by the fire afterward, his hand over his eyes.

"They should've drowned you in a bucket," Jacob had told her.

"That's enough," their father had said from his chair. "For pity's sake."

Later that evening, when William went outside, Lina had followed him.

She'd stood before him where he sat on the bench, looking up at the stars. He'd had a book with him.

"Jacob wishes I were dead," she had said.

William had put aside his book. He'd held out his hand and pulled her down beside him on the bench.

"Look up," he'd said. "Aren't the stars beautiful?"

She hadn't said anything.

"Jacob has an ugly thing crouching inside him," William had said. "I told you not to look at him."

"I can't *not* look at him," she'd said, and even as she said it, she'd felt the way Jacob's presence in a room made her heart race. He seems to *compel* her to look at him.

"My *eyes* go there," she'd said.

William had said nothing further, his gaze on the stars.

"He is the *oldest,*" she'd said. "He should know better."

"You will not change him," William had said. "Make your mind think of other things."

Lina had leaned against him.

"Look," William had said again, nudging her with his shoulder. "Did you ever see anything as beautiful as the stars?"

TODAY WILLIAM HAS BEEN PREPARING for what he calls the surprise. They have been told by William that they cannot look at the tub yet, that to look directly at the sun's reflection in the water is impossible. It is too bright for their eyes. He will tell them when it is safe to look. There is a feeling of strangeness, even dread in the air. The horse knocks and knocks in his cell. Birds fly back and forth in restless flocks, settling for a moment and then lifting off again in inky swarms that swerve across the sky. Lina cannot help herself and glances at the tub, but she sees only wavering shapes on the water's swaying surface, a bright flash.

She presses closer to William. She is happy that their mother has not joined them outside this morning. Yet alongside her happiness at being near William, her anticipation of what will take place in the tub, is her pity for their servant girl, Hilda. They have had to leave Hilda weeping inside the house, for their mother forbade her to join them. Their mother cannot be responsible for their father's and William's madness, she says, and she will need someone's help, if the event that William says will come to pass truly occurs. Hilda is better than nothing.

Their mother is furious that none of them will stay with her.

"An eclipse puts you in no danger, Mama," William had told her, but she only sat rocking by the fire, her hand on her heart, and would not look at any of them.

Hilda had come to their household at their mother's insistence when Dietrich was born, even though their mother says all the time that they cannot afford her and that she eats too much. She is a slow-moving and slow-thinking girl with a cowlick in her yellow hair and a flat, low forehead and a smell like chicken soup under her arms. She took Sophia's place beside Lina in the girls' bed. Hilda likes to tickle. At night Lina lies stiffly, steeling herself against the creeping surprise of Hilda's fingers. Hilda is a relaxed sleeper, full of grand gestures, chuckling and muttering and farting and flinging her fat arms and legs. Yet often when Lina wakes, she is curled up against Hilda's warm side, a bit of the big girl's nightdress in her fist. Sometimes she wakes to find Hilda's soft, heavy thigh thrown over hers, or Hilda's arm draped over Lina's waist. Lina lies transfixed then, lifting a hand to touch Hilda's gold-colored hair, the spray of her braids coming unwound at night like hay from a stook.

Now, in the courtyard, her father rests his hand briefly on Lina's head. He consults William, deference in his voice. William is the authority on all things. Her father says that when William was just a tiny child he took apart the twelve-hour clock and caused the cuckoo to fly out of the door over and over again.

Recently William has made her a gift of his four-inch globe. Lina likes to run her finger over the lines of the ecliptic and the equator, which he had incised with his knife.

Standing in the courtyard she feels the excitement of William and Alexander and her father. Nothing has happened yet, but already the day has been unusual, like a solemn celebration. Now the birds have quieted. All around them, the streets have become silent, except for the sudden distressed braying of a donkey nearby, and the horse's increasingly agitated knocking against the walls of his stall.

Lina moves closer to William.

"It's beginning," he says.

Lina reaches out to take William's hand, but Jacob grabs her wrist and twists her arm.

He makes a hideous face at her. "You'll be in the way!"

"Stop it," William says, and takes Lina's hand.

A cool dimness slides across the courtyard. Her father breathes hard, wheezing. Again and again he likes to tell the story of lying all night with the Hanoverian troops in a field soaked with rain, of his terrible position in a ditch, one ear underwater until dawn, his mind full of terror, his lungs gripped with damp. Afterward he was held for a time in a makeshift French prison camp, where he nearly starved to death. He always says he has not been the same since, but Lina can neither remember nor imagine him other than what he is now: often alone before the fire, playing slow, sad music on the violin. He is teary-eyed, stuttering, kindly, sometimes shouting but always, later, apologetic, begging for kisses.

William leans forward over the tub, and then he looks away, blinking.

"We still can't look at it," William says. "Amazing that it should be so bright. But in a drawing, I have seen how it occurs— the sun is gradually blackened by the solid body of the moon, passing across the face of the sun." He looks down at Lina. "Do you understand? The moon is moving between earth and the sun," he says quietly. "It's a very rare occurrence. We're in an excellent place from which to see it. And the weather is perfect, just enough haze. Were the air any clearer, we could not see the eclipse at all."

The courtyard is where Lina helps her mother scald the sheets and raise their impossible, dripping bulk, where she scrubs the knives with brick dust, where she sweeps and coughs and still there is ash and dirt and sour white splatter from the chickens. In the mornings, the sky boils with smoke from the fires. It is difficult for her to think of it as an excellent place.

Lina feels their father tremble beside her. She knows that sometimes certain kinds of excitement—his *Überangst*—precede bouts of illness, of headaches and melancholy. On these occasions, he comes home and waves away her mother to stumble upstairs, falling onto the bed and drawing the quilts over his head, shutting himself away. Sometimes the spell lasts only a few hours, but sometimes it is days before he emerges, chastened and wanting sympathy, carrying downstairs the accumulated teacups and soup bowls Lina has brought to his bedside in secret, kneeling beside him and whispering to him where he lies with his head under the bedclothes: *Papa, Dietrich has learned to clap his hands. Papa, we have chestnuts.*

And then always her mother's fury and berating follow: she has had to turn away his music students, as well as the insulting concertmaster, who came with scores for Isaac to copy. They have no money. What does he expect her to do, how will she care for all these children?

The sun ceases to exist, her father repeats now. *Die Sonnenfinsternis.*

"It will not go away completely," William says. "It is only a partial eclipse."

An ominous feeling of cold creeps across the back of Lina's neck and head. It is the same sensation her mother's gaze gives her when she stares at Lina from across the room, a rage over something building inside her.

Lina gazes across the courtyard, waiting until William tells her they can look at the tub. The cart across the way, their neighbor the apothecary's dovecote on the high wall, the roof of the stable covered in silver lichen, all have diminished somehow in the strange dim light, moved farther away. Across the courtyard, the bantams are a rusty blur, cowering together under the bench outside the door. A little light blinks forth at her from one bird's eye and then goes out.

A pale kind of darkness has fallen, but it is not like a real night. Real night comes familiarly, by degrees of color in the sky as the sun falls, fire at the horizon and at the top of the wall, bursting over the rooftops and touching everything as it goes, shadows of buildings and trees and the broom handle stretching across the ground, even her own shadow like the silhouette of a giant.

This night is sunken, colorless, unfamiliar . . . twilight in the day.

"Now," William says, and they gather around the tub. "It is almost ninety percent covered." In the tub, the round sun has been pared away. Now it is only a thin, fragile rim of glowing light.

"Don't look up at it directly, either," William says suddenly. "It will burn your eyes."

Lina freezes, staring instead at the bricks of the courtyard floor.

If she does not look up, there is no reason to be afraid, she thinks. In fact, it is strange and thrilling, this transformed world, this eerie light, just as the earthquake was thrilling, even as it was terrifying. She risks a glance about her again, keeping her gaze low. She can still see the courtyard's walls, but as if through smoke. Everything seems less defined and clear, the broom and the ax and the hatchet. Even their house with their mother and Hilda in it.

And the dimness has spread over everything that lies beyond the courtyard, too: Hanover's narrow streets and squares, the statue of Victory restored atop her pedestal in the esplanade, the river and ditches and fields and black woods beyond, the castle on its hilltop. If she could clamber up onto the roof of the stable, what would she see? A strange world, half-lit.

But it does not last. William makes them look away again, tells them that the sun will return in the tub by swift degrees.

In minutes the ordinary day is restored.

Sound rises up from the streets. Church bells in the brick steeples begin to ring, just as they did after the earthquake. Outside the gate Lina hears the sound of children's laughter and shouting, their running feet. There is a feeling that they all have been spared a terrible fate. Yet she is sad that the eclipse is over. Pigs shove their snouts under the gate as they are herded past.

William steps away from the tub.

Everything is now as it had been before.

Jacob manages to give her a hard pinch as he goes away.

How long the restored day ahead seems to her now. Across the courtyard the rooster crows and keeps on crowing.

LATER THAT EVENING, when William leaves the house, she steals after him and finds him again in his accustomed place, seated on the bench in the courtyard. He is gazing up at the stars, but when he sees her, he beckons to her and wraps her up inside his cloak.

In Finland, he tells her, they call the Milky Way *Linnunrata*, the Birds' Way, where the spirits of everything that dies soar up and throng the road to heaven.

She looks up at the sky with him. She cannot make her mind encompass what lies above their heads, beyond the scrim of sour-smelling smoke that hangs over Hanover, especially when the weather is cold and damp. Yet she feels a pull toward the dark distance and the stars that she knows William feels, too. She *wants* to think about it. How deep is the sky, how far and how wide? How many stars? Do other people like themselves stand on their own planets and gaze out into the glittering distance? William says so. But how is it that they are all held aloft, suspended in these fixed orbits? There are things moving out there, she knows

from William, spiraling planets, strange winds bulging and shifting, darting stars that cross the near sky, falling comets . . . but
from where? And *to* where?

William has shown her that if she throws a pebble into the air,
it will reach its natural apex in midair and fall back to earth. She
knows as well that the mathematical formula by which the rise
and fall of objects may be predicted comes from the application
of Newton's Laws of Motion; William has shown her the equations. Yet still she struggles: *how exactly* is it that the earth and
moon and sun do not fall? What *is* gravity? And if the moon can
pass between the earth and the sun, what is to prevent them from
colliding one day?

Sometimes she stands in the orchard and closes her eyes and
tries to feel gravity, holding out her hands, palms up. Sometimes
she thinks she does feel it, an invisible weighted ball filling her
hands. But more often there is nothing, and her hands are simply
empty.

THREE

Night

Every year it seems to Lina that winter lasts longer. Snow falls for days at a time, and the streets below the castle are captured in a frozen hush. Few people venture into the icy streets. Firelight and candlelight and lantern light glow in the windows throughout the gray days that are almost as dark as night.

The coffin maker down the street is always busy, though. Lina can hear his shop ring with the sounds of saws and hammers striking nails from dawn to past dark.

In the orchard, the fruit trees are bound in ice. Smoke from the chimneys ascends into the light of the falling snow.

When they go to church, the only time Lina is allowed outside, she sees the fires glowing at night on the banks of the *Leinestrom*. In the winter twilight they look like the pink and yellow wax flowers that Sophia used to fashion.

At eleven, Lina is smaller and thinner than other children her age, a result of frequent illness. This winter she has been kept inside most of the time, even on milder days. She is no longer allowed to go and watch the others skate on the canal.

The house has been lonely. Alexander and William have been in England for months in service to King George to protect England from an invasion by the French, but Jacob has somehow contrived a discharge from the Foot Guards and has returned to

Hanover and taken up a position with the court orchestra. She wishes it were William who had been discharged, not Jacob.

Sometimes Jacob does not come home at night, and then their mother berates their father, who is sent out on fruitless forays to search for him, even though Jacob is now a grown man.

Jacob appears eventually in the mornings, foul-tempered, with his clothes torn and dirtied and sometimes bloodied.

One morning he storms into the house and frightens Hilda by throwing his filthy boots at her. When he sees Lina on her stool by the window, he grabs her and locks her head under his arm. He is laughing, but it is an awful laugh.

He will throw her outside and bury her headfirst in a snow-bank, he tells her. No one will find her until spring.

She bites him, hard enough to draw blood.

Hilda screeches.

Her mother rushes into the kitchen at the sound of the commotion.

As punishment, Lina is made to sit for the remainder of the day in a chair by the wall.

When her father comes home, he puts bread in her lap, secretly, but she will not eat it. She hides it under her apron for later. Tears stand in her eyes, but she tips her head back so they do not fall. She understands that her father's defense of her against her mother or against Jacob lacks authority.

Her father only sits before the fire with his hand over his eyes.

Hilda creeps into the room and brings him tea, throwing fearful glances at Lina, as if even to be caught looking at her is dangerous.

LINA IS GLAD FOR the evenings when Jacob is not at home. Then only she and Hilda and Dietrich—the baby born soon after the earthquake, now a six-year-old who speaks little and who has the slow, grave manner of an old man—are there, along with the newest baby, Leonard, who arrived safely three months ago and sleeps in his cradle by the fire. Leonard is already too big for the cradle, his head in its white cap bunched up against the spindles of the cradle like a goose's fat breast. Lina makes silly sounds, pretending to play the oboe—too-tee, too-ta!—that make Leonard laugh, a baby's chortle.

Lina and her father live for William's letters from England, his account of the regiments' travels, the books he buys to occupy him while he is with the Guards, the pamphlets he reads: John Locke's *Essay Concerning Human Understanding.* James Ferguson's *Astronomy Explained.* Robert Smith's *Harmonics.* He promises to bring these books to their father when the Guards return to Hanover. When she thinks of William in his uniform, a red coat—with a swallow's nest for the drummers—and straw yellow breeches, a sprig of oak leaf in his hat, she feels a mixture of pride and fear.

Finally at sunset on the day of her punishment for biting Jacob, Lina's mother allows her to leave her chair. The sky outside the window is black. The snow has ceased falling, at least for a time. When Lina stands, her head swims, and her knees ache.

She is given a bowl of soup to eat alone in the kitchen, and a basket of wool for knitting stockings when she finishes.

Her father eats his soup in front of the fire, sighing. His gray hair is like two untidy bees' nests sprouting from his head above each ear. He sits with his feet nearly touching the fire, transcribing scores on a lapboard. He was in the duke's orchestra for a time, and he played oboe in the Foot Guards, but now the music pupils who come to the house are his only source of income. Occasionally the music director who walks with a stick raps on the door, bringing him scores to be copied or transposed. Yet the work does not bring enough money, Lina knows. The house is filled with invisible anger flowing from her mother to her father, Jacob's temper like a slow-burning fire always in their midst. The slightest puff of wind, the slightest provocation, and a conflagration flares.

Jacob has left the house again after shouting at everyone that the soup tastes like mud.

Lina goes to sit on the stairs to do her knitting.

Dietrich has been put to bed. Leonard sleeps in his cradle. He is a sweet-tempered baby, and Lina likes to pick him up and hold him close and smell his baby smell.

Her mother has said enough schooling for Lina; she is too sickly. Maybe she can resume later. Meanwhile she can go nowhere and do nothing. Her only comfort now is Leonard and the rumor that the Hanoverian regiment is expected home any day.

Inside her she feels the familiar *Überangst*.

THE FIRE SPITS, sleet ticks against the window. Finally she is unable to sit any longer. She stands up on the stairs. The stockings hang down the steps emptily, her absent brother's phantom legs. She makes them dance a little. Then she begins in a quiet voice to sing. She sings "Spring Greeting." "Goodbye, Winter." "I Walk With My Lantern."

This year on Saint Martin's Day she was allowed to walk with the other children for the first time, caroling in the streets and carrying her own lantern. Food has been scarce for some months now, but for the feast day there were bonfires along the river and gingerbread men and roast goose, its delicious crackling skin. The castle on the hilltop was lit with a thousand candles.

Now she sings: *I walk with my lantern and my lantern with me.*

Her father bends over his scores, scribbling, his hand disarranging his hair, ink on his bald crown.

"Hush, hush," he tells her. "No singing."

But then he stops the scratching of his pen and leans back in his chair. He looks up at her on the stairs. When he smiles at her, she puts down her wooden knitting needles and her stocking. She walks sedately down the stairs and around the room, singing, her imaginary lantern held before her.

There above the stars shine, and we shine here below. My light is off, I go home, Rabimmel rabammel rabum.

Her father taps the beat on his writing table. His expression is fond.

"Listen to her," her father says to her mother, who sews beside the fire. "There is great sweetness in that voice. That little voice will be a big voice one day."

Her mother does not look up. "Time for bed," she says.

Lina disdains to look at her mother.

She walks up the stairs, lantern held high.

THAT NIGHT LINA WAKES to the sound of voices through the wall. At first she thinks she is dreaming: William and Alexander are home?

She rolls over in the bed she shares with Hilda. Her head feels hot. Her neck hurts her strangely, and her ears throb and ache. She lies still and listens to the murmur of the conversation in the next room. Hilda snuffles and tosses an arm.

Lina is sure she is awake now, that those are her brothers' voices. But why do tears run down her cheeks? She thinks she has been crying for a long time, for the pillow is wet when she turns her head, and her neck hurts.

When her brothers are together at night in their room they speak of all sorts of fellows, Leibniz and Newton and Euler. When she was younger, Lina believed these were her brothers' clever friends. Now she knows that they are all philosophers. Leibniz died in Hanover in a timbered house William has shown her. These were very wise men, she knows, their ideas written down in books. Poor Euler went blind, William told her, but meanwhile he had already memorized all of the *Aeneid*! William has a copy of Newton's *Principia;* he has read passages to her. He has shown her Newton's proofs of planetary motion, too, his geometrical formulas of infinitesimal calculus, rules by which he understood the universe to be governed. She knows that William thinks Newton's drawings—the circles and arrows, the equations—are beautiful.

She writes her own equations, just making them up.

"What are these?" William had said one day, finding them and laughing.

She'd snatched them away.

But he had ignored her pique. Instead, he took her on his lap and read aloud to her some of Newton's questions: *What is there in places empty of matter?*

"Wind," she had said, guessing. "Stars."

"*Empty* of matter," William had said.

He'd continued reading: *Whence is it that the sun and planets gravitate toward one another without dense matter between them? Whence is it that Nature doth nothing in vain? Whence arises all that order and beauty which we see in the world? To what end are comets? Whence is it that planets move all one and the same way in orbs concentric, while comets move all manner of ways in orbs very eccentric?*

Lina loves the shape of William's face, his eyelashes like dark brushes. The white of his eye is very clean. She likes to touch his soft hair, which curls and is the shining color of horse chestnuts.

With her fingers she had pushed and pulled at the skin on his face, playing.

What hinders the fixed stars from falling upon one another? William had said, holding the book out of her way so he could continue reading.

"Invisible ropes," Lina had said. "Invisible horses. The good animalcules!"

She can joke about this now; William banished her shame.

"One would not advance without making assumptions," he had said kindly to her. "You made an educated guess about the earthquake—a very clever one, in fact. Anyway, you should never believe everything you're told," he'd added.

She'd tugged at his nose, pinched it closed to make his mouth open and then released it, but she could tell that he was not paying any attention to her. His mind, she saw, was far away.

NOW, LYING IN HER BED, awake in the darkness beside sleeping Hilda, she stares at a chink of light in the wall. She can tell from the tone of William's voice that he is reading aloud.

> *Did blind chance know that there was light and what was its refraction and fit the eyes of all creatures after the most curious manner to make use of it? These and such like considerations always have and ever will prevail with mankind to believe that there is a being who made all things and has all things in his power and who is therefore to be feared.*

Lina shivers. In her prayers she begs God's pardon reflexively for her sins: *I am sorry, I am sorry, I am sorry.*

Beside her, Hilda gives out a little snort.

The sheets under Lina's body feel unpleasantly rough. They are damp and cold, too, she realizes, but her head burns. She is happy that William is home, and she wants to call out to him to come to her—she has missed him so much—but she cannot make her mouth work, and she feels confused. She remembers when her brothers were first conscripted, the sound of the drums in the streets, the troops roaring. Somehow those sounds seem to be *inside* her body now.

She sleeps again but wakes at the sound of her own voice, crying aloud. The bed is empty. She sees Hilda standing by the open door, white and shapeless as a ghost, her nightdress bunched up in her fists.

Someone else is there. It is her father, Lina sees. With difficulty she opens her eyes wider.

He bends near, a candle held high, and lays a big cold finger against her wrist.

There is pain in her body, but she cannot locate its source. It seems to be everywhere.

Then she hears William's voice nearby, and she wants to say his name, but it is as though she has dropped away from her own body down into a deep well. She tries to call out to him, but her voice makes only a little disturbance in the air above her head, a visible rippling, like a lizard's streak of blue tail. The whisper of sound slides away into the silence and the darkness and is lost.

IN DAYS, a rash spreads from her abdomen across her chest and neck to her cheeks and forehead. A rope is strung across the room and a sheet draped. Her mother comes hourly with a basin. Lina raises her head and stares weakly down the length of her body, shivering as her mother washes her. She thinks of the animalcules that will die with her. She cries without tears, for there seem to be none inside her.

They scald her sheets.

Her father comes one day and shaves her head.

She weeps, wrenching away from the razor nicking her scalp.

Lina sees William, standing at the door in his red coat.

He protests the shaving, but her mother says: "Do you want us all to die?"

IT IS WEEKS before she can sit up to drink with her head unsupported, weeks more before she can crawl or stand and totter down the hall to the top of the stairs. She is not allowed downstairs, and the loneliness is awful. She sits at the top of the stairs just to hear the voices of her family. William and Alexander spend the days at the parade grounds. No one knows how long the Foot Guards will be in Hanover. A battle with the French is expected.

If he comes home before she falls asleep at night, William brings a candle and sits in the hall outside her door, reading aloud to her.

Sometimes she drifts off to sleep, but she always wakes when he stops.

"You were asleep," he says from the hall.

"I'm not," she says. "I wasn't."

"I'm only a dream," William says, laughing.

"No, you're not," she says, but she has a moment of panic. "You're real, William. You're real, you're real."

"All right," he says, soothing. "It's all right, Lina. We are both real as real can be."

ONE DAY WHEN SHE IS ALONE, sitting on the stairs, Jacob comes to stand before her.

He stares at her for a moment, and then he raises a small hand mirror; she sees the reflection of her scabbed face, the pockmarks from the rash dimpling her flesh, her shaved, patched head like that of a baby bird. Her eyes are enormous.

She stares at herself, and then she looks up at him.

Jacob drops the mirror. The glass shatters.

For a moment, he seems uncertain of what to do.

"You didn't die," he says finally. "So be grateful."

THE WAR GOES ON AND ON. In July, the Hanoverian regiment is sent off to fight the French.

They are all afraid for William and Alexander. When they learn that the Hanoverians have been defeated at a battle in Hastenbeck, their father is grief-stricken, certain he has lost his sons. But within days of news of the defeat, survivors including William and Alexander trail back to Hanover.

Lina's mother is hysterical. Rumors are that French soldiers are to be quartered in Hanover, where they will spread their diseases. The local citizenry prepares to organize a militia.

For days, neither William nor Alexander leaves the house. The regiment was in disarray following its defeat, those that survived fleeing. Lina understands that both brothers will be conscripted again if the regiment is reorganized, that they might even be viewed as deserters.

William sits in the hall upstairs, reading. Sometimes he paces.

Better that they not be seen at all right now, their father says, whispering.

Hilda cries when she is made to go to the market, afraid that even though the French have not yet arrived, she will see one and catch something and die.

"Someone make her shut up," Jacob says.

ONE NIGHT WHEN LINA WAKES, she hears lowered voices coming from the room downstairs. She can tell that it is late. She knows the hour by the sounds of the animals that live so closely quartered around them, and there is nothing but silence from them now.

It has been months since her illness, but she is still weak and unsteady on her feet from so many weeks of being confined to bed and her room. She makes her way down the hall and to the stairs on her hands and knees like an infant. She moves down the treads until she can see into the big room.

Her father holds first William's face in his hands, then Alexander's, kissing them on both cheeks.

Jacob sulks by the fire. Their mother fusses over him, murmuring something, stroking his hair. Lina watches him flinch from her touch.

William holds a pair of cloaks over his arm.

There will be a sentry at Herrenhausen, their father is saying. If the boys can slip past that point, they can make their way to Hamburg and from there to a ship that will take them to England.

"I'm not going with them," Jacob says from the fire. "It's stupid for them to travel together. They are more likely to be detained that way. Anyway, they won't draft me; they'll want me in the orchestra."

"They will have a *French* orchestra," their father, says, but Jacob shrugs.

Hilda hunches on a stool. She puts her face in her hands and begins to wail.

"Stop," their mother hisses at her. "Stop it!"

Lina stands up shakily.

She does not care about Jacob. She cannot believe that Alexander and William are leaving, will leave without speaking to her, without coming to find her and say goodbye.

But as she stands, William turns as if looking for her. He comes to the bottom of the stairs. She knows from his expression as he looks up at her that he sees what Jacob sees, what she saw in the mirror: the ruined face, the scabbed skull. But he keeps his eyes on hers.

"Now that you are recovered," he says, "you must promise to read to the horse to keep him entertained."

He widens his eyes meaningfully.

At first, Lina does not understand.

"He is bored," William says. "I fear we have underestimated his appetite for knowledge."

"What a foolish idea," their mother says. "Reading to a horse."

William holds Lina's gaze, his face serious.

Then he smiles. His eyes are shining. "Don't forget," he says quietly. "He is so very clever, our dear horse."

Jacob pushes away from their mother's embrace and storms out of the house.

Lina wants to speak, but a moment later, William and Alexander are in the open doorway, dark against the warm darkness. Lina can see the stars behind them.

And then they are gone. Hilda puts her apron over her head.

THE NEXT DAY, Lina leaves the house on trembling legs when her mother is out and finds William's books wrapped in cloth, hidden in the stable for her. She sits on a pile of straw and opens to the first page of Locke's essay, the Epistle to the Reader: *I have put into thy hands what has been the diversion of some of my idle and heavy hours.*

The door of the stable is open. The air is light and clean and the scent of the orchard reaches her.

Her hair will grow back, William has told her; she will have a crop of beautiful curls. While she reads, she touches her scalp absently, her fingertips finding the pits in the skin of her face.

A piece of paper flutters to the floor from between the pages in her hands.

It is a note from William, written in his familiar hand: *The moon you see from Hanover is the same moon I will see in England. I will come back for you.*

YEARS AND YEARS LATER, long after she has become intimately familiar with the view of the night sky through the telescope, she still begins her evening sweep of the stars by visiting for a few minutes with the moon. She notes the caverns on its round cheek, its terrain of ancient streambeds and crags, its deep, dry lakes and plains and mountains and volcanoes.

She likes to reacquaint herself with the moon, as if it is someone from whom she has been separated.

Her whole life she feels consoled by the moon's presence. Its patient head with its ruined visage follows her, keeping her in its sight.

FOUR

Friend

• ◆ •

In the years that follow William and Alexander's escape to England, Lina has one friend, Margaretta, who lives next door. They sit side by side to do their embroidery in Lina's courtyard or on the bench at the end of Margaretta's family's garden, a location Lina prefers. A stand of hollyhocks so red they are almost black towers over them, and the hives against the brick wall are alive with bees and the scent of honey. Lina has neither talent nor patience for the task of embroidery, but she loves to watch what Margaretta makes: grapes on the vine, tassels of gold thread on the grasses, snowflakes against a cloth of dark blue. Sometimes Lina lies with her head in Margaretta's lap and plays with the ends of Margaretta's long braids. Her hair is thick and soft, the color of butter. The afternoon's warmth on Lina's face, and the feel of Margaretta's hair in her fingers and grazing her cheek can put Lina into a trance. Behind her closed eyelids, the sun makes spots like the golden bees floating among the flowers.

The only cloud between them is the subject of marriage.

Margaretta is a year older than Lina—sixteen this past July. Her favorite game is to speculate about her future husband, whoever he will be, and about the many children they will have. She has already named them all and can describe their features at length to Lina.

Lina is bored by this conversation, the silliness that overcomes Margaretta when this is the topic. Margaretta is the only person other than William or her father with whom she can have a serious discussion, though usually it is Lina who does the talking. Margaretta has not had the benefit of having William as a brother, Lina understands. It is not her fault that she knows less than Lina. She is curious, though. That is enough.

Lina is uncooperative when Margaretta wants to talk about marriage.

She thinks of the old man her mother prays will one day take her.

Margaretta's own mother is a flush-faced, loud-voiced woman with plump hands and a heavy bosom draped in dingy lace, the lace at her cuffs torn and soiled, too. She likes to speak with her girls of their future weddings, and she reassures Lina: of *course* there will be someone to love such a clever girl. Lina will depend on her intelligence, her imaginative company, to attract a husband.

She never says that men will be revolted by her looks, her scarred face, as Lina's own mother does.

Margaretta has decided that Lina's husband will be a rich old blind man. This notion Margaretta finds romantic. She has developed a sentimental picture of this eventual union, Lina reading aloud to him while he strokes her hand, his eyeballs like two glass marbles. She likes to describe the servants they will have, the finery in which Lina will be dressed, the delicious meals they will be served, sweetmeats and goose, truffles and figs.

"Why *blind*?" Lina says.

Margaretta blinks, looks confused.

"It's very *sweet*," she says finally, as if Lina has hurt her feelings by not appreciating this idea. "You will help him to walk in the garden, his arm in yours, and he will adore you beyond everything."

But Lina knows why Margaretta imagined Lina's future husband to be blind: so he would not have to look at her.

Still, she thinks that maybe she could bear this future, books everywhere in her learned husband's house from before he lost his sight.

She has no faith, however, that this future will occur.

THAT FALL, Margaretta falls ill with consumption.

Lina wants to visit her, but her mother forbids it.

"You almost killed us all once," she says. "What a thoughtless girl you are, to want to bring death into our house again."

Instead, Lina leaves gifts at the gate to Margaretta's family's courtyard: eggs in a basket, wildflowers from along the river, rye rolls wrapped in a napkin, letters in which she encourages Margaretta to recover as quickly as she can.

She tells her she loves her.

The houses are close together, their walls separated by only a few feet, wide enough to allow a cart to pass between them. In her bedroom at night, Lina can hear Margaretta coughing next door. It lasts for weeks, through September and into October. Lina lies in bed, listening, her eyes on the beams running across the ceiling, her hands clasped tightly over her own chest, the pain there.

Hilda sleeps through it all, snoring and farting and muttering beside her.

Then one day in late October, there is a killing frost. No more coughing comes from Margaretta's window.

IT IS HER FATHER who tries to comfort Lina.

He shoos away Hilda, sits beside Lina where she lies on the bed under the quilts, her hands clenched so tightly they ache.

He pries apart her fingers. He has brought her one of the late-hatched ducklings, brown-feathered and leggy.

Lina turns her face aside, but she feels the creature's heart beating in her hands, and the weeping that follows finally is good.

THE AFTERNOON OF THE FUNERAL for Margaretta, Lina goes to the stable. It has been years since she has added anything to her childhood collection of pebbles and feathers, acorns and chestnuts. She unfolds the cloth in which they are wrapped and puts the items into her apron.

She has not changed yet from her good dress. She wears the brooch with the locket of Margaretta's hair given to her by Margaretta's weeping mother.

The bantams and guineas follow Lina down through the orchard to the river. She knows they imagine that her bulging apron holds grain, and she feels sorry that she has nothing for them. She is comforted by their company, their foolish air of busy industry.

She stands on the riverbank. Beside her, the feathers of the bantams ruffle in the wind. Surely a storm will come before long, perhaps even snow. The hens cluck and complain at her feet. She stares at the scene before her: the dark brown water rippling by, the yellow stubble of the field on the far shore, the gray sky. Her father had helped the others carry Margaretta from her house feetfirst, so that she should not look back with longing but will be free to go joyfully to heaven.

At the cemetery, Lina had seen that the family had been persuaded to have a bell installed. Afterward, Lina's father had complained. Such customs, he said—imagining that a dead person might revive in her coffin and pull the string to ring a bell mounted on the grave, thereby alerting the night watchman to unearth the coffin—are nothing but a way to part a grieving family from its money.

Yet surely some sort of passage awaits Margaretta, Lina thinks.

Then, for the first time, she realizes that it is *only faith* that sustains the notion of Margaretta's soul ascending toward God. The migration to heaven cannot be understood *except* as a mystery that neither science nor any man can explain.

She misses William terribly. The thought of him causes an actual pain in her stomach. Sometimes it is difficult for her to stand upright, her belly hurts her so much. She wishes he could be with her now. He is not troubled by the idea of a God he cannot understand. She knows from his letters that he is able to hold the two ideas—the unfathomable God, a fathomable universe— without compromise to his faith.

She knows, too, that ancient Egyptian kings were buried in tombs stocked with possessions for the afterlife, canisters of honey and mountains of gold coins. She does not believe that Margaretta will wake in her coffin, that her little white finger around which they had tied the string will twitch, that the bell on her grave will tinkle in the empty cemetery over which the fall leaves tumble and darkness now descends. At the cemetery she had listened to the priest and murmured the words of the prayers, but she had not felt closer through them either to Margaretta or to God. Still, she wants to make a gesture, to send Margaretta with something from her.

Hilda is in the courtyard, calling in the hens. They have settled at Lina's feet like loyal dogs, but they stir now uneasily. They are used to being brought in at night, and they sense rain approaching with the dark.

Lina steps closer to the water and shakes her apron, emptying its contents into the river. The stones and chestnuts tumble at once into the current moving at her feet, but the feathers are picked up by the wind and carried a distance over the water before she loses sight of them.

If God sees everything, she thinks, then perhaps he sees Lina make this offering. She feels that with Margaretta goes the last of her happiness. How will she bear the life before her?

She knows from maps that the river at her feet travels toward other rivers—the Aller, the Weser—and from there to the North Sea. She has William to thank for helping her to understand their place in the world, how small it is, how . . . accidental. When he had first shown Lina a map of the world, she had not believed it to be a true representation.

"But how came we to be here?" she had asked him. "Why not there"—pointing with her finger at one place and then another—"or there? What determines it?"

"Nothing *determines* it," William had said. "It is just God's design."

She looks up now. The first stars are out. Some shine with a steady light. Others are smaller and fainter. She is comforted by their presence, understanding that they are the same stars William sees. As far away as he is in England, he and she are overarched by the same sky. It feels beyond her to memorize the positions of all the stars, though she recognizes many constellations, but she knows from William's letters that others have done so. William has a star atlas, she knows, a copious record of the universe. He has sent her carefully drawn copies of a few of its pages so she may look for the constellations, and so that they may watch for them together.

No one has heard from Jacob since the night the three brothers left home. Lina is glad. Her mother cries and cries over him, but Lina hopes he will never come back.

As soon as the occupation ended, Alexander, who had struggled in England working as a tutor, returned to Hanover for a position in the court orchestra, but William was given a job as music master to the militia under the Earl of Darlington, and he wanted to stay in England. He writes that he performs as an organist, as well as on the violin and oboe and harpsichord. At one concert, he tells them, he accompanied the Duke of York, brother of King George III, who played the violoncello. One advantage of being a stranger in a strange land is that he has few diversions, William writes, and he composes new music at a great rate, seven symphonies so far. As he rides across the countryside to give concerts or to meet with his music pupils, he studies the night sky, and his mind is occupied by many cosmological quandaries and questions. He makes lists of his questions for Lina and their father: What is the size of the Milky Way and how is it to be measured? How far from the earth is the nearest star? Of what material is the sun composed? If there is life on the moon—and he believes there is—what sorts of creatures are they, and how do they organize themselves?

He has begun an astronomical observation journal. He is studying not only English but also Italian and Latin and Greek. Often he muses on the question of immortality. He writes: *My feeble understanding is not capable of pushing so far into the secrets of the Almighty. . . . I think it better to remain content with my ignorance till it pleases the Creator of all things to call me to Himself and to draw away the thick curtain which now hangs before our eyes.*

By the time she reaches the courtyard at the top of the orchard with her empty apron, the sky is dark, but Lina does not remember ever seeing the Milky Way so dense and swarming with light. It is as if a great congress takes place there.

She knows from William that they see with the naked eye only a fraction of what surrounds them. For a moment she suffers the physical sense of unsteadiness that sometimes results when she tries to make her mind calculate the extent of the universe. She gazes at the sky, its twinkling mansions.

Where is Margaretta's soul now? Perhaps it has already passed beyond the farthest star and through the gates of mystery into heaven.

FIVE

Mystery

In May of Lina's seventeenth year, the Herschel family is invited to attend the wedding of a neighbor's daughter. After the vows in the church, a fete and a ball are held in the church hall. The tables are laid with exotic fare, partridge and peacocks, loaves of white bread, honey cakes called *Lebkuchen,* dates and sugar candies, pints of the white Feldliner wine. Her mother is furious, Lina knows, at what the feast suggests about their neighbors' wealth. She keeps her fingers tight around Lina's arm the whole time, as if she needs to lean upon her. When people stop to inquire politely about her health, Lina's mother droops and simpers, affecting a limp, her hand over her heart.

Lina watches people quickly move away from them, glancing at her scarred face. She knows what they think: ugly little thing. And attached to that awful mother. Poor child.

Outside in the street, a group of boys sing the old forbidden song.

What has she got? What can she do?

There are wedding gifts of swaddling, cradles, bathing bowls. Lina, leaving her mother in a chair, wanders the hall inspecting the tables. She thinks of the old blind man Margaretta had imagined, the quiet house Lina would share with him one day, their fine possessions.

"This is the great mystery," the priest said at the church. "Your wife will be like a fruitful vine within your house. Your children will be like olive shoots around your table."

LATER THAT NIGHT, her father sits by the fire at home, slumped in his chair. He has suffered a long morose spell lately. He has only one or two music pupils remaining now. Sometimes still the music master comes with scores to transcribe, but since her father's seizure two years before, it is more difficult for him to write by hand. Like Lina, her father's greatest pleasure is William's letters. These have become long treatises William now organizes and titles by topic: Musical, Moral, Historical, Metaphysical, Characteristic. Sometimes his letters are filled with mechanical diagrams and musical notations for pieces he is composing.

Alexander has taken lodgings elsewhere in Hanover, and he rarely visits; Lina knows that their mother's unpleasantness keeps him away. Sophia has married and occasionally brings her little boy, but they never stay long. Lina sees that the child is afraid of his grandfather, the white spittle at the corners of the old man's mouth, his trembling hands, his long face, which seems to approach the boy as though he will swallow him whole, though Lina knows it is only love that gives her father's expression such intensity, such terrible fondness.

The boy squirms in Isaac's lap, throwing fearful glances at his mother, finally breaking into tears and wailing his complaint.

THAT NIGHT AFTER THE WEDDING, Lina sits at her father's feet before the fire. He has asked her to read aloud some of William's recent letters, just to hear them again, and she has complied. Now, as she folds the letters and puts them away in the box where they are stored, there is silence in the room.

Her mother and Hilda have gone to bed, her mother complaining of indigestion from the rich fare at the wedding. Dietrich and Leonard, too, are asleep.

From the shadows behind her, her father speaks at last.

"Oh, my dear," he says. "You are neither handsome nor rich. What is to be done? What is to be *done*?"

Lina looks up from the box and into the fire.

She knows exactly how she appears to others. She knows her illness stunted her growth, as well as marking her face. She is barely five feet tall, and she can hardly expect to grow any taller now. The pockmarks on her skin are less pronounced than they once were, but anyone might recognize her by running fingertips over the pitted skin of her cheeks and forehead. Her mother has declared that with her narrow hips and flat bosom and sticks for legs, it would kill her to bear a child, even if she were one day to wed and conceive.

Lina knows that the wedding and its celebration that day have made her father worry. She thinks again of Margaretta's romantic fantasies about the blind old man, his gnarled hand gentle upon Lina's head.

"Well, what hope for me then?" She tries to make her voice light to distract her father. "After all, perhaps I will attract the kindly blind grandfather Margaretta always prophesied for me."

"I believe it is your *only* hope," her father replies. "It is my fondest wish that even if you are advanced in life, an old man might take you for your excellent conversation and your sweet voice."

A familiar pain crosses her head behind her eyes at her father's words. The ghost of the fever, she has come to think of it. Perhaps it will always be with her.

What is to be said now? She blinks at the fire.

She thinks for a moment of the vanished Jacob, of how much pleasure her pain would give him now.

Why had he always hated her so?

Lina knows there will be no gentle grandfather. She imagines instead an old man with a beak of a nose and a full purse, his breath like spoiled meat, who one day will take her to his home and rap her fingers if she burns his dinner.

She would rather die.

"Perhaps if he is wise enough to recognize my excellent conversation," she says finally, though she knows she cannot disguise the bitterness she feels, "he will not be so bad."

Her father's hand falls to her shoulder.

"Of course, of course," he says. She can hear from his tone that he is repentant, that he regrets having spoken to her in such a way, betraying his fear. "You are a fountain of excellent qualities, my dear.

"Oh, how unjust it all is," he cries suddenly, "that the best of daughters should be denied a mortal happiness! It is a tragedy!"

He strikes his thigh with his fist.

Lina knows her father loves her. She has not wanted to be alone tonight. The wedding made her sad as well. But now she has had enough. She cannot bear any more of this, wants no more of his dramatics. She begins to rise from the floor.

Again he is immediately regretful.

"Child, child. Do not mind me," he says. "I am only a foolish old man. You are beloved to me, my only comfort. You will find happiness, I am sure of it."

He takes her hand and kisses it.

"Don't worry," she says. "I intend a different sort of life for myself, anyway."

"Of course," he says. But he is not listening. He does not ask her about this life she imagines, and she is trapped in the life she has, she knows. She is trapped at her mother's side, condemned to listen to her complaints. She is trapped by the walls of the courtyard and the orchard that ends at the river, trapped by the duties of sweeping and washing and cooking and sewing. All possibility in her life began with her sex, perhaps, and ended with the fever that came to her one night and left her scarred and stunted.

She has seen no fondness between her parents. She knows, though, for she has seen it between Margaretta's parents—Margaretta's father's hands on his wife's waist or cupping her bottom when they thought no one was looking—that sometimes there is love between husbands and their wives, that there is love between a blushing girl and boy who dance the *Ländler,* their arms intertwined, the girl's face upturned toward the boy's, smiling.

But that is not to be her life.

Hers is not a face to turn toward anyone.

THE NEXT MORNING she is awakened at dawn by the sound of her mother's screams and by Hilda's wailing. She comes to the top of the stairs in her nightdress and looks down. Her mother and Hilda are cringing against the bottom steps in each other's arms.

"I can't touch him," her mother says. "I can't. It's disgusting, disgusting!"

The fire is cold.

Lina wavers in her stockings on the landing, a shawl around her shoulders, her hair wild.

Her father is dead in his chair, his hands curled on his lap like bird claws and his eyes and mouth open.

THE GULF THAT OPENS at Lina's feet with her father's death lasts for five years, time that later in her memory is characterized by nothing, an empty plain almost without event, or at least events so trivial as to mystify her with their strange permanence in her mind: Dietrich being lifted to a table and playing a solo on his *Adempken* at a concert, a beautiful lady putting a gold coin in his pocket and complimenting his technique on the violin; the two months she spends lodging with a sempstress, where she learns to sew household linens and is given too little to eat; the cold floor of the garrison church where she goes alone sometimes to kneel and bow her head and ask for something, anything to relieve the barren days stretching before her. She remembers word for word a passage from one of William's letters, and which she often rereads: *There are two kinds of happiness or contentment for which we mortals are adapted; the first we experience in thinking and the other in feeling. Let a man once know what sort of being he is; how great the Being which brought him into existence, how utterly transitory is everything in the material world, and let him realize this without passion in a quiet philosophical temper, and I maintain then that he is happy; as happy indeed as it is possible for him to be.* She reads this letter so frequently that eventually the paper tears where she had folded it. At night she sits outside on the bench and looks up at the sky, at the familiar constellations. She thinks about the Being who created this life for her. She knows that it is, as William said, transitory. But she does not know where she might find a "quiet philosophical temper" with which to bear it, while it is still hers to live.

One day, her mother raises a hand to strike her. She has done so before, but this time, something in Lina's face must arrest her, for she drops her hand. They stare at each other, but it is her mother who turns away finally. Lina will make that moment last, make her mother look at her lifted hand. Yet the incident occasions no sense of triumph in Lina. It is that moment, in fact—the stark presence of her mother's fear, along with her chronic anger and lack of affection—that prompts Lina at last to write to William, to plead for his help, to beg for his rescue.

Dearest Lina. I am making plans, William writes to her after receiving her desperate letter. *I have not forgotten you.*

Finally a letter to Lina and their mother containing William's proposal arrives. He will return to Hanover in August and plans to take Lina back to England with him, where he is now installed as concertmaster and organist at the Octagon Chapel in Bath. He knows Lina's voice is a fine one, he writes, and he needs a singer he can train and keep with him all the time. The performers on whom he depends now are itinerant, their services too expensive.

He will compensate their mother for the loss of Lina.

"He will never have you sing," her mother says, folding the letter and tucking it away in her gown, as if to deny Lina the pleasure of reading his words again. "Not with your face."

But she does not say no to William, does not forbid the arrangement—she will be happy for the money, Lina thinks—and soon he writes again with a date on which he hopes to arrive.

The day William is expected, Lina leaves the house and goes down through the orchard to the river.

Finally, after years of no tears, the tears come.

When he opens the door of the house just before darkness, she is alone in the room.

She has already packed everything she owns. She stands up, but her legs are trembling.

She cannot make her feet move.

He puts down a satchel and crosses the room.

More tears. She had thought herself emptied out.

He puts his arms around her.

She knows he sees now how terrible it has been to wait.

"Lina," he says, his voice breaking. "You will be a great gift to me."

THE NEXT EVENING, William takes the chair before the fire.

He begins with a preamble: Certainly Lina's loss to the household will be felt, he says. Of course their mother will need to be compensated. He speaks to the firelight, not looking at their mother.

Lina knows that their mother has been expecting this conversation and has been scheming. Now she fretfully enumerates Lina's daily labors for William.

Lina is surprised at the length of the list of her own chores, but she sits quietly, waiting. It is all just a matter of the money, she sees now. It has always been just a matter of the money, her mother's greed winning out over her cruelty. She would rather have the money than punish Lina further.

But is it possible William does not have enough? Will her mother prevent Lina's freedom, after all? Is it only a further cruelty in her that she has allowed Lina to believe she will be permitted to go with William?

William looks away from the fire and gazes down at the paper on which he has been scratching figures.

"You have Hilda to help you," he says. "Dietrich and Leonard may assist you when they are at home."

The little boys. Lina still thinks of them in this way—Leonard's sweetness, and Dietrich's sensitivity, his feelings so easily bruised—though they are tall boys now and both apprenticed to the duke's vintner, a man who has been deprived of sons. William does not mention Jacob, of course, who has disappeared with such finality that they all believe him dead; it has been years now, and none of them has had any news of him.

"And you always may call on Alexander," William adds, "if you have need of him."

Lina thinks that Alexander would not refuse a request, but he has drifted far from the family. He has a position as Hanover's *Stadt-Musicus*, whose duty is to blow the Chorale in the middle of the day from the market tower. She hears it sometimes and imagines he is thinking of her, that the notes are for her, but he rarely comes to visit. She does not blame him.

Their mother scoffs. "*Boys* will not do *women's* work," she says bitterly.

Poor Hilda. It is a great worry to Lina that she will leave Hilda, who is now an orphan and meanwhile has developed an ugly growth on her neck like a burled knot on a tree.

William frowns down at the papers in his lap.

Lina has looked at them on the table: the familiar triangles with long hypotenuse and arrows and endless, downward-sloping equations.

"And I do not have Hilda forever," their mother says after a minute. "*She* will not stay forever, as a daughter would, though she is so ugly, I wonder that anyone even would have her as a servant now. She will only be a further burden to me."

At the sound of her name, Hilda appears like a dog, lurking by the door to the stairs. She scratches her arms, distressed by the tension in her mistress's tone. Hilda's slowness, her big ears and wet mouth, enrages Lina's mother.

Hilda stands now, empty-faced and staring, as if her brain has dropped out of her head.

"Go away," Lina's mother says. "Stop your spying."

Hilda scrambles up the stairs.

Lina feels how satisfying it would be to slap her mother. It is an effort to stay her hand.

"Certainly you will not deserve Hilda, if you treat her so," William says.

There is silence in the room, their mother sulking at his rebuke.

"You do not know how difficult it was for me, all these years," she says at last, "married to your father."

Lina is amazed at William's restraint.

At first he says nothing.

"I will send you plenty of money," he says finally, his voice quiet. "Lina will be paid for her singing. And there will be only yourself and Hilda to care for."

Lina understands that this is William's final reproach to their mother, who has so successfully driven away her children that now none will remain with her.

Lina feels her face flush at the mention of her singing. She has never sung before an audience. She does not believe William actually intends to stand her before concert patrons at Bath; her mother is right.

It is only an excuse he offers, further proof of his love and kindness, she thinks.

What will she *not* do to repay him with her gratitude?

She will do anything, everything.

Lina watches her mother turn away, her mouth pursed sourly. Yet Lina sees now that she does not intend to oppose William. There will *be* no hysterics, no false protestations of love, Lina understands. Indeed, her mother wants the money more than she wants Lina, and she will live alone except for Hilda, whom she will abuse, and one day she will die, steeped in her own bitterness. Leonard and Dietrich and Alexander and Sophia will rarely visit. No one will come to her funeral.

Lina is shocked to feel a telltale pressure in her chest, her old *Überangst*.

No, she thinks. No pity *now*!

Her mother is everything Lina knows that men believe true of women: that they are governed by heedless and selfish emotion rather than reason. That they are trivial and inclined to spite. That they are lovely when charming and obedient and kind, but when not? They are a trial for men to bear, or worse: a cause of ruination.

But all those babies, Lina thinks. Women have to bear the children. And how can they elevate themselves to the level of men when they are forever forced to spread their legs and then attend to the consequences?

She looks at her mother. She wants—she longs—to convey this strange moment of sympathy; she does not want to leave without some understanding between them. It is true that her father was a trial sometimes. Lina knows that he was weak, a sufferer by nature.

But her mother looks away.

"*Someone* might marry her," she says at last, bitterly, "and then a husband might take in a poor mother-in-law."

Lina feels these words as she used to feel her mother's hand.

How could her mother be so awful? How could she have invoked so often the cruel husband with the bald head and stick legs, the unlovable man whom she imagined would hold her younger daughter's fate?

William responds mildly. "Lina will have many admirers," he says, "with a voice such as hers."

Earlier that day, as if to persuade both Lina and their mother of the truth of his intentions, he'd had Lina sing a Te Deum, a canticle, an ode for Saint Cecilia's Day, some glees and catches. He had looked at the floor until she finished, his chin in his hand, and then he had raised his eyes, smiling.

"You won't really," Lina had said.

"Why not?" he had said.

But she does not believe him.

He glances at Lina now. *We are done,* his expression says, but there is little happiness in it.

She knows they are both exhausted by what their mother has done to them.

. . .

THAT NIGHT, Hilda weeps quietly in bed, her back to Lina in reproach.

Lina puts her arm around Hilda's thick waist, the heavy sag of flesh at her middle.

Hilda tries to bat her arm away, pinches and slaps, but Lina will not let go.

She puts her forehead to Hilda's warm back. Her own tears make cool tracks on her cheeks in the chilly room.

THE NEXT MORNING, before they are to leave, Hilda will not speak to them. She stands outside in the courtyard, her hands bunched under her apron, staring off toward the river. When Lina goes out to bring her in to say goodbye, she runs down to the orchard.

Lina stares after her for a moment and then goes back inside the house.

"I can't do it," she tells William. "I can't leave her."

The kitchen is in disarray. Their mother has not come downstairs, perhaps does not intend to say goodbye at all, and Hilda has burned a pot of porridge. Lina has no appetite. She had crept downstairs before daylight to make a cup of tea for herself and think, but she has eaten nothing.

"If I had any money of my own," Lina says to William now, "I would pay someone *else* to work for Mama, and I would give Hilda her freedom. Two of Margaretta's sisters are still at home. They could come for an hour or two a day. It's all the help Mama needs. And Hilda could go to our uncle's, where she will not be mistreated. I know he would take her in to help with the house."

William turns around from the table, where he has been rolling up sheets of their father's music.

"I can't leave her here, William," Lina says.

"We are to depart in less than an hour," he replies.

His eyes go to the stairs. Their mother remains in her bedroom, complaining of a headache they know is designed to elicit their sympathy and worry.

"I know," Lina says, following his gaze. "I *know* we are to go.

"Loan me the money," she says after a minute. "I'll find a way to repay you." She cannot imagine what this might be, but she must say it.

He fits a book into his bag.

"Run next door," he says. "Make arrangements with the Hennings. I'll give Mama a purse and write a brief letter to Uncle, explaining. He'll be happy enough to have Hilda, if I send him a payment."

Lina cannot move. She has so little power in the world, she thinks. All she has is her *wanting*.

She wants now to take her brother's hand and kiss it, but such a display would embarrass him.

"You are *very good*, William," she says fiercely.

He glances at her again, but he is smiling.

"Hurry now," he says. "You and your soft heart."

THE HENNINGS ARE PERFECTLY amenable to Lina's proposal. The girls stand by in the kitchen while Lina explains what she needs. Margaretta's mother assures Lina that she will see Hilda safely conveyed to their uncle's farm and vineyard.

The Hennings are glad of the money, Lina knows, and her own mother will not dare be cruel to the girls for fear of reproach by Margaretta's mother. If she loses the Henning girls, she loses all assistance.

Hilda is at the bottom of the orchard, wandering among the

trees and hitting their trunks with a stick. Lina is in her good black dress and shoes. She walks carefully down the hill through the trees, past the baskets of fruit gathered from the days of harvesting and left for collection under the boughs.

Hilda has stopped and leans against a tree, her big chest heaving and her face red from crying.

Lina's shoes are covered with mud.

Lina takes Hilda's hands and tells her their plan. Margaretta's mother will see that Hilda is taken to their uncle's. Hilda will go by cart and enjoy the ride into the countryside, Lina says.

She will have wine every day, if she likes. Their uncle's vineyard has been fruitful.

"Can you come and thank William?" Lina says. "William has arranged it all."

Hilda holds her apron over her face, begins again to cry.

"It will be all right, Hilda," Lina says. "Now we are both free."

William calls from the courtyard, and she knows she must leave.

She embraces Hilda, kisses her. For a moment they cling together. Then Hilda turns away.

Lina puts her hands over her face. If she does not go now . . .

She climbs back up through the orchard, holding her skirts, but her legs are shaking.

How quickly it has happened, after all, their joint emancipation.

The apples in the willow baskets are shades of pink and red and gold flecked with brown spots. The leaves shine darkly in the morning's gray light. A little white stone glints in the grass. She bends to pick it up.

The horse died long ago, but at the stable she steps inside before going into the house. She remembers the coarse hair of the horse's mane, the bones of his back from when she lay across him, her cheek resting on the prickly velvet of his thick coat. She realizes she had expected that the grief accumulated during her childhood would leave with the promise of her departure.

She sees now that it will be with her forever, no matter where she goes.

From her pocket she takes the pebble she picked up in the orchard and places it on the windowsill.

She thinks of Margaretta, the little string tied to her finger in her grave. She looks out over the orchard, thinks of its beauty in blossom and in snow. She remembers her father humming while he worked, transcribing the scores left for him by the concertmaster. She remembers the sound of her brothers' voices through the wall, remembers being a child, running across the courtyard to meet William.

Now she will never again have to be without William. She will be with him always.

The carriage is in the street. William calls to her.

From the courtyard, Lina waves a last time at Hilda, a small figure in a white apron down among the trees by the river. From this distance, Lina cannot see her clearly, but she thinks that the fluttering she detects is Hilda's apron, flapping in farewell.

In the carriage, Lina turns for a last look at the house. Though they had called upstairs, their mother never came down to say goodbye.

England
1772–1776

SIX

Storm

• ◆ •

That first night on the packet that will take them to England, as she and William stand side by side on the deck under the stars, the damp air makes her ears ache. Traveling from Hanover to the coast she had been uncomfortably hot in her black silk, but now on the sea the night is cold. A yellow lantern at the far end of the ship is the only human light for miles and miles, but the sky glitters with uncountable numbers of stars. The luminous island of the Milky Way floats overhead.

The ship had moved away from shore that afternoon with surprising speed. She'd felt the ship's collision with the waves in her body—in the soles of her feet, in her thighs, pelvis, breastbone, teeth, in a tickling buzzing across the bridge of her nose. The force of the wind against her face had made her eyes stream, but she had not wanted to retreat from the rail. Everything around her had made a sound, she realized: mast, rope, sail, straining board and joinery, wave and wind. Yet somewhere beyond all the noise she had sensed silence, too. Emptiness.

The ship had seemed so substantial when they came aboard, the sails filling with air and snapping above their heads. Now, in the darkness, it seems absurdly small for the venture on which they have embarked, this journey to England. She has never been on the sea before—never even *seen* the sea—never been *out of sight of land.* She had watched the expanse of flickering waves around them as they had pulled away from Hellevoetsluis. She knows that water obeys the same physical laws as solid objects, but how infinitely strange it seems to her now that the ocean's waters remain obediently in their place on the globe, instead of sluicing off the curved shoulder of the planet in a giant waterfall. One has only to cup a palm full of water to see how readily it trickles away through one's fingers.

It was William who told her about gravity, of course, lifting her when she was six or seven years old into the branches of one of the apple trees in the orchard. She had dropped an apple, a pebble, a green acorn, and then the acorn's hat, and finally a feather, which caught on the breeze and swung to and fro on its downward path.

Indeed, everything falls.

The rates of descent depend on the object's mass and shape, William had explained. One day he would teach her the mathematical formula by which these rates were calculated.

He had held up his hands—*jump*—and she had followed the feather into his arms.

Yet despite every demonstration of gravity's force—every day the unchanging example of its power—the astonishing idea that human beings stand on the surface of a globe rotating in space by slow degrees yet *do not fall off* still confounds her imagination. It confounds her even more at this moment.

She feels the ship shift course and the deck tilt slightly beneath her, though the sea has quieted considerably since their departure. She looks across it now as if at a frozen black lake. Clearly, she thinks, she has been deceived into absurd complacency by the material things of the world. Surrounded as one is—after all, one cannot help it—by trees and houses and shops, by cart horses, paving stones, and castles, by beds, tables, chairs each with their four solidly planted feet . . . by every example of the world's manifest presence, it has been possible for her to *forget* the extraordinary fact that the earth, as well as the sun and moon and every other planet, hovers unsupported *by any visible method.* She thinks of the planets rolled (but *from where?*) into place like boulders, stopped here and there (with a touch of God's finger?), the stars scattered like fistfuls of shining grain among them, sometimes a comet escaping the arrangement.

Yet the world and her place in it feel precarious now only in her *mind,* not in her body. William's presence beside her, holding her arm, is real, and the hard planks of the deck are solid beneath her feet. That she is earthbound is something she knows in her bones. Her struggle with the idea of gravity is only a cognitive difficulty, as William has said—one cannot *see* it except by proof of its force—but it is so much more difficult to wrestle with the *mind* than with the body, where everything is more or less irrefutable. The mind is in every way a more troublesome instrument.

She has been cocooned by the physical world, she thinks, protected, even fooled by it. Despite the steady seas now, the ship around her groans. Far away from what is near at hand—water, mast, rope, and sail—she senses the deep, dark cathedral of the universe, both terrifying and wonderful to consider. She feels . . . as small as a snail. Smaller. A little seed. A bit of chaff.

An atom. She feels as small as an atom.

The ship shifts course again, a slight adjustment. She is learning and redistributes her weight from one foot to the other, hands tightening on the rail.

The waning moon has risen just above the eastern horizon in the deep, dark blue of the sky. Its appearance now—that shadowed face—comforts her. Everything is in its place.

Yet there is a familiar pressure in her chest: too much feeling, she knows.

As often as she has gazed into the night sky, the stars establishing by the arrangement of their lights the perimeter of the universe, she has never felt nearer the mystery of the world than she does right now. It is not until this moment, in fact, that she sees exactly how small her life has been: the path from house to courtyard to church or shop, only the river running past the orchard a reminder that somewhere there was an elsewhere. That was the full expression of her hopelessness, she thinks: the idea of never being anything other than what she was and what she had always been, her miserable mother's miserable companion.

But now she is *here,* thanks to William. She is *elsewhere* after all, with a different life before her.

And she is with William.

She knows exactly what she has escaped: that grandfather who might have married her for her housekeeping, but who surely would have exacted a price for his kindness in taking her. It did not bear thinking of, that price, now or then.

Now there will be no grandfather husband to berate her.

Likely she will never see her mother again. She is not sorry.

Earlier that afternoon she had stood for a long time with the other passengers, gazing over the water. They are a quiet group, sober-faced, perhaps leaving loved ones behind or anxious about the voyage. Her tremulous joy in the presence of their gravity and apprehension—for days now this laughter inside her that is so close to tears—had felt indecent.

She'd looked up at William beside her, the wind blowing his hair away from his face.

There was no man in the world more handsome than her brother, she'd thought.

Anyone would like to look at him. But no one, she'd known, was looking at *her,* Lina with her pockmarked cheeks and forehead, and so she had let drop the shawl she customarily wore in public to obscure her features. Everyone's attention had been on the vanished shore as if by staring at it they could cause it to creep back over the horizon and reappear. Closing her eyes, she had tilted her face to the sun.

The ship will take them down the Channel and across to Yarmouth in England. She has no idea what awaits her, really, except that now she will be always in her beloved brother's company, and that is enough.

AS DARKNESS HAS COME ON, she becomes more aware of the weight of the sails above them, the weight of the air they hold. It is surprisingly loud on the deck. William speaks against her ear so that she can hear him as he explains the telescope's features above the creaking of the ship.

He puts his fingers to the back of her neck.

"It is difficult, with the ship moving, but to the south is Pegasus. You can see the box even without the telescope, of course, the big rib cage. And there's Jupiter below Pegasus, much brighter than all the others. And to the east"—she feels pressure from his fingertips again, the suggestion that she shift her view—"there's Perseus, and the Pleiades rising in the east." His warm hand cups against her neck now. "And rising in the north, Ursa Major and Ursa Minor."

Big bear and little bear. Despite seeing the moon so readily, she has no mastery over the telescope, and she feels she has lost her way in the night sky. Still she knows these constellations from childhood, the evenings when William had set forth with her on his shoulders, her hands clasped over his forehead. Sometimes he'd left the house at night to walk along the *Leinestrom*, where the banks bordering the river were ruffled with grasses that shone in the moonlight. She had learned to wait for him in the dark courtyard. Finding her there, he would stop, and she would look up at him, knowing her heart would break if he did not take her with him.

But she had never had to ask. He had lifted her to his shoulders.

They'd never spoken about what they left behind—their mother's anger, their father's melancholy, Jacob's insults.

William did not talk much on those walks, but she had not sensed that his mind was empty, or that he brooded over some unpleasantness in their family. That was his great freedom, she thinks; he could free his mind of what he did not wish to consider.

"Your mind is a world without end, Lina," he had told her. "*In saecula saeculorum*. You are free to think anything."

Sometimes, though, she had been unable to refrain from interrupting his thoughts: *What are you thinking?*

He'd never said *nothing*.

She'd understood from William that it is in curiosity, first, and then in knowledge and reflection that freedom rests. To know something is a kind of power. Even to ask a question about the world is a kind of power.

As they had walked, he had shown her the fish and the ram and the dog in the night sky, the two bright stars that formed the forepaws of the lion. He knew the names of trees. He plucked leaves and handed them up to her. Sometimes he walked for so long, so far into the country that she fell asleep, her cheek on his head, feeling the rhythm of his stride in her body. She would wake to see Hanover's steeples in the distance behind them, that world far off as in a little picture hung on the wall.

THE DECK TILTS SLIGHTLY. She feels so unsteady from looking up at the sky that she loses her balance and lurches again against William. The wet, cool breeze is in her ears. The telescope swings, streamers of light rushing past like bright rivers. The sensation makes her dizzy. Her stomach seizes.

William steadies her, holds her against him, his legs splayed to keep his balance. His body, so powerful and so close to hers, makes her shy. Ever since boarding the ship he has seemed to grow more unfamiliar to her, a stranger, his new life and identity in England approaching as their shared history at home in Hanover recedes. For the years he had been away in England, she had marked the anniversaries of his departure—all the years she lived without him—and his birthday on the wall in the stable. He will be thirty-four in November.

"It's too rough now," he says. "No use trying to hold anything in sight through the telescope."

But she returns her face to the eyepiece anyway. The sky through the telescope is dazzling, fields of darkness and light that keep folding and unfolding before her. Everything is soft and blurred, even the moon.

"The Milky Way is like a tether," William says. "You can follow the nebulae end to end, horizon to horizon. See where Capella stands, just outside the stream at the eastern edge?"

She does not know the word nebulae. She cannot identify the stars he mentions. There is so *much* to look at, but she does not know *where* to look or what she is looking *for.*

His flapping cape wraps around her skirts in the wind.

She pulls back from the telescope and takes a breath. When she looks directly at the sky, the stars are much sharper, the moon as clean as if carved with a knife. When she returns to the eyepiece, she begins to move the telescope slowly, by degrees. She feels unbalanced, as if she is being tugged into the sky. Or is falling into it.

"The telescope magnifies the effect of the earth's rotation," William says. "You'll quickly lose sight of any particular star this way. You'll learn to track a star by applying pressure to the telescope's tube. For now just be patient. Hold your gaze, if you can."

She sees after a while that if she is able to keep just a small area in view, more stars gradually reveal themselves. She begins to understand that it is not that the *stars* are moving toward her, stepping forward, but that she is *seeing* more deeply into the sky.

She has to look away again, breathing against a sensation of queasiness. But it is not seasickness, she thinks.

She blinks, returns to the eyepiece, the brass cold against her cheek.

"Don't squint," William says. "Don't close your other eye. Cover it with your hand, if you have to."

It appears to go on forever, the universe. But how can that be? How can it be *endless*?

"It's extraordinary, isn't it?" William says behind her in the darkness, his voice close by her ear. "I could look at the sky all night long. Sometimes I don't remember to eat or sleep, don't even *want* to. There is so much to see, so much to be done, and no end to the obstacles. I've found only one optician even willing to consider that it might be possible, what I want."

She turns away from the telescope to look at him.

"What do you want?" she says.

He looks up at the sky. "It is a matter of mirrors," he says. "And the length of the telescope, the materials required. And the expense."

"You are building a telescope?" she says.

"Ah," he says. He smiles. "You'll see."

She looks at him. Despite Jacob's fine clothes and manner, she thinks that it has always been with William that the family achieved real beauty. Even William's hands are well formed, she thinks, looking at them now holding on to the rail: *there is a model of a beautiful hand.* Over their travels together these last few days, she has been reminded of how, beside William, other people's flaws seem especially noticeable: a stooped back, fat in rolls around the neck, an overhanging brow or jutting teeth, eyes too small or close together. Everyone in the world looks ugly beside William.

She realizes that he has not spoken of wanting a wife. Is it because he is so busy, because of this interest in astronomy, as well as all his other obligations and employment, his duties in Bath? Perhaps he has no time for a wife. But every man wants a wife; he is a man like any other, isn't he? She can't imagine that he doesn't look back at a pretty face turning toward his own, and surely there must be many of those. William is a man who seems designed to be loved.

The thought gives her an uncomfortable feeling. Yet why should she feel bleak at the thought of William's being loved? It is only having been without him for so long, she thinks; she does not want to consider sharing him. But of course that is absurd and childish. She *will* share him, and with many people.

Still she feels the chilly vacancy at her side, the place he has left to go and stand instead against the rail.

Maybe it is true that a certain kind of life, a life of success and happiness, is reserved for those who are as beautiful as William, she thinks. But perhaps it is also true that one might stand just within the bright circle of that happiness and catch some of its warmth, even if one is not responsible for the light.

"Yes, I build telescopes," he says finally, "but the enterprise is too much to describe tonight. And we have plenty of time."

The thought sends a thrill through her. The time ahead, all the plenty of time ahead.

The moon has laid a road of light across the water, brightest at the horizon.

Once more, Lina bends to return her eye to the telescope.

Again she experiences the sensation of leaving the ship's deck, of moving into space. She reaches out a hand to grope for William's sleeve.

When he puts his arm around her, she turns away to look at him again.

The wind is stronger now. Her eyes water.

"Time to sleep," William says. "You will be exhausted."

She feels like a child being sent to bed. It is a consequence of her size, she thinks, that she is always treated this way.

The shawl she wears across her face to conceal the scars, the shawl her mother insisted she wear—because who would want her, as her mother said so often, if her face is the first thing they see?—has slipped and fallen to her shoulders.

William tugs at it now, gently.

"Do not wear this, Lina," he says. "You only call notice to yourself with it across your face. There is nothing wrong with your face."

She is horrified that he has spoken of her physical appearance. She does not want him thinking about her face.

She pulls the shawl up over her mouth. "I'm cold," she says from behind it.

He looks at her steadily. "She was unkind to you," he says after a minute. "I know she was. But it was only fear and ignorance—only her fatigue—that made her so."

Lina takes a step away from him. She had thought he understood. Their mother is a bad person. She might *not* have been, it is true, if she had been spared the burden of bearing so many children, the endless worry over money, the ceaseless labor of the household. But she is at least a weak person, disposed toward unkindness when her circumstances are trying, afraid of what she does not know, quick to blame, forever begging God not to punish her further, her prayers tinged with anger.

"*You* never felt her cruelty," Lina says.

"I'm sorry," he says. He looks away from her, gazing up at the sky again. "Now you're angry with me."

He is a big man, broad-shouldered and tall. He seems immense against the darkness now, the stars arranged around him.

"I know she kept her worst for you," he says. "Perhaps it was—I don't know. Pity."

Lina is aware of a painful pressure in her ears.

"There was no reason to *pity* me," she says after a minute. "Because I look as I do? But I never wanted *her* life."

She tries not to brood on her physical self. She is brisk about her hair—too thick, too rough and curly—plaiting it and winding it quickly into a tight knot each morning. Her body is only a constellation of parts to be assembled when required, she thinks: to carry water, to wring out the washing, to split wood, to meet her mother's gaze when told to, Lina's eye reflecting back whatever it sees but offering no entrance. She thinks of her mind—that world without end, as William says—as hidden safely within the inconsequential vessel of her body, a bird concealed in a thicket. What does it mean to the mind if its house is ugly? Nothing.

"That's not what I meant," William says.

"No, you're right. She pitied me because I am ill suited," she says finally. "Ill favored. To be a *wife*."

But now she regrets speaking. She has forced William into a contemplation of her circumstances, which, after all, he has done more to compensate for than anyone else. It is William who contrived this chance at escape, this opportunity for something other than what had certainly faced her. By her own efforts, she had been able to do nothing better than to conceal herself.

"I have nothing but love and admiration for you," William says now, "as will everyone else."

His kindness shames her.

She looks up. The sky is extravagantly beautiful.

She adjusts the shawl around her shoulders. It will take practice, this unveiling.

With her face fully exposed, she feels more acutely both the weight *and* the weightlessness of everything above her, the moon balanced overhead. She tries to remember Newton's law of universal gravitation: F and m and r and the constant of proportionality, G. Though gravity cannot be touched, she feels embraced by it for a moment. The stars and planets must be God's particular delight, she thinks, looking up at the jeweled sky, just as the orchard in flower had been her joy, and the shining scales on a trout's belly, and the beauty of the mist among the trees. She'd had all these, it was true: joys in a joyless life.

She listens to the sound of the waves. Above her the stars seem to shift a little in the wind, the whole sky adjusting itself. Truly, only a benevolent, delighted God could make a display so extraordinary, she thinks, the lights so numerous and delicate, the darkness so vast. She considers the earth planted all over with fruiting trees, hovered over by bird and butterfly, and the ocean beneath them filled with its strange creatures—she has seen drawings of them, giant whales and anemones and octopi. But the troubling question remains, as always: why would God—artist of the world, his imagination sovereign—why would God allow her beloved Margaretta to die, and the Herschel babies, too, babies with only a name on a stone in the churchyard but never a full life? Why would God bury a city and all its faithful citizens gathered to worship him in an earthquake whose tremors she had felt as a child? Why make a boy like Jacob, all hate and malice? Why make a mother who hates her child? Why make a woman and curse her with the pain of childbirth, give her nothing to do except drudgery?

She has read *Paradise Lost* for herself by now, but she has kept secret her sympathy for Eve and even for Satan, ill-favored angel. She does not imagine that even William would understand those feelings.

Above her the sky seems to pulse with light, but the moon holds steady, keeping her in its gaze.

William leaves the rail to adjust the telescope, puts his eye to it. She watches him move it, sweeping the sky slowly. He seems to have forgotten her.

Then he speaks. "In the midst of so much darkness," he says, "we ought to open our eyes as wide as possible to any glimpse of light."

Is he reproaching her?

But it seems not, for when he turns to her, he is smiling.

"You really have no idea how hard I intend to make you work," he says. "Rest now, Lina. It is all still before us, and there is much to do."

THAT NIGHT, in her cabin with its porthole, she begins the journal that she will keep—except for one long, terrible silence—for the rest of her life. She writes by candlelight, enumerating the evening's revelations: the mechanics of the telescope, her new understanding of the astronomer's tools, the illuminated world of hazy starlight revealed to her, the ancient paths in the sky. Though she had been so cold her teeth had chattered by the end, she had also been exhilarated. She had not wanted to leave the deck, leave the telescope, leave William.

She cannot believe she is free.

In her berth she can feel even more closely the packet's push through the waves, the water's heavy chop. She is aware of the cold sea surrounding her, its proximity on the other side of the wall against which she leans. She is aware that she is alone in a bed for practically the first time in her life.

There is a pinching sensation in her chest at the thought of Hilda.

She hopes Hilda is already at their uncle's, that he has greeted her kindly, toasted her health with a glass of wine.

A wind from somewhere moves through her cabin. Hot wax from the candle drips onto her wrist and onto the bedclothes. A moment later, on the next breath, the candle is extinguished. In the dark, she gropes to put aside her paper and ink.

When she closes her eyes, she does not imagine the night sky she has seen through William's telescope. The pictures that come into her head are of the world she has left behind, the world from which William has liberated her: the dirty courtyard filled with chicken droppings, the narrow tracks along the *Leinestrom* through the weaving grasses and the willows' overhanging branches, the streets of Hanover lined with familiar shops and signs, the staircase and the long hall of their house, which bends at a crook—there, where William and her father had to duck their heads to pass—and which leads to the closet heaped with linen and branches of cedar and fir.

In sleep she dreams of Margaretta, coughing in the house next door. She dreams of the horse, stamping in his stall, of the shards of daylight visible through the roof of their old home, of the snow that fell lightly into her bedroom, the lightness of its touch on her cold cheeks. She dreams of her mother, pushing Lina away, and the hard, permanent bulge of her mother's belly, swollen always with child. She dreams of Hilda, her apron foolishly over her head.

In her dreams William is there, too, his back to her as he paces on the deck of the ship. He radiates heat like the oven in the baker's wintry courtyard in Hanover, puddles of melted snow underfoot. A penumbra of light surrounds him. She tries to approach him, but he is too bright, and when his feet leave the ground, his head aimed toward the stars, she cries out, for she knows she is being left behind.

EARLY THE NEXT MORNING, when the storm breaks out across the Channel, she climbs up to the deck, covered in cold sweat, and retches over the rail into the rain. A sailor shouts at her, but she hangs on to the railing, gulping the cold air, the rain in her face. It takes a wave crashing over the deck only feet away for her to retreat. The stench in the cabin from seasick passengers is horrible. She ties her shawl over her nose and douses it with per-fumed Hungary water, another gift from William, who seemed to suspect she might need it.

William appears impervious to the nausea that plagues every-one else. He sits reading on the steps beneath one of the hatches at the end of the galley, his wool cloak around him, hanging on with one hand to the rope that serves as a handrail. Lina passes him again and again as she makes her rounds with one of the crying infants in her arms.

Finally he looks up. Her expression must be desperate, she realizes, because he stands without delay or speaking and takes the baby from her, draping it over his shoulder like a sack of meal. He secures the baby there with one hand, with the other holding his book before his face. He turns away from her to stagger down the galley, continuing to read.

Lina takes the place he has vacated on the steps. What is his gift, she wonders, that he does not struggle in the world as other people do? The world does not seem to oppose him as it opposes others.

She goes up the steps to the hatch, which she lifts aside a few inches. The sky is wild, pelting rain; the sails have been lowered halfway. She holds on tightly as the ship rolls side to side and up and down the slopes of the waves. William has explained the dynamics of ship construction to her, the reason the vessel will not capsize, but his assurances have done little to diminish her fear.

They will all die, she thinks. They will be drowned at sea. Of course she is to have no future. She always knew it. She just had not imagined *this* ending. But William is still calmly walking and reading, and the baby is fast asleep.

Lina puts her face into her hands.

William taps her head with his book as he goes past.

SEVEN

Solitude

⚫◆⚫

She stands on the sand at Yarmouth, dazed by the disconcerting stillness of being on land again. The light is milky. The ships at anchor appear not so much floating as suspended in the mist between sea and sky. She touches her hair, stiff with salt. She feels her skin, her hair, her skirt begin to soften in the warm, damp air.

She looks again for the brown-eyed man who had carried her through the waves breaking onto the shore, but she cannot find him in the crowd of people.

It is absurd to think he might return to find her, to take her hand and ask her name.

From the small boats beached on the sand, men ferry hampers and wooden boxes and trunks up the shingle toward the road. A pair of oxen being dragged through the last feet of surf, eyes rolling, lifting their noses skyward and lowing, step forward out of the mist, and suddenly she can smell them, a smell of sour animal fear. A man balancing a crate of hens on his shoulder veers toward her and then away. Feathers drift in his wake.

William is nowhere in sight.

She touches her hair again. It has come loose, no doubt when the man threw her over his shoulder. She remembers the sensation of his arms around her, her body pressed against his. She tries to secure the pins and push her curls back into place, but her hands are trembling.

On the ship she had forgotten about her face. Troubling about her appearance would have been absurd under such conditions. Now, though, standing alone on the sand at Great Yarmouth, surrounded by the bustling activity, she is aware of the condition of her clothing, her disarranged hair, her pocked skin. She has resolved to do as William proposed; she will no longer go about with her face covered. Here she has a new life, with no mother to complain about her wretched prospects. Still she has to resist the impulse to draw her shawl across her cheek.

She gathers her wet skirt and climbs unsteadily to a place higher on the rocks, where she can oversee the activity below. How will William find her among all these people? She assumes he is making his way through the chaos to recover their belongings, that he will spy her here alone against the seawall.

Unlike the rich light in the forests of Hanover or the silver haze that hovered over Holland's watery fields—William had explained to her on the post wagon about the brilliance of the higher latitudes—the gray English light is plangent, the sun a hazy circle behind the clouds. She judges by its position that the hour must be nearly midday. A moment later church bells begin to ring in the town above her on the strand. Indeed it is the noon hour.

She remembers that church bells had been ringing when they left Holland. Suddenly she wants to sit down.

She had expected happiness at this moment of arrival, but instead she feels weak in the knees. Is it the melancholy light? The sound of the bells? She realizes that she is a complete stranger in this new place. In all her expectations of this arrival, she had not imagined this: her trembling legs. Her fear.

She berates herself. Now, after so many days of terror, *now* her courage fails her? The stones of the wall at her back are covered with moss. She runs a hand over their furred surface. From the street above come the sounds of horses' hooves, the trickling of water from somewhere nearby. Silver lichen grows on the slate roofs of the houses, she sees, and the windows facing the sea reflect the clouds. She feels submerged, as if her ears are filled with water. She turns to face the ocean again, trying to breathe deeply. The Englishmen have pale skin and slashes of bright red as if drawn with a paintbrush on their cheeks. They shout to be heard over the surf, but the sound of the waves swallows their words.

In the post wagon traveling from Hanover, she and William had practiced speaking in English. She has been studying it for months, ever since the arrival of William's letter announcing that he would come to fetch her in Hanover.

"I am delighted to make your acquaintance," William had said, prompting her.

"No, kindly, beautiful sir! It is I who is very delighted to make *your* happy and many years acquaintance again," she had replied.

William had laughed.

"Excuse me," she had said to William, pretending offense. "I am very, very lost. Where is my monkey? Have you ten cows? I am twenty-two years old, and I have no feathers like a bird."

William had fallen over on the seat with laughter.

"Did you get my many thousand letters to the king?" Lina had continued. "I tell her—no, it is I *told* him, *him*—that I wish only for twenty geese and cheeses and a red frock."

William had laughed and laughed. "You are a *comedienne*, my little sister," he'd said, delighted. "I would not have guessed."

She had rehearsed many sentences: *I am very well, I am my*

brother's sister, I have blue eyes and a green dress and a red hat, you are very kind, it is satisfactory. I can ride a horse, yes.

William also had given her a book, *One Thousand and One Nights.* "It will improve your accent to read aloud," he'd said.

SITTING ACROSS FROM HIM on the post wagon, she had bent over the pages: *On the black road of life,* she read aloud, *think not to find either a friend or lover to your mind. If you must love, oh then, love solitude, for solitude alone is true and kind.*

She'd looked up.

William had been writing on the wooden lapboard he had built for this purpose. When she did not continue, he looked up, too.

"Not solitude alone," he said. "Other things, also—other *people*—are true and kind." He had reached over and tapped her knee with his knuckles, smiling.

She had felt her face grow warm at the compliment. He meant *her,* she realized.

She had looked away to gaze at the landscape through which they'd been passing. As they had moved closer to the sea, the trees had grown smaller, as if bowed under the weight of a larger sky. She had felt exposed beneath it, their tiny conveyance bearing them at its infinitesimal pace over the landscape. The world outside Hanover had been for her only a fiction, she'd realized, no more real to her than descriptions of places in stories. She'd let her hand drift outside the window of the coach, spreading her fingers to feel the cool air move through them.

They would always be true and kind to each other, she and William.

AS IF HER EARS are clearing finally, other sounds begin to reach her now as she waits on the rocks—an animated conversation between men on the street above, gulls crying. Finally she spies William making his way toward her over the sand, two boys carrying their trunks behind him. Carts and horses wait on the street; William waves to her, and then he climbs a set of stone steps to the street and speaks to the driver of one of the carts.

She assumes William is engaging the man to take them to an inn. From Yarmouth there will be diligences going east to London and stopping at nearby inns, he has explained to her.

She longs to wash. Every item of her clothing is filthy. Her hair is horribly sticky.

William comes back down from the street and gives her his hand to help her over the rocks.

"We will stay here for the night?" she asks. "Tomorrow there is a carriage to London?"

"There will be an overnight coach," he says. "We can catch that."

"William," she says. She stops on the rocks. "My clothing. I must wash. For you, it is different."

She cannot believe he will ride with her into London looking as she does. She is horrified at the thought.

They reach the street, and the driver produces a crate for her to step on so she may climb to the back of the cart. William lifts one of their trunks and fits it beside her. She remembers her promise: she will do anything.

"All right," he says finally. "We will stop."

Then, more kindly, he says, "I understand. All will be well. But from now on," he continues, "we will speak only in English. Yes? It is a good idea."

"William," she says. "No."

If William will not speak to her in their native tongue . . .

But he has left her to climb up beside the driver. He turns

around in the seat, and she has no difficulty with his meaning when he points to his cheek, pulls up the corner of his mouth in a smile.

LINA HANGS ON TO the side of the cart as they make their way through the streets. The horse is clearly young and unused to the shafts, lunging ahead; the driver has the animal under poor control. From having driven their own horse and cart through the orchard at harvest to collect the baskets of apples, she knows enough of horse behavior to see that this one is skittish. She used to like standing by their old horse's head while the wagon was loaded, murmuring nonsense into his feathery ear. It would be wonderful if she could ride a horse sometimes in England, she thinks.

When the horse shies at something, the driver uses the whip.

Mistake, Lina thinks.

Traffic on the roadway eases as they leave the crowded streets of town, but away from the constraints of other vehicles, the driver has even greater difficulty holding the nervous animal in check.

As they turn onto a narrow lane, a cow bellows from behind a hedgerow.

The startled horse tries to rear in the shafts—Lina lurches against the side of the cart—and then takes off at a gallop. The driver stands up shouting, raising the whip. When the horse swerves toward the far side of the lane, the cart tilts, pitching the driver and William and Lina into the ditch along with their trunks.

Lina has the breath knocked out of her. She stares up at the blue of the sky, feeling as if her chest is collapsing. Pain shoots along her leg and her hip, her shoulder and into her neck. She tastes grit in her mouth.

The driver is nearby in the ditch, sitting up and holding his head and groaning.

William runs down the lane after the horse, which has stopped, after all, only several yards away, the cart wedged at an angle against a tree.

Lina takes a breath at last, gasping. She stands painfully, but she is not sure she can walk. There is a bloody gash in her knee.

William gathers the reins under the horse's chin, and speaks to it in soothing tones. She sees that the cart's wheels are fortunately intact. She watches as William persuades the horse to back up in the shafts and dislodge the cart from its position against the tree. The horse shakes its head up and down and rattles the bit in its teeth.

"You're all right?" William calls to Lina. "Come take his head."

She limps across the lane.

She holds the horse, stroking his damp neck, while William and the driver recover their belongings. The wooden case for the telescope is cracked, but the telescope itself is unharmed. She looks down; her skirt is torn and covered in mud and blood. She does not dare look too closely at the wound on her leg.

At last the complaining driver is restored to his seat, and William helps Lina into the cart again. Lina cannot understand everything the driver says, but she understands that when William speaks to him, he reproves him for handling the horse poorly and for using the whip. William is very confident with the man, she notes. He has the bearing of a gentleman, and obviously he feels his authority, as well as conveying it to others. Everyone on the ship had taken him for someone of importance, his detachment from the general terror marking him out.

William announces that he will walk beside the horse the remainder of the way.

Lina sits in the cart and pulls her torn skirt aside to view the damage to her leg. It is not so bad, after all—only a bad scrape—

but it is painful. She suspects she will be bruised, as well. She tries to stanch the blood on her knee with her handkerchief. Her dress is ruined, she fears.

Yet she feels—how can it be, after such a fright?—*happy*.

In fact, it is as though everything suddenly is a great joke. What does it matter if she is covered in mud and blood and is nearly dead with fatigue?

She did not drown at sea.

She is free of Hanover and her mother and the narrow cell of her future.

She turns her face to the light filtering through the leaves of the trees whose branches arch above them. It is the first of September. The air has a grassy sweetness. Something fragrant blooms in the hedgerow; bees ascend and descend among the unfamiliar white blossoms. Though the coast had been misty, here the afternoon light is clear and warm. The green fields glimpsed between the trees lining the lane glow, their color so vivid it seems almost unreal.

She thinks again of the brown-eyed man who threw her over his shoulder in the surf, the movement of his chest and belly against her as he pushed through the water.

She has stepped away from the fate she faced in Hanover, the old husband with bony knees and knotted hands who would take her for her good qualities, beat her for her bad ones.

She will never again be her mother's servant.

Sitting in the cart now, she has again the sensation of too much feeling inside her, but this time—the surprise of it is like a beautiful flower opening in her chest—it is only too much happiness.

AT THE INN, William arranges to have their filthy clothing attended to before their departure the next day. A dinner of soup and bread, a pudding of berries and cream is provided for the travelers. There are three others at the inn, an elderly woman and two young girls who are her grandchildren, Lina learns, also on their way to London.

After the meal Lina steps outside to see the innkeeper's garden. It is a pleasure to be on land again. She feels she cannot get enough of it. She walks slowly, her leg paining her. She touches leaves and flowers: English flower, she thinks. English vegetable. English tree.

Returning to the inn, she stops in the doorway, open to the early evening. In the big room William sits near the fire, a book in his hand. The two little girls play with paper dolls at the table nearby.

Lina gazes in at the scene. The room is tranquil, the little girls whispering to one another, their grandmother in her black dress and shawl dozing in a chair in a dark corner. William's posture is graceful, one long leg extended and inclined on a footstool. His jaw rests in the cup of his palm as he gazes down at the page before him. Anyone might mistake William for the father of the little girls, she thinks. Then one of the children approaches him and lays one of the paper dolls familiarly on his thigh. He looks up, smiles at her, touches her head. He says something to her in a quiet voice, and she skips back to the table.

William returns to his book without seeing Lina, waiting in the doorway.

In his white shirt, open at the neck, he seems to gather all the light in the dark room toward him.

THAT EVENING, as they part company in the hallway, Lina is surprised when William takes her shoulders and kisses her forehead. He has rarely kissed her, even when she was a child.

"It would be a great misjudgment," he says, "to assume your size equals your courage. This has been an eventful voyage for you already, has it not?"

He speaks to her in German, as if he has forgotten his rule about English. The familiar sounds make her feel close to him again.

"It's not luxury I offer, you know," he says. "But I hope you will be happy with our arrangements in Bath. It is not a . . . conventional household."

The hallway in which they stand is narrow and low-ceilinged. Standing so near to William, she feels suddenly shy again.

"I wish only to be of help to you," she says. "I am so grateful to you."

He still holds her shoulders. "She did you a grave disservice, Lina," he says. "I see that more clearly now."

She knows he means their mother.

"Well, she is gone," Lina says. "Or *I* am gone, thanks to you. I don't want to think about her."

She means: *I want to forget.*

"From now on then," William says, "we will think only of the future. It will be only the future, for us."

SHE UNDRESSES IN HER ROOM before the fire, discarding her filthy clothes in a basket that she leaves in the hall for the innkeeper's servant girl, who has been instructed to wash them and dry them overnight before the fire. This luxury, to have someone attend on her behalf to tasks that have always been hers to execute for others, feels strange. A further luxury: the innkeeper has assured her that Lina will have the room to herself. The two little girls will sleep with their grandmother.

The room is warm. She opens one of the casement windows

under the thatch. Rain is falling, the sound heightening her sense of privacy, safety at last after so many days and nights of peril.

What she has come through already, she thinks. She would not have imagined herself brave enough for any of what has happened so far. And yet here she is.

In the firelight, she examines her body. Her arm is swollen, bruised from elbow to wrist, but she does not think the injury severe. She unwinds the strips of cloth that the innkeeper's wife had given her from around her leg and washes the wound on her knee again. She does not want to trouble anyone for further attentions, wants no further interruption at all, in fact. She tears the hem of her nightdress to use as a fresh dressing. She can mend it later.

She stands before the fire. She feels herself profoundly changed already from her former self, but her body is familiar: the narrow hips, little belly protruding like a child's, small breasts with soft flat pink nipples. She takes in a breath and puts her hands at her waist, turns before the fire as if regarding herself in profile. She holds in her stomach, palms flat on her belly.

She will have to become stronger, if she is to be fit for this life with William. She knows that had it not been for her discomfort and fatigue, the trouble to which women must go over their clothing, William would have spared the expense for this extra night, let alone the luxury of this privacy now. He would have proceeded to London despite his dirty coat and trousers. But a man never needs to worry about what impression he makes with his attire. Or about his face, she thinks. In any case, William's face is an asset to him.

She feels the fire's heat on her thighs and belly and breasts, the cool air from the window on her back. She stretches out her hands to the flames. She is too tired now, she thinks, but she will have to remember these first impressions of England in order to write them down in the morning when she wakes: the glowing fields, the sweet-smelling shade of the lane, the bees hovering above the hedge, all of it lovely, really, despite the accident with the horse. She had sat restored to the cart, blood running down her leg, and she had felt her body overflowing with happiness, sweeter perhaps for its delay, her initial bewilderment at their arrival, her loneliness.

When before in her life has she ever felt such happiness?

She takes up the sponge from the washbasin and draws it over her neck and shoulders. She can still smell the salt on her skin and in her hair, despite having poured a full pitcher of warm water over her head in the yard earlier.

Her arm and leg throb; she knows the bruises will be worse by morning. So, of course, she thinks: the body is also the house of longing and pain.

She closes her eyes and crosses her hands over the soft hair between her legs, pressing gently against the bone for a moment. She cups her breasts.

Then she opens her eyes and finds her nightdress, pulling it swiftly with its newly ragged hem over her head.

She has William, she thinks. To be of use to his greatness— for she is sure that he *is* great, that further greatness lies before him—this is all she wants.

She will have to make her body incidental in that other way.

A REMINDER OF THE DAY'S JOURNEY, a raised bump on the bone of her elbow, will stay with her forever, a lump like a stone under her skin. Even when she is an old woman, she will be able to run her finger over it and recall the clatter of the frightened horse's hooves, the driver shouting, the green leaves shifting gently overhead as she'd lain stunned in the ditch. Now, looking into the fire at the inn, she knows she will never forget that the new life she commences in England begins with her first sight of the moon through a telescope, with a sea crossing during which she nearly drowns, with her fall from the cart, and then with this night, when she stands alone before the fire. It begins with a renunciation of her body for any purpose except work, a final farewell, she imagines, to the kind of love shared between husbands and wives. She will have this other, different future, a different kind of love, her love for William.

Such a love as the sort poor Margaretta once dreamed of for herself—the kissing and tickling and other sport in bed . . . it grieved her, but she knew that was never to be hers.

She buttons her nightdress, climbs onto the high, unfamiliar bed. Already there is this extraordinary fact of being *alone*. In the ship, she had given up her solitary berth to take one or the other of the babies into bed with her each night, though there had been little sleeping taking place.

She had hated that cabin. If they were to drown, she'd thought, she would rather jump from the deck into the waves than go down trapped inside the ship.

She thinks about Hilda, whom she hopes is safely installed at their uncle's farm. All the years they were bedfellows, Lina reading at night by candlelight, Hilda complaining . . . she misses Hilda now.

The bedsheets are cool. She stretches out her arms and legs, turns her head to watch the fire.

There are other kinds of love in the world, she thinks. There is the love of music and of learning, of good work for the brother she loves. A body is made for many uses.

She closes her eyes. She knows she wants to think again about the feeling of being held by the man who carried her through the froth of the shallow surf to shore.

She remembers, too, the horse's body beneath hers as she lay against his back in her childhood. She remembers Hilda's warmth beside her in the bed, the weight of her big veiny breasts and the soft skin of her plump feet. She remembers the smoky smell of her mother's apron over the hard bulge of her pregnant belly. She remembers her father's heartbeat in her ear.

She is almost asleep.

She thinks of *One Thousand and One Nights*. Solitude alone is true and kind.

Yet the body is not so easily ignored. She crosses her arms over her breasts and hugs herself. She brushes her hands over the soft hair between her legs. She takes her hands away, places them palm down on the sheet. Then she allows one hand to return and rest between her legs.

A comfort.

EIGHT

Seeing

In the coach on the way to London, William promised to show her the sights, but in fact she has only a glimpse of one, William pointing out Saint Paul's dome with its golden ball and cross. It is opticians' shops where William takes her instead, hushed palaces furnished with settees and ottomans and Oriental rugs, displays of swan's-neck barometers, terrestrial and astronomical telescopes, thermometers and theodolites and spirit levels. Italian merchants handle the goods with reverence. Lina is afraid to touch anything in these establishments, but William appears to know his way around, conversing in a mixture of English and Italian and French with the proprietors. She understands only some of what is said, but the tone of the shopkeepers—resistance and doubt—is unmistakable; William pulls out papers, spreads them on the tables, draws figures, but they shake their heads.

The day is rainy. The wide streets are full of traffic, black horse-drawn carriages shining in the rain, the sounds of horseshoes striking the wet stones, sometimes a spark thrown. Gentlemen in top hats and bowlers dart across the streets between double-decker carriages with curving staircases leading to the open seats on top, advertisements printed on their sides. She is amazed at it all.

William has an umbrella, and she holds on to his arm as they make their way through the streets. They visit six or seven shops; she loses count. By midafternoon her feet are cold and wet and the hem of her dress is muddy. She is hungry. She is tired. William was not exaggerating, she sees, when he said he could forget to eat or sleep.

Toward the end of the afternoon, after more of William's protracted but apparently unsuccessful negotiations at yet another shop, they step into the street to find that the rain is falling even harder than before. She steps into a puddle and feels cold water drench her boot. She cannot prevent her cry of unhappy surprise, but she will not look at William. She has promised herself not to complain.

Again, it is as if he reads her mind. He catches her arm. "Tea," he says.

At a hotel on Jermyn Street, a fire burns in a crowded parlor, and William finds them seats near the blaze. Lina spreads her skirt. She is famished and, she realizes, annoyed. How does William manage with so little sustenance? She is a quarter his size, and she feels ready to faint. Also, in the city the troubling sensation of having her face unmasked in public feels more acute. Now, in the noisy dining room of the hotel, she is aware of the gaze of others who glance between her and William; the two of them bear little resemblance, she knows. No doubt people in London are surprised to see a woman such as herself in handsome William's company.

So, she will have to get used to this, as well. She turns in her seat to face the fire.

The tea, when it comes, looks delicious: a cake with raisins, brown bread and cheese, and a dish of gherkins.

After just a few hours in the city it is clear that her attire is more provincial and shabby than she had supposed. If she can have some material, she thinks, she can do a better job for herself. She can ask William for that, at least. About her hair ... she glances at the sleek heads of the women around her and touches her head self-consciously. In the damp weather, curls have escaped her plaits. She will have to take greater pains, for the situation will be no easier in Bath. William has told her that the town is a gathering place for fashionable people.

A couple walks past on their way to a table, the woman with a pretty, heart-shaped face, her dark hair brushed into two smooth wings on either side of a straight part. Lina sees the woman's gaze fall on William, who has sat forward to pour the tea.

"Little sad face," he says in German. "I have kept you hungry all day. I warned you. I forget to eat."

She is unnerved by his way of reading her thoughts. How is she to protect herself from his perceptiveness? And yet what is the harm in being seen, after all, in being known and understood? William *loves* her. So this, too, this shying away, is a habit in her that needs breaking. She *wants* to be known. It is just that so much of her experience is with unkindness.

"My clothes, William," she says quietly. "And my *hair*."

He glances at her, but she is grateful that he does not brush away these worries with false compliments. He hands her a cup of tea and a plate with a piece of cake.

"I need material for dresses," she says, resorting again to German. "I can make them myself. I will embarrass you, looking like this."

He adds sugar to his tea, a spoonful in her cup. "I can give you an allowance for clothing and hairdressing and so forth," he says, speaking pointedly now in English. "Niceties appropriate for when you perform."

"William," she continues in German. "You don't *really* mean to make me sing."

"Of course you will sing," he says. "You need practice, but you will do very well for what I need."

He takes a piece of bread and cheese and leans back in his chair, opening a catalog of some sort.

She looks at the fire. She does not doubt her singing voice, though she knows she needs further training. It's just her . . . *face.* Her body. Her *person.*

She wants to change the subject. There is no use dwelling on what she cannot change. She puts down her cup.

"Tell me what you are trying to do, why we are going to all these shops," she asks.

William frowns at her over his catalog, for she has spoken in German again.

"I know, I know," she says, "but I cannot say everything I mean yet and it is too frustrating. Just for a little while." She hurries on before he can argue with her. "I can see all these people are in some way reluctant. They cannot help you?"

William puts down his catalog.

"They can't imagine what I can imagine," he says, and when he resumes in German she feels relief and gratitude. "Not just the instrument. The *view.*"

"I don't understand," she says. "Explain it to me, please."

He leans forward toward the fire and pours them both more tea. She picks up the cup, grateful for the heat of it in her hands.

"What I want is a mirror," he says. "But I want a mirror so large that no one believes it can be made. Or that if it could be made, anyone could afford to purchase it. They're very expensive even at the usual size"—he holds two fingers apart a few inches. "More important, though," he continues, "it's that they can't understand what might be *revealed* with a larger mirror, a mirror of the dimensions I imagine."

He unfolds a piece of paper from his pocket. "Look," he says.

Quickly he draws a model of a telescope. "This is the original refractor telescope designed by Galileo. So, there are lenses at each end, as you know, one fixed and the other—at the eyepiece— adjusts. You advance or retreat from an object to bring it into focus."

Lina drinks her tea. She feels better. This is what she has come for, she thinks, to be not only in William's company but also in his confidence.

The refractor is fine for looking at the moon or planets, William explains. It is a serviceable tool for the sailor or soldier. But for astronomical viewing, for looking at the stars, he tells her, the refractor has limitations. First, for viewing an object at any real distance, it must be very large, so large that it is unwieldy. Also, he says, the magnifying lens creates distortions—prisms, or rainbows—around the image.

She watches his hands, drawing cones and arrows.

"But a *reflector* telescope—" he says.

"Newton!" she says.

He looks at her and smiles. "Our old friend Newton. Yes." He returns to the drawing.

"As the name suggests," he says, "the reflector functions by reflecting light. The concave mirror at the base of the telescope, here—the speculum—gathers and concentrates light, collects it—and sends it back to the top of the tube. There a flat mirror deflects the light at a right angle to the eyepiece. There is no chromatic disturbance at all."

He glances at her. She nods her understanding.

"The bigger the mirror," he says, "the more light it will capture. And the more light captured without distortion—"

"The more you will see?" she finishes.

He leans back, holds up a hand.

"The *farther* I will see," he says. "It's not just that I might see, for instance, the moon in greater definition. Though there is that, too.

"You must understand, Lina," he says, and now his voice quickens with excitement, "that we possess no accurate sense of the extent, the *depth,* of the universe. For that, we need a much bigger surface for gathering the light. Much bigger. The sky is not a *dome.* At least, not as we have imagined it, I think. We are accustomed to believing that the universe ends with what we can see, that stars are smaller or larger based on their size or degree of brightness, not as a result of their distance from us."

She feels lost, and her face must show it, because he tries again.

"Here is the problem," he says. "We imagine that what we see now *is necessarily all there is to be seen.*"

She looks at his drawing, trying to take in what he suggests.

"We need better tools," he says. "But more significant, we need a greater imagination. This is what all these opticians lack."

She sits back, trying to take in what he is suggesting. She looks up from the sketches he has made and across the crowded room. People drink their tea. A freckled boy comes with an armload of wood for the fire. All around her are the domestic clatter of dishes, the smells of smoke and damp wool, the scent of the dark tea in the cup on her lap. She also can hear the rain outside, the downpour's volume. Through the windows' thick glass, vague shapes of passing traffic can be made out. The afternoon is already dark, verging toward evening, and the figures outside the window are indistinct: horses, carriages, a passerby bowed beneath a black umbrella. Against the glass is also the reflection of the fire, a tiny distant brightness as if contained in an unreachable realm.

During the days when she was so ill, the fever wrought effects in her brain so bizarre and memorable that she has never forgotten them. Folds like the wings of Victory in Hanover's esplanade

closed around her at the height of the fever, a feathery, hot darkness. Sometimes there had been explosions of light, like the flar-
ing of the fires burning at night in the orchard after the early
spring pruning, or like a window in a darkened room flung open
to sunlight. These flashes of brightness made a shattering pain in
her head. Sometimes she has dreams in which these visions recur,
and she wakes from them with a headache. Sometimes still she
sees lights pulsing in her peripheral vision; these episodes, too,
inevitably augur a headache. Around her now she senses the city
teeming, webs and spokes of roads leading away from London to
other towns, to the edge of the sea, to the black darkness of the
ocean.

She turns as something in the fire cracks and then collapses.

William is looking into the flames.

"It's not only that a mirror of the size I want is difficult to
fashion," he says without transferring his gaze to her. "There is
the expense of it, as I said. I have designs for both telescopes and
mirrors. I can show them what I want, but so far no one has been
willing to undertake such a task. Every optician I have consulted
says either that it is impossible, that the size of the mirror I imagine cannot be made, or that the price—even if it *could* be made—
would be exorbitant."

He shifts his gaze at last, gathers up his papers.

"What I would give," he says, "for a fortune."

He puts his papers into his satchel.

"There are still one or two others we can consult before we
leave for Bath," he says. "But I am coming to the conclusion that to
achieve mirrors the size I want, I will have to make them myself."

He stands up now. "Indeed, the work is already under way in
Bath. You shall see."

She looks up at him. She really knows nothing at all, she realizes. She had thought she was coming to England to keep house

for William. Instead, she is being ushered into a place where the size of the universe is in question.

He gives her his hand.

"It's good you're here, Caroline," he says. "I feel better, having eaten."

He smiles, that blazing smile of his.

"You shall remind me that I am human," he says. "That shall be your primary obligation."

THE NEXT DAY, late in the afternoon, they visit a shop where William and the proprietor appear on friendlier terms. The shop's interior is full of gleaming glass and polished wood and ticking clocks. The clerks are dressed in black, their wigs bright white, and their manner to William deferential. In company with the owner, a small, finely dressed man with a limp and an ivory-topped cane, William makes his way familiarly to the back of the shop to show Lina the glassmaking work. At the end of a flagged passage, he cracks a door to show her. The courtyard is filled with the roar and heat of brick furnaces. Red-faced men in grimy aprons and sweat-stained tunics fire the mixtures—sand and soda, potash and lime, William tells her—to make glass, grinding the glass on lathes. Lina can feel the heat on her face.

Back in the shop, William shows the man his drawings and they bend over them together, consulting in a mixture of Italian and English. After some time they come to the end of their discussions. William rolls up his papers, and the man sees them to the door, bowing briefly over Lina's hand when they leave.

In the street, William takes her arm, but his face has a stubborn set.

"Of *course* it will require experimentation," he says. "Undoubtedly failure will precede success. But if one is always afraid of failure, one will make no progress at all." He falls silent.

"They think I mean to glimpse God's face," he says then. "*That* is why they are afraid."

It is nearly dark. She has no sense of London except that it is full of ticking clocks and the eyes of telescopes, driving rain and muddy water inches deep in the streets.

William steers her along.

"They listen to those who say it is wrong to probe the heavens, that an astronomer aims to expose God, to . . . reduce him. They misunderstand. I aim not to diminish our awe, but to expand it."

Lina looks up at him.

"They simply have no idea what there is to be seen," he says. "So. I will have to show them."

AT THE INN on the edge of the city where they stay that night before the next day's journey to Bath, she is brought supper in her room: a wedge of meat pie, a baked apple, sponge finger biscuits to be dipped in a cup of wine. William leaves her alone for the evening while he dines with the Royal Astronomical Society, a dinner to which he has been given an invitation from a friend who supports his astronomical investigations; he is considered an amateur, he tells her, but some have become interested in his ideas.

Good Henry Spencer, William tells her. She will meet him in Bath.

She is glad to hear there is a friend, someone else to support William in his endeavors. If it all falls to her, surely she will fail.

William returns to the inn in high spirits, knocking on her door and wanting to talk. At dinner a hare had been served on a platter, he tells her, whole and with tufts of fur left for decoration on the tips of its ears, its little tail tucked between its legs.

William had thought this very funny.

He had engaged in a conversation with Dr. Maskelyne, the royal astronomer, he reports. They had argued about the existence of volcanoes on the moon and the possibility of life on other planets.

"He's a devil of a fellow," William says, leaning back in the chair by the fire in her room. "He thinks me a lunatic, because I suspect the moon to be inhabited. But *we* inhabit the earth. Why should it seem a surprise that life exists elsewhere in the universe? It is a symptom of man's arrogance, when he believes there is nothing between himself and God."

Yet despite his arguments with the royal astronomer—Lina can scarcely believe that her brother is in the company of such famous men—William is cheerful, and she can tell that the conversation this evening has energized him. He is not yet a member of the society, but he hopes that with Henry Spencer to help put his work before its members, he will soon be admitted into their ranks.

How extraordinary he is, she thinks, gazing at him.

Only a few years ago, he was nothing but a soldier in the Hanover Foot Guards.

"Tomorrow for Bath," he says. "I will be glad to be back at work."

AFTER HE LEAVES, she turns to her journal.

I am almost annihilated with fatigue and excitement, she writes, *but my brother is a great commander of his resources and returns from his engagement this evening with his mind afire. I expect that his will one day be counted as among the greatest minds of our time.*

She thinks again about what he had said to her earlier that day as they had sat at the hotel, that the difficulty with man's understanding of the universe is not what man can see. It is that he believes that what he can see *is all there is to be seen.*

There had been such a look on William's face as he had spoken to her, his expression fervent. Against her legs she had felt the heat of the fire.

"There is an art to seeing, Lina," William had said this evening. "It involves the human eye and the astronomer's tools and his familiarity with what is known, of course. But true vision—*true* vision—rests with what can be imagined *beyond* what is known. Do you not agree?"

She thinks of her brother in his own room now, closing his eyes. What moves against those closed eyes? she wonders. William's dreaming life . . . it must not be like the dreaming life of other people. Though they are of the same flesh and blood, there is really no comparing them beyond that. Their father was right. William *is* a genius.

YEARS LATER, reading through William's daybook from that time, she will find a single reference to their voyage from Hanover to England, those first days of her emancipation that had been— for her—so full of revelations.

Set off on my return to England, William had written, *in company with my sister.*

The brevity of this mention of herself—not even her name— does not take her by surprise when she discovers it. By then, she knows intimately that though her gaze had been trained always— and only—on him, *his* mind forever had been elsewhere.

NINE

Andromeda

William's voice reaching her in her attic bedroom wakes her, but she is caught in a dream's paralysis: a storm on the Channel, the sound of rain, one of the twin babies crying somewhere out of sight, a lantern swinging in the darkness and then going out.

The dream dissolves finally at the sound of William's voice, calling her again.

She opens her eyes. Watery morning light brims in the room's dormer window. There are drops of rain on the glass. In bed, her nose and cheeks are cool, but she is warm under the quilt.

Last night it had been too dark to see her surroundings clearly, but in daylight the room reveals itself. The walls are not papered, though one plastered wall has been painted the color of egg yolk. A brown stain like a spider's web darkens the ceiling in a corner. Arranged against the far wall is a battered three-panel screen decorated with elaborate urns of flowers with drooping blossoms and scattered petals. One panel bears a dent as though kicked by a careless foot. A small chair and a wooden table holding a basin and pitcher, very plain, have also been supplied. Someone has thought of her comfort, she sees, but perhaps there is not much in the way of resources.

In the carriage last night they had driven over the Avon and into Bath across a long humped bridge, the horses moving fast, Lina holding on to the strap. William had asked the driver to make a turn around the Royal Crescent, so that Lina could see the houses arranged in their astonishing, beautiful arc. It was past dark by then, and the driver had gone around the enormous circus once and then again to satisfy William. Lina had sat forward in amazement, looking out the window at the curved façade of the splendid houses, a lamp at every door, seemingly every window lit, a galaxy of lights.

Throughout the evening's ride, William had asked the driver to stop from time to time. He had leapt out, trained a small collapsible telescope at the sky for a few minutes, made notations in a book.

"Tremendous," he'd said, getting back inside and shaking his head like a dog coming in after a rain. The night's cool air had flown off him.

He had given her the telescope on one of their stops, but she had trouble focusing it.

"With practice," William had said, "your eye will become accustomed."

LAST NIGHT she had been too tired to take in much of the new world she now inhabits. William had led the way up four flights of stairs to her bedroom in the attic. There was no room available on the lower floors, he had explained. All the others have been given over to work on the telescopes.

"The kitchen is on the ground floor," he'd said, "as well as the workshop. And there is a garden behind the house."

Apparently the vegetable garden is to be her responsibility as well, she had learned. Soon, too—when there is enough money— work will commence on construction of a larger, separate workshop in the garden to accommodate the size of the furnaces he will need if he is to fire mirrors of the dimensions he imagines.

He had been full of plans and purpose, talking away as they climbed up the stairs, his hand cupped around a candle's flame.

She'd looked up at his shadow on the ceiling, at her own, trailing behind his.

"You'll see it all tomorrow," he'd said. "I have furnished a parlor for the instruments, and the harpsichord is truly excellent. I've recently acquired a good harp, too. Mrs. Bulwer has seen the room papered in stripes. I think it suitable for the ladies who come for lessons. But you will recommend further improvements, I know."

He had turned on the stairs to look at her.

She'd thought of the plain rooms of their house in Hanover, the uneven floors and rough furnishings, soot stains on the walls, snow drifting through the roof. She'd thought of the horse in his stall.

"Of course," she had said. "Yes."

NOW HE CALLS AGAIN from below.

"Caroline! Lina! Prepare yourself!"

An eruption of sound—hammers, saws—explodes from the formerly silent floors below. She hears men's voices.

She gets out of bed quickly, wrapping the quilt around her. Is this the usual din of her brother's household? She has no idea of the time. Last night she'd been so exhausted that she'd fallen asleep without writing in her journal. She will have to build greater endurance, she knows, if she is to keep pace with William.

She is still buttoning her gown when a boy appears on the landing outside her door, carrying her trunk on his back. His ears are enormous, curved outward as if they would catch things flying past his head. His chestnut hair is roughly cropped. He's a happy-looking child, no more than ten years old. A forest creature, she thinks . . . with lovely blue eyes.

He looks up at her from under the trunk, which seems far too large and heavy for a boy of his size, his cheeks puffed with exertion.

"Say *guten Morgen* to our friend Stanley on this Saturday morning," William calls from the landing below.

The child smiles. He appears delighted to be there, in fact, heavy trunk or no.

Herr Herschel's house in Bath is a great adventure, she supposes. In what other household are they sawing and hammering *inside?*

She is forced to retreat further into her room to allow him to ascend the remaining steps.

"Good day, missus!" he says.

"*Danke schön*, Stanley. *Danke*," she says, trying to help him slide the trunk from his shoulder. "Thank you very much."

He gives her a comically exaggerated bow.

She gathers up the garments she had shed last night and heaps them on the chair.

William calls again from downstairs.

"I made everyone give you an extra hour to sleep," he says, "but that is the limit of my consideration. It is time to work. Come down!"

She glances out the window. The cobbles in the street are wet, gleaming in the morning's opaque light. A finely dressed lady— blue hat, matching dress, a little white dog on a lead, and carrying a folded umbrella beneath her elbow—hurries past on the far side of the street.

She comes to the door of her room. A draft moves up the staircase to meet her. William waits on the landing three floors down.

His skin and eyes are glowing. His hair, combed away from his forehead and tied at the back of his neck with a ribbon, is dark and wet.

"I have been for my swim," he calls. "You must come see the swans."

Stanley runs down the stairs; William gives him a playful swat as he goes past.

"And now you have met our Stanley," William says as she begins to descend. "You will see there is nothing the boy cannot do. Come down and have tea and something to eat. Mrs. Bulwer is here to show you everything. Are you rested?"

She begins to reply but jumps at another explosion of banging that commences from somewhere outside, now joining the commotion from within.

The house in Bath is narrow, two rooms to every floor except the attic. She had seen that much on their arrival last night, though the doors had been closed. Now, as she passes down the stairs, she sees workmen busy in the rooms on the third and second floors, rooms that in any normal house, she thinks, would be bedrooms or parlors. A few scant furnishings, some covered with sheets, so she can guess what they are only by their shape, have been pushed against the walls to make space.

She glances in the door of one room, which contains a collection of large wooden stands of various sizes; these must be for the telescopes under construction that William has described. He has already sold several models of his own design, he'd told her on the carriage ride last night—it is partly the success of these instruments that has furthered his reputation with other astronomers—and he has given away many others as tokens of his esteem or friendship. An astronomer works mostly alone, but until another viewer of the night sky confirms his findings, he will achieve no success; it is good to have friends.

The floor of the room is covered with shavings. Partly erected tripods and rests lean against the wall, and the air smells of sawn wood. A young man with a plane in his hands and an apron around his waist turns and gives her a little bow. He bears some resemblance to the young Stanley. Brothers perhaps?

In another room two older men, burly hands and forearms revealed where their sleeves are rolled, stop to nod at her. They are setting up a lathe.

William had said that the whole house had been turned into a workshop, but she had not quite imagined this.

"How many people do you employ?" she says, reaching him on the landing.

"They come and go, as I have funds," he says. "So it depends."

A GOOD FIRE BURNS in a big fireplace in the basement kitchen, and the room is much warmer than those upstairs. A long table occupies the center of the room, and a smaller gateleg table with several rush-seated chairs arranged around it is situated near the window, its deep sill piled with drying onions.

She moves to look out the window. The garden is long and narrow, ending in a brick wall and gate. A vegetable bed—she sees potato greens and the heads of cabbages—runs along the wall. In the garden's center stands an enormous telescope, mounted on a wheeled platform. It looks to Lina like a strange, rare creature contained in a too small pen.

"The fourteen-footer," William says, speaking from behind her. "That's the length of the tube."

The garden is no good for viewing, he explains, so he rolls the telescope out to the street at night.

"I have permission now to take down the garden wall," he says—he gestures to the wall with its gate at the garden's end—"and then I'll set up the twenty-foot telescope near the river."

"*Twenty* feet?" She turns to look at him.

"Ah. Yes, and with a mirror eighteen inches in diameter," he says. "One day a forty-foot reflector. Its mirror must be—well, at least forty-seven inches."

"*A forty-foot telescope?*"

He smiles. "You doubt," he says. "Doubt not."

He looks out at the garden again.

"You should have seen the place when we first came," he says. "The beds needed trenching four feet down before I could have anything planted, and I had to have it all scythed. It was so overgrown that I almost fell down a well concealed by the tall grass. But we've had a good supply of vegetables, once we had it trenched properly. Stanley is a fine hand at gardening."

"*Forty feet?*" Lina says again. "A telescope that is *forty feet long*?" She cannot think about *vegetables*.

She looks at the fourteen-foot telescope and tries to imagine something nearly three times its size.

Lina turns from the window as a woman in a cap comes in from the passageway, her arms full of linens. The woman has a plain face, but her smile reveals good teeth. She shifts the washing to one arm and curtsies to Lina.

"Mrs. Bulwer," William says. "This is my sister, Miss Caroline Herschel."

Some politeness with Mrs. Bulwer is called for, Lina knows, but she feels shy about her command of the language.

"I am pleased to know you," she says.

"Mrs. Bulwer will come occasionally, if you need her," William says, "but it will be a great savings to have you here, instead. All our resources must go to the work." He bows to Mrs. Bulwer.

Mrs. Bulwer, hanging several shirts over the drying rack by the fire, says something, but Lina cannot understand her accent.

William laughs. "She says you have come to live in a mad-house with lunatics," he tells Lina.

Mrs. Bulwer makes a dismissive motion with her hand—it is obvious she understands William as ringleader of this circus, Lina thinks—and returns down the passageway from which she had come.

Lina looks around the room. Everything here is new to her. How is she to take charge? How many people is she to feed? And there is no servant at all except little Stanley in the garden? Who will empty the chamber pots? My god, she thinks. Surely there is a privy.

The unpleasant prospect of attending to her brother in this intimate way sends humiliation flooding through her. She is sure he has not thought of this. He has forgotten what work it is to run a household, she thinks, or—being a man—he never knew at all. How has he managed all these years?

"Mrs. Bulwer will take you to the market today," William says. "She will show you where to buy what you will need for the household. You'll have an allowance, of course. But I will leave the accounts in your hands. I am glad to be rid of them."

He must see that she looks daunted. He stops talking and steers her to the gateleg table, pulls out a chair for her.

"Come," he says. "Sit."

"William," she says. "I cannot. My English—"

"You are already proficient! It's not difficult!" he says. "And you need no words to recognize a chicken or a rabbit or a dozen eggs."

She remembers that she has vowed to be obedient, to serve William in all things. She sits down. But how is she to ask for anything at the market or say how much of what she wants or to understand what is to be paid? She will only point at things like an idiot, shrug and gesture? And then she remembers: there is her face, too. She will have to go about in the world unmasked.

He pulls out a chair at the table and sits down beside her, runs a hand through his damp hair. She imagines him emerging from his swim. Perhaps people here truly think him mad, with his morning ritual in the river and his enormous telescope in the street at night. She thinks of him plying through the water alongside the swans.

"So," William begins. "There are household duties. Cooking and so forth. No one is fussy about what we eat, so you shouldn't worry. We eat anything."

"We?" she says.

"Midday dinner for the workmen, when they are here," William says. "Morning tea. Afternoon tea. Very simple. Bread and cheese. Cake."

Lina feels as though small hands are pressing fingertips against her throat.

She does not want to remind him about the singing lessons he has said would begin immediately. She has been worrying about this, imagining herself standing before an audience at the Octagon Chapel, her face uncovered. They had passed the chapel last night on their way to the house. William had pointed out the public baths as well. Such pursuits are not to his taste, he'd said. "Very strange, very mystical, I think, people walking slowly through the warm water and the mist in their fine clothing as if they are in a dream.

"Some say it is therapeutic," he had continued, but it was clear he had neither time nor inclination for such pursuits.

But again now it is as if he hears her thoughts without her speaking them.

"Three singing lessons a day," he says, "and you will practice the harpsichord two hours as well. We will make much music, I assure you. That is how I earn my income, after all. No one pays an astronomer except the king." He smiles at her. "One day I shall have some of the king's money."

She cannot think about the king any more than she can think about the vegetable garden. She can't imagine how she is to accomplish everything he has set out for her. How will she practice her singing and play the harpsichord and go to market and cook and clean and—

William takes her hand.

"There is everything to teach you, Lina," he says.

He speaks to her in German now.

"I will give you as much to learn as you can bear," he says. "I need someone who understands what I am trying to do. I need someone who will not judge me or doubt me or chastise me or trouble me about unnecessary things. I need someone who will only *help* me. And your mind is quick. I think you will be an even greater help to me than I had foreseen."

It is vain to be pleased by his compliments, she knows, but she is flattered.

And that he speaks to her in German . . . she is touched by this. It is a concession to her worry.

"It is what I want, also," she says carefully in English. She wants him to know she will make an effort. She closes her other hand over his.

Her frustration from a moment before, her anger at his apparent failure to understand her trepidation, her fear that she cannot do everything he seems to be prescribing for her, abates but only slightly. The little hands release their grip on her neck, but she can still feel them there.

Mrs. Bulwer returns, fusses before the fire, and then brings to the table plates of toasted bread and sausages, boiled brown eggs in a bowl.

She sets down a tray with a teapot and two mismatched cups. Mrs. Bulwer pats Lina's shoulder.

"She's a tiny thing," she says to William, as if Lina is deaf. "You didn't say. Pity, about the pox scars. I suppose she's lucky to have survived, though."

Lina looks stoically at William. She has understood Mrs. Bulwer perfectly this time.

William avoids Lina's eye.

"I did not tell you, Mrs. Bulwer," he says conspiratorially. "My sister is indeed tiny, but she is a very powerful German witch. You'll have to watch out for her. She's very clever."

Mrs. Bulwer's face bears no expression for a moment, and then she laughs.

"Mr. *Herschel*," she says and turns back to the fire, but she pats Lina's shoulder again.

Lina does not look at William. She picks up an egg. It's warm in her palm, familiar.

"Mach dir nichts draus," William says. "Never mind."

WILLIAM WAKES HER when he returns in the mornings, smelling of the river. Drops of water from his hair fall onto her as he bends over her, shaking her under her quilts in bed.

"Sleepyhead," he says, though it is barely light outside. "You waste the good day."

She dresses and makes tea, and then they sit together in the kitchen, pulling the gateleg table near the fire for warmth, for the autumn weather is already cool. William gives her an hour of instruction every morning. He covers diverse subjects: music, arithmetic, astronomy, English, the practice of keeping the household accounts. He aims to make her a useful companion, she understands and, as with all things in William's universe, in short order.

She is tired during these dawn sessions. William berates her for yawning. But one day after a few weeks of this routine she finds she has awakened before William has come to fetch her. She is downstairs in the kitchen before he returns from his swim, and she has already made bread dough, two bowls of it rising near the fire.

He is clearly pleased to find her there, the kettle steaming.

It is early October, and there has been a first frost.

"Isn't it too cold?" she asks him as he sits down by the fire, rubbing his head dry with a shirt.

"When there's ice on the river," he says. "That's when I stop. The exercise sharpens my thinking."

It is difficult not to look at him, the shape of his strong shoulders and arms, the muscles moving as he dries his hair, his skin flushed. She wonders again about a woman, but there has been no sign of one so far.

He mentions no friend except Henry Spencer, whom she has yet to meet.

She will delight in Henry Spencer, he assures her.

She finds herself thinking often of him, wondering about this friend of her brother's.

SOON THE DAYS of rising early, of asking her mind to move quickly, create the habit of it. She wakes with her head already occupied with questions for William, as if they have been turning themselves over in her mind while she has been sleeping, questions about the nebulae that so interest him, about the moon, about parallax and its importance in astronomy. He teaches her the quantitative formulas and algorithms and geometrical diagrams used to compute the distances between celestial objects or to establish their positions in the sky.

Little lessons for Lina, William calls these hours of tutoring.

At the midday meal, which she prepares for William and however many workmen are about, there is often further instruction.

One day, while they are gathered in the dining room, he makes her guess the angle of the slice of apple pie she serves him.

She is flustered to have attention called to her in this way. She looks at the slice and makes a guess.

"Wrong," he says.

He reaches over and takes away her plate with its serving of pie. He takes an enormous bite. There is silence around the table. He looks over her. "What?" he says. "You must answer correctly, or you will have no pie."

The men look away, smiling. William takes another bite, and then another. He presses the tines of his fork to the plate to collect the crumbs.

She sits, her face flaming.

"I cannot believe it," she says. "You are eating my pie. Where is my pie?"

He pats his mouth with a napkin.

"Delicious," he says. "Unfortunate that you missed it."

She stands up abruptly and begins to gather the dishes. She is mortified, furious with William for embarrassing her. She feels every day all too aware of her ignorance in relation to her brother's knowledge.

The men hand their plates to her as she comes round the table, thanking her politely as if to make up for William's treatment of her.

"You can have mine," Stanley says. He lifts his plate with his uneaten slice toward her.

"Do not coddle her," William calls down the table. "You will see. She's cleverer than all of you put together."

At the end of the meal, when the men have gone back to work, the table is covered with William's papers, and there is ink on the cloth from his scribbling and his notations on musical scores. He leaves the table finally, a book in hand, a napkin falling from his lap to the floor.

Later she finds a plate on the gateleg table in the kitchen, a piece of pie untouched. On the back of a scrap of one of William's papers, someone has drawn an arrow pointing toward the plate.

She hears a sound in the passageway, and when she turns, she catches sight of Stanley's coat. She sits down at the table and eats the pie—it would seem ungrateful not to do so—but her stomach hurts and her mouth is trembling.

"My brother is a monster," she says aloud. "You are my only friend in the world, Stanley."

But she turns her back to the passage and wipes her sleeve quickly across her face. She does not want Stanley to see her tears.

OVER THE DAYS AHEAD, she runs continually from the kitchen to the garden or the workshop or to one of the rooms upstairs. She cooks for the men. Sometimes there are only one or two workers present, sometimes half a dozen, sometimes none at all, but Stanley arrives every day as soon as school is finished, and there is no end to the chores with which he can assist her: peeling potatoes, sweeping the rooms, working in the garden. His elder brother, James, who serves as William's foreman, is with them most days, as well.

She practices the harpsichord for an hour every afternoon.

She practices singing, as William had proposed, three times a day.

She copies William's letters, so that he may keep a record of them.

She washes their clothing.

She keeps on the table in the kitchen a list of the mathematical equations needed to compute exact positions of celestial objects, so that she might refer to it throughout the day, trying to memorize them.

She plans and cooks the household's meals.

She adds and subtracts figures from the accounts, gauges the weather and if there might be sufficient hours fine enough to hang out washing that day, calculates how long it will take her to copy the musical scores William has set aside for her.

She would never have imagined her head could hold so much. It is like the spoon from her childhood in Hanover with its magical convex bulge, she thinks, as she runs up and down stairs. More and more is added to her mind every day. She has never worked so hard in her life. She has never been so tired or so overwhelmed. Also, she realizes, she has never felt so happy.

It is only sometimes that she thinks about Margaretta, her friend's joy in contemplating the husband who would love Lina, the pleasure he and Lina would have under the quilts, the babies they would make. She tells herself—again and again—that she would not trade that imagined life for the one she has now, the excitement of being with William in England, of being part of his ambitions, of feeling her own store of knowledge grow so rapidly.

SHE LIKES BEST their morning lessons. The household is quiet then, just the two of them, and they sit close together by the fire. On these occasions, William sometimes strays from teaching her something particular to speak more speculatively about his investigations, the hours he spends with the telescope each night when the sky is clear. She likes the intimacy of these conversations, likes watching William as he looks into the fire, thinking and talking to her, eating the porridge she makes or the egg and cheese pies.

One morning he explains what he sees as the limitations of Flamsteed's *Atlas Coelestis,* his enormous star catalog, one of the atlases William consults so often. He believes, he tells her, that there are many more double stars than have been identified so far—she knows now that these are stars bound with another in a perpetual orbit—and moreover that these star pairs serve as gateways into the greater depths of the heavens, as well as keys to achieving more accurate measurements of the sky. If one can accurately measure the distance between double stars in a pair, he says, then one will have a basis for other, greater distances.

He pours more tea for himself, takes another piece of toasted bread. He intends, he says, with Lina's help and with the greater strength of his new, bigger telescopes, to begin a new catalog.

Lina understands enough by now to be daunted by the scale of this ambition, the painstaking hours ahead of sweeping the night sky to find these stars, of even knowing how and where and when to look for them. It is one thing to look at the sky at night in a purely appreciative way, uninformed about its contents, she has learned. One simply marvels lazily at the beauty of it. But it is another thing to *know* the stars and to imagine—as William does—that only a fraction of the universe has so far been revealed.

"This is a task for many, many months, is it not?" she says of the planned atlas. "I cannot imagine how you will do it, William. My mind already feels as if it will explode."

William laughs. He reaches over and puts his hands on either side of her head, waggling it back and forth as if testing the weight of her brain.

"Yes," he says. "Definitely bigger than when you arrived. I think it will not explode. I believe, Lina, that you possess the biggest brain in the smallest woman in England. I imagine it is plenty big enough for what lies ahead."

He smiles at her. "You are happy, Lina? I know it is a great deal of work for you here."

"I am exhausted, and you are a slave driver," she says. "I have never been happier."

"There is nothing you miss about Hanover? You have only to say so, and I will take you back."

She stares at him, astonished. "I wish *never* to return to Hanover," she says. She stands up. "Please, William. Do not think of it!"

He looks up at her. "Do you write to our mother?" he says.

She turns away. "You may send her my greetings, if you wish, when you write to her yourself."

William says nothing for a moment, and she moves away to begin making the day's soup.

"You are a most determined person, my sister," he says. "I am learning that about you."

She lifts turnips and onions from the basket, dumps them on the worktable.

William stands up. "One day you might wish to forgive her, Lina," he says. "I am thinking only of your conscience after she dies."

She will not look at him. "I can keep my own conscience on the score of our mother, thank you," she says.

But she is surprised to feel tears in her eyes. She stops and presses the backs of her hands to her face.

William comes and puts his arms around her. "I'm sorry," he says. "I am—how do they say it? An oaf."

"It is the *onions*," she says. "Only the onions."

WILLIAM CARES THE MOST about astronomy, Lina learns, but there is a living to be earned, and he must spend his days at the Octagon or giving music lessons or composing music or traveling to conduct at churches and concert halls nearby. Every hour when he is not occupied with music, however, he spends in the low-ceilinged, narrow workshop that extends into the garden, working on the mirrors for the telescopes he and the men he employs build to sell, testing different compounds of copper and tin, as well as the polishing techniques that will yield the perfect concave parabolic curve. She discovers that he cannot take his hands from the task of polishing a mirror, as any change in pressure on the soft metal will mar its surface and ruin it. She can see that the work is taxing.

Day after day that first fall in Bath, Lina watches William standing at the lathe in the workshop, sweat running down his face and soaking his shirt, despite the fact that the temperatures outside fall further with every passing week. He rubs the mirrors with a solution of ground sand and water, and then finally with a putty to achieve the necessary curve. A polishing session can last for twelve or even fourteen or sixteen hours, but in the face of every optician's refusal to help him, he is determined to find for himself the perfect formulas that will allow him one day to build mirrors of the enormous size he imagines.

"William, please," she tells him one day when he has been at the lathe for nearly nine hours. "You must eat."

He doesn't answer her. He can be like that sometimes, she has learned, so absorbed in whatever he is doing that he does not hear her when she speaks to him.

"*William*," she says again.

"Yes, yes," he says, impatient. "When I finish."

She returns to the kitchen. Where does he find the strength and perseverance? She does not want to think about how or whether he relieves himself during one of these marathons. It's possible, she realizes, that he has achieved such discipline over his body that he can in fact last for many hours without either food or bodily relief.

But his exhaustion after these long sessions of work troubles her. When William finally staggers away from the workshop, or comes in at dawn after a long night at the telescope, she does not like the look in his eyes, the way he seems not to see or hear her or anyone else. She is reminded at these moments of their father, his temper and his fragility.

Finally, one evening while William is at work polishing a mirror, she approaches him with a plate.

"All you have to do is open your mouth," she says. She keeps her voice quiet, noncommittal.

She extends a bit of chicken toward him.

This is how it begins.

When he works on the mirrors, or if he spends many consecutive hours at the telescope at night, reluctant to turn aside or to pause for sustenance, she stands nearby and feeds him, bits of cooked potato and meat, bread and cheese. She holds a wineglass to his lips, a napkin beneath his chin.

Even as she is aware of the intimacy of these exchanges, she sees that somehow William does not recognize her at these moments, is not exactly aware of her as a person separate from himself.

As on their walks long ago by the river at night in Hanover, they speak little.

It is not that there is anything wrong with her ministrations. He must eat, or he will surely faint from fatigue and exertion. But somehow she is glad that there is no one there to witness these moments.

ONE DAY IN EARLY NOVEMBER William suggests that she read aloud to him while he works, both to entertain him and to continue to improve her pronunciation for when she consents to sing in public at last. She will only embarrass him and herself, she tells him, if she cannot speak correctly. In truth, she would be content never to perform—the house has become a complete world for her, with plenty to occupy her, and she does not like to leave it even for the marketing—but William is resolute.

If she cannot feel confidence yet in her speech, then she will have to work to better it.

Despite the cooling weather outside, he keeps the workshop's door to the garden open. Wrapped in shawls, she makes her way over many days through *Don Quixote*. She struggles, but it is true that her English improves. Stanley often comes to listen, prompting her when she stumbles, though sometimes the way she says things makes him laugh.

"I like to think of you in my old Hanover, Stanley," she says, pretending offense. "Who would help you when you understand nothing of what is said to you? Me, Caroline, whom you like to mock, ha ha ha. I would be the one, and you know you would be grateful for my kindness."

AS THE WEEKS PROGRESS from November into December, darkness comes earlier and earlier. Lina reads to William every afternoon he is in the workshop; she reads aloud very slowly, uncertain about how to pronounce many words. Looking up from the page to rest her voice one day, she gazes into the garden. Doves call to one another from their places hidden in the ivy. Along the river and in the garden, the seed heads of weeds have turned to black powder that the wind scatters. The trees on the far side of the brick wall are bare of leaves, and the river has taken on the slate color of the winter sky. The sunsets are often brilliant, the colors reflected in the water. Hawks slide past along the river, their backs alight in the setting sun. She is aware of a vivid quality in these quiet moments—a bird on a branch, the river on fire, the mirror gaining brightness under William's hands. She has the sense that she is, for the first time, truly and deeply present in the world.

EVERY NIGHT when the sky is clear, she and Stanley help William wheel the fourteen-foot telescope into the street. Lina wraps herself in cloaks and shawls to take notes on William's observations of the stars' positions. It takes her time to understand the method and language of the star atlases, their maps of the regions of the sky. Sometimes William is irritated when she asks him to repeat something. But the following day they go through her notes together, and gradually the night sky becomes more familiar to her. William gives her turns at the telescope; it is true that gradually she learns to see more. And what she sees amazes her. After a few weeks, the moon's surface, its desert ridges and changing shadows and dark craters, feels as recognizable to her as the landscape around Hanover once had been, as the streets and fields around Bath are gradually becoming.

Stanley often stays overnight to assist them through the hours of observation, holding a lantern for her so that she can see to write and bringing hot bricks for their feet. She and Stanley are almost the same height; she knows that soon he will be taller than she is. She is touched by his loyalty to her; he follows her to market when he is not in school, helping her to speak with the fish women and the butcher—their accents are still difficult for her to understand sometimes—and carrying her packages for her.

Sometimes he brings gifts from his widowed father: a pair of perch, a basket of black walnuts, or a side of bacon. She understands that his father, with no wife to help him, is glad to have Stanley in the employ of William Herschel. She knows, too, from the account books, that William pays Stanley as much as any of the grown men in his employ.

One morning as she and William go through the month's expenses together, she observes that he pays Stanley, only a boy, wages commensurate with those of his older brother. "I think it is good," she says. "But I worry—maybe we ask too much of him? He is only a child."

"I have told him to be attentive to you," William says. "I pay him according to my esteem for you."

She colors. She does not want a companion *paid* to attend to her. William is paying Stanley to . . . to *love* her, she thinks.

She looks down at the account book, the columns of figures, her neat handwriting. For the first time in William's company, she feels—she cannot identify it at first. Then she realizes: it's loneliness.

It is because William understands that she will have no husband, she thinks. And what is a woman without a husband? He means to surround her with surrogates who may be compensated for their devotion.

William looks up at her from the pages laid out before them on the table.

"Stanley has displeased you?"

"Nothing Stanley does would ever displease me," she says. "He is the best of boys."

"I think so," William says.

There is silence between them for a moment. She reminds herself again of what she escaped.

"I am grateful to you, William," she says at last. "You know that."

"And I to you, little Lina," he says. "So there is no imbalance, no disproportion, between us."

It's not true, she thinks. The distance between what *she* does every day and what William manages to accomplish is vast. Her mind—it is like a little satellite star to his mind, and his mind is a planet, a sun. If he pays Stanley to help her, she should be grateful. He is only being considerate. Yet she cannot completely put away her discomfort.

He has recommended that she copy phrases in her journal

from time to time to practice her hand. That night before going to sleep, she opens one of the many books gathered at her bedside. She reads, even after only a few months, with improved command now. For her copybook she searches for sentences whose meanings not only do not elude her but also hold some significance for her.

Great joy, she reads, *especially after a sudden change of circumstances, is apt to be silent, and dwells rather in the heart than on the tongue.*

She copies these words, blowing on the page to dry the ink. She thinks about her joy. It *is* a great joy, whatever the complications.

Then she blows out the candle.

AGAIN AND AGAIN in these early months William mentions Sir Henry Spencer. Lina learns that he owns a farm in Hampshire and, like William, is an avid astronomer, as well as a physician. He is apparently a frequent visitor to Bath, where his mother, a widow, enjoys the company of society, but Henry himself is rather shy, William reports. He sees patients, though mostly those men and women and children who belong to his estate. He prefers to spend his free hours at home at the telescope rather than at parties and balls. He is also an excellent horseman; on several occasions that fall he has loaned William a horse for his travels, sending a well-dressed groom from the family's stable in Bath.

Lina looks forward to meeting this Henry Spencer, this man who appears to revere William as she does.

Through Henry's influence, William has been elected to join the Bath Literary and Philosophical Society. She has already copied one of William's papers—"On the Utility of Speculative Enquiries"—for the edification of this group.

"Oh, you will admire Henry," William assures her. "His mind is very quick."

A quick mind, Lina has learned, is William's highest praise.

Yet Henry Spencer does not come. His mother has been indisposed, William reports, and Henry has not wanted to leave her. He has had trouble with flooding on some of his fields. He is engaged in the purchase of some new horses. He has had difficulty with his farm manager. There has been an outbreak of measles in the village, and he has had business dealings in London. Every time Lina asks about him, there is some reason he will not visit them in Bath.

"You are very interested in Henry Spencer," William comments once.

She colors. "I am not," she says. "It is only that he is a friend to you."

But she knows that it is also true that she has imagined Henry will be a friend to her as well.

Other than Stanley and the men working for William, she has met few people since her arrival in Bath. She avoids her brother's music pupils, hiding in the kitchen when they come to the house, to his annoyance. She fears she will be forced into social circumstances during the approaching holidays. But she wants an intimate, she knows, not meaningless polite chatter. Henry Spencer with his quick mind and his affection for William might be an intimate.

She has purchased material for new dresses at last, but she has had no time to sew for herself. She will not show herself to the finely attired young women who come for singing lessons, often accompanied by their mothers, until she can put forth a better appearance, she decides. But to make a new dress requires hours, and there is always something else to do.

She is aware of their neighbors, of the glances of passersby who surely are acquainted with her brother. She wonders what they think of the handsome organist and choirmaster sitting all night at the telescope in the center of the street with his sister at his side. To those who wake from sleep and cross to the window to close the curtains against the moonlight, William and his huge telescope mounted on its rolling platform must seem, she imagines, like a strange invention from a dream.

OFTEN AFTER HIS HOURS at the telescope, William likes to sit in bed working for another hour or so. When he deems her proficient enough in English, he asks her to join him and to write as he speaks, because then he can be drawing or writing something else at the same time.

"How can your mind do two things at once?" she says to him.

"Two?" he says. "Why not three or four?"

To sustain them she goes down to the kitchen and heats a basin of milk or barley water. She sits beside him on the bed. He drinks and talks. He spills milk on the sheets.

Her eyelids droop.

"You are asleep," William chides. "Wake up."

He likes to read aloud to her from his transactions, the conclusions he is reaching, the assumptions he is making, as if by hearing the sound of his voice advancing his arguments, he can come to a greater understanding of his own mind: he is trying to calculate the height of the lunar mountains by measuring their shadows. He is obsessed with attempting to determine a method for measuring the distance between stars, information he is certain will help him begin to approach a correct scale of the universe. He is eager to prove the existence of some form of life on the moon or the other planets. She understands during these nights that it does not matter that he speaks to *her,* only that the ideas in his head need a voice.

All the rest of the world is *asleep,* she thinks. She and William are the only people on earth.

His shoulder beside her is warm.

She cannot help it. She is so tired.

When she wakes in the morning, William already gone and the sheets beside her cold, she is aware that he has allowed her to spend the whole night at his side.

ONE NIGHT, William retires early, after only a few hours at the telescope. Clouds have moved in, cutting short their viewing, and they are both weary. William has been working on a symphony, along with his usual labors, and Lina is glad to see him agree to climb the stairs to bed at midnight. Yet she feels unusually alert and restless.

She goes to the kitchen for the fire's warmth. She has begun to develop greater facility with the lamp-micrometer, the device William has built to arrive at more precise measurements of double stars he sees through the telescope. A flat wooden disk, three feet in diameter, the micrometer has mounted on it two oil lamps inside separate tin boxes; each box is pierced with a single pinhole and situated on an arm that can be rotated on the disk. At the telescope, William sights two stars and then adjusts the boxes on the arms and moves the arms on the disk so that the pinpricks of light emanating from the boxes appear identical in orientation and separation to the two stars seen through the telescope. From night to night it is Lina's job to measure the changing separation of the illuminated pinholes using a string stretched between the boxes. Then she must perform calculations to deduce the true angular separation of the two stars from the measured distance between the two boxes. The calculations are time-consuming, and in the beginning her mind is slow-moving.

Yet this evening it is as if the formulas have become second nature to her; she does not have to refer to them again and again to remember them. She makes coffee for herself, pulls the table close to the fire. By two a.m.—in just over an hour—she has all the evening's observations fully calculated and recorded. Already with the fourteen-foot telescope William has been able to see much more in the sky than anyone before him; the number of double stars in their atlas increases weekly.

She goes upstairs to slide the papers under William's door, holding her boots in her hand. She likes imagining what he will think when he sees what she has been able to do.

The next morning William looks up at her when she comes into the dining room with tea for him.

He has her papers before him.

"How long did this take you, Caroline?" he asks. "You must have been awake all night."

When she tells him, he looks at her for a moment. Then he smiles.

"Ah," he says. "I have been waiting for this."

THAT NIGHT when she goes outside to empty a bucket of water into the garden, she can see the constellation of Andromeda quite clearly. She knows the myth of Andromeda, the poor girl chained to a rock to await her possession by the sea monster Cetus, and the hero Perseus rescuing Andromeda by flying to her rocky island on his winged sandals.

It is true that she wants more. She knows she does. What she is beginning to understand inflames her imagination as it inflames William's, though she is aware that her mind's readiness lags far behind the movements of his. The universe contains *numberless* phenomena, she has realized—islands upon islands of nebulae, each possibly its own Milky Way.

They are, as William says, surrounded by worlds upon worlds. She thinks of the animalcules and her old childhood understanding of them.

She looks up at the sky. Occasionally when she and William are in the street at night with the telescope, she has the odd sense of being observed in return, perhaps by beings that watch the earth from their own distant stars, as William has suggested. The sensation makes her slightly uncomfortable, in fact, even as it excites—what *sort* of beings? But she does not mention this to William.

Sometimes in her dreams the brown-eyed, laughing sailor who carried her to shore at Yarmouth rises up out of the water and finds her on a rock. She sits, arms wrapped around her knees, waiting for him. She can never go to him, though—the water is too rough, and he cannot approach her—and eventually he sinks below the waves.

"Just as I predicted," William had told her. "You are ready for more."

TEN

Winter

• ◆ •

A span of clear, cold weather keeps William and Lina at the telescope for many hours each night. Often they sleep early in the evening for a few hours and then take advantage of the interval between midnight and dawn to focus on the southern sky, where they have an unobstructed view from just a few degrees above the horizon to the zenith.

The night sky in winter has a sharp, polished clarity, Lina has learned. This particular night is bitterly cold, and as they stand in the street, she knows her hands will ache when she returns indoors. She looks up; the Milky Way seems inflamed, as if the stars it contains multiply before them. She knows that the view of the winter sky from the Northern Hemisphere contains fewer stars than in the summer months, so her sense of their greater numbers now is only an illusion. It is actually the greater expanse of darkness surrounding them, those black depths, William has explained, that makes the stars seem so bright. But knowing this does not interfere with her impression that the sky, winter or summer, is—as William believes—in a constant state of flux, new stars continually dying and being birthed, arriving at and departing from the near sky, the whole firmament a brilliant—and active—hive of light.

William is determined to work as many hours as he can in

such fine conditions, but Stanley has developed a bad cough, and Lina has asked if his father will let Stanley remain with the Herschels, so that she might tend to him. This evening she is torn about staying at William's side for too long. She works alongside him for a few hours, adjusting the lateral motions of the telescope at his direction, taking notes, but she hears annoyance in his voice when she tells him she wants to go back to the house to check on Stanley.

She is tired tonight. This life of constant work is all right for William, she thinks, as she heats tea, boiling it with dried lemon peel, but she is worried about Stanley, who often pleads to spend evenings with them at the telescope. He is only a child, and he is ill now; it is unkind of William to be impatient.

She sits with Stanley for a while, waiting while he drinks the tea and until he falls asleep again. Then, an hour or so before dawn, when William has not yet come inside, she wraps up in her cloak and shawl and returns to the street.

A gentleman is with William, looking through the telescope. From time to time passersby stop and ask for a look. William is gracious about such requests; she has seen him detain visitors with his enthusiasm for longer than they might have wished, in fact.

William turns now, smiling as she approaches, his irritation with her from earlier entirely gone.

"See who it is," he says.

The man turns from the telescope. He is very tall. In the lantern's light, she is struck by the extreme paleness of his skin. At his temples are pronounced declivities, as if his head has been squeezed in a vise. His hair is red and wavy, brushed forward on either side of a bald spot; she has the impression that his brain presses painfully against his skull. His nose is pointed, with a deep groove at the tip.

A horse she assumes belongs to the man has been tied to the

post. At the market she often stops to stroke the necks of the big cart horses, to breathe in their pleasant, familiar smell. It is almost the only thing about her life in Hanover that she has missed, the happy hours she spent on their old horse's back, when she let him wander through the orchard, finding the occasional windfall apple. Now, this horse's beauty—it is a chestnut, gleaming in the moonlight—seems to throw the man's unfortunate appearance into even greater relief.

"At last he comes," William says, clapping the man on the back. "Here at last is our good Sir Henry Spencer."

The gentleman bows. He addresses her formally in excellent German. He welcomes her to England. He holds William in great regard, he tells her; he is grateful for the telescopes William has made for him, for the observations about the night sky he has shared. He is sorry that it has taken him so long to come to Bath and make her acquaintance.

Then he clears his throat. He understands from William that she likes to ride. He has brought her a horse, which her brother tells him she will greatly enjoy. He hopes she will accept the horse as his gift.

"Did I not tell you?" William says to Lina. "He is the best of men."

Again he claps Henry on the back.

"For me?" Lina says.

Henry bows again.

"Who has contrived this?" Lina asks. She looks at William. "This is your idea?"

"No, no," William protests. "I said only that you loved to ride. Henry intuits how best to meet a friend's desire."

"Tomorrow afternoon?" Henry proposes. "You will join me to ride along the river?"

Lina colors. She is glad of the darkness so that her blushing will not show. Yet this pained-looking man, his unflattering appearance . . . he is not at all what she has expected.

THE NEXT DAY IS LOVELY, despite the cold. The sky blazes bright and blue. No snow has fallen recently, but every night there is a frost, and the grass in the morning is furred with silver. Shortly after the midday meal, Henry rides up on a black gelding, leading the chestnut mare, which is to be hers.

He has arranged with William that she may keep the mare in the Spencers' stable in Bath. The Spencers will undertake all expenses for the horse's care.

"He is very generous," Lina had said to William at breakfast, when she learned of Henry's arrangements. "Why? It is his esteem for you?"

William had shrugged. "I have given him many fine instruments," he'd said. "But the horse is no great cost for the Spencer fortune. He wants us not to worry about what to him amounts to only a few pennies. That is his kindness."

In the daylight, the extreme paleness of Henry's skin is even more noticeable than had been revealed by lantern light the night before. His eyes are red-rimmed, his nose red also.

She feels sorry for him. It looks as if being in his skin pains him.

Outside the garden wall, William helps her to mount, her boot in his cupped palm. As soon as she is seated, she realizes she has forgotten how wonderful it feels to be on horseback, the sense of the animal moving beneath her, her body in contact with that of another living creature.

Her pleasure must be evident, for William laughs up at her.

"Lina will enjoy herself today," he says to Henry, as if she is up to some mischief.

She gives her brother a look—she feels embarrassed enough

already by the extravagance of Henry's gift to her, the prospect of their time alone together without a chaperone—but he only laughs.

They begin at a walk, moving into the meadows along the Avon, where the tall grasses near the water have fallen and form a brittle surface that shatters beneath the horses' hooves.

She expects that Henry will speak. It seems polite to wait for him to begin, but he says nothing, and after a few minutes the silence has lasted so long that she cannot imagine how to break it. She looks at the river in despair. The swans have kept pace alongside them for some time. When Henry moves a little distance ahead on his horse, she lies down quickly for a moment over the mare's neck and rests her cheek along the horse's mane. The pleasure feels secret, stolen, a comfort in the face of the strained awkwardness she feels in Henry's presence.

Finally, as they emerge from a copse into a long meadow, he turns to her. "You are comfortable if we let them run?" he asks.

She is nervous—her experience is limited—but when they rein in the horses after a few minutes, Lina is breathless.

"Oh, *thank* you, Henry Spencer," she says. "I had forgotten it, how much I like it."

He reaches to pat his horse's neck. He glances her way, smiling, but he says nothing further. Silence descends between them again. They turn around and begin toward home. Perhaps William pressured Henry into this generous gift after all, she thinks. Or perhaps Henry is sorry to have had to commit an afternoon to her company. She thinks of her scarred face; could even a man as unattractive as Henry Spencer be made unhappy by her appearance?

Why should it matter—she feels a momentary anguish—what a person looks like? *She* would be willing to be Henry Spencer's friend, as ugly as he is. She can do *nothing* about her face.

They ride side by side along the river. After a few moments, looking away from her over the water, he says, "Forgive me, Miss Herschel. Your brother will tell you. I am a poor conversationalist."

She does not look at him.

"I, also," she says. "And of course my English is still . . . Do not worry."

No more words are exchanged between them. They have disappointed one another, she thinks. They have mortified one another in some way she cannot fully understand.

William comes out from the workshop to greet them when they return.

"Join me at the telescope tonight?" he says to Henry.

"With pleasure," Henry says. He turns to Lina and bows from the saddle.

"I am very grateful to you," she says, but she feels her face color, and still she cannot look at him. Things between them had been so difficult.

William helps her dismount. She strokes the horse's neck. She would kiss her nose, but the presence of the men embarrasses her.

They wave goodbye to Henry as he rides off. As they walk into the house, William puts a hand on her shoulder.

"He is a very good man, is he not?" he says. "But I think he is—how do they say it? Not of this world, exactly."

THAT EVENING CLOUDS MOVE in and the sky is too overcast for observing. William sends Stanley with a message for Henry that their viewing will have to be postponed. Lina is glad that she will not have to face Henry Spencer again immediately.

But William is annoyed, pacing restlessly through the house. Finally, near midnight, he announces that he will use the time instead to polish his tools on the grindstone in the garden. He is frustrated, Lina knows, with the bad weather, nights of rain or now, possibly, snow. All evening the temperature has been dropping.

She is in the kitchen, scrubbing one of William's shirts, watching him march around the room, rubbing his head.

"You need sleep, William," she says. She feels weary from her afternoon with Henry, despite its pleasures. "*I* need sleep."

He has worked several days at the lathe—she has lost count of how many hours—as well as at the telescope each night. He *must* be tired, she thinks.

William ignores her and moves past her down the passage to the workshop.

She leaves his shirt soaking and follows him. He begins to gather his tools.

"Why don't you rest tonight?" she says. "Surely that can wait. What are you doing?"

"If you are in need of sleep," he says, "no one is preventing you from taking it. I will just sharpen some of these. They are no good to me if they are dull."

She watches him for another minute. She has the sense that he has insulted her in some way, accused her of laziness.

"Fine," she says. "Go sharpen your dull tools."

She leaves him, untying her apron as she goes and dropping it on the floor of the kitchen. She has had enough for the day. Suddenly their life—the constant work, William's obsessive ambition and drive—makes her feel profoundly, unmistakably lonely.

She climbs the stairs to her attic and washes her face in the basin. She sits on the bed, looking at the stack of books on the floor. Yet what she feels is not just anger at William, she knows. She had hoped that Henry Spencer would bring into their lives a third party who might sometimes distract William from work, that he would be someone with whom she could converse as well. She puts her face in her hands for a moment.

She has, she admits it to herself, entertained foolish romantic fantasies about him.

She does not mind that he is ugly or shy. These are superficial qualities that should mean nothing to a person of discernment. It means nothing to her, what Henry Spencer looks like. But he is not interested in her company. William is right; Henry Spencer is not of this world in some way. He doesn't *need* to work, so he may choose what medical cases interest him. Like William's, perhaps, his head is occupied with a higher order of thought than that of ordinary people, ordinary people who want—what? What? she thinks. What does she—an ordinary person—want?

Ordinary comforts.

So she is full of a woman's common stupidity after all, she thinks. But why can she and William not lead a more normal life? Every month they are out of money, and progress on the new workshop has ceased until he can procure further funds by performing somewhere. Night after night they spend in the cold and dark, looking at the stars; her labor of recording William's observations is never-ending.

Only Stanley is a joyful presence to distract her from William's needs.

She picks up a book and leafs through the pages in a desultory way. She has decided to blow out her candle when she hears William downstairs, calling to her.

In the kitchen she finds him white-faced, holding one hand wrapped in her discarded apron. Blood has soaked through the cloth and drips onto the floor.

"Sit down," she says, frightened at the amount of blood. "Sit *down*, William. For god's sake."

She fetches hot water, a basin. He is too stubborn! It is a selfishness in him to be so obstinate, to sacrifice his health and safety in these ways. On the nights when he cannot go out to look at the stars, he is morose and silent, withdrawn. He reminds her at those moments of their father. And what would *she* do if anything were to happen to William? What would happen to *her* life? She is entirely dependent on him. Once her music career commences, there may be some income there, but she still feels that she is not ready yet, and that the likelihood of her supporting herself by her voice is so small as to be worth nothing. Perhaps it will never come to pass at all. And of course there will be no husband for her, none of that protection—whatever its price—which is afforded most women.

She recoils when she unwraps the apron. One of William's fingernails has been ripped off completely. The exposed flesh is the white of a fish's belly and pulsing blood.

William turns aside.

"Yes," she says. "*You* cannot look, but I will have to."

SHE DOES NOT SPEAK again while she dresses the wound and wraps it in a length of clean linen. When she submerges the bloody rags in a bucket, the water blooms bright red. Standing to lift the bucket and carry it out to the garden, she realizes her legs are shaking. Outside, she stands in the cold air, breathing hard. She feels sweat break out on her forehead and over her scalp.

A moment later, she leans over and is sick onto the grass.

When she straightens finally, the world spinning before it settles, she looks up, tilting back her head and breathing deeply. The clouds have parted in places, revealing scraps of black glittering with stars. An acquaintance of William's, an astronomer from whom he has purchased some grinding and polishing tools, has written to William recently about the notion of "dark stars," as he calls them—chasms of deep darkness like wells in space—where the force of gravity is so powerful that no light can escape. She and William have discussed this idea. She finds the notion as terrifying as it is compelling. Again now she has the sensation of looking not up but down, as if into well water that reflects the sky, stars floating there.

She stares up at the sky for a few minutes, trying to conquer the old sense of this unsteadiness that sometimes possesses her when she thinks about the universe, the "island universes," as William calls them, beyond the Milky Way, stellar systems he believes to be in the process of formation or death. There are, he surmises, thousands—perhaps thousands upon thousands—of suns lighting up distant worlds.

The white tail of a rabbit running across the garden startles her. She looks down and sees that William has left his tools in the grass. If they stay there all night, they will rust.

She gathers them up and returns them to the workshop, drying them with rags before putting them away.

When she goes back into the kitchen, William is standing before the fire and pouring two glasses of spirits. He has taken off his bloody shirt and stands bare-chested, his belly slack. His face is very white, and the pupils of his dark eyes, when he turns to her, have dilated.

He hands her a glass, and then he turns away.

She looks down and sees that her nightdress is streaked with William's blood.

"You can say it," he says. "I am a trial. I know it."

She says nothing. The muscles in his arms and chest are well defined and powerful. His regimen of physical work has made him strong. There are a few gray hairs on his chest. Yet as he ages he becomes only more beautiful, she thinks.

He lifts his arm to drink, and she sees a corresponding movement in the dark window across the room, where their reflections are captured. Their images are almost comically disproportionate. She is so small. She has yet another apprehension at that moment of the distance between them, the gifts that William has been given, her own portion scaled as if to fit her size. Perhaps this distance between them will only increase, no matter how much she learns. Certainly she will never be less ugly than she is now.

She tilts the glass to her mouth and downs the sherry in one swallow.

"Oh," she says, surprised at the heat in her chest. She puts her fingertips to her lips.

"I'm going to bed," she says, when she can speak.

She turns away from William, his expression of confusion and contrition, and puts her glass down on the table. She knows that he is sorry for worrying her, sorry for injuring himself. Yet she also knows that he does not believe those costs constitute any reason to compromise his ambitions, nor will they change his behavior. He will go on this way until it kills him.

He follows her up the stairs, however. When they reach the door to his bedroom on the second-floor landing, he puts a hand on her arm.

"There is no one else, Lina," he says. "There is no one on whom I depend, as I depend on you."

She softens, looking at him. He is still very pale; his hand must hurt terribly.

"Good night," he says. She pats his arm, but she turns away and climbs the stairs without speaking to him.

He will not be satisfied, she knows, until he has done the thing that everyone says is impossible, until he has built a telescope so large and powerful that he can look beyond the perimeter of the known world and into the infinite—into worlds of light separated by unfathomable moats of darkness, she imagines—until he can make a mirror large enough to reflect all the light in the universe.

It occurs to her again that perhaps she is not ready for what will be revealed, if he can do as he hopes. She dislikes this coward who crouches inside her and sometimes bleats forth a protest. Her hesitancy reminds her of her mother's ignorance and fear, those two qualities so inevitably linked. Still, sometimes she has bad dreams, nightmares in which she falls through an endless sky, the trails of comets brushing past her—soft hands closing her eyes—as she reels into an abyss.

She does not like to think of *endless,* she has told William.

"Consider it bounded, if you like," he has said. "But, so, what is beyond the boundary, then? Nothing? How can there be . . . nothing?"

She strips off her bloody nightdress and exchanges it for a clean one. She does not want to return to the kitchen to put the filthy one to soak. It will have to be used for rags if she cannot wash out the blood tomorrow.

One *cannot* conceive of *nothing,* she thinks. One cannot imagine *forever.*

But she will have to, if she stays at William's side.

ELEVEN

Shadow

• ◆ •

The holidays come and go. Lina avoids having to perform by coming down with a sore throat and then with a bad cough that lasts for weeks. One day early in March, as she is tipping a bowl of peeled potatoes into a pot of water in the kitchen, William appears in the doorway. He is holding a letter and smiling. She scarcely has time to set down the bowl before he picks her up and heaves her over his shoulder. He carries her down the passageway and outside to the garden.

"What are you doing?" she cries. *"William!"*

He has recently conducted two oratorios, and the household is once again flush with money. The relief for them both has been great. After a period when construction on the bigger workshop had to stop for lack of funds and William was morose, now James and two other men—newcomers to the household—have been hired to continue the work. They turn at the sight of William jogging around the patch of grass in the garden with Lina over his shoulder. In his free hand, he holds the letter. Stanley, kneeling in the beds at Lina's instruction and mulching the cabbages with additional leaves for protection, looks up.

"It is from the Royal Society," William announces. "At last."

He sets Lina down. Then he embraces her, lifting her from

the ground for a moment. When he lets her go, she staggers backward and puts her hands to her head. Her hair has slipped loose.

Stanley falls over into the grass, holding his sides and laughing.

"And what is so funny to you?" She turns to Stanley, pushing
the pins back into her coiled braids and brushing down her skirts,
but she is laughing as well.

William turns to the others. "Today we will celebrate," he
says. "Lina, let us have cider for everyone."

The Royal Society, she learns, has confirmed William's observation that the Pole Star, *Stella Polaris*, depended on by sailors and
caravans of travelers across the deserts and lone wanderers to help
point them north, is not one star, but two. Moreover it also has
accepted his expanded catalog of the sky's double stars, his work
of the past several months. William has identified 269. Of these,
227 have never been seen by anyone before. The achievement, she
knows, is nothing short of astonishing.

She knows that most of William's observations that fall and
winter have pointed to the probability that the universe is not,
after all, in a stable state—a limited number of fixed stars revolv-
ing in predictable patterns—but in motion . . . or, rather, in *evo-
lution*, as he has told her. That William has revealed even the
familiar Pole Star to be not a single star but two in fixed orbit . . .
with only this single observation confirmed, the universe is suddenly much larger than anyone has yet imagined. She knows, too,
that Henry Spencer has helped persuade his colleagues in the
Royal Society of the truth of William's claims about the magnification powers of his eyepieces, traveling himself to show various members—with equipment built and furnished by William
himself—what he has been able to see.

William keeps a duplicate record of all his correspondence,
and she had copied the letter he'd written to Henry in which he'd

asked for his assistance. Lina knows the gentlemen of the Royal Society have been slow to accept William's findings; he has not come from within their own ranks, after all, and his discoveries are not only startling but also challenging.

It would be a poor fate to be condemned because I have tried to improve telescopes & practiced continually to see with them, William had written to Henry with some exasperation. *They have played me so many tricks, and it would be hard if they had not proved kind to me at last.*

Nearly everything William surmises has to do with his assumption that the solar system is one of uncountable numbers of other solar systems. She knows that one hundred nebulae have been identified so far, for instance, and that it is William's sense that these glittering vaults, star clouds rich with color and light, are like doorways into other, secret realms in the universe that he—and at least a few others—suspects exist.

Henry had sent William a reply.

If it lays in my power, you shall not be sent to Bedlam alone, for I incline much to be of the party.

They have much to be grateful for in Henry's friendship, she knows. Still, she wishes he would not be so painfully awkward around her.

"How can I put him at his ease," she asked William, "so that we may be friends?"

"What do you want with him?" William said, though not unkindly. "He wishes only for the company of his books."

"He makes me sad," she said.

"Why? It is only sad if you imagine him to be longing for something else," William replied. "I assure you: Henry is happy with his books and his horses and his farm and his patients and his telescopes. He wants for nothing else. Only for his mother to stop worrying him to marry."

Yet sometimes when Henry comes to visit with William, she catches him glancing at her with an expression she cannot quite read. They are like two stars in orbit around William, she has thought. They circle each other endlessly, but they will never meet.

That afternoon, as she works in the kitchen, she listens to William singing in the smaller workshop. She is glad of the day's news, the Royal Society conferring its blessing on William and—at long last—extending its formal invitation for him to become one of its members. She has copied enough of her brother's correspondence with other astronomers to know the widespread doubt that surrounds his findings. She feels offended by the stiffly worded hesitancy of his skeptics, though William appears to welcome invitations to prove his theories. She is touched by the earnestness and the civility of his replies, the effort he makes to send detailed drawings to other astronomers so that they might see what he sees, the gifts he has made of telescopes to enable others to share his own triumphs. There is little of selfishness in William in this regard.

Throughout these months, in fact, she has seen little in William she does not admire. He possesses qualities—confidence, charm, enthusiasm—that draw people to him naturally. And he is not afraid of hard work, a trait that endears him to those he employs and that earns him, in the end, the trust of those whose views he challenges. The men William hires to help build the outer workshop shake their heads over him, but Lina knows that they respect him, too, for he works alongside them with equal vigor. They are all excited by what he envisions, the construction of the twenty-foot telescope—one day, a forty-foot—that will allow a view into the heavens such as can hardly be imagined.

But every man William employs needs to be paid, and his supplies cost money, and sometimes they go hungry.

She had not expected that.

"Again, soup?" William says, when there is nothing but turnips and potatoes and carrots in the cellar.

His unhappiness at these moments pierces her.

She has come to hate evenings of poor weather, despite her gratitude for the intervals of rest they provide. She hates the silence of the house when there is no money to pay the workers, when William comes, dejected, to the meal she prepares at the end of day. He does not talk much then, but sits by the fire with a book and reads as if he is alone. On these nights, when his eyes are turned to the page, she supplements his bowl with potatoes from her own, and she watches the room fill with shadows.

YET THESE SPELLS of relative poverty never seem to last long. William organizes the musicians at the Octagon for an additional series of performances, and he recruits several new music pupils. Even in bad weather that winter, he has traveled to conduct concerts or to rehearse orchestras elsewhere. To improve the chorus in Bath and to encourage greater audiences, he has recruited singers with no experience at all, including from among the carpenters and joiners he hires for work with the telescopes.

Lina slips into the chapel one day to hear them rehearse, and she is amazed at the success with which these untutored men and women, under her brother's direction, render the choruses of the oratorios he has put before them. Such a sound he has coaxed from these common people! But it is their happiness, all their faces turned toward her beloved, handsome brother, conducting them with his customary energy, that most touches her. Of course people want to be in his company, to follow him on whatever untraveled path he charts. Flowers naturally turn their faces to the sun.

· · ·

SEVERAL DAYS AFTER THE LETTER from the Royal Society arrives, a cold rain falls. That evening, Lina heats bowls of lamb stew for herself and William, and they pull the table close to the fire. William is disappointed to be prevented by bad weather from the hours he would prefer to spend at the telescope, but a copy of a book by Erasmus Darwin, *The Botanic Garden,* has arrived, and it has offered William some happy distraction. Darwin is a member of the Lunar Society in Birmingham, where William goes occasionally for meetings and conversation, Lina knows, and William was pleased when a messenger delivered the book earlier that day.

William sits down at the table with the book. Lina looks at the titles of the two long poems it contains: "The Economy of Vegetation" and "The Loves of the Plants." William is not usually much interested in poetry, but the book has caused a stir among his scientific acquaintance, he tells her. They eat in silence for a while, William reading.

After a few minutes, however, he sets down his spoon.

"Listen," he says. He reads aloud:

> *Star after star from Heaven's high arch shall rush,*
> *Suns sink on suns, and systems systems crush,*
> *Headlong, extinct, to one dark center fall,*
> *And Death and Night and Chaos mingle all!*
> *—Till o'er the wreck, emerging from the storm,*
> *Immortal Nature lifts her changeful form,*
> *Mounts from her funeral pyre on wings of flame,*
> *And soars and shines, another and the same.*

He puts down the book.

"He predicts . . . catastrophe?" Lina says.

She looks at the fire. How exactly is one to understand Immortal Nature and her wings of flame? As a force unleashed by God?

William stands up and takes an apple from a basket on the table, polishing it on his shirt. He goes to the window, looking out at the darkness and the rain.

"Yes, catastrophe," he says, "but then a new universe to follow, a new beginning. Worlds without end."

Lina turns to look at him, his back to her as he stands at the window. She can see his reflection in the glass.

"Do *we* face catastrophe?" she asks. He has not exactly suggested this before.

"One day, perhaps," William says. He takes a bite of apple and then turns to smile at her. "Some think our magnificent sun has sufficient energy to last . . . only for ten million years. But there can be now no question of instability in the heavens," he goes on. "These explosions, if you will—these *systems crushing systems*—are perhaps the *source* of all the stars and nebulae that surround us, including our own planets and Sun. It is as Darwin says. He knows what I have seen, what others have seen."

Lina remembers the earthquake from her childhood, her worry that the moon had fallen from the sky.

William returns to the table and picks up the book again.

"He is a brilliant thinker, Darwin," William says. "I believe there is no one quite like him, really. But he has made some enemies, and he will make some more."

He lifts the book. "Even with this," William says. "A volume of poetry."

He takes another bite of the apple.

"They say *I* am a lunatic," William says, "but do you know that Darwin has made an organ able to recite the Lord's Prayer, the Creed, and the Ten Commandments?"

Lina laughs.

"It's true," William says. "He is not much for Christianity. This organ of his is a bit of a joke, but some have taken it badly.

He believes the world has evolved purely according to physical properties inherent in the universe, not by the hand of God. He says man's terror of hell is a disease of the mind."

William takes another bite of apple. "He is not afraid of much, Mr. Darwin," he says.

Lina stands and picks up their soup bowls. She knows, of course, that some people object to what her brother and other astronomers attempt. They perceive these efforts to understand the universe to be contrary to the quest for God, even an assault upon God's throne.

"These physical properties," she says. "This would be Darwin's Immortal Nature?"

William has opened the book again. "I suppose so," he says. "Yes."

"But *you* believe in God, William?" she says. It has not occurred to her to question this before—his faith as a younger man had been so secure—yet now the thought of God, somehow waiting just beyond the reach of her brother's telescope, gives her an uncomfortable feeling.

William closes the book, finger between the pages to mark his place, and looks over at her.

"How could anyone look through a telescope," he says, "and not believe in God?"

LATER THAT NIGHT when the rain stops, Lina steps outside. The sky is still overcast, the moon invisible. She takes a lantern with her into the darkness and walks along the garden beds where she and Stanley have been working during the day. The garden is temperate, thanks to the protection of the brick walls and the lingering heat of the furnaces in the new workshop. She has been able to start spinach and lettuces much earlier than usual, protecting them under a carpet of leaves. She moves the leaves aside with her foot. Her light catches the glint of tiny new green shoots. She holds it higher and passes it over the row of winter cabbages, their ornate pink and white and green furled heads beaded with drops of rain that shine in the lantern light. She lowers her lantern over the cabbages, bends down to inspect the bejeweled leaves glistening in the darkness.

She stands upright again. The streets around her are silent. She remembers the "dark center" in Darwin's poem. She is aware of the night's cool air on her face, the scents of wet earth and woodsmoke. She touches her fingertips to the soft skin of her neck, finds the pulse there. The manifest miracle of the world, its astonishing structures—cabbage or man or star cluster—has been William's inspiration from the beginning, she thinks. Of course his interest was eventually attracted by the deepest mystery, the vast unknown, the tantalizing beauty of the heavens.

It must be some smallness in her that sometimes she finds it crushing—she realizes she has Darwin's words in her head—to contemplate the numberless stars, the innumerable systems that surround them. Under her fingertip, she feels the quiet beating of her blood. She tries to concentrate only on the sensation of occupying her own body, but she cannot sustain it. The universe is all around her, and it, too, seems to pulse with a hidden force, commanding her attention.

THROUGHOUT THE REMAINING cold weeks of the spring the Avon has a border of ice on both banks, a thin stream of black water moving in its center. The rear garden wall now has been fully demolished to allow access into the meadow that borders the river with its commanding view of the sky, and the low-roofed workshop is nearly finished, built of heavy timbers and with a stone floor to withstand the heat of the furnaces. William has begun firing the furnaces and testing small mirrors made of various compounds of metal, and though the days have been bitterly cold, the heat of the furnaces when lit and the high brick walls to the east and west protect the garden.

One day in April, Lina goes outside with a basket of wash to hang to dry in the afternoon sun. The air in the garden is warm, the men working in shirtsleeves. She decides to bring tea to the table outside, and the men take their cups there, blowing on them and munching on bread and cheese she provides, as well as lady apples from the baskets stored in the cellar.

She is used to the men's company by now, more confident around them. They are polite fellows, grateful for the soup she ladles up at dinner, the breads and puddings she bakes. She stands with them for tea, her face turned toward the sun.

Later that afternoon, she rehearses with William in the music room, "Lo, How a Rose E'er Blooming." It is a favorite of his, the melody sad and sweet.

"And in German now," William says.

Es ist ein Ros entsprungen.

She stops when she notices him look up from the harpsichord. She turns around.

Thomas, one of the bricklayers, stands in the door.

William smiles. "She has a lovely voice, Thomas, does she not?"

"Yes, sir. Very lovely, sir," Thomas says, and he blushes. "Excuse me." He bows and turns from the door.

William looks at Lina.

"*You* are ready," he says, pointing at her.

"Nearly," she says. She does not meet his eyes. "Perhaps."

After William leaves the room, she stands by the harpsichord, depresses a key. The note lingers in the quiet room. She touches her fingertips to her face, the pitted surface of her skin.

• • •

A FEW DAYS LATER, William tells her that Henry Spencer will be in Bath for the weekend, and that he has invited him to dine. Lina has taken out the mare often that winter. Each time she has sent Henry a letter of thanks, telling him of her ride and some news of William or the household. He rarely writes a reply, but on several occasions she has opened the door to a servant delivering gifts from the Spencer estate: small and exquisitely wrought landscape paintings—she learns from William that Henry is an amateur painter as well as an astronomer and, like William, a musician. Once he sends them a pair of silver candlesticks, then a finely woven shawl for her, bottles of wine and claret.

William appears unimpressed by these gifts.

"Yes, of course. It is very kind of him," he agrees, examining one of Henry's paintings when it arrives one day, holding it up to the light of the window.

Then he looks at his sister. "I hope, Lina," he says, "that you do not imagine that he *admires* you."

She has been sitting at her writing table, but she stands up quickly.

"Of course not," she says, though she can feel her face coloring. "It is *you* he admires."

She realizes as she speaks that she has wondered this, if perhaps Henry is in some way in love with William himself.

"I have offended you," William says, though he does not sound contrite. "Do not misunderstand me, Lina. It is only as I told you. Henry is . . ."

"It is men," she says boldly. "He prefers . . . men."

William looks surprised.

"You go about so little in the world, one might think you know nothing of it," he says. "You surprise me. But I think it is not that, though of course I cannot be certain. I think . . ."

She has been touched by the extravagance of Henry's gifts. She feels—she wants to feel—that they are, whatever William says and though she has no evidence of it, tokens of Henry's esteem . . . for *her.*

William holds the painting against the wall as if to test how it will look there. It depicts the curved shoreline of a seaside bay, darkened winter fields, a sky of beautifully painted clouds.

"I don't know. It is as I have said," William says. "Henry wants for *no* companion."

He touches his temple. "He is not a man of the body. Only of the mind."

Lina looks down at the papers on the table.

"You have . . . spoken about this?" she asks him.

"Can you imagine such a conversation with Henry?" William says. "Of course not. And it is not that he has no feeling for a friend; you see that. But he has no interest in—intimacy, I think. I don't know how else to say it."

Lina straightens some of the papers on the table. Her feelings about Henry, rather than becoming less complicated, have only become more so as the months have gone by. She feels grateful to him for the gift of the mare. His attentions to their household and to William's career have been steady and kind. All around her are his gifts: a pretty Chinese bowl. One day a full silver tea service arrived, packed neatly in a hamper. A pair of soft kid gloves, cloud white, clearly intended for her.

She has never asked William about women, about whether he imagines a wife for himself. It would have seemed . . . an intrusion. They do not speak of such things. But she has wanted to, she knows.

"*You* have no companion," she says now.

She looks up and watches him examine Henry's painting; she wants to see his response.

But William only laughs. "How can you think so? I am *surrounded* by companions," he says. "And I have you."

"But . . . you have no *wife*," she says.

"Too busy," he says. "And no money. A wife is expensive."

She sits back down at her writing table, takes up her quill.

She is glad. She knows she is.

May they be poor forever, she thinks, if this is poverty's happiness.

THE NEXT EVENING, Henry and William sit at the gateleg table in the kitchen while she prepares supper. She has been anxious about the meal—they eat simply, and she imagines Henry will have expectations about the food—but William has told her not to worry. Henry is no more interested in food than he is in love, he says. They will eat in the kitchen, where they may all be comfortable. They have a ham, and Lina has made onions in cream and roasted turnips. Later, they will take out the fourteen-foot telescope. William is eager to show Henry his recent observations about the moon.

When they are finished with the meal, William pours more wine for them. He has been writing about the Lunarians, he tells Henry; he would be glad now of his friend's thoughts.

Lina and William have been looking at the circular shapes—the circuses, William calls them—on the moon's surface.

"You will indulge me?" William unfolds papers from his pocket.

Lina glances at Henry; she knows that some do not countenance her brother's theories about life on the moon.

But Henry sits forward with apparent interest.

She notices with sympathy his red-rimmed eyes, the strange way in which he holds his hands gripped together in his lap, as if it is necessary to contain them somehow. There is an unhappy pressure in her chest. Truly he is the most awkward man she has ever known. She has to look away from him.

William reads aloud:

As upon the earth several alterations have been and are daily made of a size sufficient to be seen by the inhabitants of the moon, such as building towns, cutting canals for navigation, making turnpike roads, etc., may we not expect something of a similar nature on the moon? There is a reason to be assigned for circular-buildings on the moon: as the atmosphere there is much rarer than ours and of consequence not so capable of refracting and reflecting the light of the sun, it is natural to suppose that a circus will remedy this deficiency. In that particular shape of building, one half will have the directed light and the other half the reflected light of the sun.

Lina looks over at Henry, but he gives no sign of surprise. William continues.

Perhaps, then, on the moon every town is one very large circus. Should this be true, ought we not to watch the erection of any new small circus, as the Lunarians may watch the building of a new town on the earth? By reflecting a little on the subject, I am almost convinced that those numberless small circuses we see on the moon are the works of the Lunarians and may be called their towns. . . . Now, if we could discover any new erection, it is evident an exact list of those towns that are already built will be necessary. But this is no easy undertaking and will require the observation of many a careful astronomer and the most capital instruments that can be had.

When he finishes, he looks up at them. He puts his papers on the table.

Lina looks over his shoulder at the drawing he has made, something that looks like an inky copse of trees.

Henry, too, leans across the table. William turns the paper so Henry can see it better.

"What is the illustration?" Lina asks.

"A lunar forest," William says. He bends over it with his quill and makes a few further scratch marks. "And I believe I have detected *growth*," he adds.

Something about this drawing of his, the little hash marks to suggest trees, and how close he bends to the page, makes her feel protective of William. It is not that she doesn't believe his theories; she has spent enough time at the telescope now to be able to see at least some of what William sees, though she knows her eye is not as acute or her mind as informed as his. She never knew William as a young child, of course, for too many years separated them, but she has an apprehension of him at this moment as childlike, the little boy gazing up at the moon. She remembers her own fanciful notions about the creatures that might—or might not—inhabit the other worlds around them. She lets her hand fall to William's shoulder for a moment, resting her fingers lightly there.

He continues to draw, but he reaches out to her with his other hand, palm up, surprising her.

After a moment, she puts her hand there, and he closes his fingers around hers.

"How much better," William says, "now that you are here, Caroline."

WHEN WILLIAM AND HENRY prepare to go out that night to the street, Lina says she will remain inside, that she has tasks to complete. Henry can assist William in her place.

"Another time, I hope," Henry says, bowing, as she prepares to go upstairs.

It is only a formality, him speaking this way, she thinks. It is just what people say. She knows that he will be happier if he can be alone with William.

It only occurs to her later, when she looks out the window of the music room at William and Henry in the street with the telescope, that perhaps William was laying claim to her in some way with that gesture, that hand opening and expecting hers to rest in it. He was telling Henry that Lina is not free to leave him and love another. That indeed she would not choose to do so.

After a moment, before one of them can sense her there, looking out at them, she turns away from the window.

THE NEXT WEEK BRINGS another book loaned to William from a fellow astronomer. It is part of her regular duties to copy such books, even this one in Latin, which she cannot read, and today the task gives her one of the headaches from which she sometimes suffers, the flashes of light and queer blank spots in her vision. William frequently prepares papers on his investigations. These, too, she copies, but she has fallen behind, and many pages await her. She sits by the window in the parlor reserved for music lessons, where the light is good, but when William leaves the house for an errand, she puts her head down on her folded arms, willing the pain to pass.

She is woken sometime later by Stanley, by his hand jostling her shoulder.

"He's back," Stanley says, quietly.

Lina sits up, blinking. At least the headache is gone. Usually there is no remedy for them except sleep.

"Thank you," she says. She touches her hair.

Stanley moves away, but he lingers in the door, a worried expression on his face.

"It's all right, Stanley," she says to him. She smiles to make him feel free to go.

She looks down at the papers before her. There are so many of them, an infinity of papers.

THAT WEEK, William begins holding rehearsals at the house with the performers he has engaged for the spring concert series. He composes chants and anthems and psalm tunes for the choir, the morning and evening services set in two different keys. The speed with which he transposes music astonishes her.

Yet every penny goes toward the household's needs and his pursuits in astronomy. He wants no horses, no comforts, no fine furnishings or clothes. Painful moments between Lina and William occur when there are not sufficient funds to pay their creditors, and Lina must present to William the difference between what they owe and their income.

"Every time I must go off somewhere to perform, I lose time," he complains.

That week during one of her music lessons, they argue.

"You are ready, Lina!" he says impatiently. "Anyone listening to you would say what I say. It has been months! You are *ready.*"

She feels guilty; it is true that if she began to sing in public, William would not have to pay another performer.

But she is *not* ready, she knows. She is not ready *inside.*

Gradually, though, she has begun to gain confidence in front of his pupils, mostly young ladies in town for the baths, including "dear Miss Farinelli," as William refers to her. He bends—archly, Lina thinks—over her white little hand.

Miss Farinelli's behavior around William is besotted. She issues peals of laughter, ringlets jiggling.

Though Lina feels less shy now, sometimes she has to contrive an excuse to leave the room when Miss Farinelli comes for her lessons, though William prefers for Lina to stay and sing duets. Miss Farinelli's pitch wobbles without a counterpoint.

One afternoon that week, Lina sees Miss Farinelli to the door.

When she returns to the music room, William has seated himself at the harpsichord again. He is in the midst of composing a sonata for it. He does not look up when Lina enters.

"Thank you for your help," he says, speaking over his playing. "Dear Miss Farinelli would go straight over the cliff without you to hold her back."

Lina smiles. "It is true that she cannot carry a tune. But her bosom is *very* practiced at heaving."

William laughs, plays a few more measures, his eyebrows lifted.

"I believe," Lina continues, "that her bosom is in danger of escaping her dress entirely, if you continue to encourage her to sing in the higher octaves."

William laughs again. He stops playing and writes something on the score before him.

"Miss Farinelli is a delightful creature," he says.

"You're *enjoying* looking at that bosom," Lina says.

"I have looked inside her head, too," William says. "And do you know? It's a perfect miracle. There is absolutely nothing there."

Lina goes away to the kitchen. She stuffs a brace of chickens. For a while there is a pleasant feeling of sunlight in her chest. She sings to encourage it, but as the afternoon wears on, her happiness fades.

One day, she thinks . . . one day William will take a wife.

Or a wife will take him.

TOWARD THE END OF APRIL William finally asserts that she is ready for her first performance at the Octagon, and that he will have no more delaying tactics from her. The evening she is to sing, he has been busy finishing a small mirror, and they are both late getting ready. At last they race out of the house and through the streets. She is breathless when they arrive—she will *never* be able to sing! Why must William always require her to be doing ten things at once?—but in the vestibule outside the big room of the chapel, where she can hear the musicians tuning their instruments, there is no time to worry. William adjusts his wig, tugs the tails of his coat, pats her on the head as if she were a puppy, and then throws open the doors, bowing to the audience, who greet him with smiles and applause. He indicates Lina with his hand—there is further applause—and then he sits down at the harpsichord.

She comes to stand beside him. She feels every eye upon her. She clutches her hands together and looks at her brother.

The audience is arranged in small groups in the little parlors throughout the room, the women in a rainbow of dresses that Lina can tell, even at a glance, are expensive. People have turned expectantly toward her. Silence fills the room, the musicians poised. She is aware of her face beneath her wig—she has powdered it and dotted rouge on her cheeks—and she suffers a moment of paralysis. She has no guide for such ministrations; perhaps the effect is terrifying, especially with the green of her dress. But William has nodded at the first violin, and the music has begun, and then he looks up at her, smiling.

She has had months of training from William, endless solfège exercises—*solfeggio per gli dissonanzie, per la falsetta,* and *per la sycopatione.* Now, almost without realizing she has begun, she hears herself move effortlessly into the music.

I heard a voice from heaven.

AFTERWARD, SHE IS KISSED. There are cakes and sweet wine. Ladies press her hand between their own, offer greeting cards, say she must call, how delightful, of course Mr. Herschel's sister would have such a divine voice. Where has he been keeping her?

Mr. Herschel, they say, teasing, why have you been hiding this little jewel from us?

Her cheeks feel warm. The ladies' gowns are beautiful, fields of silk. There is laughter in the room. Everyone seems to be turning toward her for a moment. She finds herself smiling and smiling. When William moves away from her side for a moment, she sees across the room to a mirror. Who is that little white-faced child? she thinks, and then she sees that it is herself.

From henceforth blessed are the dead which die in the Lord, she had sung.

Even so, saith the Spirit.

AFTERWARD SHE AND WILLIAM walk home under the moon.

Along with his other investigations, William has been sweeping regularly for comets since last October. She knows that, despite the occasion of tonight's concert, there will be neither rest nor celebration when they arrive home. She and her brother will haul the telescope up to the street, as usual.

William says nothing, either about her singing or about her green dress or her hair, over which she had taken a good deal of trouble.

"We shall have a good night of it," he says at last, looking up. "The moon in partial phase . . . but none of this English *rain*. I weary of the rain."

Lina follows his gaze to the sky.

There is her old friend the moon, its gray face scored with shadows.

TWELVE

Planet

Weeks of bad weather ensue. Wind and rain blow in visible gusts like giant hourglasses bending across the meadows by the river. Finally, there is a lull in the relentless clouds. On the first warm day—the sky the pale blue color of milk, the long branches of the willows along the Avon swaying in the breeze, wrens busy in the damp grass of the garden, the scents of running water and thawing earth in the air—Lina boils kettle after kettle and washes everything she can.

William has to work in the music room with a woolen blanket over his shoulders, as she takes every last one of his shirts. Stanley helps her string lengths of rope across the garden, so that they can hang everything to dry in the rare interval of sunshine. They carry chairs outside and stand on them to pin things to the lines. Stanley and James lost their mother to pneumonia when Stanley was an infant, and Lina knows that Stanley has found in her not exactly a replacement for his mother, but an affectionate companion; they are more like sister and brother than parent and child. When she throws a damp sheet playfully over his head, he clowns under it. *Where am I? Where am I? Someone bring me a light!*

With Stanley she feels truly lighthearted.

Over the days since her debut at the Octagon, William has

planned a series of performances for her, including a first principal role in Handel's *Judas Maccabaeus,* but by the end of the day of laundering she again has a fierce sore throat. Before nightfall she has lost her voice. William, perhaps so pleased to be restored at last to his place at the telescope after the long spell of bad weather, seems unconcerned; the performances are still weeks away. He encourages her to stay in bed and recover. Stanley attends to her, walking carefully upstairs throughout the day balancing cups of tea.

Henry Spencer, who is in Bath, hears of her illness and sends oranges. Stanley brings the crate upstairs to her, and she rolls the oranges between her palms, releasing their fragrance into her attic room. She tells Stanley to take as many as he can eat, to fill his pockets with the fruit, and she peels and eats one orange after another. Henry's kindness is remarkable, as always, but she has not forgotten the evening when William appeared to lay claim to her in front of Henry, taking her hand in his. That gesture—so unlike William, who is rarely demonstrative with her—has continued to trouble her. She doesn't like what it suggests about her brother, that Lina somehow belongs to him, and that William had wanted to be sure Henry understood that. What right has William to determine to whom she might give her affections? What if Henry Spencer had been a different sort of man?

Her head aches. She rolls over and closes her eyes. A different sort of man would not be drawn to her, in any case, she knows.

She cannot make herself comfortable. Orange peel litters the bedclothes. She stares up at the cracks in the corner of the ceiling. Perhaps it was only that William wanted Henry to be assured that Lina is happy, that she is cared for and loved, that Henry need feel no concern for her, or any hopes that she might have about him. Still she has avoided Henry on the most recent occasions he has come to join William at the telescope. Some unhappiness makes itself felt between them—his desire not to wound? Her sorrow, perhaps, for what cannot be given? And William's gesture did nothing to dispel it.

She gathers up a handful of orange peels from the sheets, bringing them to her nose. If she is sometimes weary or lonely . . . well, these feelings are nothing in the face of her contentment. It is a fool's sentimentality in her that persists, perhaps, echoes of her years at Margaretta's side when her friend would prattle about the natural affections between men and women, imagining the hand of Lina's gentle, blind husband falling to his young wife's head in kindness and concern.

An idle fantasy, that had been.

SHE COMES DOWNSTAIRS after two days of rest to find William at the harpsichord.

He looks up. "Ah! You are well at last," he says, as if she has been absent for weeks. "Good. I have left you my notes."

He resumes playing. Lina goes down to the kitchen and makes coffee for herself, toasts bread. She comes back upstairs with a plate and her cup and sits at her writing table. Her illness has left an odd ringing in her ears, and she shakes her head now, trying to dispel it.

It is one of Lina's tasks to record William's notes neatly in his observation book, which is organized by date. She turns her chair so that the light from the window falls over her shoulder and onto the page of scribbled notations before her. William is playing one of the sonatas he has written, repeating certain phrases.

She pulls the papers toward her.

Pollux is followed by three small stars at 2' and 3' distance. Mars as usual. In the quartile near Zeta Tauri is a curious either nebulous star or perhaps a comet. A small star follows the comet at 2/3rds the field's distance.

She looks up at William.

"A comet?" she says. "You didn't tell me." This would be news.

Her brother stops playing for a moment. He looks out the window. "Perhaps," he says. "We shall see."

But the next night, Lina at his side, he finds the object again, some distance away from its former position. Over the following two weeks, apart from two evenings of rain that interrupt them, he is able to track the object, which reveals itself as a small disk, with a pale greenish cast. Lina measures it using the micrometer. Whatever it is, it appears to be approaching.

But stars do not move, Lina knows, and this object, unlike most comets, has neither beard nor tail.

ON THE THIRTEENTH NIGHT of viewing the object, clouds move in from the south. Lina and William come inside just before three a.m., but William goes to the kitchen and uncorks a bottle of claret. He pours two glasses, handing one to her.

His expression is serious. He raises his glass to her.

"To my faithful assistant," he says.

"It is not a comet, is it?" she says. "It's a . . . planet. A *new planet*, William."

She reaches for the chair behind her, sits down.

William leans forward and touches his glass to hers.

"There is still much to see and learn about this object," he says. "Weeks—even months—of observation and measurement lie before us. You should know that by now."

"But still," she says. "I think—and I think *you* think—that it is neither star nor comet. It has none of those characteristics. Oh, *William*." She feels unsteady at the thought of it. "How did you know *where* to look?"

"It is not that I knew where to look," William says. "It's that it was *there*. I only built the device by which to see it."

He turns to the fire.

"Be in no haste, Caroline," he says again. "It will take a long time for the scientific world to acknowledge what I have found. Many eyes will have to see what I have seen, and they will need my tools to do so with any accuracy. Meanwhile, there is much else to do."

She looks up at him.

She remembers her father, bemoaning William's premature death, what a loss to the world it would be. He had been right, though not about the death. William has always had the shine of immortality around him, and now—somehow she knows it is true—he has stepped onto the stage of world history. The universe is suddenly exponentially larger, for this planet—if indeed that is what it is—must be orbiting the sun *far beyond Saturn*. It is almost unthinkable. She stares at William gazing into the fire, his handsome profile. How strange it seems, that it should be *her brother* who would become the first man in history—in recorded history, at least—to discover a planet, to expand the universe around them as surely as if he had put his shoulder to the ceiling of the sky and pushed against it, heaving it open like a door. She remembers the evenings in her childhood when William lifted her to his shoulders and walked with her into the soft, quiet night beyond the lights of Hanover.

He has always carried her, she realizes, and he carries her still. In a way, he carries them all into a future so much brighter—and yet so much more complicated—than anyone could have imagined.

WILLIAM IS CORRECT. As soon as he furnishes his account to the Royal Society, letters begin flying back and forth between Bath and London, and before long from around the world. Half of those delivered in the next weeks and months misspell William's name. Several are insulting, accusing him of outright lies.

One writer says he is "fit only for Bedlam." The magnifications of William's telescopes far exceed those commonly available; he has made lenses with powers greater than ten times those in use by even the most expert and well-equipped astronomers.

William writes patient descriptions of the object's location, and Henry helps transport telescopes to London, as well as to other interested astronomers in England. Meanwhile debate about William's finding rages on.

Regardless, the discovery distracts him surprisingly little, Lina sees, as if, having guessed that there was more to be seen, he is neither surprised nor satisfied. As soon as the workshop and furnace are completed in May, William's experiments with the larger mirrors he envisions begin in earnest. Construction on the twenty-foot telescope has proceeded in the house and in the old workshop attached to the house, where the men have been building sections of the new instrument, as well as the eyepieces and necessary bits of joinery, along with a supply of smaller telescopes to be sold or given away to William's colleagues.

William continues to test various mixtures to find the right combination for the mirrors he imagines for the giant reflector. Lina writes letters to suppliers all over England trying to procure sufficient quantities of copper and tin. William and James and another workman experiment with amounts of wrought and cast iron, arsenic and hammered steel in dozens of small models, but again and again William is unsatisfied with the results. Some materials improve the polish of the mirrors, he discovers, but either they do not reflect much light or they make the final product too brittle. The work is painstaking—they must keep careful records of the formulas—and exhausting. The furnaces are menacing, and the lathes for polishing the mirrors are vicious instruments.

One morning a workman appears in the kitchen, blood spattered across his shirt. "Missus," he says, breathless. "Can you come?"

Lina drops the basket of onions she has been holding.

In the garden, she finds James helping to support William outside from the workshop, one hand bound in linen but copiously bleeding.

"It is nothing," he says, as they help him to lie on the grass. "Truly, nothing . . ."

James approaches her. He keeps his eyes on her face, his hand closed tight around something.

"We ought to call for the surgeon," he says quietly.

When he opens his hand, the tip of William's finger is there. Lina stares at it.

The next moment, William has fainted.

THAT AFTERNOON, after the surgeon has sewn up William's finger and departed, Lina sits beside her brother on his bed with a basin of hot water.

In polishing one of the mirrors on the lathe, his hand had slipped, William had told the surgeon.

"It was only carelessness," he says now to Lina. "Do not punish me with your eyes like that, Caroline. I will be more careful."

"It was your *exhaustion*," she says. "You push yourself too hard, William."

He smells of the iodine the surgeon used on his finger, and of the lavender with which she has scented the water she uses to wash him. There is blood all over his arm and chest, where he'd held the injured hand. She runs the cloth over him now. His skin, where it has been little exposed to the weather and the sun, is soft and white. She has set his blood-soaked shirt in a kettle of hot water with lye.

She moves away the basin and helps him now into a clean

shirt. He leans back against the pillows, and she settles again beside him. His eyelids flutter.

She has so rarely seen William asleep that when his head drops to her shoulder, she is afraid he has fainted again. But his chest rises and falls evenly, the bandaged hand propped and held high over his heart, as the surgeon has instructed. The fingertip could not be restored, of course. The surgeon was only able to stitch up the end of his finger. She worries that William will never again be able to play the harpsichord as he once did, though perhaps he will manage on the organ, which requires less delicacy.

The house is quiet. She had sent James and the other workmen home.

"That is enough for today," she'd said to James. "I fear he will kill you all with his endeavors."

James had demurred, protective of William. "It was only an accident," he'd said. "Could have happened to anyone."

But he had seemed relieved to close the door to the workshop when she said she would take care of the mess inside.

"Take Stanley with you," she said. "He works too hard as well. Everyone here works too hard."

There is much to be done now—she will have to face the blood in the workshop, a task she does not relish—but she does not want to leave William just yet. In the silence, she realizes how accustomed she has become to the noisy chaos of the household, music emanating from one room, the sounds of construction from the workshops, even messengers at the door, knocking or ringing the bell, delivering letters or packages. It is only at night, when she and William are alone aiming the telescope into the sky, that the world's ceaseless chatter falls away.

A WEEK LATER, Lina looks from the kitchen window to see a farmer arrive at the end of the garden with a raggedy cart heaped with manure and pulled by a pony. Two little boys running along beside the cart climb into it when the farmer pulls it up and stops, and at once they begin pitching the clods into the garden. William appears with shovels, and he and the farmer start shoveling the manure to a spot just outside the door of the old workshop.

The growing pile steams. She cannot imagine what William intends to do with it; it is far too much for the vegetable beds.

Lina leaves the window in the kitchen, where she has turned a bowl of dough for a last rising. She has been awake, as usual, since before dawn. From the window of her bedroom, as she had buttoned her dress in the dark, she had seen Aquarius tipped on the horizon. The seasons are progressing. There are loaves to be punched down now and pea soup to be started. Later she will roast two ducks brought to them by Stanley's father. She has learned that if she wants to complete the work of feeding the household, she must find time for it before William requires her for other tasks.

She wipes her hands on her apron and goes down the passageway and out to the garden.

The cart has been emptied in short order. The boys wave to her from the back of the wagon as it tilts and rocks away down the track running alongside the river. William, his shirt loosened, sweat on his forehead, stands by the heap. The smell reminds Lina of their old stable in Hanover, the hours she had spent in the horse's shadowy stall, watching the progress of the spiders laboring in their high cobwebs.

William leans the pitchfork against the wall of the workshop.

"It's a good supply," he says, "but I fear not quite enough. Well, I can get him back for a second trip, if we need more. No shortage of manure in the world, after all."

He turns to her. "When shall we begin? I think it will be easy enough work."

She tucks her hands beneath her armpits. The air is warm, but her hands suddenly feel cold. "Begin *what*?"

"We discussed it, surely," he says. "It's for making the molds, for the mirrors."

She must look baffled, because he continues with some impatience. "The manure. We will pound it in a mortar and sift it fine. It will be the perfect material, very strong and yet sufficiently flexible."

"William," she says. "I do not understand you."

From among the tools leaning against the workshop wall, he produces what she understands after a moment is a giant pestle, a wooden post that has been sanded neatly to a cylinder and rounded at one end. From the doorway beside the pile of manure, William drags forward a large barrel sawn in half.

"Better outside than in, I think," William says. "It will be dusty work. But fine exercise, of course." He claps his hand against his chest.

She looks at the pestle, the barrel that will serve as mortar bowl, and then at the heap of dung.

"You want *me* to do this work," she says. "In addition to everything else. You're serious."

"Stanley will help you," William says. "He is a big enough boy for such labor. And Henry has said he will come take a turn when he is here. In fact he has built the sieve we will use to sift it. I expect it to arrive any day. I don't think it will be too big for you to manage."

She hears defensiveness in William's voice now, the aggrieved tone he is capable of taking with her when she is not wholly enthusiastic about some enterprise. His face—his expression in concentration like that of a statue of an emperor, she has thought, both grave and noble—can take on a spoiled hauteur when he feels he is being resisted.

"You cannot really mean for me to do this," she says.

He does not answer.

"*William.*" She knows her tone is sharp, but she can't help it. "To pound *manure?*" she says. "To sift *dung?*"

His jaw is set, his expression truculent.

"There is no other way," he says. "The mixture must be very fine before we can mix it with water. Otherwise it's likely to crack when we fire the mirrors."

"Get the *men* to do it!" She feels outraged.

"It's *pointless* work for them, Caroline," he says, and now he actually raises his voice. "*You* cannot do the work *they* do. It's a waste of their time!"

He takes up the stick to be used as a pestle, pounds the ground with it a few times, as if she has failed to understand how it is to be managed.

"And *my* time?" she says. "What of *my* time, William?"

He frowns and says nothing.

"You don't know what to say to me right now, do you?" she says. "You have no answer for me. It is not enough for you to find planets and comets and to catalog every star in the heavens and build a telescope as tall as—as a house," she says. "I see now it will *never* be enough for you. Nothing will ever be enough."

He does not look at her.

"I thought you were happy," he says. He turns away from her and stares at the river.

"I *am* happy!" She puts her hand over her heart. "I am *happy*, William! That is not it! You are being . . ."

She looks at the heap of dung and then around at the garden. James and another workman have appeared in the open doors of the big workshop. She supposes she has raised her voice as well.

"I shall find someone else to do it," William says, more quietly.

"No," she says. *"No."* She will be involved in the great work of their life, even if it means sifting dung. She doesn't want anyone *else* to do it. But why can he not see that what he asks of her is so . . . unfair?

She unties her apron and then reties it more tightly around her waist. She runs her hand over her head, the braids wound there. She raises her other hand, holds her head between her palms for a minute.

"We begin *now*," she says. "As always."

SHE SPENDS THE NEXT few weeks helping to make the molds, pounding the manure into dust for hours at a time. At the end of the day, her back and shoulders are so tired and sore she cannot lift her arms above her head to unpin her hair without pain. There is filth in her handkerchief when she coughs and blows her nose, the cloth stained black with dust and red from nosebleeds.

The only thing that keeps her going is her fury at William. He *is* a lunatic, she thinks. She doesn't care if he *invented* the universe. He has no feeling for other people.

One morning while she works, a scarf over her nose and mouth, grinding the pestle into another barrel of manure, a tremendous blast sounds from within the workshop. The ground shakes beneath her feet.

Holding their hands over their heads, the men run from the workshop out onto the grass.

One of the furnaces has exploded, she understands. The mirror on which William has been working must have shattered.

She drops the pestle.

William and James have stopped and stare at one another. Then, surprisingly, they begin to laugh.

"My god," William says. "That was a near escape. Look—"

He bends down and picks up a glittering shard; the force of the explosion has embedded fragments of the mirror in the earth. James doubles over, howling, as if it is all a great joke.

She cannot understand why they are laughing. She keeps the accounts, and she knows that nearly five hundred pounds of metal has been lost—who knows whether any of it can be salvaged? And the furnace will need to be rebuilt. They have no money for such endeavors right now! William has found a new planet, he is the greatest astronomer on earth, and yet they have hardly a shilling, and he is laughing like a madman, wandering around and picking up pieces of the shattered mirror. They might have been killed. *She* might have been killed, a piece of the mirror lodged in her heart!

Her legs are trembling. It is as if she has not seen the mad enterprise of their household clearly until this moment; other people *do not live this way.*

She puts her hands over her face.

William approaches her. "No harm was done, Lina. Look. No one has been harmed."

"It is only relief," he calls to James, patting her back. "She is only relieved we are all right."

She does not want William to touch her.

"I must go for a walk," she says.

She takes off her filthy apron and drops it on the ground. She wrenches away the scarf from around her neck. She knows William is bewildered by her reaction, but she doesn't care.

"Don't," she says, when he tries to put an arm round her shoulders.

"I can't, I can't . . ." But she cannot finish her sentence.

THE AIR IS COOLER by the river. She walks quickly, her hands under her arms.

She is exhausted. It is her fatigue as much as her fear that has upset her so; she knows that. Yet why does William appear to thrive on the furious pace he keeps, at work all day on the twenty-foot telescope or the mirror, up all night looking at the stars, and meanwhile composing music, directing the choir, conducting the orchestra?

He is truly the happy genius of his own company.

He needs no companions, she thinks—not even her—unless they are useful to his ambitions.

He loves no one. Not really. He lives only for the work.

How would he have felt if she had been killed in that explosion?

On the river a pair of swans keeps pace with her. She puts the backs of her hands to her eyes, wipes her dirty face. She never forgets that she owes William her freedom and the privilege of this position at his side, watching as scientific history is made. She owes him the welcome expansion of her mind and even her body—her voice, these newly strong arms. Yet why, why when the furnace exploded . . . why were *they* laughing, while *she* feels so angry? And so sad?

She glances at the river. The two mated swans have become four, she sees, the reflection of each white bird mirrored in the water's surface as the light has changed. Afternoon closes in toward evening. There will be a mess back at the house, she knows. The men are no doubt already working to clean up what they can from the accident: the broken bricks of the furnace, the cracked flagstones. She can't exactly imagine the extent of the damage, but she knows that days and days of work will have been lost. There will be filth everywhere, filth that William and the men will track into the house. She thinks of the kettles of water she will need to heat so that they might wash. Their faces had been black with soot, and their clothes filthy.

She stops by a willow tree and looks at the river.

The young ladies she sees on the streets of Bath stroll arm in arm in their lovely dresses and tiny slippers or in the company of finely dressed gentlemen. That is not her life, and she knows she would not trade the life she has now for theirs. She finds the conversation of the women who come for music lessons uninteresting, though it is not their fault; they have no tutor such as she has had in William. They seem childish to her, these young women, even unreal, somehow, with their powdered skin and fine clothes and elaborately dressed hair and long gloves. They sing for William, their eyes heavenward—some of them prettily enough, a hand resting daintily on the harpsichord—and their stout mothers look on approvingly. But she would not want to be them. Not for a minute. The life she has with William is as provocative and exciting as she could ever have imagined for herself. Yet still she cannot seem to prevent the sadness that overtakes her sometimes, her old familiar, her loneliness. Her *Überangst.*

It is the ghost of her father in her, perhaps.

There is some longing in her that she cannot name or assuage . . . except she knows that it only goes away with work, work, and more work. Perhaps this, too, is William's dilemma.

It's strange to her that sometimes she feels this longing most piercingly when she looks up at the night sky with William. How oddly alone she feels then.

What would it be like to lie down beside a husband every night, someone whose steady breathing comforted her in the dark hours?

She would marry Henry Spencer, she knows. She loves him for his kindness and his generosity, and she does not want to feel alone in the world, as she sometimes feels when confronting—or being confronted by—the endless distances of the night. But Henry Spencer will never ask her to marry him, though likely there is not another woman on the planet with whom he could share so many of his interests.

It is time for her to turn back.

She is hungry, she realizes. Lately, working in the garden so often, she has been much in the company of the men. She brings tea outside to the garden most afternoons when the weather is fine and eats with them. She likes being with them. They even tease her—how is it that such a tiny woman can put away such quantities of bread and cheese? they ask. No one expects her to be silent on these occasions. She is as much a part of the shared endeavors as any.

The swans proceed away from her down the river, the two white bodies side by side. When they disappear beneath the canopy of a willow tree's long wands hanging over the water and touching its cold surface, she turns back to the house. The hours ahead seem very long indeed.

THAT SUMMER, after deliberations by the Royal Society, which has amassed many excited reports confirming William's observations from other astronomers around the world, the object William saw is determined finally to be a new planet.

William wishes it to be named for the king, the *Georgium Sidus*.

With the Society's official recognition, and thanks to support from Dr. Maskelyne, William is awarded the Copley Medal by the Royal Society and named a royal astronomer for a salary of fifty pounds a year. It is not anywhere near enough to support him and to pay consistently the men in his employ, but Henry Spencer succeeds in lobbying for additional sums from the king toward the construction of the forty-foot telescope. Lina, balancing the books, calculates that with occasional concerts and performances of William's music, they can make do for a time, but she knows that her brother's ambitions will soon outstrip their income, and there is the problem of where the forty-foot telescope will be built as well.

William makes frequent trips between Bath and London or Windsor in the weeks after the announcement. He takes the seven-foot telescope with him, and uses it to instruct King George, who is very enthusiastic. He writes daily to Lina when he is away. On one trip to London, when the sky is cloudy and William cannot provide his usual entertainment with the telescope, he delights the princesses with elaborate displays of lamps lit in the gardens at Kew and pasteboard models of Saturn mounted on the garden walls. Of this pretty conceit for the royal young ladies, he writes to Lina with undisguised pride: *The best astronomer might have been deceived! You know vanity is not my foible, so I tell it all to you without fearing your censure.*

Gradually, their life in Bath begins to change. With the Royal Society's recognition, William has garnered greater numbers of friends in the scientific community, and he is away from home more often. Lina knows from the letters he receives that he has risen from his status as an eccentric amateur to a leader among astronomers of the day: more enterprising, bolder in his approach, and with a genius for mechanics and invention, as well as a gift for writing and explanation. Henry Spencer tells her on one visit that William's charm has won over even the most reluctant and stodgiest members of the Royal Society. It is impossible to resist the combination of William's intelligence, his obvious accomplishments—as Henry says, no one else is building telescopes the size of William's or with mirrors so large and fine—or his good humor and delight about it all.

Lina is busy almost every day making copies of William's papers, his endless reports on his observations, as they are now in great demand. Conversation flies among poets and philosophers and scientists about William's theories and conclusions, the new view of the solar system emerging from his observations. There is still argument from those who believe his investigations a threat to piety; William has shown the universe to be not the "immortal tent" described by some poets but rather a wild and unbounded place, its deepest recesses in a continual state of colossal and spectacular dissolution and decay and reconstitution. He has, as one writer tells him—and with some fear as well as awe, Lina thinks—taken the roof off the dome of the world.

Every week words of inquiry come by post from other astronomers wanting to compare their own findings to William's, to ask questions and confirm sightings.

Well-born and highly honored sir, these letters begin.

Very highly respected sir.

William has become the most famous astronomer in all of Europe. And she has become the sister of the most famous astronomer in Europe.

THAT SUMMER, when Lina is released from her daily labors, she falls asleep instantly, but it is as if her mind can never rest. On some nights her dreams are so vivid that she feels she has hardly slept. The old horse from Hanover appears in her dreams, knocking at the walls of his stall. Hilda cries in the orchard, or the blackbirds lift over the river, their swarms in the sky like the scratched drawings of William's lunar forests or the cities he imagines within the moon's circuses. Sometimes she dreams of her childhood illness, the light of a candle approaching and receding, her father's sad face, and in her body is the phantom pain of the fever. Again and again she dreams about the laughing brown-eyed man who lifted her from the boat at Yarmouth and carried her through the white surf, gulls calling over the sound of the waves.

As he is so much in demand elsewhere, William leaves her alone more often now for her to continue sweeping the sky in his absence, looking for comets. She sees nothing out of the ordinary—William reviews her daybooks without comment when he returns from his journeys—but she makes an important discovery for herself. The nights when she is alone pass more quickly than those she spends with William, when sometimes her mind falls into vacancy as she waits for him, his eye to the telescope, to convey information to her. She uses the smaller of the telescopes, and there is no need for Stanley to stay awake and help her, though sometimes he wakes in the middle of the night and comes outside with sleepy eyes to bring her tea. Though her endeavors in William's absence are purely solitary, she feels peaceful in the dark fields of the universe. It takes her eyes a little while to become accustomed, and often at the start of a night of viewing she feels fearful, alone in the darkness; in the quiet, the sounds of the world around her have the power to startle her with unexpected force: the human coughing sounds made by deer moving through the fields near the river, wind stirring the leaves of the trees, the high rattling chorus made by the many species of grasshoppers in the tall grass of the meadow, a sudden pained cry from shrew or mouse meeting its end. But gradually the presence of the physical world around her recedes, and she is filled simply with wonder at the stars and planets taking their places in the night sky above her. After some time looking west, she might turn after midnight to greet Mars rising with Pisces, and she feels then as if old friends surround her. Sometimes there are moments when the atmospheric turbulence disappears completely, and she sees details in sharp focus—the ice caps on Mars, the ribbons of markings, canals or canyons, on the planet's surface—and it is almost as if she can put out her hand and touch them. Not until she closes her notebooks and prepares to retire does she realize how exhausted she is, stumbling with fatigue into the house, because during the hours she has been gazing at the sky, time has had no hold over her.

It is simply more engaging, she concludes, to be the stargazer than to be the stargazer's assistant.

THIRTEEN

Observatory House

•—◆—•

Lina has known for some time that the house in Bath, even with the addition of the new workshop, is too small for what William envisions, the great ambition of his forty-foot telescope. When the twenty-foot is finished in June and erected in the meadow along the river, William spends every clear night there in the grip of the nebulae, continuing to look closely into their depths.

That summer, sometimes in the company of Henry Spencer, he begins searching the countryside for another property to lease. Eventually he locates a house with sufficient acreage and a good aspect for viewing in Slough, near Datchet. Located on the Windsor toll road and surrounded by pastures sloping toward the Eton flood meadows along the Thames, with Windsor Castle on the horizon, the property has a large barn and stables in addition to the house. These outbuildings are its chief advantage, as all the work William imagines can be accommodated there. Reviewing their accounts, Lina worries about the additional cost in rent, but Henry Spencer assures them that he will pursue with Sir Joseph Banks the matter of further sums from the king, who has already made one investment, beyond the awarding of a salary, in William's endeavors. Surely, Lina thinks, the king's royal astronomer will want for nothing in pursuit of his grand design, the success of which will cause England and its king to shine brightly in the eyes of the world.

William announces that he has named the new property Observatory House, and he orders a brass sign to be mounted by the front door. Lina is surprised by this gesture, the caprice of it is uncharacteristic; it suggests William is more aware of—and takes greater pride in—his public stature than he generally admits. Perhaps it is the nearby presence of Windsor Castle, she thinks, reminding William of his relationship with the royal family. But overall he is not much distracted by his new notoriety. As usual he wants only to get to work; finally he has found a forge in London that will work on the mirror he wants, now that he has determined the proper mixture of metals for it, and he decides to go immediately to Slough to begin hiring men to commence work on the telescope itself and the enormous scaffolding that will support it.

One warm afternoon in July, Lina trails him through the house in Bath as he prepares to leave, gathering up books and papers he wants to take with him.

She will not mind being left behind to arrange for the household to be packed up and moved? She understands there is no time to waste.

"It's fine," she says. "But—

William has decided that James will go with him to Slough, along with the twenty-foot and fourteen-foot telescopes disassembled and loaded onto carts, and with a supply of tools as well.

She has seen very little of her brother over the last few weeks; what time they have spent together has been largely at night when the sky is clear enough, and she has assisted him at the telescope, taking notes as he calls out his observations. She looks around the music room. It will be no easy matter to find someone to help move the instruments—the harp and the harpsichord, especially—not to mention all the equipment in the workshops. It will take weeks to pack up everything.

William moves aside a globe and a heap of books, looking for something.

"You are not taking a bed? Or a table?" Lina says now. "Where will you sleep? And what will you do about your meals?" she asks.

William leafs through a set of drawings, models for the scaffolding that will support the forty-foot telescope.

"Do you not remember that I used to sleep on my cloak on the moors when I was first beginning in England, traveling here and there? You must think me very soft. I can manage!" His tone is impatient, or at least distracted.

She feels slighted. "Well, you have trained me to be your cook and housekeeper, because I imagine you enjoy the comforts," she says. "I could give up those tasks and spend more time performing . . . or helping you with all these papers." She gestures at the untidy piles. "I will need time to organize all this."

William has done little in the way of music since the confirmation of his new planet, the *Georgium Sidus,* and he has scheduled no further singing engagements for her. She is not surprised, given the new demands upon him, but it is disappointing nonetheless. Now he doesn't even seem to hear her.

"Yes, yes," he says. "Well, come as soon as you can, Lina. I can hardly wait for you to see it."

Then he turns to her, and she knows that once again he has read her mind. He puts down the papers he has been holding and takes her head in his hands. He tilts her forehead toward him and kisses the crown of her head.

"I will miss you," he says. "Undoubtedly, I will be a perfect wreck by the time you arrive. You have spoiled me."

"Take Stanley, at least until school begins," she says. "Stanley's very good in the kitchen. He can see that you get a proper meal."

"I wouldn't hear of it," he says. "Stanley won't leave your side anyway, and you know it. You will need his help here. I shall just be very, very glad to see you instead."

THE NEW HOUSE AT Slough is covered with ivy, giving it a comfortable, settled appearance. On the September afternoon when Lina finally arrives with Stanley, whose father has agreed to let him miss school for a few weeks in order to help with the move, the weather is hot, the air still. She can smell the nearby river meadows, the sedges and rushes. She and Stanley walk through the rooms together. The house is much larger than the one in Bath, and with endless fireplaces. She will have her work cut out for her, Lina thinks, keeping them all lit in the winter.

It pains her to think of managing without Stanley once he returns to Bath. He is now almost a full head taller than she is—such growth in a year!—a fact that seems to have increased his sense that she requires his protection. That he is motherless has made him more attached to her, she knows, yet she has always felt that they are friends in some other, unspoken way. Perhaps, though she had a mother, she, too, has always felt the lack of that care and kindness.

Their furnishings and supplies arrived ahead of them and have been set willy-nilly everywhere. It will take days to create order, she sees. William clearly has made no effort with any of it. But after the cramped rooms and low ceilings of the house in Bath, she finds the light in the new house wonderful. Nor will she miss running up and down the many flights of stairs as she did in Bath—there are only two stories here—though she suffers at the loss of the snug garden that even in winter retained a

Mediterranean warmth, thanks to the heat of the furnaces and the pleasant enclosure of the brick walls. She had loved looking out the kitchen window across the grass to the open doors of the new workshop, the men moving around inside and heat rippling in the air. She'd been able to grow spinach throughout the winter, and they'd had lettuces as early as March.

No one has come out to the street to meet the carriage, so she and Stanley follow the sounds of industry coming from behind the house, banging and sawing and men's voices. A parlor with French doors leads onto a wide flagstone terrace and a flight of two steps down to a sunken, overgrown lawn, perhaps a half acre in size, she estimates, and badly in need of scything, where the twenty-foot telescope has been erected. The lawn ends at a low stone wall, beyond which she sees the orchard William had mentioned in his letters.

The barn, a huge affair of rubble and brick—Lina can see from its size why William was so pleased to have found it—is on the east side of the orchard a distance behind the house. Stables and a cobbled stable yard are nearby. A lane leads to the complex of buildings from the Windsor turnpike that passes before the house.

In the barn, they find a team of men at work. She knows from William's letters to her in Bath that the scaffolding for the forty-foot telescope will be erected in the meadow beyond the orchard, but meanwhile the barn will accommodate the contraption he has designed to support the huge mirror while it is polished.

She and Stanley step from the sunlight into the shade of the doorway. William turns and sees them.

"Here you are! Here you *are!*" He waves. "It is wonderful, is it not?" He crosses the barn to greet them. His shirt is filthy, but he embraces Lina and claps Stanley on the shoulder. He looks as he often does when most energized, Lina thinks—eyes bright, color high in his cheeks, smiling as if he lacks for no pleasure other than the work before him. But he is preoccupied as well, interrupting himself to call instructions to two of the men lifting beams to sawhorses.

"The house is *very* good, yes?" he asks Lina, turning to her again. "I know you will soon have everything arranged. I thought it better to leave it all to your . . . instincts."

"It's beautiful—" Lina begins.

"Good, good. You have just arrived? Well, go then." He opens his arms wide before turning away again. "Go and explore our new paradise."

LINA AND STANLEY WALK through the tall grass of the lawn and through a gate in the stone wall into the orchard. Though neglected—the trees will require a good pruning next spring, Lina thinks—they hold surprising amounts of fruit: damson and greengage plums, apricots, figs, and perry pears. William had written to report that the orchard contained greengages—her favorites—and they find many on the ground already split and being feasted upon by bees.

That afternoon, before doing anything else, she and Stanley search the house for vessels with which to gather the fruit, and return to the orchard with baskets and bowls. Stanley locates the well and brings in water. In the kitchen at the old deal table they cut away the spoiled flesh and cook big kettles of greengage and damson jam.

It is near dark when William appears. He has washed his face and hands, but he has not changed his filthy shirt. He seems surprised to find Lina and Stanley sitting at the table spooning jam onto bread, surrounded by crates and hampers. He eyes the pots on the fire.

"Tomorrow Stanley and I will set up house and go to market," Lina says. "Jam for supper tonight."

She sees Stanley look back and forth between her and William; she knows he, too, senses William's perturbation that they have not begun to unpack their belongings, and that no supper is prepared.

"It's lovely jam, sir," Stanley says.

Lina offers William a thick slice of bread and jam, but he waves it away—she recognizes his expression of controlled displeasure—and leaves the room.

"I think he was expecting a three-course dinner," Lina says, handing the bread to Stanley instead. "Soup and roast and pudding. All made from magic. By the little fairies."

She takes a bite of bread and licks her fingers. "Only with you do I keep my sanity, Stanley. Mrs. Bulwer was right. We are in service to a lunatic in a madhouse."

Later, though, she sends Stanley off to search for bedding for them for the night, and she looks through their belongings for one of the hampers in which she packed the plates. She fixes a makeshift supper for William from the summer sausage and cheese and bread she brought from Bath.

She finds him sitting on the flagstones of the terrace in the last of the day's light. He has drawings spread out on his writing board and a bottle of ink beside him.

He looks up when she appears with the plate and a bottle of cider.

"I cannot find the glasses," she says.

He reaches up and takes the plate from her.

"Tomorrow I will begin to organize everything, William. I promise." She sits down beside him. She wants to make up for having been cavalier with him earlier. As maddening as her brother can be, and as famous and brilliant as he is, why does he inspire these feelings of protection in her? It is his good intentions, she

thinks, the innocent quality of his optimism and faith, the endless battles he must wage to persuade those who doubt him and
to procure funds sufficient to accomplish what he intends. Why
cannot *everyone* see what he will do, if only he can have enough
help? Why must their household always scrape by in this maddening way?

Lina has prepared the statements of their costs for the materials William has estimated he will need, and the wages for laborers,
who also will need to be kept in food and beer; surely, she hopes,
Sir Joseph Banks will persuade the king to be more generous.

She feels contrite now. She should not have spent the afternoon
making jam with Stanley when she could have been unpacking,
hurrying to create domestic comfort for William. It is all he has
ever asked of her, that she not oppose him in any way. He has
been sleeping in rough conditions, surely—it would not surprise
her to learn that he'd done as he suggested and slept outside on
his cloak—and eating in whatever haphazard fashion he has been
able to manage.

She feels the sun's lingering heat in the bricks against her
back. The weeks of packing in Bath had been boring and lonely,
organizing William's papers and books—she is resolved to make
a proper catalog of everything now—and complicated arrangements had needed to be made to convey their possessions. She
had negotiated endlessly over prices and the bills to be paid. She
is competent at such housekeeping tasks now, but it had been tiring business.

Something about the bright light in the rooms of this new
house, the freshly plastered walls, the warmth of the afternoon,
the sleepy quiet of the orchard and the scent of the plums . . .
It is rare for her to have indulged, as she did with Stanley this
afternoon. Yet she had stood there by the fire and taken a spoon-

ful of jam and closed her eyes—the delicious sweetness of it had almost made tears come to her eyes. She had needed the interlude of pleasure.

So she is not sorry, really, except that she has disappointed William.

"Everything goes well here? You are happy?" she asks him now.

"The men are good workers, though I will need more, when the mirror arrives," William says. "But I am content." He brushes crumbs from his shirt and looks up at the sky. He puts aside his now empty plate. "It's a beautiful night, is it not? Let us have some hours at the telescope."

The stars have begun to come out. She turns to look back at the house. Through the windows, the ghostly light from Stanley's lantern moves from room to room, as he searches among their belongings for mattresses and bedding for them this evening. She closes her eyes again. She had been imagining going to sleep, lying down. She feels as if she has not really rested in weeks and weeks.

She will not think of what needs to be done in the house. Not now.

She rests her head briefly against William's shoulder. "Of course," she says.

His shoulder is both soft and strong against her cheek, and he smells of his own sweat but also of sawdust and fresh air. This is what she has missed over this last month, she realizes: William's companionship.

"You are happy here," she says. "This is good. I will be happy here, too."

William drinks from the bottle of cider, passes it to her.

"Now that you are here," he says, "I have everything I need."

This, too, is like him, she thinks. Of course he was unhappy earlier when he came inside, hoping for a hot supper after so many weeks of working without anyone to tend to him. But he never *remains* bad tempered. For a moment she thinks of Jacob, his evil moods. There has been no word, still, of Jacob's whereabouts. Though she never asks for news of their mother in Hanover, William writes occasionally to her, she knows, and to Alexander. Lina has sent letters to Hilda through Dietrich and Leonard, who read them aloud to her, for she was never taught to read.

William stands and holds out his hand to help her up. "Soon— very soon now, I think—we shall see what our forty-foot instrument will reveal."

IN THE DAYS THAT FOLLOW Lina works to the point of exhaustion, moving furniture and making order in the house. She decides that the room formerly used as the laundry, a long, narrow one-story wing that looks out over the terrace, will make an ideal library, and she borrows one of the carpenters from William's endeavors for a few days to have shelves built. She and Stanley, who is very quick with needle and thread, sew long muslin curtains that may be drawn across the shelves to protect the books and papers and certain pieces for the smaller telescopes from dust, and she has some of the workmen move a heavy table—too cumbersome for her and Stanley to lift—that will serve as a writing desk. The wing has a flat roof, and after consultation with the carpenter, she has him build a sturdy ladder attached like a trellis to the outside wall. She intends to set up one of the smaller telescopes there. The roof will make an ideal viewing platform. The new library space gives her pleasure; she likes its flagged floor and clean plaster walls, its view of the twenty-foot telescope and, beyond, the moving treetops of the orchard. Stanley makes a footstool for her out of a bale of hay packed tightly and covered with Hessian burlap, which he sews while sitting on the terrace in the sun. It serves very well as a place for her to rest her feet, which otherwise dangle clear of the floor, when she sits at the desk.

As long as the nights are clear, Lina fixes supper for William and Stanley and herself at nine p.m., and then William sits for hours at the twenty-foot telescope set up in the garden. As always, Lina attends him.

One rainy morning, sitting wearily in the kitchen, she counts the hours and realizes she has slept for a total of only twenty hours over five days.

Sometimes she sees odd spots before her eyes. A headache lurks but does not take possession of her. The fresh air and sunlight protect, she believes, as well as William's excitement and the visible progress of the labor on the forty-foot. And she is relieved, more than she realized she would be, to be away from Bath and the scrutiny she felt under there. Here she sometimes walks barefoot in the grass, lies with Stanley in the orchard, and sings as she goes about her work.

It is, after all, a paradise, as William had said.

WITHIN WEEKS THE SCAFFOLDING to support the iron tube of the forty-foot telescope begins to rise in the meadow beyond the orchard, and work proceeds on the giant contraption in the barn, a massive twelve-sided structure designed by William that will hold the mirror to be polished to the ideal parabolic curve.

As Lina watches the work progress over the early weeks, she marvels again at William's ingenuity. His design for the contraption is astonishing: twelve long handles protrude from the huge frame that will support the 120-centimeter mirror, which will rest on a convex sort of nest at the center of the structure. Twelve men each will be assigned a handle. Each handle will be numbered, and linen smocks with corresponding numbers are made for the men—Lina sews these on the nights when the clouds prevent their work at the twenty-foot telescope—to protect their clothing as the polishing liquids are applied. Twenty-four men will need to be employed in total, William estimates, twelve men per shift, working hour after hour to turn the platform on which the mirror will be suspended, and adjust its position by exact degrees. William devises names for the combination and direction of the movements necessary to create the proper curvature and thinness of the mirror—the glory stroke, the eccentric stroke—to teach the men exactly how to polish its surface.

The planning for all this takes hours. The mirror, weighing nearly half a ton, will be fired at a forge in London according to William's instructions and transported to Observatory House, first by barge up the Thames, and then for the last miles in a cart lined with hay to protect it. Finally the mirror arrives on a glorious October day. William is in charge of seeing the men conscripted to unload it and lift it to the polishing apparatus. A cheer goes up among the workers, who have stopped their labors to witness this endeavor.

While one crew of smiths and carpenters works on the scaffolding and the tube for the forty-foot reflector, the business of polishing can at last begin. Lina and Stanley take to sitting in the open doors of the barn to pit fruit from the orchard—they can't afford for any of it to go to waste—watching the men move through their rotations at the strange machine. They're all simple country fellows recruited by William, but it does not surprise Lina that they have taken to the task of working for him like acolytes to a priest. Indeed there is something occult about their efforts, Lina thinks, the teams of men in their white linen smocks, working with concentration and care in the shadowy barn.

Stanley's father has agreed to allow Stanley to remain with the Herschels through the winter ahead, with Lina serving as his tutor. As they sit working together they discuss mathematics and history, philosophy and natural science. Stanley turns twelve the day the mirror arrives; as they watch the wagon proceed slowly up the lane from the toll road toward the barn, Lina takes his hand in excitement.

"I'll never forget this birthday," he says. "I know I shan't ever forget it."

She squeezes his hand.

Sometimes when Lina looks at Stanley, working sums beside her or sitting with a bowl of pitted plums between his knees, juice on his mouth and shirtfront, she thinks that between William and this beloved boy with his rough hair and big ears, she has everything in the world she wants. Indeed, despite the constant air of industry and excitement at Observatory House, it is a surprisingly peaceful place. Flocks of white butterflies hover over the tall grass of the lawn. No one has had time to scythe the whole area, though Stanley has trimmed a path to the twenty-foot and down through the orchard and into the big field where the scaffolding for the forty-foot is being erected. The grasses in the meadow move with the wind as if a big hand passes gently over them, and Lina feels a kind of benediction given to their enterprises.

In the early evenings before dark falls, she works in the old laundry, beginning to develop a proper ordering and index system for William's papers. She purchases additional long tables for the library from a church rectory she learns from one of the men is being refurbished; some of the pieces of joinery for the telescope are stored there under sheets, as well as supplies of mirrors for the smaller telescopes, for William is never content to have only one enterprise underway, and now his reputation has put his telescopes in even greater demand.

The weather remains unseasonably warm and sunny into late October. Lina is able to work with the doors of the laundry open, even as the sun descends behind the orchard. Now when she looks out across the lawn and past the orchard, the enormous scaffolding for the forty-foot telescope looms against the sky in the meadow. William has spent weeks out there under the sun, along with the parade of workmen led by James; he lies on his back or stomach on one beam or another—sometimes perilously high above the ground—supervising every screw and bolt. The behemoth structure, fixed on a two-axle mount so that it can be rotated, looks to Lina like a fantastical animal. It seems vaguely mournful to her, like a creature that is the last of its kind, a beast that might shake itself one day and begin to move, to creak slowly through the meadow at night toward the house in search of its master. She imagines it standing at the upper-story windows and inclining its long neck, looking for the man who will be lifted to the viewing platform thirty feet above the ground to tilt the biggest telescope in the world toward the stars and the deepest recesses of the heavens.

Certainly the telescope's claim on William—on them all—is utterly complete.

She feels sometimes that it is they who serve it, rather than the other way around.

ONCE THE SCAFFOLDING and the iron tube are completed, every evening when the sky is clear the mirror is removed from the polishing machine in the barn and laboriously transported in a cart to the tube, into which it is lowered by means of yet another complicated apparatus that William has designed.

Two men are needed to raise and lower the viewing platform, working in careful unison to prevent the platform from tilting and pitching William to the ground, an accident Lina is certain would kill him. William designs a further system to ensure that the platform will rise smoothly—two bells, which must ring in unison, letting the men know they are hauling on the ropes with equal pressure—but the process fills Lina with anxiety. The first night of this experiment, she stands in the grass with a shawl over her shoulders, watching William hoisted into the evening sky, and listening to the bells. Not until the sound dies away and William waves gaily from the platform at its fixed location does she realize she has been holding her breath. From her position on the ground, he seems so small.

Beside her, Stanley whoops and cavorts through the grass.

And each night the process is repeated, as William judges how closely the mirror approaches the standard he imagines.

No other man, Lina thinks, would have had the patience for this endeavor.

Yet they are all inflamed by what William imagines he will see when it is finished, and though he walks like a prophet among his workers, he is as familiar with the use of a hammer as he is with the arcane business of the cosmos, and this endears him to the men he employs.

One windy afternoon, as she is bringing in washing from the line in the garden, she hears the unearthly sound of voices from the far meadow. She can see no one, however, and it is with a start that she realizes a few of the men are actually standing *inside* the telescope's enormous tube, which has been lowered to the ground for some adjustment.

After a moment, she realizes that they are singing.

ONE AFTERNOON LATER THAT MONTH, Stanley comes running to find her in the old laundry. "The royal carriages are in the drive!" he says.

"What?" she says. "It is the *king*?"

"And the archbishop, I think. They've gone round to the meadow." Stanley's eyes are wide. "But they've left a lot of others behind, as the king told them to wait in their carriages in the road. They don't look very happy."

"Go. Go and wash your face," she says. "Then come help me."

She hurries to change her dress and then to the kitchen to prepare a tray of tea and cake and wine.

The archbishop and William are standing in the meadow below the scaffolding, but the king has already ascended the short flight of steps to the viewing platform and the cage, where a viewer may be raised securely thirty feet in the air. As Lina crosses into the meadow through the gate, Stanley behind her carrying the teapot, the king waves gaily down to her.

Once on the ground again, he greets her familiarly, though they have met only once, in the Octagon Chapel, at a performance of music composed in his honor by William. He allows her to kiss his hand but then raises her up. He turns to the archbishop.

"Come, my lord bishop," he says, getting down on his hands and knees and beginning to crawl into the tube on the ground. "My royal astronomer here will show you the way to heaven with this great telescope of his!"

Lina watches the king's rump disappear into the tube. The archbishop, a fold of fat around his middle and with wagging dewlaps, seems less inclined, but there is nothing to be done but smile politely as he gets to his knees, the heavy chain around his neck swinging, and follow the king. Lina meets William's eyes for a moment—even a king's or a bishop's bottom is foolish—but she must look away or laugh. When the archbishop's backside vanishes completely, Stanley falls helplessly onto the grass in mirth, his hands over his mouth.

William gives them a warning look; she knows that they depend on King George's money to finish the work, and that he has been known to be erratic in his behavior and commands lately. They have already petitioned twice for additional sums—nearly four thousand pounds now—and she knows that the king expects nothing less than miracles from this enterprise in which he has invested so heavily. They must cause no offense.

"Stanley," Lina whispers. "Come with me."

They run back toward the house. At the orchard they stop to look again at the telescope. William is helping King George from the tube. She can hear his enthusiastic tone of praise. The archbishop, she supposes, is still inside the telescope.

"Run ahead," she tells Stanley. "Bring baskets of the plums for the king and the archbishop to take back with them."

She watches him for a moment as he runs through the tall grass. The afternoon is drawing to a close, and the moon is already visible. Smoke rises from the kitchen chimney. She turns back to the meadow. William and the king stand beneath the scaffolding, gazing up at it.

Every night William leaves the earth, leaves all that is familiar to men who walk on solid ground, and aims his gaze into the unknown. He seems an oddly lonely figure to her at this moment, despite being in such private and intimate contact with the king of England. As, in his way, does the king himself. She has never before doubted that the telescope, once the mirror is perfected, will yield great discoveries, but looking at the strange structure now, with only William and the king dwarfed beside it, she suffers a moment of pure terror.

What if it is all for nothing?

What if William has already seen everything there is to be seen?

YET EVERY EVENING as the stars emerge, William has the telescope raised and the mirror inserted into the tube. He can direct the telescope toward whatever celestial object he wishes to view, and that fall and winter he continues to experiment with the mirror and eyeglass and the necessary focal length. Sometimes he crawls into the tube, holding the glass in his hand. By December, he and Lina spend every clear night working together, focusing particularly on Saturn and its satellite moons. Once the mirror is perfected, William expects—hopes—to discover more of these moons, as he is sure they exist. This event, too, would suggest that the contents of the universe are far greater in number—legions of planetary moons surrounding every planet, perhaps—than anyone has yet imagined.

The mechanism for adjusting the position of the telescope, despite its enormous weight and size, is clever—more of William's ingenuity at work—and Lina has no trouble managing it alone. In a little hut built at the base of the scaffolding, she sits at a table with the sidereal clock and Flamsteed's atlas open before her, and hot bricks at her feet. From the information William calls down to her through the speaking tube, she records the declination and right ascension and any other circumstances of his observations. In a single night, William often finds as many as four or five new nebulae.

It feels to Lina as if the universe is exploding around them.

But still the mirror is not quite right, William frets.

The weather has cooled considerably. The temperature now frequently drops well below freezing at night. William dresses in extra layers of clothing and hardly seems to notice the cold. Before he ascends to the platform, he rubs his face and hands with the cut side of a raw onion, a prevention he believes protects him from the ague.

Lina suspects William would not eat or drink at all over these long, cold, dark hours if she did not from time to time over the night climb the ladders to the cage with sustenance for him. He does not want to take his eye from the telescope for fear of missing something critical. As in their early days in Bath, when he was beginning to practice polishing mirrors of the size he imagined, she feeds him by hand—cheese and bits of soft cooked beef, boiled eggs, apples and plums she has dried that summer.

She speaks quietly—or not at all—on these occasions, only asking a question from time to time about what William sees in the sky above them. She does not want to disturb his concentration or the communion she knows is established between astronomers as skilled as William—he can find anything in the sky almost instantly—and the stars. The only sounds are the creaking apparatus of the telescope when its position is adjusted, and the occasional hooting call of the owls that fly at night through the fields and woods and down along the river. In the cold, empty meadow, the sounds have an ancient clarity, carrying far in the chilled air, and the ground, hard with frost or light snow, shines under the moon's light. She remembers the creatures she once imagined on the sun and moon; William has never abandoned his theory that planets other than their own are inhabited, or his belief that the moon is studded with volcanoes, though she knows that many in the Royal Society doubt him. She thinks now that those beings, if indeed they exist, are far stranger than those she had pictured when she was a child: the old, dark-faced priest from Hanover with his turnip nose—surely dead by now—or the tall, gentle creatures she had imagined, their eyes like those of her beloved old horse.

William's lips close around her fingers, the morsel of meat or bread and cheese or fruit she offers.

She wipes his mouth for him.

She brings hot tea in an enamel jar wrapped in flannel. She holds it to his lips, a napkin under his chin, so that he can drink.

She feels as always at these moments a mixture of awe at William's stamina and tenderness at his helpless submission.

In her apron pocket is a flask with brandy. She uncorks it and holds it to his lips.

No one else, she feels sure, would ever care for him in this way.

She cannot imagine, from all the women she has met—including those she is certain would regard William Herschel, with his proximity to the king, as a very fine catch—a wife who would do what she, Caroline, does, staying awake all night with never a care for her clothes or her hair or her own fatigue. In the darkness, she stands below William on the spectators' viewing platform for a long time.

Above them the stars glitter, a beautiful pageant, brilliant and mysterious. There is a language being spoken in the silent distances, Lina feels, music played. She and William lack the tools or faculties to hear it, but she knows he inclines toward it, certain of its existence.

TO WILLIAM'S ANNOYANCE, the king now calls frequently for his presence at Kew or Buckingham Palace or Windsor, wanting news of the telescope's yields or further instruction with the telescopes William has built for him. When William is away, Lina spends some hours alone at the smaller refracting telescope she has set up on the platform that two carpenters have built for her on the flat roof of the old laundry, now their new library. Along with the ladder on the outside wall, one of the ironmongers has fashioned her a clever circular stair that leads to a skylight in the ceiling, which may be pushed easily aside. At night she regularly sweeps the sky, trying to teach herself, as William has said, *how to see.*

It is not easy.

She has lost her old sensation of the stars being fixed points pasted against the sky. Everything around them, she now knows, is moving. Yet if she closes her eyes, the knowledge of this still makes her dizzy. Often at the telescope she has to steady herself—her hand reaching for something solid—against the sensation of falling. It is only the ticking of the clock beside her, its metronome set to assist her in timing her observations, which reminds her that she is on terra firma. When she looks down, she sees the garden below, even in the dark illuminated by lights from within the house. She sees the shapes of the barns and the curve of the orchard rows beyond, the scaffolding standing at its distant spot alone in the meadow. In William's absence, the telescope is lowered, as if hanging its head in weariness.

Much of what she sees on earth now reminds her of the sky with its planets and comets, its blooming nebulae full of clusters of stars: the English hawthorn branches she has come to love, full in spring of white flowers. Falling snow. The shining flagstones of the terrace on rainy nights, the lights from the house falling across them in bands like the Milky Way. From the rooftop she can see down to the small pond, and on clear nights its surface reflects the stars, so that they seem both above and below her. When she stands alone in the darkness at her own little telescope, sweeping by orderly degrees across the night sky, she knows now that she will never tire of it.

She is grateful for this joy, the joy of being amazed, this transformation of her gaze from admiration—for anyone can see the stars are beautiful—to astonishment.

This is William's greatest gift to her, she thinks, the gift of awe. She lies down with it at night and wakes with it in the morning. Somehow, her awe makes what is quotidian or tedious—the tiring business of making meals or beds, or washing clothes—almost holy.

• • •

AND THEN ONE NIGHT it happens.

William has been frustrated by the persistent imperfections of the mirror, imperfections that interfere with and distort his vision, but now, at last, he thinks it is perfect. He aims the telescope into the sky, and within only a few minutes, he calls down triumphantly through the tube: *A sixth moon of Saturn, Lina. There it is.*

Lina, sitting in the hut, lifts her hand from the page and stares out the little window into the dark. The ink in her bottle has already frozen. Her feet and hands are so cold she can scarcely feel them.

A moment later, he speaks again, his voice strangely near. She thinks of the first night of their crossing to England, when he held her against him and spoke into her ear above the sound of the waves and the wind in the sails.

"And a seventh moon," he says now. "Lina. There is a *seventh*." Silence follows.

Then he says, "I'm coming down."

Lina leaves the hut and begins to lower the telescope, but her legs are shaking. Had the telescope failed them, she cannot imagine what would have happened. But it has *not* failed them. William was right.

He descends from the viewing platform by ladder and comes to help her fix the telescope into its resting position.

His eyes are shining, and he reeks of raw onion, but he takes her face in his hands and kisses her on one cheek and then on the other. It is so cold that the muscles of her face feel frozen. She tries to smile.

"My monster," he says, and for a moment she thinks he means *her* . . . what can he mean, addressing her in that way?

She thinks of the moon, her face.

And then he laughs. "Our forty-foot *monster*. It has obliged us, after all."

THE NEXT EVENING, Henry Spencer comes to see for himself. First he and then Lina ascend in the viewing chair, William giving them directions through the speaking tube about where to look.

Later that night, after they return to the house and have a late supper, William excuses himself to write letters to Dr. Maskelyne and Sir Joseph Banks and to the king. Henry will take them with him when he leaves the next day for London. He will be proud to serve as messenger with such news, he says.

Lina's relief at the immediate and profound yield of the forty-foot is immense. She realizes now how worried she has been that the king's investment would turn out to be for naught, and that William's assertions about the capability of the new instrument might be exaggerated.

Henry has been a frequent visitor to Observatory House over recent months. She knows that he, too, has staked his reputation on William's success, many times adding his endorsement to William's petition for additional funds. At Henry's direction, Lina has meticulously calculated every expense: every candle, every pint of beer, every log for the fire, the accounts with their suppliers, the wages they pay, even to Stanley. Surely Henry, too, is relieved now. Yet it has occurred to her that their expenses will not disappear with the completion of the telescope. They still must eat, must light the fire. William's salary from the king of fifty pounds a year will do little to approach meeting their needs. And William will not be satisfied with these discoveries, she knows. There are other endeavors: the catalog of nebulae he wishes to publish, which will require hours and hours of her time, as well as his.

And yet *these* sorts of ambitions—to support the work of other astronomers, rewriting the sky for them—are not so sensational as to attract the king's financial support.

From the parlor where she and Henry sit, she can see William's light in the old laundry through the window—they have continued to call it that, despite its transformation into a well-stocked and useful library. William had put more wood on the fire before leaving the room. She feels its warmth at her back now, though a draft moves around their feet. The remains of the night's supper are on the table, a roast chicken, stewed cabbage, a plum tart. The house is empty but for the three of them. Immediately following the forty-foot's revelations about the moons of Saturn, Lina recommended that William send James and Stanley home for a visit with their father, who has been ill. They are both in need of a rest, she senses. Before leaving, Stanley hugged her, and she realized—her cheek against his shoulder, his arms around her—what a big man he would one day become.

"Wee Stanley," she said, using her pet name for him. "I will miss you. Come back to us soon."

She wishes he were here now. How both he and James would be rejoicing with them.

With William's departure from the room, the usual silence falls between her and Henry.

She begins to stand to clear away their dishes, but Henry moves his chair abruptly, its legs scraping against the floor.

"I have been thinking," he says. He looks away from her out the window into the darkness.

She stops, her plate and William's in her hands.

"I have been thinking," he repeats, "that the *queen* might be very glad to be invited to support the work being done here at Observatory House. Especially *your* work, Caroline."

"I do not see why that would be," she says. "I am only an assistant—and a kitchen maid—here. You know that I would do anything for William, but—"

"Nothing William has done would have been possible without you," Henry says. He turns to look at her. It is the first time he has held her gaze for any length of time. She feels her face coloring.

Henry had eaten little at dinner, she'd noticed. He seems even more gaunt than usual. She looks past him. On the wall, they have hung two of his paintings, both still life arrangements. A dead hare hangs its head in one, a tiny window of light in its black eye.

Henry continues. "I do not mean that William lacks for intellect or imagination, obviously, or that you have made up for some deficit there. It is extraordinary, what he has accomplished. Truly he has changed our understanding of the universe more than any other human being of our time, and I suspect for some time yet to come. And he has given all the rest of us the tools to continue his work, the knowledge of *how* to see. That may turn out to be his greatest contribution."

Henry looks around the room, as if its spare furnishings might somehow suggest proof of William's abilities. "You live in such a simple way, the two of you," he says quietly, as if speaking to himself. "I envy it." He pauses. "But that is not what I mean to say." He turns back to look at her. "I mean that your hand is in everything, is everywhere, Lina—the workshops, the gardens, the library, in every paper or letter William writes, every list and map and notation in an atlas. I know that you are with him night after night. Few women—few *people*, man or woman—would be capable of such devotion. But it is not just your loyalty that must be rewarded. Your *intelligence* is absolutely necessary to these endeavors. I believe you *know* that. I would think less of you for false modesty."

He has never made such a long speech to her, she realizes, nor spoken so fervently.

She stands still, holding the plates. It is true, she knows, that she has been more than a kitchen maid or housekeeper to William. Why would she say such a thing to Henry, of all people? She has William to credit for training both her mind and her eye, but it is unbecoming to be self-deprecating, and meanwhile it is insincere, too. She *has* learned things. She *has* been of use. It is true.

"I believe I must thank you now," she says quietly. "I know what I have done for William. I am grateful to you, Henry, for seeing it truthfully, for neither more nor less than it is."

Henry stands up abruptly. His cheeks are flaming red.

She looks with sympathy at his poor sore, watering eyes, his long nose, which is pinched and blue. She notices, too, that there are ugly lesions, little eruptions, at his high collar, as if it chafed him. It pains her, as it has always pained her, to look at him, to look at the discomfort he seems to be in. What is it that has caused this man to be so deeply uncomfortable in his own skin, meanwhile showing the world—as a painter and gardener and scientist and physician—such generosity, attending devotedly to both its beauty and its pain?

He stands and takes the plates from her and sets them on the table, but his hands are shaking, and the forks clatter. Then he reaches out and takes her hands in his. She can feel in his grasp how he trembles.

"Believe it or not," he says, "I have never held a woman's hands like this until this moment."

He looks down at her hands. "So tiny," he says. "And yet so extraordinarily capable."

He is to make a proposal to her. She cannot believe it. She looks quickly across the room, out the window. Through the darkness, as if at a great distance from her, she sees William's light burning in the old laundry. She has a sudden, almost frantic desire to go to him—she has difficulty not removing her hands from Henry's—to rest her hand on William's shoulders as he sits at the table writing, to set a cup of tea at his elbow.

"Do you not feel very small sometimes, Lina, in this vast universe William has illuminated for us?" Henry says.

She looks up at him. He is smiling, but the expression in his eyes is sad.

Once she wished for this, she thinks. What has changed? She cannot leave Observatory House. She cannot leave William. Once she had imagined she would be glad to be relieved of her labors for him; she had not understood at all—even though he had warned her—that he would ask so much of her, that she would work so hard. Yet she has come to love even more fully—though she would not have thought greater love possible—not only her brother but also the work itself. She would not give it up. In a way, William has given her *herself.* Anything else, any other life, she realizes, would be a small life, a narrow life, compared to the one she has now. There will always be a . . . lack; she thinks of the empty bed, the desires she feels at night, heat in regions of her body that at times is almost painful. But there is no having *both,* for she cannot have a husband *and* her brother and her labors with him.

She never believed she would have a choice, but in fact, she sees now, there is no choice to be made anyway. She would not consider it. And she imagines in any case that Henry acts now only out of his great regard for William, and that he believes it would be a comfort to her, before she is too much older, to be wed. He aims only to provide for her, she suspects.

"Henry. There is no need," she begins. "You must not feel sorry for me."

His expression changes to one of dismay. "No. Caroline. You misunderstand. *Never* would I feel pity for you. I admire you beyond any woman I have ever met." He stops and looks down.

When he begins again he speaks very quietly, and she can feel in their joined hands their pulse, which seems to have become one.

"It is not easy for me to say this," he says. "But if there were a woman I was free to marry, I should choose *you*. I wish now to convey, to convey . . . my love."

He drops her hands, reaches for a handkerchief, and presses it to his nose and then his eyes.

Lina is horrified. Pity—and, yes, a kind of love—sweeps her. She twists her hands together. "Henry—" she begins.

"But I am *not* free," he goes on. "I am not free in so many ways it is almost—" He laughs, but it is a bitter laugh. "I would say it is ludicrous, but it is too terrible to be funny. I should like nothing better than to give you any comfort in the world, Lina. I know you will not simply take my money, though I intend to give you and William as much of it as I can now, despite that I am constrained in some ways. And I cannot give you my . . . body, my *self* in any way other than as a poor, pitiable companion. For the purpose of companionship, you have already an ideal companion in William anyway."

"Henry." She does not know what he means, but she fears she does not *want* to know, either. "What is it?" she asks. "What is the matter?"

"You know that I am a physician, Lina, so you will trust me when I tell you I am absolutely certain. You have heard of the disease," he says. "Some have called it the great imitator, for it presents in so many different ways."

Lina thinks of Jacob, of a conversation overheard long ago. Her father had warned Jacob, shouting at him, that his behavior with women—with prostitutes, she knows now—would endanger him.

Syphilis. She knows what it is. She knows how it is contracted.

Henry must see on her face that she understands him, because he continues.

"There is more, I am sorry to say, in some ways the worst yet. For I am in fact to marry, though I will have no contact with the lady at all. It will be a marriage only on paper, in secret, in order that the Spencer estate may be transferred to her father at my death. You see, there has been a debt, a gambling debt from my father's time, gone unpaid these many years, interest accruing. It must be paid now. They have exercised some kindness in not removing us earlier, wishing to protect my mother. It has been a kindness, in that regard."

"Henry! Henry, you are not *dying*!" She stares at him, horrified. She was right; it *has* been painful for him to live in his body. She lifts her hands to touch him, but he steps away.

"I cannot bear for you to know how I must have brought this on myself. Some . . . instances of foolishness," he says, as if reading her mind. "Fatal foolishness. I never imagined myself—desirable."

She sits down, because she fears she cannot stand. Behind her, a log falls from the fire, and she smells smoke in the room. Her eyes are burning. It is as if he is leaving her, leaving them *at this moment*, as if she is watching it happen.

But he takes a seat and pulls his chair near to her. "I intend to convey what I can to William in goods—furnishings, silver, paintings," he says, "before the event of the marriage takes place. But they have a good idea of my assets, and they will notice losses of any significance. What I want to do, as well, is to speak to the queen about you, especially before the news of the circumstance spreads, as surely it will, once I am gone. What she will give is little, though heaven knows the royal coffers are deep enough, but it will be something to help you, and I believe she will enjoy the autonomy of the gesture."

. . .

LINA REALIZES NOW that he *is* saying goodbye. And she had thought he intended to propose marriage to her. What a foolish woman she is, to have apprehended so little. She looks up at Henry's paintings, the sensuous mound of grapes on the plate, the flowers at the end of their season, petals touched with pink or drops of red blood scattered over a cloth white as a cloud, the hare's shining fur, its eye holding a window of white light. She does not want to cry. She puts her hands over her mouth.

"Listen to me," Henry says. "There is no reason you should not have an annual salary, as William does. It cannot equal his, of course, but it will be something. I think I may suggest to the queen that her investment—her private investment in the work of another woman—will be to her lasting credit in history."

Lina drops her face into her hands. She cannot bear it.

She hears him stand up. "I am so very sorry," he says. "Believe me, my dearest Caroline, when I say I wish . . . I wish I could do more. So much more."

She takes her hands away from her face. "You are not leaving us," she says. "You must not leave us, Henry. William will be—*I am!*—*heartbroken*. There is no need for it, for you to leave! Stay here. Stay with us! We will care for you, gladly."

She stands up. She knows that she did love him once. "I would have said yes," she says.

He looks at her, and at that moment she thinks she has never seen an expression of such kindness on the face of any person, even William.

They look at one another for a long moment. "I think we might have been happy," he says finally. "I would have tried very, very hard to make you happy."

Lina thinks of the moons they witnessed earlier that evening, the ghostly ring of satellites orbiting the planet.

"How beautiful and strange a phenomenon," Henry had said. "Every celestial object with its attendants and companions."

"I will collect William's letters from him and ride out this evening," he says now.

It feels difficult for her to speak. "He does not know. William does not know?"

Henry drops his head. "The coward in me . . . I have written to him." He produces a letter from his pocket. "I will leave it with you . . . to give to him. Later, please. After I am gone."

WILLIAM DOES NOT LOOK UP when she comes into the laundry. She places Henry's letter on the desk beside him.

He looks up at her, and she fears her face will give her away, but he seems to notice nothing amiss. "Going to bed?"

"Yes," she says. "Good night, William."

There is a coward in her, too. She can neither warn him nor stay to comfort him. She goes to bed, where she expects to weep, but instead she feels a rage so powerful it is as if it will lift her body from the bed or burn her up. She lies rigidly in the cold sheets, her hands clenched, her throat aching from suppressing her grief. Tears run down her face anyway.

At one point, she realizes that William must be standing in the hall outside her door, for candlelight shows beneath it.

He knocks softly, but she does not answer.

Later, regretting this, she opens the door, but the hallway is dark. No light shines from beneath William's door or, when she goes downstairs, in the old laundry.

So they are both alone in the darkness.

England
1788–1822

FOURTEEN

Hooked

• ◆ •

It is Stanley, grown as a young man into an experienced orchard-
ist, who tends capably to the old trees and plants new apple
varieties—Bramley Seedlings and Flower of Kent—caring for
them through the years. In the market he sells pears and apples
from Observatory House's orchard. The income helps sustain the
household.

In the flower borders along the terrace wall, he and Lina have
planted delphiniums and roses, phlox and alliums and asters. In
every season, Lina likes to keep a vase of flowers on William's
desk in the old laundry, even when he is away. In the cold months
she cuts a frosted sprig of boxwood or a stem of holly, its berries
bright, for the silver bud vase that was one of Henry's last gifts to
them.

She never fills it with water without thinking of Henry;
indeed, she feels sometimes oddly close to him, as if he is present
along with the constellations and planets—and their inhabitants,
should such inhabitants exist, as William says—looking down on
her as she goes about her work.

The vegetable garden, dug in during the spring after their
arrival and maintained mostly by Stanley, yields potatoes and cabbages, squashes and beans and peas and lettuces.

They have, in this way, enough.

In the old laundry, the muslin curtains sewn by Lina to protect William's papers and books are bleached and hung to dry in the spring air once a year. They are fastened along polished wooden rods at the tops and bottoms of the high shelves, so that they may be easily drawn aside or closed. When the windows are open to the breeze, the curtains ripple like water. It is pleasant to Lina, while she sits alone working, to feel as if the walls shift responsively around her. Her hand moves swiftly, covering the pages: William's papers on astronomy, his letters, his Philosophical Transactions, as he calls them. The wooden boxes Stanley builds for William's correspondence, each letter copied and ordered by Lina according to date and to writer, grow in number. By now she answers alone many of the letters William receives—asking for assistance in locating various celestial objects or for clarification of his ideas—without needing to consult her brother at all. She can sign his signature as easily as she signs her own. There are too many letters for him to attend to himself.

The old linen smocks worn by the twenty-four men who polished the first big mirror for the forty-foot have been washed and folded long ago and put away in a trunk with wormwood and rosemary to protect them from moth larvae.

Lina has the sense, growing as the years pass, that everything of William's life and work must be preserved. There is no object too small to be worth discarding.

The world will want to remember William, to know him even when he is gone.

WHEN LINA APPROACHES FORTY, her monthly bleeding, never strong, becomes suddenly painfully heavy for a short time and then in a few months dwindles to almost nothing. She suffers a few fainting spells during these weeks of heavy bleeding, one in which she falls, cutting her head, from several rungs up on the circular staircase she has had built to her rooftop telescope. She has been discomforted more frequently over the years by her old headaches, rolling spherical objects and explosive flashes in her vision, sometimes areas darkening in odd patterns like frost on a windowpane. But the disturbances rarely last long, and they appear to cause no permanent harm. In general she feels increasingly vigorous, in fact. Her arms are strongly muscled, her hands rough from outdoor work and from so many seasons of cold at the telescope. Sometimes at night in the winter she slathers them with lard and wears gloves to bed. Adapted over the years to little sleep, she does not find it difficult to make do with only a few hours each night.

She is surprised only occasionally now to find a little brown stain of blood on her undergarments, to feel the rare telltale cramping in her lower belly, a reminder of one of the uses of a woman's body.

One Saturday morning in March she works in the kitchen, baking a cake from a supply of hazelnuts and dried currants and orange peel. The smell of the cake rising recalls for her one from her childhood, a round-domed treat studded with candied fruit and cloves and nuts, baked every year by Margaretta's mother to celebrate her daughters' birthdays.

And then Lina calculates and realizes that it is her own birthday today.

Such events were rarely celebrated in the Herschel house when Lina was a child, and she and William have never observed each other's birthdays. Often, it seems, they simply do not remember them at all. She realizes that she has lost track of her own age; she sits down at the table, wiping her hands, staring out the window. When she calculates it, she is surprised to find that she has turned thirty-eight.

William, she realizes, will turn fifty in November.

Their mother has been dead for a decade. William saw her once before her death, on an ambassadorial trip to Göttingen, when the king dispatched him to deliver a telescope to the duke.

On his return to Observatory House, though Lina did not ask, William reported that he had found their mother "much changed."

Lina did not answer him, busying herself with a task in the kitchen.

"But not in the essential ways, Lina," he said after a moment, and he rested his hand on her shoulder as he left the room. "You may regret nothing, except what you could not have changed."

Their mother never wrote to Lina, nor Lina to her.

"I should convey your greetings?" William would say, whenever he sent a letter.

"If it pleases you," Lina would reply, but she is annoyed at his dutifulness to their mother.

She turns now at the sound of footsteps in the passage outside. Stanley comes into the kitchen. He has become, as Lina predicted, a big man, taller than William, who was once well over six feet tall, though he has lost some height as he has aged. Stanley's ears are still enormous, his chest muscled as a cart horse's. His hair—that bright shade of ginger which when he was a child made him seem so much the comic character—has darkened to rusty red. His wife keeps it cut very close to his head. Today he has one of his little boys with him, the baby's eyes as blue as his father's, his feathery hair the same color as Stanley's when he was a boy.

Stanley hands the lad to Lina, who takes him on her lap. The child—this youngest, named William, since the names of both grandfathers now have been used for his older brothers—puts his soft hands up to touch her mouth.

His fine hair and pink cheeks smell of the fresh air, his breath of milk, both sour and sweet.

"I'll chop some wood for—" Stanley begins, and then stops.

To her embarrassment, Lina has begun to cry. She turns her face aside, but she cannot hide her heaving shoulders. Her tears fall on the head of the heavy infant in her arms. The baby opens his mouth, reaching for the knuckle she raises to his lips.

Stanley's expression is stricken.

"It's all right, Stanley," she says. "I've only realized. . . . Sorry."

"*What?*" he says. "What is the matter?"

"Nothing," she says. She bends her head over the infant, dear little William. "It is only my foolishness."

She raises her face. "No. No, it is only my good fortune, Stanley," she says. "It is all around me." She bends her face to the infant, little William, who reaches up to touch her cheek.

EVERY WINTER WILLIAM CATCHES a bad cold. This February, despite his habitual precautions, he develops a serious cough that will not leave him. Nor will he abandon the telescope at night, despite her entreaties. Stanley, too, has fallen ill, as has the baby. Lina has forbidden Stanley to join them outside, though sometimes he stays overnight anyway, sleeping in the kitchen and building up the fires for them there and in the old laundry, for Lina and William often work for an hour or more after they come inside.

There are frequent visitors to Observatory House—some traveling even from overseas—curious about the famous telescope, and they often want a look at the night sky through the celebrated instrument. This evening the temperatures have fallen very low, usually a deterrent to the casual onlooker, and Lina is alone with William. Owls call back and forth for over an hour. She has come to recognize the notes of different species—William's ear is so good he can usually name the exact notes.

It's often the tawny owls they hear, with their distinctive cry, *ke-wit hoo hoo.* William imitates both the male and female sounds with great success, cupping his hands and blowing through the aperture between them. The owls always answer him.

"You make them fall in love with you," Lina says.

"I make them fall in love with each other," William says.

BY MIDNIGHT THIS EVENING, despite the fact that she has brought a greater supply than usual of hot bricks for William's feet and for the little hut under the telescope in which she works, her hands are numb, and her throat feels as if it is on fire. She tells William through the speaking tube that she is going inside for hot tea, but he does not answer. She wraps her shawl about her head and goes outside, calling up to him again.

"William!" She can feel her temper rise. It pains her to speak.

He answers her at last, coughing. "Yes, yes. I heard you," he says.

Then why did he not *answer?* she thinks. She stands beneath the scaffolding, looking up at the long, dark arm of the telescope raised toward the moon. "I'm going in to make tea," she calls. "I'll come back shortly. Do you want brandy?"

William makes no reply.

She knows she should be careful—there have been freezes and thaws for weeks now, and where there has been standing water in the meadow, patches of black ice have formed—but in her irritation she turns impatiently. At once she feels her leg slide out from beneath her. She grabs for one of the beams of the scaffolding, but to no avail. When she falls, the pain in her leg is so fierce she nearly faints; she feels certain one of the iron hooks for the mechanism by which the tube is hoisted has pierced her calf.

"I am hooked!" she calls up, when she recovers enough to speak. *"William!"*

An owl calls, and then another, as if her alarm has spread

among them. She does not know if her brother hears her. She stares up through the crossed bars of the scaffolding at the stars. The full moon is above her, approaching and then receding. She closes her eyes for a moment.

Then Stanley is there, coughing, his arms under her. He has come with a fresh supply of hot bricks for her. She cries out when he lifts her, and he gasps as he realizes that he has pulled her leg free from one of the hooks.

"Missus!" he says, aggrieved. "Oh, missus!"

"Sir!" he shouts up to William, and she hears a rare anger in Stanley's voice. "Sir, your sister has fallen!"

At last she hears William's voice coming from far above. The effect is strange in the otherwise silent night, as though he speaks from the stars themselves.

"What is it?" he calls down. "What has happened?"

"Come. Come quickly, sir!" Stanley calls, and it is an order, not a request.

STANLEY CARRIES HER to William's bed, as William insists. The fireplace in his room is bigger, and the room will be warmer. When Stanley gently lifts her torn skirt from her calf, she sees William, standing at the side of the bed, blanch at the sight of the wound.

He turns away, but she can see his hands shake as he lights candles in the room.

She faints once, she thinks, and when her eyes flutter open, William sits beside her in a chair he has drawn close to the bed. He holds her hand, and his fingers are very cold. He coughs.

"Stanley has gone for the surgeon," he says. "You will be all right, Lina. Don't worry."

He is speaking to her in German, she realizes. How strange, after so many years, to hear their old language.

She feels sick to her stomach and light-headed. It must be the loss of blood, she thinks.

Dr. Onslow arrives sometime before dawn, Stanley having ridden the distance to his farm to fetch him.

He is grim at the size of the puncture in her calf.

She lifts her head as he unwraps the bandage Stanley applied, but the sight of the wound on her leg makes her throat fill with bile. She must have left behind on the hook two ounces of flesh. The hole is enormous.

"No more work for her, until she has healed," Dr. Onslow tells William, washing his hands in the basin of hot water Stanley brings, "unless you want her lame for life."

"Of course," William says. "She will not work for a moment."

"This will hurt, I'm afraid," Dr. Onslow says, warning her.

He glances at William. "Give her something to hold between her teeth," he says, "and have the brandy ready."

When Dr. Onslow takes the first stitch, she faints again.

When she wakes, it is over. William stands at the end of the bed. He does not look well. He is pale and still coughing, and the cords in his handsome neck stand out. He has lost weight over the winter, Lina observes, as if she has not seen him for some time. His hair is shaved short under the wig he wears, but he has on no wig now, and she sees in the room's candlelight that his hair is fully silver. She is aware of the smell of him; he is in need of a hot bath. And they are both in need of new clothes. William looks like a scarecrow, shabby to the point of embarrassment.

Now that her brother performs almost no music—and she hasn't sung in public in years—they have little need of fine attire, except those clothes they wear to church when they attend, or when William must visit London. Since the king's mysterious illness, William has been called to Windsor Castle only once. He reported that the encounter had been strange indeed, with the king ensconced in a sort of rolling chair, his spirits very low and his manner odd. He had rolled away from William at one point, waving his hand, while William was speaking to him, and he had not returned to the room in which they had been seated. William had been left alone, gazing at the paintings and the gilt ceiling, until a servant wordlessly appeared and escorted him from the chamber.

Dr. Onslow is still in the room, packing his bag.

"She shall stay in bed as long as necessary," William is saying to the doctor. "Stanley's wife can come to attend her." He coughs, puts a handkerchief to his mouth.

The surgeon looks at him. "You must mind your own health, sir," he says. "These are cold, damp nights for a man your age to be outside looking at the stars until dawn. I mean no disrespect"—he bows slightly—"but perhaps it is not worth your trouble. In such weather, I mean."

WILLIAM SEES DR. ONSLOW to the door and returns to Lina in his bedroom. "The man means well, I daresay, but he understands nothing of why the *winter* sky is as important as the *summer* sky," he says irritably. "If an astronomer thought only of the climate and his own comfort in it, we should still be living in ignorance."

"You must sleep, William," Lina says. "Let Stanley help me to my own room. I'll be more comfortable there." She begins to struggle to sit up.

"No!" William comes to her bedside and with difficulty kneels beside her.

He takes her hand. "I have asked too much of you," he says.

"Sometimes." She encloses his hand with her own, smiling faintly.

But when he bends his head lower over her fingers, she realizes that he is struggling to control his emotions. Except for when the news of Henry's death reached them, it is the first time she has seen him so moved.

"I am all *right*, William," she says. She reaches and touches his shaved head. "It is nothing, really. I shall heal in no time. Please."

"I have taken your whole life, Lina," he says. "You have no husband, no child. . . . You must have a life for yourself. Before it is too late."

She does not like this line of maudlin reasoning, and she feels insulted that he appears not to consider that her labors in his behalf—either as housekeeper or as his assistant in astronomy—have been of abiding interest to *her*. Also, it seems disingenuous of him, she thinks, or at least thoughtless at this moment of her suffering, to suggest that he is only now appreciating what sacrifices she has made for him. And in truth—except for dear Henry, and she has never confided to William what Henry said to her on the last night she saw him—there have been no alternatives to her life with William. Those other pleasures she might have enjoyed, the pleasures Margaretta so longed for, but which were denied even her by her premature death. . . . Lina has always *known* they would not be hers. And what can he mean, *before it is too late*? It is already too late for any other sort of life for her.

She looks at her brother's bowed head, his shaking shoulders.

"I *gave* my life," she says. "William, I gave it. Without you I would have had no life at all. You know what I escaped. And you have given me so much in return. *More*—much more—than I have given you."

She remembers the day they left Hanover, how he had not hesitated when handing over a purse to free Hilda from her servitude to their mother. She remembers Hilda weeping, foolishly holding her apron over her face. The trees had been heavy with apples that day, the mud deep underfoot, and the morning sky full of clouds as fragile as lace. She remembers it clearly, that moment when her life divided, her past left behind as if it had died and been buried.

Their brother Alexander joined his younger brothers, Dietrich and Leonard, at the vineyard eventually, when their uncle passed on. They'd written to William after their mother's death that Jacob, after decades of silence, had surprised everyone by returning to claim the house. No one knew where he had been, or how he'd heard of his mother's last, fatal illness. He had said not a word of explanation to anyone, apparently, about all his years of absence, though Alexander reported that he looked badly used, and that he kept to himself. Whatever money Jacob had, Alexander wrote, apparently came from gambling.

Lina wonders what the old house looks like now, whether Jacob has kept up the orchard. She imagines disarray, rats in the corners, Jacob with his devil's face and dark teeth before a dying fire, cinders on the kitchen floor. She knows that Jacob wrote once asking William for money, and that William sent it, without question. Perhaps there have been other entreaties, other payments. She doesn't know. She hasn't wanted to think about him. It comes to her suddenly that had William not taken her away so many years before, she might have been first her mother's slave, and then Jacob's.

"William," she says now. "*Please.* I shall be well in no time."

But there is fear in her. He will *not* send her away—he must not, he *must not!*—because he imagines her unhappy or now unsuited for their labors together, lame or otherwise incapable.

He will *not* banish her from the life—the *work*—she has come to love. She delights in her hours alone on the laundry roof, her contributions to the catalogs of stars on which William works. She does not want to abandon her own investigations, any more than she wants to abandon his.

"I can manage without you, Lina, I feel certain," he says. "You must take as much time for yourself as you like, as much time as you need to be well. You must enjoy yourself."

"I am *fine*, William," she says. "It is only a little wound, after all. I will heal quickly, I am sure."

She feels her panic subside a little—he means only for her to rest, she thinks—but she is hurt by his remark that he can make do without her. She had thought herself indispensable. Indeed, she knows she *has* been indispensable.

"Truly," she repeats. "A matter of a few days. Or less," she goes on. "I am sure of it, William."

He bows his head lower. He brings her knuckles to his mouth, and his hands tremble. When a cold tear falls on the back of her hand, she is shocked.

"I am worried about *you*, William," she says. "This is not like you!"

He looks up at her then. He withdraws his hands from hers and wipes his eyes and mouth with his handkerchief.

"I know that you have been practicing economies," he says. "Your stipend from the queen, mine from the king . . . allow us no luxuries."

She does not like the look on his face. Something is there beyond his worry over money. These are old familiar troubles. "Surely Sir Joseph will help you, or Dr. Maskelyne," she says, but she knows even as she says it that William cannot be truly concerned about this. Though it is always a challenge, finding enough money, eventually it comes from somewhere. And William could spend more time with his music, as he once did. She could sing, perform again. They could easily work up a program for the season. It has been many years, of course, but . . .

"He is such an admirer, Sir Joseph," she says. "Of course he will—"

The fire has died down. One of the candles on the mantel gutters. William should call for Stanley, she thinks, or soon they will be in darkness.

William looks away from her. "I have met someone," he says.

In the bed, Lina moves swiftly, involuntarily, shifting her body away from his. The pain in her leg is shocking, and she stifles a cry.

William coughs again, wipes his nose, still without meeting her eyes. Instead he gets to his feet and goes to the window.

"She is a widow," he says. "She has a sizable fortune."

The night has been long, but now she sees that the palest light has arrived at the window, a fragile light, low on the pane. Lina does not want to see it, does not want what is coming toward her, this new day.

"She is quite young," he goes on. "You know her family; she is a Pitt, now—a brief marriage, unfortunate. She was married for only a year. An accident. Her husband suffered a riding accident. Her family . . . they are the Baldwins."

Lina cannot speak. All the years she worried that a wife would replace her in William's affections . . . and yet it had never happened, not even during all his visits to London. Eventually she had ceased to think of it. They would grow old together, she and William. They would be enough for each other.

She is acquainted with the Baldwin family from church, where they must come in two carriages, there are so many of them. Their house commands a fine view of Windsor Castle, she knows, and is very grand. Has she ever seen this young woman? She must have, in church.

"She is very kind," William says. "Very sweet-natured. A lovely girl. A lovely woman."

"You will take a *girl* as your wife? You are an *old man*, William," Lina says. "How old is she? Surely, you have no—"

She raises herself in the bed. She feels her pulse thrashing in her sore throat, matching the throbbing in her leg.

"You mean—" she says. "Now I understand you. You mean to take her to solve your difficulties over . . . *money.*"

He continues to stand at the window.

"That is not why," he says quietly.

"Then what? What *is* it?" She hears that her voice has become angry.

He is silent.

"I have not made up my mind," he says finally. "I do not know if she would even have me. Indeed it is true that I am her elder by several years."

"William," she says. "What can she do that *I* cannot do for you, except to give you *money?*"

But she hears herself then, hears the horrible nature of her question.

She feels how dry her lips are, cracked from the cold.

"I *worried* you would respond like this," he says. His tone is weary.

She is shocked. William is *never* weary.

"Have I not been excellent company for you, Lina?" he says. "My wanting to marry now, finally, is not the same as wanting to hurt you. I have *never* wanted to hurt you. Mary believes in our investigations. She has the resources to assist me. I believe she would like to be of use."

He coughs again into the handkerchief, as if this speech has brought it on.

"I hope you will be *happy* for me," he says finally, "if happiness with Mary is to be mine."

"William!" she says. She can feel how big her eyes have become, as if her face has been stretched tight over the bones.

She can feel the old pressure in her chest, her *Überangst*, feel her mother's hands, pushing her away. *Don't do that.*

"I shall go find Stanley," he says, "to build up the fire." And then he has left the room.

AFTER SOME TIME, Stanley appears at the door carrying a tray with tea and a boiled egg. Steam rises from the pot. He sets down the tray beside the bed. "You're all right? I'm going to get more wood," he says.

Lina has been staring at the day rising outside the window.

"I wish to go to my own room," she says. She begins to sit up.

"There's no need for that," Stanley says. "You're fine here. Your brother said so. Dr. Onslow wants you to rest."

"I can rest in my own room," she says. "I will be happier there."

Stanley regards her for a moment. "Eat, first." He sets the tray on her lap.

Obediently she drinks the tea, eats the egg. She has no appetite, but the hot tea feels good against her swollen throat. Stanley sits down on the bed beside her. She is afraid to look at him, afraid of what her face will reveal. He says nothing. It is like him, she thinks, to be sensitive to her. Surely he knows nothing of William's intentions, but he knows something beyond her accident has transpired.

"Why not stay here for now?" he says gently. "You've had a bad fall. Rest yourself."

She looks up at him. "Help me. Please. Truly, I want to be in my own bed."

He does not argue further with her. He takes the tray away, and she begins to try to move, but the pain in her leg is awful, and despite herself she cries out.

Stanley looks down on her.

"You are determined on this," he says. "I don't know why. But you can't walk. You can hardly move."

She looks at her leg, the bandage there.

"If I lift you," he says, "it will hurt you."

She nods. "Yes, I know it. Thank you, Stanley. *Danke schön.*"

He leans down then after a moment and slips his arms beneath her carefully, picking her up and holding her as he would a baby. She closes her eyes against the pain. She puts her arms around his neck.

She remembers the laughing, brown-eyed man who carried her to shore so many years ago.

Stanley makes a sound of sympathy; she knows it is his love for her that makes him sad now.

"It's a mystery," he says, "how someone so strong could weigh so little, in the end. If one was to judge only by your behavior, anyone would think you must be made of iron and weigh a ton."

In her room, when he lays her in bed, she is panting from the pain.

"I wish you hadn't made me do that," he says.

"Sorry," she says. And again she thanks him.

"I'll make you a fire," he says. "And then you must have tea and broth. Or wine. Dr. Onslow said so. Sarah has come, with the babies. Shall I ask her to come up and help you now?"

How tactful and considerate he is, she thinks. Someone must help her with her clothes and to wash, and she must empty her bladder, which aches.

The babies. It is how he always refers to his boys. She loves that about him.

"Sarah will stay until you're on your feet," he says. "She's a good nurse, and it's no bother to us. The boys love to be here. You know that."

She speaks from the pillow. "I never could have managed all these years, Stanley. Never without you."

"I'd say you were a match for him." Stanley stands up from the fire. "You'd have done all right." But his face shows his pity for her.

She manages a smile, but what she feels is that somehow she has begun to die a little, will die a little more every day now.

"Where is my *Bruder*?" she says, using the old German.

"He's in the laundry," Stanley says. "I think he went in there to work, but he's fallen fast asleep over his papers."

He wipes his hands free of dirt from the logs. "What do you know? He's mortal like the rest of us after all, the old man."

WILLIAM COMES TO HER ROOM that evening, after Sarah has taken away her supper tray. He has washed, and he wears a fresh shirt. Sarah must be busy downstairs with their filthy clothes, washing and drying, as well as cooking, Lina assumes, and managing the children, too. Earlier Stanley had brought the little boys up to say hello, reminding them to be careful of her bad leg. The eldest boy, Anthony—as sweet-tempered as his father—said, "Poor Missus Caroline. She is hurting very, very badly," and he kissed her hand again and again instead.

William's sleep—however little he intended to take it—has done him good. He looks better.

He has a bottle of sherry, and he pours her a glass.

"Is the pain any better?"

She nods.

He looks out the window. A hard rain sounds against the glass.

He goes to the mantel and takes up the clock, another of Henry's gifts. It's a lovely thing, bronze and ormolu. A female figure seated at a desk with an open birdcage before her is mounted on the top. The pendulum swings behind the frieze, a blur of gold like a bird's wing. It must have stopped, she realizes, just before dawn.

She does not want William to touch the clock, but he winds it, sets it back.

She knows he is at a loss, unable to sit at the telescope tonight.

"Have you everything you need?" he asks.

She nods again.

"Now you are not speaking to me." He sighs. "It was my fault, your accident. If it were not for me, you would have been safely inside last night, asleep in your bed like all the other ladies in England."

"I do not *wish* to be *safely inside*, William," she says.

He comes and sits on her bed. "What can I do?" he says.

"Nothing," she says. "I'm fine."

"Caroline."

"If you think I am unhappy, William, you are mistaken," she says.

He colors.

"I will go on," she says. "As usual." It is what she has decided. He may take a wife, but she will do as she has always done for William. He will love her no less, and perhaps there even will be happiness in it for her as well. "I shall stay here in my place and do as I have always done."

At this he does not meet her gaze. He looks down at her legs beneath the quilt.

"We are friends, Lina?" he says. "As usual?"

"Do you know what I have remembered?" she says. "From long ago. I read it in a book you gave me. I wrote it down. *If you must love, oh, then, love solitude, for solitude alone is true and kind.* But I do not think it is true."

William looks at her.

"Solitude is not always true and kind," she says. "Neither are some people. But some are good, very good. And there are things to love other than solitude. So not every bit of that passage I wrote down is true, and though I once thought it very wise, I no longer think so."

"You are quite right," he says quietly. "I agree with you."

"We are friends, William," she says. "True and kind friends. As usual. Nothing will change."

But to this, it seems, he has no answer.

FIFTEEN

Comet

•——◆——•

The winter seemed endless. Lina thought she had never been as glad to see summer arrive at last with its long, hot days and droning companies of bees from Stanley's hives in the orchard, and even the mosquitoes—despite the fear of malaria—which congregate in the damp meadow where the forty-foot rests. In the late afternoons she likes to take a cup of tea and rest on the terrace, looking out over the garden and the orchard and the scaffolding of the forty-foot beyond, enjoying the feeling of the heat on the top of her head and on her back and shoulders.

Her leg has healed, though it was three months before she could walk without limping. The wound left a divot in her calf into which she can fit her knuckle.

During the remaining cold months of that winter and into spring, months when it was impossible for her to walk any great distance, William worked instead at the smaller telescope near the house in the garden. He could not do without her assistance, however, and so he devised a system of string leading from his hand at the telescope to a window in the laundry. By pulling on the string, he could get her attention where she sat at the desk. She would open the window, and he would ask for information from the astronomical tables before her, or he would call out to her to communicate his own sightings, which she would then record.

After a few days of this, they developed a kind of language using the string, one tug or two or three having specific meanings that needed no words. She sat by the window for hours that winter, the string in her hand connecting her to William.

She could not see him, but every time she felt the pull on the string, she knew he was there.

Nothing, she thought—not even William's marriage, should it come to pass—could break this bond between them.

WILLIAM VISITS FREQUENTLY with Mary Pitt and the Baldwins over the winter and spring. He makes no secret of this, but Lina does not ask where he is going when he takes a horse and rides out, and she will not speak to him of his relationship with Mary, despite having been a guest at the Baldwins' home now on two occasions, invitations she knew she could not reject. She ceases to attend church with William, however, and pleads work when he asks her to accompany him.

Late one afternoon in June, Lina comes across the terrace from the laundry, where she has been working on William's catalog of nebulae and copying one of his papers, to hear voices from inside the house.

In the sitting room, she finds damp-eyed Mary gazing up at William with a look of adoration on her face, and two of the younger Baldwin children.

Lina's hands are ink-stained, and her back is sore. The evening before had been cloudy, and she had gone to bed early, but this morning she had been awake before dawn. She'd spent an hour in the kitchen, setting bread dough to rise, and then the early morning hours weeding in the vegetable garden, and then finally the afternoon in the laundry, first with the new atlas, listing William's most recent notations, and then copying more of his letters. Mercifully, they have had no visitors at Observatory House for a few days, though there is often a steady stream of them. Now she wants nothing more than to walk in the orchard for a bit, to lie down in the grass on the warm earth and watch the stars come out.

But here is Mary, and Lina was not expecting her, which makes it worse.

The day has been hot, with no breeze. In the laundry the muslin curtains have hung without stirring. She had been aware of the sound of bees outside, but William had been in town on errands, and the house had been quiet. She had not heard horses or a carriage. Perhaps they'd come on foot, she thinks, traipsing across the fields under an umbrella to protect Mary's complexion from the sun.

Now the day will end in tedium, exactly the sort of housekeeping—being a hostess—Lina finds most tiresome and, in the case of Mary, most upsetting.

She will have to serve them something to eat, when she and William might just have helped themselves to cold chicken and bread and cheese and sat on the terrace together as night fell. With almost no one in William's regular employ anymore except Stanley, who tends the gardens and the orchard, and Sarah, who comes to help sometimes with the washing, Lina does not cook as she once did. She knows there is little in the larder beyond a half a chicken and the end of a cold pork roast, some wine jelly and cabbages and potatoes. The bread will take an hour to bake, even if she puts it in the oven now.

William holds Mary's little hand in his big fingers as if it were a butterfly's wing.

"Surprise!" He turns to Lina, smiling.

She watches him take both of Mary's hands in his own and pull them playfully. They both laugh.

Why does Mary always look so wet about the eyes, Lina

thinks, as if everything either thrills or frightens her to teary speechlessness? Her skin is so pale that it seems clear liquid rather than blood pools beneath it.

The grass in the meadow has not been scythed in nearly a month. Lina walks alone every day in the fields, no matter the height of the grass; she likes the meditative state of this exercise. The hems of her dresses, however, are always covered with brown burrs and little black stickles like arrows. She sits down now and adjusts her skirt to hide the worst of the disarray. Despite all of William's accomplishments—most recently the comets he has seen, his numbers greater now than any counted by other astronomers—they have debts, and the expense of maintaining the house and the mirrors and the telescopes, not to mention their manufacture, is not diminishing. Since William's announcement about his intentions toward Mary this past winter, Lina has been careful with their expenses—more than once she has suggested he turn to music again—but she is aware that they are in worse condition financially than ever before.

Since the staggering revelations of the forty-foot early on, there has been no further investment from the king beyond their small salaries from the royal coffers.

"Doesn't he understand that you cannot support yourself or your work on fifty pounds a year?" Lina had said.

"The king has no idea what *anything* costs," William had said. "He is the *king*. He's never had to purchase anything."

Lina looks down at her ink-stained hands now, the poor condition of her dress.

Mary is dressed beautifully all in white, as seems to be her habit.

"I brought the children to see the telescope," Mary says, turning to Lina and smiling.

Mary is the eldest of the children in the Baldwin family. Her marriage to John Pitt, when she was twenty, was short-lived. Lina learned from Stanley that after the death of her husband—a wealthy merchant—Mary returned immediately to her family, also possessed of considerable fortune, in Datchet. As inheritor of her husband's estate, she is now extremely well-to-do.

Twice this summer Lina and William have been entertained for dinner at the Baldwins' manor house. There appeared to be a dozen Baldwin children present for the midday meal, some in their teens, others still so young they peered at her from over their soup bowls, only their round eyes showing. They are all pale-haired, like Mary and like their mother, who clearly sees William as an ideal match for her widowed daughter: he is nearby, so he will not take her far away, and he is distinguished. As wealth and property are no longer an issue for her daughter, Mrs. Baldwin wants for Mary what all mothers should want, Lina thinks: happiness. And it is clear that William and Mary, unlikely though their union seems given their difference in age, seem happy.

Mary's voice contains an apology now, as if she knows she has trespassed against Lina by arriving unannounced and without any escort but two of her younger brothers.

Lina, turning to look out the open French doors, sees that the boys have crossed the garden to climb the stone wall.

"They mustn't go near the scaffolding," Lina says. "I hope you told them, William."

Mary's mouth trembles, but she holds her ground on the settee, her little hands still drooping like a pair of empty gloves laid in William's palms.

"Of course," Mary says. "They want only to look at it."

"I've promised them a glimpse of *Georgium Sidus* one night," William says, "or Jupiter or Saturn. We will like that, won't we, Caroline?"

· · ·

IN THE KITCHEN, Lina puts her hands to her blazing face.

If they wed, Mary and William—and now it seems inevitable, given the smitten looks that travel between them—it will be the end of something for her, even if Mary cannot compete with Lina in terms of her assistance to William's astronomical investigations.

She kicks off her boots and strips off her stockings. The kitchen's tile floor is cool under her bare feet. She must prepare some sort of tea for William and Mary and the two little boys. In the larder she finds a stale ginger cake, slices it, and spreads it savagely with butter. There are apples in the cellar; these she heaps into a bowl. The pork loin can be hacked up and decorated with pickles. She finds a tiny spoon for the wine jelly in the drawer of the hutch, and a piece of cheese—she sniffs the green rind—in the icebox.

In the dining room she shakes a tablecloth with a snap, sets out the dishes. Flies hover. She lights candles, puts the backs of her hands to her cheeks again.

She will serve them barefoot.

She looks out the window. Beyond the rippled glass, the green world of the summer glows.

She should be happy for William, as he says.

She should endeavor to like Mary.

Who would not be happy to see a beloved brother married? Only a *monster* would not.

HE TELLS HER LIKE THIS: one day later that month he announces that he must go to London for two days. He is vague about his purpose.

Stanley comes to harvest the honey on the morning after William's departure. Lina follows him out to the orchard, where he dons his bee veil. When he turns to her, she cannot make out his face clearly.

"The Baldwins have gone to London," he says. "I thought I ought to tell you."

She is silent for a moment. She turns and looks into the orchard.

"You have done a good job here, Stanley," she says. "How beautiful the orchard is now. Remember it when we came? That first day, we made the jam?"

She does not want him to look into her eyes.

"Perhaps it will be for the best," he says.

"I know," she says. "Thank you for telling me."

"I think he ought to have told you himself. Everyone knows he is to make a proposal." He pulls on his gloves and faces her again before turning to the hives.

"There's no one can take your place," he adds. "You know that."

TWO NIGHTS LATER, when William comes home, she is working in the laundry.

"Stand up," he says without preamble from the doorway. His eyes are glowing, and his color is high. He looks wonderful, as healthy and fit as he has in years. "You are to have a new sister," he says.

He stops. "Well? What have you to say to me?"

"It is very good news, William," she says with formality. "I am very happy for you."

He stands still. For a moment they regard one another. A breeze from the window stirs the papers on the table.

Then he comes forward and grabs her shoulders, gives them a shake.

"I knew you would come round," he says. "I told Mary that you would. She's terribly afraid of you, you know."

He kisses her cheek.

"Well, we shall be a family now, yes?" he says.

THAT NIGHT WHEN LINA retires to her room, she picks up her daybook. She sits at the table by the window, a candle beside her. She looks out into the darkness. There are clouds—it is no night for viewing the stars. Only the moon is visible from time to time, its familiar face appearing when the clouds part.

She writes the date, August 12, 1788, and one sentence: *My brother is engaged to marry.*

There seems nothing more to say. Or nothing more she will commit to paper.

She closes the book.

THE WEDDING IS SMALL, just the two families—though the Baldwins are great in number—and a few friends. The littlest Baldwin brothers and sisters strew rose petals outside Saint Laurence's church in Upton.

Lina seats herself across the aisle from the Baldwins. She hears people enter the small church behind her, but she does not turn around. Then she feels a hand on her shoulder. She turns. Stanley has taken a seat in the pew behind her. Sarah, beside him, smiles at Lina, but there is sympathy in her expression.

Lina touches Stanley's hand and then turns back to face the priest, and to regard William's and Mary's backs as they stand together at the altar.

When they kneel, Lina looks up at the sunlight pouring down through the narrow stained-glass windows, dropping color across the floor and over her hands, folded in her lap.

She wears the green dress that she wore for her first performance at the Octagon. The silk is thin in places. Sarah, who is clever about such things, has trimmed it for her, but she feels patched and shabby. She is aware of her scarred face for the first time in many years, of the oddity of her physical presence; she is smaller than many of the Baldwin children, with their perfectly milky skin and fine yellow hair.

Her gloves, too long for her arms, have had to be rolled at the elbow.

She remembers the wedding in Hanover so many years before, the boys singing in the street afterward.

This is the great mystery, the priest had said. *Your wife will be like a fruitful vine within your house. Your children will be like olive shoots around your table.*

And she remembers her father, moaning from his chair before the fire. *Oh, my dear. You are neither handsome nor rich.*

AT THE BALDWINS' HOUSE after the ceremony, Mr. Baldwin brings her a glass of sherry where she stands by the long drapes at one of the windows in the parlor. The day is warm, and she is nervous, the conversation around her loud. She drinks thirstily. A servant returns again with another and then another glass. She is embarrassed when her glass is always empty, but she is grateful to have something to do with her hands. Though Mr. and Mrs. Baldwin and their guests have many questions for William, who stands with his arm around Mary's waist, no one asks Lina anything about herself or her role in the work. The children run past her, shrieking. Outside, two dogs chase each other over the grass.

Across the room, Mrs. Baldwin speaks with a lady Lina does not recognize; when Lina sees them glance at her, she turns quickly to look out the window—she does not want to be caught staring—but the movement makes her dizzy. She grasps the curtain to steady herself.

Then William is at her elbow. "Lina?"

Children's merry laughter sounds. Someone plays the pianoforte in another room. A smell of roses comes to her. She watches the sunlight move across the rug, a pattern of pink and yellow blossoms—and little black bees? She leans closer—and curling vines. Slowly she brings her gaze up to William's face.

"You're unwell," he says, his hand on elbow. He bends near. "Too much wine, Lina," he says in her ear. "Take no more, please."

Somehow Stanley is found to escort her home.

Mary stands at the front door, her hair wound prettily with flowers. She leans forward to kiss Lina's cheek.

"Sister," she says. "I know we shall be friends. I have told William that we shall find the nicest lodgings for you. And you must have whatever you like from Observatory House, of course."

The front steps under Lina's feet tilt. She feels nauseous.

"What?" she says.

Stanley's hand appears under her elbow. "Come, missus," he says. "Sarah is at home, waiting for us."

Lina stares at Mary.

Mary's eyes flit unhappily to William's.

An uncomfortable expression crosses his face. "Go with Stanley, Lina," he says. He leans forward and kisses her forehead. "We will see you in a couple of weeks."

She dislikes it when he kisses her on the forehead. It is a kiss for a child.

She knows he and Mary are going on a wedding trip to Wales and to the Lake District. It will be the longest period she has spent away from William since her arrival in England.

Stanley leads her down the drive toward the horses and their carriage. She wobbles, feeling the pebbles of the drive beneath the thin soles of her shoes.

When she is seated beside Stanley, Lina turns back. William and Mary stand at the front door of the Baldwins' house. William has his arm around Mary's waist again. He lifts his hand to wave.

Stanley raises the reins, and the carriage lurches forward. When they round the bend and are out of sight of the house, Lina leans quickly over the side of the cart and is sick.

Stanley begins to pull up on the reins to stop the horses, but she sits back up, wiping her mouth with her glove. She then takes off the glove and throws it into the tall grass by the road.

"Go on," she says. "Please. Go on."

She finds a handkerchief and presses it to her mouth.

Stanley glances at her. "It's very hot," he says. "You'll feel better now that you've been sick. Could happen to anyone. All right now?"

The carriage rocks. The trees on either side of the lane bob up and down. She holds on to the seat.

"What did she mean by that?" she asks Stanley. "That they shall find other lodgings for me."

Stanley looks straight ahead. He says nothing.

She looks at his profile for a moment. Understanding dawns.

"Very . . . kind of them. Of my *Bruder*," she says faintly.

Stanley reaches across the seat and takes her hand.

"Not how I would put it," he says, squeezing hard, "if you ask me." He glances at her. "It's just how I feel," he says. "Sorry."

"You *knew*," she says. "You already knew."

"I *offered* to look for you," he says, and she hears now his anger and frustration, "but she said their servants will take care of it."

"I see."

He squeezes her hand again.

"Why?" she says. "Why must it be this way?"

Stanley shakes his head. "I don't think they've thought it through," he says. "It's a poor decision, I'd say. Sarah says so, too."

Lina closes her eyes, but it makes her feel sick to do so, and so she opens them again. She wants desperately to get home, to shed her sorry old dress, which now smells of vomit, to wash her face, and to mount the stairs to her rooftop observatory.

SHE DOES NOT BELIEVE the day could be any worse, but when she arrives home, she finds on her desk in the laundry, propped against a wrapped package, a letter written in Mary's hand and signed by both her and William. They have given her—as a gift—five days in London, while they are on their wedding trip.

Lina knows Mary imagines that this perfect holiday, as Mary refers to it in the letter, will be a great luxury for her. All the arrangements—and many amusements—have been planned for her.

In the box is a soft Indian shawl, ivory, with a delicate red and gold pattern of teardrop shapes.

Lina is to enjoy herself and to *rest*, Mary writes, after all her hard work. She thanks her for taking such good care of William for all these years.

LINA CAN SEE NO WAY to refuse to go to London. Too much effort has been made, and so much already spent on the arrangements, apparently.

She discovers when she arrives in the city at Mivart's Hotel that Mary also has supplied her with a maid for the week and with a wardrobe of new dresses, a kindness that stings.

The maid says nothing when Lina begs her to return the gowns, asking instead for a few simple things in gray or black or brown, but Lina can see the young woman is surprised. Once the maid has returned with the dresses, Lina dismisses her for the week.

What would she do with her assistance? She has no idea. She has had no servant except Stanley, and he is more friend than anything else.

She attends none of the parties or concerts to which she has been given invitations, though it pains her to miss the music. She spends the days instead at the British Museum, gazing at the Greek and Roman and Egyptian artifacts. For a long time one afternoon she stands before the colossal bust of the Pharaoh Rameses with his cobra diadem. All afternoon the light in the giant room moves slowly around Rameses. Lina leaves the museum at last when his face falls into shadow.

She has brought a small telescope with her, but the lights of London are too bright for her to see the stars at night.

After four days, she can bear no more of it.

She returns to Observatory House.

FOR TWO DAYS, she sleeps through the mornings and wakes at noon, spending all night, from sunset until dawn, at the telescope on her rooftop observatory. It is strange to be alone in the house without William for so many days running. Stanley comes to check on her once a day, but with the death of Sarah's father a few months before, he has inherited their family's small farm, and he is busy making improvements to the house, so that they might move there eventually.

Most of her work at the telescope over the years has been at William's direction, tracking objects for him or taking measurements. Now, in her brother's absence, it is as if his voice is silenced, too. There are tasks she could undertake for him, but she feels in some way as if she has been unleashed. Her time, for almost the first occasion in all the years she has been with William in England, is her own.

The nights are warm. She takes a coffee before beginning her labors, standing at the door of the laundry to watch the shadows lengthen over the grass. In the meadow, the forty-foot telescope has been lowered to the ground. The scaffolding against the horizon has a deserted look.

When she climbs to her rooftop just after sunset, swifts and little bats move around her in the sky. Sometimes she hears the beating of wings near her head, feels the movement of the air.

She uses the five-foot Newtonian telescope made for her by William. By now she knows by sight all the nebulae, and so she also knows therefore that her chances are better than for most at sighting a comet. William has used the Greenwich method of scanning the sky quickly with a field glass and binoculars, then proceeding to make detailed observations, but over these days alone she develops a method of sweeping that allows her to scan as much as a quarter of the entire sky in a single night, moving the telescope along the meridian from horizon to zenith and back to the horizon, and then, after a few minutes, beginning again. A clock helps her keep a steady pace. She also knows that comets are most likely to be glimpsed on their orbit around the sun either in the west at sunset or in the east just before sunrise, and so at those times she moves horizontally before beginning her vertical sweeps. She knows, too, that a comet's orbit—whether an elongated ellipse or parabolic or hyperbolic—would affect how often it could be seen and whether it would return in her lifetime. She has learned from William that the comet of 1661 was observed by Polish astronomer Johannes Hevelius, and that Edmond Halley, in his analysis of several comets using Newton's Laws, had found a similarity between the orbit of the comet of 1661 and a comet seen earlier in 1532. She thinks of Halley, on his high hill at his lonely island observatory on Saint Helena in the South Atlantic, and then at the side of Hevelius in Gdańsk, where he helped confirm Hevelius's observations. She thinks of all the astronomers, often alone, but sometimes accompanied through the night. She is glad tonight to be alone. If the sightings in 1532 and 1661 were not of separate comets but instead two apparitions of the same returning comet, then Halley predicted it should return again in 1789. But in any case, it is not Halley's comet she wants to see, or any other comet already witnessed and recorded. She wants to see one of her own.

THE COMET APPEARS TO HER on the third night. She sweeps as far as Beta Lyrae, and then there it is, coming from the south, surrounded by a burr of light. Though she has seen William's comets, she feels now much as she did on her first glimpse of the moon through a telescope on the deck of the packet that brought them to England. It is one thing to see an object someone else has been clever enough to detect. It is another thing to discover it for yourself. She feels as if she is seeing a creature long thought to be extinct emerge blazing from the dark forests of the sky, out of the past itself. She understands now, as she did not on that first night on the ship, the *time* the universe contains, the depth of its history truly beyond her comprehension. Comets seem like messengers from another epoch, another world altogether.

She knows that if she is the only person to see it that night—and that is the likely circumstance—then she must find another pair of eyes to witness it, at her direction, before it is gone entirely.

There is no time to be lost.

She stays at the telescope for only a few more minutes, long enough to make precise notes about the comet's location and to make an educated guess about its path.

Then she goes downstairs.

WITH A GOOD HORSE and in good weather, it is at least an eight-hour ride by horse to London, another two hours beyond that to Greenwich Park and the observatory there, where she will find Dr. Maskelyne. She has not been on a horse since Henry's death, but she walks into the village now and rouses the man who owns the stable. He is reluctant—surely she does not intend to under-take this journey without escort?

"My brother should be most unhappy to learn you refused me," she says. "My errand is at his orders, and it is of the greatest importance."

It troubles her not one bit to lie to him.

WHEN SHE APPEARS at the observatory the next day, the sun has just set. She has ridden for many hours, but she has felt not at all weary or even hungry. The excitement of her discovery seems echoed by the wind that moves the tall trees around her in the darkness and then into the next day, giant clouds like mountains piling up low along the horizon. She is desperate that the sky remain clear, that her comet appear again.

At the great telescope at Greenwich, she gives Dr. Maskelyne the coordinates, and he directs his gaze.

When he turns away to look at her after a few minutes, his expression betrays both his astonishment and his admiration.

"My *dear*," he says, with warmth.

He bends and takes her hand, kisses it. Then he looks seri-ously at her. "You are truly a most extraordinary family. Know-ing your role in your brother's endeavors, it should not surprise me that you are indeed a powerful astronomer in your own right. And a woman who could ride so many hours alone and without pause . . . I would venture to say that you are brave and strong, as well."

He shakes his head. "I think the heavens themselves must have decided to obey you. You have conjured forth a comet, Miss Herschel, and it has appeared at your command. Congratulations."

Back at Observatory House—Dr. Maskelyne insisted on ordering a carriage to take her home, and she wants only to return to her own rooftop viewing platform—she sleeps for a day. The next night, she returns to her rooftop for another look, perhaps her last, at her comet.

Indeed, it appears again, exactly where she expected to see it. Yet despite what Dr. Maskelyne said, she feels as she has always felt in the presence of the stars, not the reach of her power but rather the dominion of the vast universe.

There will be other comets to follow. Of that, she now feels oddly certain.

THE NEWS TRAVELS FAST, and soon, even before William and Mary are home, letters of congratulations begin to arrive, addressed to her at Observatory House.

High Priestess of the Heavens, one letter begins, from an admirer in Lisbon, a physician and amateur astronomer with whom she and William have had friendly correspondence over the years.

Still on his honeymoon, William writes, as well, in reply to her letter—she had made it brief and formal—and to an additional letter from Dr. Maskelyne.

William's excitement and pleasure—and his pride—are evident in his words, but they bring tears to her eyes, nonetheless.

I wish I were with you, dear Lina, William writes, *to share in your victory.*

SIXTEEN

Silence

• ◆ •

Another letter from William arrives: he and Mary have decided to extend their trip for a few more weeks, he writes, and meanwhile new lodgings for her finally have been arranged.

Eventually a place of your own choosing might be found, if you wish, he writes, *but for now these new quarters will keep you close by us, which is our only desire. Mary has seen to it all.*

Lina packs her belongings at Observatory House. There is very little she wants, after all, just her clothing and books, a few pieces of household furniture and effects to supply her needs. She assumes she will be able to return to use her rooftop observatory as often as she likes, though nothing has been said about this directly. William appears to imagine that she will continue to help him, that her expulsion from the house to rooms nearby is neither surprising nor regrettable, nothing to be mentioned or to occasion complaint. That she must leave Observatory House— her *home*—is a decision that appears to have been reached without any discussion, as if everyone naturally agrees that such a change in circumstances is mutually desirable, and her opinion is unnecessary.

She does not know if Mary suggested it to William.

Perhaps Mary's mother proposed it, the maiden sister being unwelcome in a house with a new bride.

Two servants from the Baldwins arrive to take Lina's belongings for her, but Stanley has given her orders to wait for him. He will not hear of her going without him, but he must be at an auction in the morning. He will be there by two o'clock, he tells her.

She tries to work in the old laundry, but she cannot keep her mind on even the simplest of tasks. Everything seems to impress itself upon her as if she were seeing it for the last time.

Finally, she gives up. She goes into the orchard and sits on the grass near Stanley's hives, which make a pleasant buzzing sound. If she leans her ear against the wood, she feels the vibration in her cheekbone, the bees going about their business. After all, it is just an ordinary day.

HER NEW HOME, she discovers, is a pair of rooms above a butcher's shop on the Windsor Road in Upton.

Her belongings have been delivered ahead of her, as promised, but they have been deposited every which way, boxes and hampers crowded into a narrow hall. The men had taken no care. It seems to her, in fact, that they have been deliberately careless. She looks around, bewildered. Do the servants at the Baldwins' dislike her or her brother or Mary Pitt to treat her things in this way? Has she or William given offense?

Stanley is outraged, repeating again and again his complaints.

"I *told* them before they left that *I* would make arrangements for you," he says, "but Miss Pitt"—he corrects himself—"Mrs. *Herschel* said their servants would take care of it, that she wouldn't trouble me."

Lina finds that some dishes in a crate have been broken, including a small Chinese vase that was a gift from Henry.

You should have some things you like about you, William had written, *so of course take anything you wish from Observatory House. We want only for your comfort.*

She'd noticed that he writes of himself and Mary together as if they are of one mind. He writes *we* now, never *I*.

The disorder in the rooms is terrible. The walls are dingy, and the windows in the front room overlooking the street are grimy. Moving from the first room into the second, seeing the smoke stains up the plaster above the fireplace and the narrow mantel, she feels disbelief. Had William not seen this place? Perhaps he thought the rooms perfectly located in the village, that she would no doubt enjoy the convenience of being so near to everything. Perhaps he did not understand how small it is.

She looks around. How is she even to cook a meal for herself? After so many years in William's company, after all her service to him, such great happiness between them, she cannot believe that this is where fate—where *William*—has deposited her, that he could imagine her to be happy here, coming to Observatory House and knocking on the door like a guest.

Stanley is behind her. When she turns from the window, she sees he is having difficulty controlling his face.

"Missus," he says. "Oh, *missus.*"

She stands motionless in the center of the front room. She can hear the sounds of activity from the street outside: horses' hooves on the stones, the bells ringing the hour at the church, the conversation of passersby below. She has a sudden memory: sometimes, when William grew weary from sitting too long at his calculations in the laundry, he would call for her, and she would oblige him by taking off her shoes and walking barefoot over his back.

Had anyone ever come upon them doing this, surely they would have thought it strange.

How unobserved they had been at the house.

How often alone and yet together.

· · ·

THAT NIGHT SHE CANNOT SLEEP. There is no help for it, she knows. She sits up, feels for her boots. She will go for a walk. She is not afraid of the dark. She has never been afraid of the dark.

She has spent so much of her life awake at night that the Windsor Road's emptiness now, its silence, does not trouble but rather consoles her. She passes the last dark building—the blacksmith's forge, smoke still rising from his chimney and a smell of burning in the air—and walks along a quiet stretch where the road runs past a small pond. There is plenty of moonlight, the moon's reflection floating in the pond. She stands for a while and listens to the deep bellowing of the bullfrogs, the light chirping of the tiny green frogs. She walks on until she thinks she has tired herself sufficiently, and then she turns back.

It is William who discovered the *Georgium Sidus*, William who was—who *is*—the king's genius, William who has understood the stars and the planets and all their places in the universe better than anyone else. What is she? She knows that her accomplishments, though far less than William's, amount to something, of course. But perhaps her accomplishments are only the rewards of the dullest virtues—*women's* virtues—of effort, interest, and consideration. Even her comet, though it required experience to know where to look for it—as William has always said, seeing is an art—is mostly the result of her patience.

Will there be forever now only these few rooms and a narrow hall over a butcher's shop, the smell of blood below her?

When she returns from her walk, it is nearly dawn. A mad rooster crows in a nearby garden. In bed again, she closes her eyes. Then she opens them in the darkness.

From the window, she can see the constellation of Aquarius resting like an urn tipped on the celestial equator. It pours forth its stream of stars, a beautiful deluge sprayed across the sky. In

China, William once told her, the constellation was called *Heu Leang*, the Empty Bridge.

She thinks now about the Scotsman Ferguson, the astronomical instruments he developed for showing the motions of the planets, the places of the sun and moon. This man—no doubt a genius like William—began life as a shepherd boy, she knows, lying on his back in the meadows at night surrounded by his flock, measuring the distance between stars with a knotted string. The thought of others who, like her, have spent their nights alone watching the stars consoles her now.

It had once comforted her to be reminded that she and William, though he was in England and she in Hanover, looked up at the same moon.

The rooster crows again. Her head aches. She turns on her side. Her eyes are dry. Anger keeps her grief at bay, she thinks. She shifts again, lies on her back on the unfamiliar bed, and stares up into the dark. She has taken off her boots, but she has not undressed. By refusing to put on nightclothes, she can somehow postpone her acceptance of her new home, the dreadfulness of it. She feels certain now that William did not see this place before the arrangements were made. Maybe even Mary didn't see it; maybe the task had been left to a servant—*find somewhere for the sister*—and it had suited a servant to see that rent was paid to some relation.

Surely if William had seen that there was no garden, no kitchen, just these low ceilings and crooked stairs . . . surely he would not have sent her here. And of course there is no place at all for her telescope.

She will not stay here.

She gets up again and wraps herself in a shawl of soft pink wool, a gift from one of the princesses several years ago, sent to her via William on one of his trips to Kew. She reaches down beside the bed and takes up her daybook. She draws up the blanket around her and props her back with a pillow.

She must find another place to live. Surely there will be a cottage nearby—she's seen enough of them on her walks—with a good aspect for viewing the sky, somewhere close enough that she can walk to Observatory House, if she chooses. She has no money of her own, of course, beyond what is paid to her monthly by the queen, hardly enough to live on. She will have to depend—depend yet again—on William's kindness, on Mary's conscience and her fortune.

She will not desert William. She will continue to work for him, to help him in all his endeavors. She will not forget what she owes him.

But she is not sure she can forgive him.

She looks down at her journal. She has nothing she wishes to write about what has happened. After so many years at William's side, after a life as interesting and varied, as adventurous and wondrous as that of any woman in England, of any woman's in the *world* . . . now, she realizes, she has nothing at all to say. Or nothing she is willing to say.

She ties up the book tightly with a cord like something she means to weight with a brick and drown.

The rooster has stopped crowing. She blows out the candle.

She listens.

Silence.

This is the shore on which she has been washed up, she sees. It is an ill-prospected shore, dark and stony, Andromeda's lonely rock, nothing at all like the shore at Yarmouth where the laughing, brown-eyed man once took her in his arms and carried her through the waves.

No. She will never be able to forgive William for this.

. . .

IT IS YEARS LATER, crossing the field between Observatory House and the cottage where she finally took up residence, when Lina slips in the snow one winter night and sprains an ankle. She has intended to join William at the telescope, but it is clear when she attempts to stand that she cannot manage the walk.

The village boy paid to escort her every night with a lantern as she goes between her cottage and Observatory House runs for William.

Back in her own cottage, where the boy's father carries her, she confesses to Dr. Onslow, who has arrived after being alerted by one of William and Mary's servants, that she fell during a spell of faintness. Her old headaches have been bad recently, the spots before her eyes during these episodes more numerous and prolonged. Sometimes her vision clouds completely, as if a fist were closing, the aperture of light shrinking to a pinprick.

Dr. Onslow, holding her wrist, recommends a fortnight in a darkened house, if it can be contrived.

She should rest her eyes, at least. And then, should she lose her sight altogether, he tells her—and William and Mary, who stand anxiously nearby, Mary despite the late hour—that it would be well, while she still has some vision left, if she has time to rehearse how she might navigate the world as a blind person. It would be perhaps a prudent precaution.

"I remind you," Lina says, "that I am well accustomed to the darkness. Are you recommending now that I *practice being blind*?"

"Just rest, Lina," the doctor tells her. "I confess . . . I don't know what will happen to your eyes. But heaven knows it will not harm you to *rest*."

He shakes his head. "I have treated no woman as determined as you or so little inclined for leisure." He pats her hand. "How old are you?"

She thinks. "Fifty-seven. No, I don't know. I don't remember," she says crossly. She grimaces.

"As I said," Dr. Onslow repeats. "Rest. In the *dark*. Let us see if that helps with the headaches, at least. And meanwhile you can give your ankle time to heal, as well."

"You shall want for nothing, Caroline," Mary says. "I shall supervise it all myself. You should not be accompanying your brother in such conditions anyway. I don't know why you let him order you about."

"I come of my own accord and interest," Lina says, but she knows Mary means her words kindly. As William's wife, Mary has proven herself loving and dutiful and generous, not only to William over the years but to Lina, as well. Her attentions to Lina have been affectionate and steady. About that first set of rooms, Mary had made tearful, embarrassed apologies; the servant left in charge of that transaction had been sacked. Yet it had taken Lina time to forgive her.

The morning following her first and only night in that unhappy place, which reeked of pig's blood and from which no stars could be seen, Lina had walked to Stanley's farm. She would not go back to Observatory House, though William and Mary were not due home for several more days.

A gamekeeper's cottage near Observatory House stood empty, Sarah had said, conferring with Lina and Stanley over their kitchen table. It wasn't much, but it had once had a beautiful garden and a lovely big fireplace. She'd gone there often as a child, she said, as her mother had bought wool from the gamekeeper's wife, who'd raised a few sheep in the meadow, as well as bees.

Stanley had ridden directly into Upton with a wagon to retrieve Lina's belongings, and then he had returned to take her to see the cottage the next morning. That night she had slept in the boys' bedroom under the thatch—she could not go back to Observatory House—listening to the voices of Stanley and Sarah in the room beside hers, the boys downstairs before the fire. She knew they felt sorry for her, appalled at her treatment by William and Mary. How wonderful it must have been for Stanley and Sarah's boys to grow up knowing, as they did, how much they were loved, she had thought.

YET SITTING IN THE WAGON the next day beside Stanley, when they came upon the cottage in its clearing, neglected leaves piled up against the doorway in a heap, Lina had known that she could be happy there.

Within a week, Lina had set up house for herself. She did not go to see William, even when she knew he and Mary had returned from their honeymoon. And when William rode over one afternoon a few days after his return, obviously puzzled about her failure to appear, she had heard the sound of a horse coming while she worked in the garden, and she had hidden in the woods. When she had seen William appear, she had felt a painful pressure in her chest, equal parts grief and anger and longing.

From behind a tree, she had watched William knock at the cottage door. When she failed to answer, he had gone to cup his hands around the glass of a window to peer inside. Finally he had turned around, hands on his hips. He had called her name, but she had retreated, her back pressed against the tree, and she had not answered him. She had thought of the night Henry had left them, when she had not replied to William's knock on her door, their separate grief. What could they have done for one another that night?

William had waited for over two hours that afternoon—a sacrifice for him, she had known, given how little he liked to be idle—walking around the garden and picking bits of leaves and bringing them to his nose. As Sarah had said, the garden had been lovely and had needed only weeding and pruning to restore it. Lina had wondered if William would let himself inside the house, but though he had knocked again and appeared to consider turning the handle, he had not done so, and she thought then that he had felt at that moment her parting from him, her barred door, where before he had experienced their separation only in terms of his happiness with Mary.

Finally, he had taken paper and ink from his saddlebag and written something on a piece of paper he had left at the door, weighted by a stone.

Come tonight, dear sister, he had written.

Then he had added: *Conditions are most excellent.*

When he had ridden away at last, she had returned to the cottage. She'd felt no victory at having denied William her presence, only an embarrassed foolishness. And sadness.

At some point over the years, Mary had been forgiven.

About William, it has not been so easy.

But she is not proud of that.

SARAH MEETS MARY at the cottage the morning after Lina's fall in the snow to drape the windows in black cloth to shut out the daylight. Only the thin lines of brightness around the edges of the material tell Lina that it is day . . . those quivering lines and the birdsong.

"Are you frightened, Lina?" Mary asks, gathering up her cloak to depart. "I will stay with you, if you are at all uncomfortable."

"It is a fool's idea," Lina says. "One cannot practice becoming a blind woman."

Mary leans down and kisses her cheek. "Please do as Dr. Onslow says. There can be no harm in it, at least."

A servant from Observatory House, supervised by Mary, brings Lina her meals. Mary visits in the afternoons and reads to her. Stanley comes every day, once in the morning and again at night. His farm nearby is thriving, but on horseback he can be with her in less than half an hour, and he sits with her in the darkness at breakfast and dinner while she feels over the dishes on her tray, their heat or coolness.

When she spills a bowl of soup one afternoon, she erupts.

"This is ridiculous," she says. "I feel a fool. Take down those cloths, so I can see what I'm doing."

"Be patient," Stanley tells her. "Be patient."

She discovers after a week in the dark that her sense of smell has sharpened: onion soup, tea made with mint leaves, the approach of snow or rain. And every person has an individual smell, she realizes.

She sleeps a great deal over these days. Her dreams are populated by creatures—foxes and stoats—that hurry through the night over the white surface of the frozen field surrounding the forty-foot telescope and its scaffolding. In her dreams, when she holds aloft a lantern, the animals turn to her for a moment, their eyes flashing in the dark.

Though she behaves as if she thinks Dr. Onslow's warning is absurd, the thought of going blind frightens her so much that in fact she scarcely opens her eyes at all, much less to practice trying to feel her way around her bedroom, hobbling on her sore ankle. She lies in bed, her ankle bound tightly. She hopes that tears, when she cannot prevent them, do her eyes no harm.

She awakes one night during this confinement to the sound of her bedroom door opening. A candle flickers in the hall; she shrinks from its light.

A man's shape appears: William. He is carrying something large. He enters the room. She smells snow.

She struggles to sit up in bed.

"William?" she says. "What time is it?"

William is in his seventies now. For some months Lina has written all his letters for him, passing them to him for his shaky signature, for he can no longer control a steady trembling in his hands.

Yours most constantly, he appends, the words falling down the paper. *Yours most faithfully.*

Adieu.

It seems impossible that he should be with her now on this night, that he should have walked from Observatory House to her cottage in the snow . . . and carrying a cello.

He takes a seat on the small chair by her bedside, the cello balanced between his knees. He bends his head, lowers his familiar profile, lifts the bow. She smells the rosin used to make the bow's action smoother. She sees bright epaulets of snow on William's shoulders.

"Do you remember this, Lina?" he says.

He plays "Suppose We Sing a Catch," one of his own compositions. He plays parts of a sonata for violin, cello, and harpsichord. He plays some capriccios, part of a concerto for oboe, violin, and viola. It is as if he cannot remember all of any of the pieces he has written, and he plays back and forth between them, losing the melody and then picking up a different one. It is a concert most disjointed and strange, William's head hanging lower and lower as the night goes on, as if the notes he wants are in the floorboards at his feet and he must coax them up from the ground. She knows he has not played much of late, but the music, the bow drawing out the note, is both sweet and sad, holds in it every season and the singing of the stars. She remembers what it was like, all those years when they were alone together, how happy she had been. She gazes at him from her pillow, making no effort to rest her eyes now. She wants nothing more than to hold this picture of him beside her.

They are alone together again, just the two of them. Even late at night at the telescope over these last few years, Lina has been aware of Mary asleep in her and William's marital bed at Observatory House, aware that William would join Mary there before the sun rose. She hated herself for her lingering anger at him. It was only reasonable that William should want a wife. And Mary is a good woman, thoughtful, eager to please.

The years when Lina was everything to her brother seem to have taken place long ago.

"We never speak of love, you and I," William says over his playing. "Do you know that?"

Later, she feels his fingertips on her face, the back of his hand brushing her cheek.

In the morning, she thinks she must have dreamed it, her brother's appearance in her room at some dark hour, the notes of the song, the snow that fell from his coat to her bedclothes when he bent over her. His touch.

Had he said it? "Never could have done any of it without you. *Dear one.*"

He had.

"Nonsense," she had said. "It was all you, William."

She remembers the music, remembers putting out a hand and touching William's cold sleeve, his warm fingers closing over hers.

When she puts her bare feet to the floor and stands up that morning, the boards are still wet, where the snow had fallen from his coat and melted.

DESPITE EVERYONE'S WORST FEARS, Lina does not lose her sight, though she continues to suffer from the headaches. She resents the way they incapacitate her—there is nothing for it but to sleep, to close her eyes—but eventually she is able to resume her work for William. Still it is her greatest happiness to work alongside him, though there are more pleasures in a day for her than she once had thought possible: Stanley and Sarah and their boys, who tease her, little William now grown and quite able to pick her up and carry her around, though she laughs and protests. She loves her garden, the bees climbing the hollyhocks. She has a violin, and she plays occasionally, alone in her cottage. Her contentment seems complete. She reads some poetry, poor John Keats's "Endymion:" *A thing of beauty is a joy forever: Its loveliness increases; it will never pass into nothingness.*

SHE IS TAKING NOTES from William when it happens.

The month of August has been still and hot, and William has been confined to bed for a week. His voice is weak, his thoughts often confused.

From her seat at his bedside, she reaches forward from time to time with her handkerchief to touch his face where sweat beads on his skin. Sometimes, shuffling among his papers on the bedclothes, he becomes agitated and asks her to find something in the laundry. In her haste to calm his anxiety, she runs downstairs and snatches up whatever she can find; any piece of paper will do. She returns, sitting back down in the chair beside his bed and holding up as proof whatever paper she picked up.

By then his mind has moved on.

Through the years William has been beset by many curious and admiring visitors, sometimes forty or fifty people gathering at a time—princes and lords and admirals and countesses—who come to see the telescope and the famous man who built it. Sometimes they have heard of her, too, the stargazer's sister, the great comet huntress.

By now, Lina has found eight comets with her reliable little sweeper.

The crowds keep William outside for hours at night, sometimes for several nights in a row. Despite Mary's and Lina's entreaties, he almost always makes an appearance when someone arrives hoping for an audience. He is so pleased by people's interest that he turns no one away. He is unfailingly generous in that way.

Now, as the hottest days of summer approach, he falls ill. No man could be expected to recover again and again from such assaults upon the body, Lina thinks, even a man as vigorous as William. He is very strong; usually he suffers for a few days—he is deviled by persistent coughs—and then, his energy and spirits apparently restored, he seems himself again, sometimes even undertaking to travel, though he goes nowhere now without Mary.

Arriving at Observatory House from her cottage earlier this summer, Lina had often found him in the barn working on a telescope, for he continues to sell them, despite Mary's fortune. One day, crossing the meadow, she heard singing—William's voice like a far-off echo—and only as she approached the telescope did she realize he was inside the tube and scrubbing rust from a spot where moisture had gathered, singing as he worked.

He appeared to be invincible.

But this most recent bout of sickness has weakened him more fully than ever before. They had one fine day in late July, when he seemed better—they walked in the garden and picked and ate raspberries—but every day now since his being ordered to bed by Dr. Onslow, Lina finds him seemingly more fatigued, more distraught.

On this day, she sits by his bedside throughout the morning, writing down whatever he says, even though he makes little sense. It seems difficult for him to finish a thought. It pains her to see in his face the struggle of his great mental effort, his awareness of and humiliation at his confusion. Still, he talks on.

"William, my hand grows tired," she says at last, "and surely you are fatigued, as well. Why not rest? Why not—"

But he appears not to hear her.

"And I have . . . on the moon . . . distinguished a tall building," he says, and there is wonder in his voice. His eyes close, and then open again. He meets her gaze for a moment—she knows he sees her—but then his eyes slide away.

She begins again to write. Later, the record of his disordered thoughts will be far too painful for her to read.

"—it is perhaps the height of Saint Paul's Cathedral," William says. "And soon . . . I feel . . . confident that I will provide a full account of its inhabitants. They are . . ."

His voice pauses.

She has been writing. She looks up.

His head has fallen to the side against the pillow.

She overturns the small table between them on which she has been writing. Ink floods the sheets. His face is warm between her hands, but his chest is unmoving beneath her cheek.

She cries out—William, William, *William!*—and they all come running, but it is too late.

A MONTH AFTER WILLIAM'S DEATH, Lina sits in the chilly dining room at Slough, opening letters. September has come, and with it unceasing days of cool rain. Many letters come each day, offering praise of William and sympathy to Lina and Mary. Mary has returned to her family's home—at least for a time, she has said—to be in the company of two sisters who still live there. Lina is aware of how in Mary's absence the rooms at Observatory House have been emptied of much of their warmth. Even as she became a mature woman, Mary's childlike qualities—her pleasure in comfort, her innocence, a certain fragility—never left her entirely. It did not surprise Lina that Mary fled to her old childhood bedroom after William's death, though her parents have long since died and are not there to comfort her.

The salutation in Dr. Silva's letter of condolence to Lina is characteristically hyperbolic.

"He adores a metaphor, your Dr. Silva," William—amused— had said once of Silva's beautiful though occasionally absurdly formal English.

Dr. Silva, a Portuguese physician and amateur astronomer, is a great admirer and has written often over the years, corresponding with William but more often with Caroline about her comets, in which he, too, is most interested.

Letter after letter has arrived, as word of William's death traveled, but she is touched especially by the kindness of Dr. Silva's concern. She pulls her shawl closer around her shoulders. Stanley has come that morning and built fires for her, but the persistent damp weather and gray skies seem as much inside the house as outside.

Princess of the heavens, this letter begins.

I write to you of my great grief at the news of your brother's death, for a bright light has indeed left the world. What can be done to comfort you now? I know you to be in the darkest of dark nights. May I extend to you, please, an invitation I most sincerely hope you will accept? Come to Portugal, Miss Herschel. Come to Lisbon. Let the beautiful sunlight of my island heal you. I know the journey to be a long one, but I can make every arrangement for your comfort, and you may work here undisturbed but with my full support. Your good work must go on.

Over the years of their correspondence, Dr. Silva has had other names for her: *Astronomer Célèbre. Priestess of the Temple of Urania.*

These titles made William laugh. He liked waving Silva's envelopes in the air at dinner in the dining room at Slough—she would try to snatch them from him, but he held them beyond her reach—reading aloud their salutations in delight.

"He only teases, William," she'd always said, protesting. "He makes a joke with me."

She, too, finds Silva's honorifics a bit silly—her pleasure in them embarrasses her a little—but still, she is touched by them, pleased at the recognition of her own skills they contain.

She looks up now from Silva's letter. Rain falls in the garden, softening the trees in the orchard past the row of elms. The scaffolding and the telescope are completely obscured by the mist.

Into the darkness of her grief: a small ray of light.

WILLIAM WAS BURIED on the seventh of September in the churchyard at Upton. The day was cool and damp, water beading on the horses' backs, on Stanley's black sleeve where she held his arm, on her own black gloves.

William's friend Dr. Goodall, provost at Eton, was present, along with a few others, but both Lina and Mary had wanted the funeral to be small.

As the prayers were said, Lina had thought of Henry. Though she finds certain romantic notions about heaven absurd, perhaps after all there would be a reunion of some kind for William and Henry. That is a comfort.

It was Dr. Goodall who supplied the sentence that Lina appreciated so much on the marble slab above the vault.

Coelorum Perrupit Claustra.

He broke through the barriers of the heavens.

In the churchyard afterward, she and Mary stood side by side.

Mary took Lina's hand. "He was so proud of you," she said. She folded her other hand over Lina's.

"You always had most of him, Lina. But I never minded, you know. Thank you for sharing him with me."

Lisbon
1823–1833

SEVENTEEN

Star

The pillows on the heavily curtained bed in the room she is given in Dr. Silva's villa in Lisbon are the most sumptuous on which she has ever laid her head. Not that she is laying her head. Since William's death nine months ago, she has been able to sleep only for brief intervals, sustained like a prisoner fed doses of bread and water by helpless moments of unconsciousness into which she falls for a few minutes, her chin dropping to her chest. She wakes, her mind teeming, finishing the sentences and thoughts abandoned moments before. She feels as if she is condemned to read from an endless stream of documents, passed to her continually by unseen hands, and every word she must speak aloud. She is afraid she will forget something, overlook some detail of William's work that then will be lost to history, and he is no longer there to remind her of what she might have missed.

Will it go on forever like this, her mind awake and in pain? She misses him so much. In the first weeks after his death it was only with a great effort of will that she got out of bed.

I could not have imagined, she wrote to Dr. Silva when she accepted his invitation, *the strange blank of life after having lived so long within the radiance of genius.*

DR. SILVA LEFT HER two hours ago, after their dinner together. Since then she has been sitting up in bed, leafing through her day-books, making notes. It seems the most natural task with which to follow William's death, to finish his uncompleted articles from the notes he left behind, to make a concise and clear and complete history of William's accomplishments, to write the story of his life . . . which is also the story of her life, she realizes.

She stops from time to time to reach out and touch the bed's rainbow silk tassels, to gaze up at its canopy—extraordinary material, the color of blood oranges. She cannot believe she finds herself surrounded by such luxury. It is long past two in the morning. Her head is woozy from wine and sleeplessness and the other thing, the thing that she knows truly keeps her awake, will keep her awake until eternity.

There had been many lonely days and nights at her cottage, many years of nights when rain or snow fell or clouds covered the sky, and she and William could not work at the telescopes. Then there was only a lasting silence in her little house.

In the end, it had been all right. She had gotten over it, some-how. The old habit of their affection, their mutual interest, had sustained them. She was glad that had been their way. Out of the black unhappiness of their childhood, the darkness of that little house in Hanover with its resentments and anger and misery and disappointment, she and William had made a good and lasting light between them.

And she would never have wanted to stand between William and a right and good happiness.

Yet it was true that her pain and resentment had been there inside her for a long time, that he had known they were there, and that he understood his own hand in them, his thoughtlessness, how easy it had been for him sometimes—so strong and sufficient unto himself—to neglect or ignore ordinary human cares. *Let whatever shines be noted.* William had lived by that motto. But sometimes, she thinks now, it is both wise and kind to attend to the dark, to put your eye to it and to acknowledge it. Pain belongs to the darkness, for instance.

And anyway, without the dark, there would be no light at all. Regret, regret.

She had never told him how much he had hurt her. But she had never told him she had forgiven him, either.

And now that silence will be with her always.

SHE SEES NOW THAT she has spilled ink on the glorious sheets. She wets her finger and rubs at the stain but only makes it worse. What will the servants think of the mess she makes?

She has all of William's writings with her, the entirety of his *Philosophical Transactions,* in which together she and William summarized and enforced his views, clarifying his arguments. It took her months to organize things in England. Mary had been bewildered when Lina, after many letters back and forth with Dr. Silva, announced that she intended to voyage to Lisbon.

"It is so far!" Mary had looked astonished.

"Not so very far. A pleasant voyage, I think, in many respects." She mentions an acquaintance of William's, a member of the Royal Academy, and his family, with whom she kindly will be allowed to travel; they are continuing on to Seville.

"And when will you return?" Mary had asked, seated in the drawing room of the Baldwin family home, where she seemed to have settled in for good. "What will happen to . . . everything, to the telescopes at Observatory House?"

A different woman, Lina thought, would assume more owner-ship of William's estate and his scientific legacy, but the money had always been Mary's anyway, and William's astronomical investigations had been beyond her. Had there been children, Lina knew, things might have been different; early in the marriage Mary had suffered two miscarriages, on both occasions returning home to be nursed by her mother. But there had been nothing after that.

Every day during those convalescences, Lina had ridden over to the Baldwins' and sat with Mary.

"It would have pleased William so," Mary had said through her tears, "to have a son." Lina had held her hand.

"He is grateful to have *you*, Mary," she had said. "He wants only for *you* to be well and returned to his side. Please don't worry."

It *had* pained William, Lina thought, though he had never spoken of it. And indeed it had pained Lina, too. How wonderful it would have been, she thought, had there been a child—girl or boy—with William's brilliance and Mary's gentleness.

"IF YOU WILL BE SO GOOD, MARY," Lina had said, "I believe Stanley can serve as caretaker for the property. He will look after it all until decisions are made about the telescopes and other equipment. Both Dr. Maskelyne and Sir Joseph Banks will work on it."

"But *your* return?" Mary had repeated, looking bewildered.

"I'm not . . . certain," Lina had said.

Mary had looked away from Lina, out the window. They had both lost weight, Lina had thought, gazing at her.

"It will comfort you to undertake such a voyage?" Mary had asked, sounding incredulous.

"I believe so," Lina had said. "I hope so."

BEFORE SHE LEFT FOR LISBON, Stanley had come to Observatory House, and they had walked through the rooms together, as well as the barns. Lina had made an inventory of everything, so that Stanley could oversee its care until its fate was decided.

They had stood together in the shadowy barn. Lina had draped most of the equipment in canvas coverings, including the gigantic old apparatus on which the big mirror had been polished.

"It was like a dream, wasn't it?" Stanley had said. "What he was doing all those years. What *you* were doing. A strange dream." He had shaken his head.

"It feels like a dream now," Lina had said. She'd handed him the inventory.

"But you'll keep working," Stanley had said. "You'll keep looking at the stars."

She had smiled, though by then she had begun to cry. "I will."

"Good for you," he'd said, fiercely. "*Good* for you."

She had taken his arm, going back to the house, and he had put his hand over hers.

"It was a beautiful dream," she'd said. "Wasn't it?"

SHE HAS BROUGHT ALL of William's papers with her to Lisbon, leaving copies of many of the documents for Dr. Maskelyne and the others to decide what to do with them.

Earlier that day, shown by a servant to the suite of rooms prepared for her, she had seen that the volumes and papers she'd sent ahead had been arranged in a room adjoining her bedroom on a long table set before doors leading to a balcony. At another table a chair intended for her to sit in while writing had been supplied, its arms concluding in lion's paws, its seat upholstered in a blue silk cushion embroidered with a design of the constellations and the planets, the yellow sun at its center, Jupiter on the ecliptic. She'd smiled at that.

Now, spread out on the sheets around her, are the pages of notes from William's final weeks, most in Lina's hand.

She picks up one sheet and holds it to the candlelight.

Somehow here in Lisbon it is easier for her to read these than it had been back in England. During his last weeks, though at the time they had not understood they were his last weeks, she and William had often worked in the old laundry, William resting on a chaise Mary had seen moved there.

William and Mary had added a small conservatory to the old laundry. From his chair at his desk, William had been able to look directly into the glass-walled room, where the air was moist and scented with geraniums. Lina was grateful for the funds that had allowed Mary to make Observatory House so comfortable for William. With Mary's arrival, the untidy and often impoverished world of Lina's years alone with William had vanished as if it had never been. The gift of Mary's fortune had helped spare William much mental anguish over money.

In those last weeks, resting on the chaise, a rug over his lap, William had dictated to Lina.

"We can then pronounce," he'd said, "that if our gauges cease to resolve the Milky Way into stars, it is not because its nature is doubtful, but because it is fathomless."

She closes her eyes now, remembering.

"Have you ever been frightened by what you see, William?" she had asked him once.

They had been alone at the time, as they so often were, he at the old twelve-foot telescope set up in the middle of the street in Bath one spring night.

"Of what?" he'd said. "Frightened? What do you mean?"

She had surprised him enough that he had removed his eye from the telescope . . . and you could miss so much in an instant. His expression had been puzzled.

She had waved at the night sky above them. "All this," she had said. "Wherever it ends. Or doesn't."

A Scottish theologian and amateur astronomer interested in William's discoveries and his reports to the Royal Academy had written to William of his own personal sense of renewed faith that had followed William's conclusions, despite the wails of those who decried the astronomers' labors as an intrusion into heaven's sanctified realm. She could recall that man's letter word for word; she had carried it within her for years, in fact, for he had said better than she could what William's work had meant, in the end.

You have left me no room to doubt that countless globes and masses of beautiful matter lie concealed in the remote regions of infinity, far beyond the utmost stretch of mortal vision. To consider creation in all its departments as extending throughout space and filled with intelligent existence makes certain beyond all ardent doubt my own sense of the God who inhabits immensity and whose perfections are boundless and past finding out.

That night in the street in Bath, Lina had gestured again at the sky.

"You know," she had said to William, "what is *out* there . . ."

William had turned back to the telescope. At one level, her question had not interested him. He had adjusted the eyepiece.

"One day, we will know truly that we are not alone in the universe," he had said. "That is a day I long to see."

She had stared up at the dark windows along the street, thinking of the plump and bonneted wives asleep in bed beside their husbands, the fires burning in their bedroom grates, their curtains drawn against the dark. How was it that William had been able to imagine so much? Had been so fearless? Perhaps it was a kind of faith, all along. Her notion of God was no clearer than her old childhood drawings of the moon's inhabitants, though she had felt more certain of God's presence—of some presence, whatever one might call it—not less, over the years.

She opens her eyes now and puts aside the sheet of paper she holds. She chooses another from those fanned out upon the bed.

With the forty-foot telescope, William had written—this is in his own hand now; she touches the words with her finger—*the appearance of Sirius announced itself like the dawn of the morning. The brilliant star at last entered the field of the telescope with all the splendor of the rising sun.*

There is a fragment at the bottom of the page: *diffused nebulosity exists in great abundance. Its abundance exceeds all imagination—*

She goes for a moment into the oblivion that passes for sleep.

It does not last, of course.

ONE BEGINS AT THE BEGINNING, does one not?

But where *is* the beginning, after all? How will she tell the story of the life she led at William's side? For many years after William's marriage to Mary, Lina did not write in her daybooks. Now she knows what foolishness that was. Who was she punishing with her silence? Only herself. Those years of her daily life are mostly gone to her now. She can reconstruct them only by painstaking comparison with their astronomical journals, various correspondence, piles of receipts. How easily things slip away.

She thinks of the tawny owls flying through the meadow at night, crossing beneath them as she and William had sat at the forty-foot.

She thinks of the comets' tails, disappearing.

She closes her eyes again and tries to visualize the old house in Hanover.

What *is* the first thing she can remember about William? What is the first thing she can remember at all?

And then there it is, at the threshold of her memory: the day of the Lisbon earthquake well more than half a century before, the day the city had been destroyed and so many had died, the day Winged Victory fell to the grass in the square in Hanover so many miles away from the earthquake's epicenter. How strange, she thinks, to find herself now in the place where the event of her earliest memory originated, the shifting place deep inside the planet that had rippled that day across the earth to disturb the water balanced in the bowl of a spoon held by a girl kneeling at a plain deal table in Hanover.

She remembers the peas leaping on the tabletop, the logs collapsing in the fire, the instruments crashing to the floor in the next room. She remembers her mother's stinging hand on her face. She remembers the smell of burning coming from the orchard later in the day, when she was allowed outside at last, the way the bantams, still nervous, had followed her through the trees like loyal dogs.

And *there* is William, holding her hand as she kneels to touch the cold stone feathers of fallen Victory's wing.

William had been correct about Lisbon. In a year, the devastated city had been cleared of debris, the populace harnessed for an extraordinary effort, and progress made toward building an entirely new city. She has seen now the results: the beautiful broad avenues lined with trees whose leaves capture the light and caress the walls of the buildings with their shadows. She has seen now from Dr. Silva's carriage the wide squares and smooth plazas floored in marble.

The engineers were careful, William had said at the time, reading aloud to her from accounts of the city's reconstruction. They created wooden models of all the structures planned for the new city, and they tested them against earthquakes by marching troops around and around them in great numbers.

Lisbon, William had told Lina, would be as beautiful and as safe as any city ever built by man.

Certainly it is as beautiful as any place she has ever seen. And Dr. Silva was right about the sunlight. It *is* glorious.

How can it be that so much time has passed since that earthquake?

When Dr. Silva had greeted her at the port earlier today, he had presented her with a bouquet of lavender. It grows wild all over the peninsula, he had told her, putting it into her arms.

"It is true," he'd said, smiling at her. "You are as tiny as the reports of you claim you to be. And yet—you have given so much to the world."

Crowds had parted around them, porters with baskets on their shoulders, ladies disembarking from the ship in their lovely dresses.

He'd kissed her hand. He is small himself—only just over a foot taller than she is. His beard is gray, his hair jet-black except for two silver bars at his temples. When he bowed over her fingers, she smelled a fragrance—something pleasing and herbal—clinging to his skin, his garments, his hair.

He hoped she would be his guest as long as she liked, he'd repeated, as long as it took her to finish her writing.

It would be my greatest honor, he had written to her in England, *to offer you a sanctuary in which to work, where you may be cared for with discretion and kindness. Please consider it a tribute to your great brother, as well as to yourself.*

On his arm this evening she had been escorted through his enormous villa with its flights of terraces, its urns and marble statues, a profusion of shining waists and breasts and shoulders and thighs, shadows falling discreetly here and there. A declivity at the throat, the crossed thighs, dimples low on the back, the span of tendon across a calf, an arm retracted to hold a bow's string, the swell of muscle under skin . . . how transfixing it all is.

She had inspected the telescopes arranged on the highest parapet, the magnificent view of the shoreline of the Iberian Peninsula leading away in both directions. The view of the night sky will be extraordinary, she knows. Together she and Dr. Silva had stood in silence, regarding the undulating curves of the cliffs, and she had felt that he appreciated her marveling at it. Their silence was, she feels, not an uncomfortable one for two people who had not met face-to-face until this day. She feels she knows him, at least in some way, from their years of correspondence, and he does not seem a stranger to her.

The way he had written to her, with such intimacy, about William's death . . . he had understood her feelings, she was sure. And in person his formality is gracious rather than stiff, his manner kind and respectful. She had been correct when she had defended him to William; there was humor in him also.

"Little queen of the night," he had said, bending over her hand when he left her at the door of her chambers after their splendid meal that evening. "It is an honor to be of service."

She had never eaten such food: delicate, thin slices of cured ham, roasted prawns and oysters, a cod whose sweet white meat had been prepared, Dr. Silva told her, with sea salt and herbs, a green wine, a silken rice pudding. They had eaten alone on a small terrace, two servants—a beautiful young man and an equally lovely young girl, Lina thought, turning helplessly to watch them—coming forth silently to bring dishes and then to take them away, to pour wine, to leave them alone.

Seeing Dr. Silva notice her watching the young servants, she had felt herself blush.

"They are—well, how do you say it? They catch the eye," she'd said.

"The young," Dr. Silva had said. "They seem more beautiful every day, the older I become."

"My brother, also, was that way," she had said. "Very beautiful."

And then she had bowed her head. The power of her feelings, after so many months: it would never leave her.

Dr. Silva had reached across the table. When he held out his hand, she had taken it.

She had looked at his distinguished face, the sympathy in his eyes. But there had been another feeling present in his expression, too, something in the way he beheld her that seemed completely new to her.

Her own face perhaps had improved with time, she thought, the old childhood scars softening. Still, no one would ever call her beautiful.

At the door of her bedchamber, Dr. Silva had lingered over her hand. His mouth had been warm. At last he had raised his eyes to hers. They had looked at each other for a long moment.

"I am glad you have come, Caroline," he had said. "I may call you that, I hope. And I hope . . . you will stay."

Now she pushes aside the papers and slides down in the bed to rest her head at last on the pillow. She listens to the waves breaking along the shoreline.

She is perhaps too old for this. Well, she will not count up the years of her age. What is the point of reminding herself? She closes her eyes.

In her dreams, when she falls asleep finally—a deep sleep for the first time in weeks and weeks and weeks—the sound is confused with the percussion of troops on horseback, marching round and round a castle, trying but failing to bring it down. Sunlight is reflected in its windows, hundreds of bright mirrors.

. . .

AS SHE BREAKFASTS the next morning, Dr. Silva joins her for coffee and reiterates—as if he is worried she is thinking of leaving, despite the trouble it has been to her to journey this far—that she may stay as long as she likes. She asks about the recent political unrest in Portugal, but he waves a hand; it is always one thing or another. She will be in no danger, and she will create no inconvenience to his household, he insists. His own offerings to astronomy have been modest; it would give him the greatest pleasure to be of assistance to her now, as she tries to finish William's work. Among William's papers, she has with her his "Book of Sweeps" and the "Catalogue of 2500 Nebulae"; with these she intends to prepare a new catalog of the nebulae, more conveniently arranged in zones and beginning from the North Pole.

"Not a small endeavor," Dr. Silva notes.

He pauses, before taking his leave of her. He, too, is curious about the lower region of Scorpio, he says, an area that had so puzzled William. They might look at it together, he proposes.

She imagines it, the two of them side by side at the telescope on one of Silva's terraces.

She cannot explain exactly why she accepted Silva's invitation, she who has hardly gone anywhere in her life.

It was his description of the sun, she thinks. The light.

SHE WORKS ALL DAY, every day. From time to time she goes to stand on the terrace outside her workroom, to rest with her face upturned to the sun. Sometimes she spies Silva on the terraces below, moving among his pots of flowers, among them bougainvillea, he had told her one morning at breakfast, which after a while they had begun to take together. He had stood up and plucked a blossom, bringing it to her.

He is seventy-one, he tells her, and he sees patients now only three days a week. Mostly he confines his practice to children; it is a great joy to him to help effect a cure for a child, for then there is a double happiness.

"Both parent and baby smile," he says, smiling himself.

Under the table, she folds her hands over her belly.

"Your children?" she asks.

"Alas," he says. "There were none."

THAT EVENING, after their meal is concluded, he sends away the servants.

He stands to pour more wine for her.

She wears her hair in the old way, braids wound tightly around her head.

He fills her glass and then puts the bottle on the table. He does not return to his chair. He looks down at her.

"May I?" he says.

Her hair has not so much turned gray as it has silvered. The touch of his hands as he unpins and loosens the braids, his fingers as he spreads the strands, is gentle.

She closes her eyes. She does not know where to look. She has never been touched in such an intimate way, not since her mother's diffident hands combed her hair and braided it when she was a child.

"My wife," Silva says, "liked me to brush her hair. She suffered from headaches. It was a therapy of sorts."

Lina finds it difficult to speak.

"I, too, have headaches," she says. "Since I was a child."

"I thought so," he says. "In certain lines on the face, one can see the headache. I do not offend you?"

Lina moves her head a little—no, no offense—but she does not want him to stop. The feeling of his hands . . .

"You lost her," she says finally. "Your wife."

"Many years ago," he says. "She died when she was quite young. I have been alone for—"

When he stops, she turns to look up at him.

"A very long time," he says.

THE SILK CANOPY ABOVE her bed with its rainbow tassels ripples in the night breeze from the open windows. She smells oranges, lavender, the ocean's salt, the unfamiliar, strongly herbal scent of the man lying quietly beside her. From somewhere distant in the villa she hears a young woman's laughter. Outside the window, stars and more stars.

She whispers, "The servants will not come?"

"They will not," Silva says.

"You are sure?"

"Absolutamente."

She shuts her eyes.

He blows out the candle and holds her against him. His skin is warm and soft. He is trembling, too.

"THANK YOU," he says later into her neck, and she can feel that his cheek is wet against hers, as hers is wet against his, though they are both laughing a little, too.

"We are not too old!" she says. "I had thought—"

"No, no. The body—" He touches her face. "Amazing what the body can do."

Later still, when he is laughing again, she teases: "It is the custom in the great city of Lisbon to greet lady visitors in this fashion?"

"No custom," he says. "Only my good luck."

She turns her face to his shoulder.

"You know," she says. "My first."

EIGHTEEN

Dark

Two years after her arrival in Lisbon, Lina and Silva make a trip to Hanover. Silva suffers from gout, and he is afraid that if they wait longer, he will be unable to accompany her.

"You want to go," he says, as they make their plans. "You are sure."

"I can't explain it," she says.

What she feels is irrational, she knows. It is that William is there, in some way, and also that some lost part of her is there, too, drifting. Untethered. More and more, as she tries to reconstruct William's life, her life, it is her memories of her childhood that feel most clear to her.

She wants to go back, she tells Silva finally, to *put things to rest* for herself—that is how she says it, for she cannot think how else to describe what she feels—and she means somehow that she feels in Hanover she can close something, a window left open, a door.

She wants, too, to banish the shadow of her old hurt, to put it away forever.

Her mother. She thinks of her unhappy mother. How to resolve that? There is no resolving it. It is over, unfinished forever.

But she remembers tossing her childish collection of nuts and feathers and pebbles into the river on the afternoon of Margaretta's funeral. She wants to stand in those places again as the woman she is today.

Once she thought she would die of despair, but after all she has survived. She has outlived, in fact, her sister and all her brothers except Leonard. After William's death she wrote to Leonard and Dietrich, who were then still alive. They sent condolences by reply, mentioning, too, that Jacob had again disappeared, his whereabouts a mystery. It is possible, she thinks, that Jacob is still alive, somewhere. The thought of him abroad in the world, still able to inflict torments and injury, is not a comforting one, though by now he surely would be too old to do anyone any harm.

Her sister's children and Alexander's and Dietrich's sons are grown, all with young families of their own. Leonard and his wife are shy as strangers with Lina, yet they are hospitable to Lina and Silva, whom Lina introduces as her great friend and as a friend of William's as well.

From Leonard, Lina and Silva learn that Hilda is still alive. Considered too old for work, she is accommodated in a corner of the kitchen of the Herschel relatives who run the vineyard where her brothers labored for so many years.

One afternoon Lina and Silva hire a carriage to take them to the vineyard. When Lina steps into the doorway of the kitchen, she has to reach for the wall to steady herself; Hilda is slumped in a chair in the corner, the goiter on her neck grown so large that she must hold her head at a savage tilt, her ear nearly touching her shoulder.

When Lina wakes her, Hilda startles, eyes rolling, and then cries and cries.

Silva believes Hilda too old and feeble to withstand surgery to remove the goiter. Instead, they see her settled as comfortably as possible at the convent outside of Hanover. A sister of the order comes and admires Hilda's fine friends, which pleases Hilda. She smiles—toothless, eyes watering—and she reaches out her hands to Lina and Silva.

Silva speaks to a sister and makes particular arrangements for Hilda's care, compresses for her neck.

In the cold, echoing corridor outside the dormitory after they have left Hilda, Lina puts her face in her hands.

Silva takes her in his arms. "She is all right," he says. "It does not *pain* her, Lina. Only it is uncomfortable, perhaps, and the compresses will help, the kindness."

She remembers William smiling at her on the day of their departure from Hanover so many years ago, telling her to hurry. She remembers the money he gave to their uncle for Hilda's care.

She is glad that Hilda's life has not been unhappy. William had once read aloud to Lina a letter from Alexander in which he related that their uncle always gave Hilda a glass of wine at night, over which she smacked her lips loudly, making them all laugh.

The Angelus bell rings. Lina and Silva stand in the corridor.

"Tell them that they must feed her cake every day, if she wishes it," Silva says. "Wine, if she likes. Whatever she wants. I can leave them with plenty of money. She may have every comfort."

Lina kisses his hands. "Obviously I am never to have money of my own," she says. "I am grateful to you."

"You should have had a fortune," Silva says, "for all your work."

"I should have had independence to do my own deeds, for good or ill," she says.

Silva kisses her. "Yes," he says. "That is what I meant."

"I don't know if I shall see her again," Lina says.

Silva takes her arm. "You are both happy now," he says. "Listen to the beautiful voice of that bell."

· · ·

ON THE LAST DAY of their visit, Lina and Silva go to the Herschels' old house. They inquire of the neighbors—some relations of the Hennings still live next door—but no one seems to know what has become of Jacob. Lina imagines him, a bent little old man, his face even darker and more contemptuous than ever, his fingers bony and grasping.

The occupants of the house have heard of the great William Herschel and his telescope, of course, and they welcome Lina and Silva with courtesy, offering wine and cake in the front room. Some of the furnishings are the same—a bench before the fire, a table, two chairs. Lina finds that she cannot sit down anywhere.

Her mother's ghost, her father's ghost. They are all around her. But not William's.

She tries the bench but stands up quickly.

She has been waiting to feel William near her—longing for it—but it has not happened yet.

"May I walk through the orchard?" she asks.

Night has fallen, but the moon is full. Though it is late fall, the air is mild. She crosses the courtyard, and she can smell even before she reaches the stable that there is a horse inside. She opens the door, closes it behind her. The stable is in darkness, but she moves by memory to the old stall, slides the smooth wooden latch, and steps inside, her hand finding the horse's neck. He bobs his head up and down in agitation until she blows into his nostrils, as she used to do for their old horse. He quiets, only stamping his foot from time to time, while she rests her forehead against his shoulder. The smell of his feed—bran laced with molasses—is sweet.

Inside the house, she knows, Silva will be doing his gallant best in his limited German.

She runs her hand along the horse's back, then turns to reach up to the windowsill. In a corner she finds the pebble she left there so many years before, the little white stone she had picked up in the orchard on the day she and William left for England. It is ice cold and smooth in her hand. She slips it into her pocket.

THE SHOPS IN HANOVER are lit prettily with gas, and in the marketplaces lighted booths are open in the evenings. She and Silva stroll back to their hotel that night, her arm tucked in his. Festive garlands of greenery have been strung along the streets. Everyone—cooks and housemaids, gentlemen and butchers—walks among the booths and purchases hot wine and sweets and pretty indulgences: knitted bags and purses, framed embroideries, hats and gloves. The air is warm from braziers where the chestnut roasters stand shaking their baskets.

At the hotel, she lies beside Silva in bed.

"You are missing the sunlight, my dear friend," she says. "You are tired."

He turns to her on the pillow and strokes her hair. "You have done what you need to do?"

"I don't know," she says. "But thank you. Let us go back to your lovely island."

IN LISBON, Silva sits for long hours in the winter sun.

The next October, they observe a great number of shooting stars. They sit side by side on the villa's terrace at night. The sky is illuminated with extraordinary streaks of light. They stare, transfixed at the sight, surrounded by the beautiful anatomy of Silva's marble sculptures, the scents of lavender and plumeria.

Lina makes her way through many years of her journals, working to create a complete narrative from notes and lists of visitors, records of William's travels and purchases. Her silence—her failure to write anything at all about their daily lives—lasted almost eight years, those years now mostly lost to her by comparison with the years for which she has recordings in her daybooks.

Her hurt and her anger had been so great.

What had made her pick up her journals again, after so long? She considers the date on which her more recent entries begin, calculates, though her journals make no reference to it, that she must have begun to write again soon after her quarantine for the blindness that the doctor feared would afflict her forever. Perhaps it was the thought of losing the visible world that made her return to recording it: the day's weather; what had been served at dinner; shooting stars, comets, and partial eclipses; once, a bat in the chimney; any event, no matter how trivial, as if she felt the numbers of them before her diminishing.

She remembers William at her bedside playing the cello in the darkness, his head bent, his palm on her cheek. Remembers the snow on the bedclothes.

William had loved her. She had always known that. That had never been in question.

After years of silence in her daybooks, there is simply an entry, ordinary as anything, about a visit from Stanley and the boys at Observatory House for Sunday dinner, an order for a spring lamb, and an amount to be paid for ink.

That is how forgiveness is made, she thinks. Patiently.

SILVA DIES IN HIS SLEEP beside her one night after ten years together. When she wakes, his body is turned toward her, and she lies for a long time next to him, looking at his face, watching the beautiful light creep slowly across the ceiling until full sun lies across them.

It costs her a great deal to leave their bed.

When she stands at last to draw the sheet over his face, she finds she cannot do it.

She calls the servants, who help her to a chair beside the bed, Silva's hand still held in hers.

It is her only consolation that she believes he knew how much he gave her: that first night, unbraiding her hair. All the nights that followed.

Indeed. Her body had many uses, after all.

Hanover
1833–1848

NINETEEN

Light

Why, in the end, does she return to Hanover?

Why not remain in the sunlight in Lisbon surrounded by the comforts of Silva's villa? Why not go back to the familiar, lovely mists of England, to Observatory House or her little cottage?

At Hilda's bedside in the convent, leaning on a stick, Lina entertains the young postulants, ticking off the events of her and Hilda's long lifetimes for them: the great earthquake in Lisbon, the American War, the old French Revolution, the rise and fall of Napoleon, the development of the railroad and electric telegraph and gaslights, two kings crowned in England, and now the reign of Victoria begun.

The nuns hold their fingers before their mouths, amazed.

"We will live forever, two old monkeys," she tells Hilda, but in the corridors of the convent, Lina walks slowly through the bands of light and shadow, one hand on the wall to support her.

Sometimes, on nights when William sat at the forty-foot telescope for many hours, his voice in the speaking tube would startle her after a long silence.

"Lina? Are you there?"

"I am here," she would reply.

"Are you awake?" Teasing now.

"No."

His laughter then, coming from far away, among the stars.

At night from the window in Hanover she looks out at the moon. She can sit for many hours without moving.

William taught her that. Patience.

SHE GIVES HER COPIES of Flamsteed's volumes, along with the final star atlas, the catalog of omitted stars, and most of her papers and William's writings and books to the observatory at the university at Göttingen. There is a ceremony to acknowledge her gift, the years of her work, her and William's contributions to astronomy. She is feted and fussed over.

It is done now mostly, the last additions completed in Lisbon, the lives written down. Only the end remains.

But what is the end?

She lights twenty candles at the church when the Duke of Cumberland is pronounced the King of Hanover, and she feels, as a result of these political changes, finally and permanently separated from England.

She writes often to Stanley, closing always: *I send my great love to you and Sarah and the little boys.*

Stanley writes to her that the forty-foot telescope is in disrepair, that Mary has provided funds to have it restored, but that it is difficult for him to find workmen suited to the job.

It is strange to have the house still empty, he writes. *It is as if you will come back any day.*

There might have been a moment, after Silva died, when she could have returned to England. But she let it pass, she thinks, compelled by an impulse . . . to finish something she cannot articulate, or to find something. Now she is too old for such difficult travel. It was enough, she knows, to extricate herself from Lisbon, to reestablish herself, with the help of Leonard and one of her nieces, in Hanover. Everyone had thought her mad, undertaking such a move, but again, friends—a nephew of Silva's and his wife—assisted her, accompanied her.

She is held in esteem by many, friends and strangers alike, she understands, but she knows the measure of her worth, its extent and its limit.

In Hanover she is much alone. She often sleeps through the day and is awake at night.

She writes again to Stanley: *I made a mistake, coming back here.* But she does not mail this letter.

Instead she sends funds to have the forty-foot telescope dismantled and stored at Slough, along with what equipment remains, and the house purchased from Mary and given to Stanley, along with sufficient funds for its upkeep and their needs.

He and Sarah are glad to find a tenant to run their farm and to move into Observatory House instead. He has planted new trees in the orchard, he writes.

People still come to the house, he says, wanting to see where William Herschel and his famous sister lived and worked.

You are missed here, he writes.

SHE CANNOT EXPLAIN the emptiness in her she is trying to fill, nor why she feels there is some hope of comfort in Hanover.

The house she has taken is across the street from their old house. She wanted it, and Silva left her enough money that when she tells the occupants what she will offer for it, they move in a day's time.

She knows Silva would be horrified. The place is miserable in many ways. Small rooms. None of his beautiful sunlight. Yet she feels oddly at home.

The smells of the forests nearby and stable across the street are familiar. She feels, despite the loneliness of her days, as if she is being brought into greater proximity to the past, to her child-hood, and to William. The feeling excites her in a way that is deeply complicated and private; she both longs for it and then cannot bear it.

Her front windows overlook the wall of their old courtyard. From her bedroom window on the third floor, she has a clear view through the rooftops of the northern sky. She sees the tops of the trees in the orchard and, beyond them, the river.

Sometimes she walks across the street to their old courtyard and asks to sit on the bench outside.

SHE GOES TO THE CONVENT and sits beside the sleeping Hilda. "I am looking for my *Bruder*," she says aloud to no one.

IN 1835, when she is eighty-five years old, the Royal Society in England confers upon her its honorary membership. Three years later, she receives the diploma of membership of the Royal Irish Academy. In 1846, she is awarded the gold medal for science from the King of Prussia. It is sent to her, with compliments, through Baron Alexander von Humboldt. Two years later, when she is ninety-seven years old, the crown prince and princess of Hanover send her a velvet armchair.

"What shall I do with this?" she says to Betty, the young woman who comes every day to help her.

"Sit in it!" the maid says, bouncing upon the seat.

Sometimes when Lina looks at her hands, she is shocked by their condition, so old and twisted and knotted. William's hands had been beautiful, even at the end of his life, his fingers graceful. She remembers him holding up his index finger to stop her from interrupting him, remembers leaning over and swatting away his hand.

At her house in Hanover, admirers occasionally come to call, and she dresses carefully on these occasions in readiness for visitors.

When guests appear, Betty brings tea and coffee.

She writes in her daybook on December 30, 1839: *In the afternoon Fraulein S. came to see me, but she is deaf. I talked with her for a couple of hours without either of us being the wiser.*

She writes, *O, why did I leave England?*

She remembers: owls in the meadow; Stanley on a ladder in the orchard, picking pears; William, thirty feet in the air, looking though the telescope; the ocean of stars—above and below, reflected in the water—from Silva's terrace. She remembers Silva's hands, their gentleness on her face.

WITH HER LITTLE TELESCOPE, she watches one year an eclipse of the moon, and the next year, two comets. Many evenings she studies the moon, William's circuses. She imagines the Lunarians' gleaming white metropolises, their inky-dark forests, their deserts and lakes.

It is always a comfort to glance out the window and see the moon there. Yet she has a question she is trying to formulate, something she wants to know.

She needs very little for herself and Betty: a few tables and chairs stained like mahogany, a few chairs with cane bottoms. A bedstead and bedding. A clothespress, a glass globe, a black Wedgwood slop bucket, a cupboard with tea things for company: milk pot, tumblers, cups and saucers, a cake basket, sugar tongs. Four plated candlesticks. A dressing glass.

For many years after her return to Hanover, she takes a daily walk. The owners of the Herschels' old house become accustomed to seeing her open the gate—as if she still lived there—and cross the courtyard, making her way down into the orchard toward the river, leaning on a stick. They do not disturb her.

One day the youngest child from the family, a little girl with black curls, comes running after her; they have found in a cupboard an old almanac that belonged to William. His name is written inside.

The child holds it up to her.

Lina presses it against her breast with one hand, trembles upon her stick.

The child waits for a moment, and then runs away back up the hill through the flowering trees.

LINA REMEMBERS WHEN PIGS were forbidden in the streets of Hanover. Now oxen and cows are also not allowed. Yet she crosses the street between her new house and their old family courtyard fearfully, for such an undertaking is more dangerous than it once was. There are so many carts and carriages.

Now there are some days when Betty comes and Lina cannot rise from bed.

She wants only to sleep.

She remembers the ringing of the bells, the muffle of snowfall in winter, the calls of children skating on the *Stadtgraben*. She remembers the nightwomen who came to collect the waste. She remembers the beadle, summoned to move along beggars who lingered. She remembers her mother, the smells of making soap and candles for the household. She remembers her mother's angry face, the hard bump of her pregnant belly, remembers her hands, pushing Lina away.

Don't do that.

One day she wakes and dresses and feels full of a worried, inchoate urgency. Betty hurries to bring tea and soup, and Lina gets up and dresses and walks down through the orchard to the river and stamps her stick into the ground and feels a bleak rage at a childhood so unhappy.

But it does not last.

Gentleness comes upon her almost as quickly, William's hand brushing her cheek as he took his farewell that night during her blindness.

The surprise of it. This, *this*. Here it is, after all. She can *choose* what to remember. Summon it. She closes her eyes in relief, this gentleness to replace the old hurt. It is what she has been waiting for. She had not known she could ask for it.

That night she lies on her side, knees drawn up as she had done as a child, and thinks of William holding up his arms to her when he had helped her to sit on the branch of an apple tree.

She is lifted to his shoulders, and he carries her away into the moonlight by the river.

Her father holds her against his chest, her ear to his heartbeat, his hand stroking her hair.

There is the scent of Silva, her forehead pressed to his soft back at night in bed.

Then she is standing on the roof of the old laundry in Slough, and a fox barks across the frozen meadow. The moon is full above her head. The stars carve fantastic shapes into the darkness.

Worlds within worlds are in all things.

ONE EVENING IN DECEMBER, the black-haired child finds Lina seated on the bench swept clear of snow in the courtyard after nightfall.

The night is very cold, and the old woman is breathing hard, and her eyes are wide with distress. Both hands are clenched on her stick.

"Did you see that man just now?" she asks the child. She shrinks down on the bench and makes a face, eyes like slits under her frilled white cap. "A little dark-faced man? I was sure I saw a man go into the stable."

"No one's there, missus," the child says. "I was just in there. Only the old horse, Jango, is there. You know him."

"I had a bad brother," the old woman says. "Someone told me that he was found strangled in the cemetery."

The child's eyes widen. "We heard about that," she says.

The old woman shakes her head.

The child holds out her hand. "Do you want to go home, missus?"

The old lady looks around. "Where are the others?" she says.

"I don't know," the child says. "What others?"

The old woman looks up at her. Then her eyes move past the child's face to the sky.

"Do you know the stars?" the woman says. She points with her stick, traces shapes: horse and fish, swan and dragon.

Then she falls quiet.

The child sits down beside her.

"Your mother is kind to you?" the old lady asks.

"I love my mother," the child says. *Ich liebe meine Mutter.*

The lady nods. "That's good.

"I had another brother, my brother William," she adds after a time. "We used to sit here on this very bench, and he would show me the stars. I loved him very much."

The child is quiet, looking up at the sky.

After a while the old lady stands up. "Now I'm ready," she says, and holds out her hand. The child takes it and sees her across the street.

At the door, the old lady leans down. "Give me a kiss."

The child obliges.

"Thank you, my dear," the old lady says.

· · ·

SHE LIES IN HER BED that night, breathing hard. Betty the servant and various Herschel relatives gather round. Fans are supplied. Tea is brought.

"I'm sleepy," someone says.

"Hush," says someone else.

At midnight, Lina turns her head at an odd angle on the pillow, as if trying to see something.

"It's the moon," someone says. "The moon at the window."

Someone else says, "Let her see it."

Hands are beneath her, turning her, until her face is full of moonlight.

"Look. She's calmer now," someone says.

Lina does not leave her house again.

IT IS JANUARY. Snow lies deep and undisturbed in the fields and weighs down the boughs of the fir trees in the forest. Fresh snow falls now on the procession as it moves through the streets, the cold mourners gathering their cloaks about them. The churchyard has been kept warm by fires, and the ground is muddy. Above the shimmering radiance of their heat, a few snowflakes whirl.

The retinue that follows Lina's body to the churchyard of the *Gartengemeinde* includes the royal carriages. Garlands of laurel and cypress and palm branches, sent by the Crown Princess from Herrenhausen, adorn the coffin. The service is held in the same garrison church where Lina was christened and confirmed nearly a century earlier.

The slab has been carved with an inscription supplied by her servant, Betty, who reported that her mistress had made a draft of the words, her exact age, of course, left blank.

The gaze of her who has passed to glory was, while below, turned to the starry Heaven; her own Discoveries of Comets and her share in the immortal labours of her brother, William Herschel, bear witness of this to later ages. The Royal Irish Academy of Dublin and the Royal Astronomical Society in London numbered her among their members. At the age of ninety-seven years 10 months she fell asleep in happy peace, and in full possession of her faculties; following to a better life her father, Isaac Herschel, who lived to the age of sixty years two months seventeen days and lies buried near this spot since the 25th March, 1767.

With her in the grave, according to her instructions, is the old almanac that had been William's. Her head rests on a pillow of lavender brought from Lisbon.

BY NIGHTFALL, the snow has stopped.

The skies have cleared, revealing the magnificent Pleiades high in the sky. Gemini and Orion appear in the east. The great king, blazing Jupiter, accompanied by its attendant moons, slowly makes its magnificent march across the heavens among legions of stars.

The black-haired child across the street had followed the impressive retinue through the streets to the churchyard earlier in the day, but she'd felt afraid of the group of mourners and the coffin, and sad about the old lady, and she'd gone home.

That night she lies in her bed and looks out the window.

She thinks of the old lady sitting on the bench in their courtyard, pointing out the constellations with her stick.

"You're not afraid of the dark, are you?" the old lady had said.

"No, I'm not," the child had said.

"That's good," the old lady had said.

The child had leaned against her. In truth, she *was* afraid of the dark.

"You understand that the stars are always here," the old lady said. "They do not go away in the day. It is that we can *see* them only in the dark. That is the good thing about the dark."

The child had looked up at her.

"Let whatever shines be noted," the old lady said. "That is the Royal Astronomical Society's motto."

She was quiet. Then she took the child's hand. "Let us look always toward the light," she said.

The child gazed up at the old lady for a moment, and then she turned away and tilted back her head to take in the sight of the stars above them. "Our companions," the old lady had called them, "on the long road."

"All right," said the child. "We will."

ACKNOWLEDGMENTS
─────────────

Fortunately for the world, brother and sister William and Caroline Herschel left remarkable and detailed records of their lives in the form of letters, lists, catalogs, journals, musings, "day books," and scientific papers. The habit of such recordkeeping is not unusual, either for the Herschels' time or in general among people who believe their work holds implications for history, and indeed, the Herschels', especially William's, investigations into astronomy were proven to be of great significance to the world's understanding of the universe, both then and now. History is often recorded in words as well as deeds.

Extraordinary people individually and together, William and Caroline—divided by the twelve years between them and by their different genders but united in so many other ways, including their great affection for each other—were active correspondents and chroniclers of their separate and combined scientific endeavors and achievements, as well as the more prosaic details of their daily domestic experience. A scholar in search of the story of their lives will find no shortage of material, written both by the Herschels themselves and, as the years progressed, by others— scientists and biographers—who understood the significance and scale of their contributions to astronomy, and who worked with diligence and skill to produce narratives that reflect the fullness of the lives of these two singularly fascinating people and their place in scientific history.

I am grateful first for William's and Caroline's shared habit of letter writing and of keeping records of their experience, and especially for Caroline's effort later in her life to fashion a narrative from the deep and rich trove of material left by her brother and contained in her own notebooks. Historians and novelists are fortunate when the subjects of their interest leave behind richly furnished rooms so easily explored and from which a story can be understood.

So it is first to William and Caroline themselves that I owe the greatest debt, not only for the inspiration of the remarkable story of their relationship, one perhaps unparalleled in scientific history, but also for their generosity toward those who would come after them and wish to understand what it had been like for them to work side by side, as William once said, in the "laboratories of the universe."

A historian seeking to understand the Herschels' lives would approach their story very differently than I have done, though we might depend on many of the same sources for information. Historical novels hove to varying degrees of factual "truth" about their particular subject or place or time, according to the writers and their concerns. It is Caroline's life in which I have been chiefly interested for the years of my work on this novel. In telling her story in *The Stargazer's Sister,* I have made several deviations—some minor, some dramatic—from the historical record, sometimes for purposes of narrative design and sometimes out of an impulse to shape the material for purposes other than historical accuracy. The character of Dr. Silva and his relationship with Caroline is entirely invented, for instance, and various chronologies and details of the Herschel family or William's scientific work or his and Caroline's movements from house to house have been collapsed or altered or compressed. Stanley is an entirely invented character, for instance, as is Sir Henry Spencer, though William in fact had many friends among the British aristocracy.

William Herschel and Mary Pitt had a son, Sir John Herschel, who went on to become an astronomer of great importance in his own right, but the fact of his existence has been omitted from this story. William and Caroline's brothers played a role in their astronomical endeavors, though to a lesser degree than Caroline or William himself, obviously, but they appear only as minor characters in this novel.

In some cases I have used Caroline's or William's words—written or spoken—exactly as they are reported by various sources; in some cases I have changed those words slightly, and for much of the novel, of course, the dialogue is entirely invented. In any case, when I used their actual words I tried to do so in a way that represented circumstances and motivations accurately.

The dates of some historical events have been altered for chronological consistency or compression within the novel (such as the date of the Battle of Hastenbeck, for instance). I likewise made changes to the scene in which the Herschel family views a partial solar eclipse in a tub of water in their courtyard in Hanover. This event occurred, in fact, in 1764, later than I have presented it in the novel, and while in the novel William explains the phenomenon for his family, he was not actually present for it. Likewise, William's discovery of the sixth and seventh moons of Saturn were separated by nearly a month, but in the novel they occur on the same night.

The epigraph to Penelope Fitzgerald's extraordinary historical novel *The Blue Flower* comes from the poet known as Novalis, who is the novel's protagonist: "Novels arise out of the shortcomings of history." Writing on *The Blue Flower* (and other novels) in *The Nearest Thing to Life*, James Wood argues that it is the specific and extraordinary feat of fiction to "rescue those private moments that history would never have been able to record . . . when we read historical fiction the characters take on lives of their own, and begin to detach themselves in our minds from the actuality of the historical record. When characters in historical novels die, they die as fictional characters, not as historical personages." In *The Stargazer's Sister,* I have sought to illuminate those "private moments" unrecorded by history. Yet for all the changes—inventions and omissions—to the historical record of William's and Caroline's lives, I wanted to capture the truth of what has felt to me from the first most intriguing and most moving about Caroline's life: that she clearly loved her brother, that she admired him and served him and his endeavors with unquestionable loyalty and intelligence . . . and that her devotion was not without complexity and perhaps sometimes cost for her. Her life ran alongside his, and their parallel tracks were rarely divided by distance of any significance in terms of time or space, but their lives were not the same life, and for all their closeness, their experiences occurred in very different universes.

In September 1798, Caroline wrote to Dr. Nevil Maskelyne, England's royal astronomer from 1765 to 1811, from her and William's home in Slough, England. She wished, she said, to thank Dr. Maskelyne for his support in seeing printed her index to John Flamsteed's famous star catalog, at the time among the most complete atlases of the night sky since Tycho Brahe's catalog of the 1500s. The letter contains a paragraph that shows exactly the degree to which Caroline understood that her and her brother's lives, for all their closeness, were both regarded and influenced and shaped by the conventions of the times and by prevailing notions about men and women. Caroline was born in 1750; if she had been born one hundred or two hundred years later, of course, her life would have been very different indeed.

"Your having thought it worthy of the press has flattered my vanity not a little," she wrote to Maskelyne about his interest in her index. "You see, sir, I do own myself to be vain, because I would not wish to be singular; and was there ever a woman without vanity? Or a man either? Only with this difference, that among gentlemen the commodity is generally styled ambition."

This careful bit of wit contains an important clue to Caroline's understanding of the world's perception of her role in her brother's life.

THOSE WHO WISH TO READ about the Herschels will find ample material, and I am much indebted to the following works for the light they helped shed on the significance of William's and Caroline's contributions to astronomy and overall to the world in which they lived and worked.

Two volumes in particular provided helpful and substantive records of the Herschels' lives.

The Herschel Chronicle: The Life-Story of William Herschel and His Sister Caroline Herschel, edited by William's granddaughter Constance A. Lubbock (Cambridge University Press, 1933), uses letters, Caroline's journals, and various selections from among William's writings, including his scientific papers "On the Construction of the Heavens" and "On Nebulous Stars."

Caroline's papers are contained under the title *Memoir and Correspondence of Caroline Herschel,* compiled by Mary Cornwallis, the wife of John Herschel, William's only son. As she writes in her introduction to the volume, "Great men and great causes have always some helper of whom the outside world knows but little. There always is, and always has been, some human being in whose life their roots have been nourished. Sometimes these helpers have been men, sometimes they have been women, who have given themselves to help and to strengthen those called upon to be leaders and workers, inspiring them with courage, keeping faith in their own idea alive, in days of darkness . . . These helpers and sustainers, men or women, have all the same quality in common—absolute devotion and unwavering faith in the individual or in the cause. Seeking nothing for themselves, thinking nothing of themselves, they have all an intense power of sympathy, a noble love of giving themselves for the service of others, which enables them to transfuse the force of their own personality into the object to which they dedicate their powers.

"Of this noble company of unknown helpers Caroline Herschel was one."

Mary Cornwallis's sensitive and perceptive reading of Caroline's writing and correspondence creates a nuanced portrait of Caroline that was immensely helpful to me.

I am indebted as well to the work of many others who have written about the Herschels, chiefly Michael Hoskin, perhaps the foremost scholar of the Herschels' lives, who has written voluminously about both William and Caroline. I relied heavily on his work *Discoverers of the Universe: William and Caroline Herschel,* published in 2011 by Princeton University Press. It is my hope that should he ever read this novel, he would appreciate the story's deviations from the historical record and see in my changes to that record an altered but not unrecognizable truth.

Also invaluable to me were *The Georgian Star: How William and Caroline Herschel Revolutionized Our Understanding of the Cosmos* by Michael D. Lemonick. This book, released in 2004, is among the titles in the Great Discoveries series published by W. W. Norton & Company. In addition, *The Comet Sweeper: Caroline Herschel's Astronomical Ambition* by Claire Brock, published by Icon Books in 2007, offered further insights into Caroline's life. Richard Holmes's marvelous *The Age of Wonder: How the Romantic Generation Discovered the Beauty and Terror of Science* was hugely helpful in its portraits of several figures from the scientific revolution of the later part of the eighteenth century. There are likely few better sources than Holmes's brilliant book for capturing the excitement of that period, and the figures of genius, wit, and bravery who characterized that era.

Another volume vastly useful to me, especially for an understanding of Caroline's early years, was *Flesh and Spirit: Private Life in Early Modern Germany* by Steven Ozment.

Of additional assistance were several small books—by Patrick Moore, Frank Brown, Michael Hoskin, and Brian Warner— prepared for The William Herschel Society, which maintains The William Herschel Museum in Bath.

I owe a great debt of gratitude to the indefatigable Dr. Tom Michalik, retired Professor of Physics from Randolph College in Lynchburg, Virginia, for his vast knowledge and experience as an astronomer and for his skillful, painstaking, enthusiastic, and patient review of the manuscript and his advice about many scientific aspects of the novel. Any errors of that sort remaining are mine alone. He did his best with me.

Edd Jennings—man of many talents—was also an attentive and kind and informed reader, and his letters to me about the manuscript were thoughtful and full of rich detail.

Many graduate students at the University of Virginia were generous about sharing their knowledge with me over the years at the university's McCormick Observatory.

A trip to Bath, England, and the surprisingly modest Herschel house and museum there helped me envision more clearly the years Caroline and William spent on New King Street in Bath.

Jennifer Brice—gifted writer, sympathetic reader, dear friend—heroically read multiple drafts of the novel. I am deeply grateful to her for the comfort and joy of her companionship, and for her continued faith, interest, and patience over the decade of my work on the story, as well as her endless store of good advice and her empathetic understanding of Caroline's life.

My daughter Molly McCully Brown was a faithful—and attentive and sensitive—reader of various revisions, and her suggestions were enormously helpful. Her deft touch informs many important scenes in the novel.

To my brilliant editor, Deb Garrison, and my wise, faithful agent, Lisa Bankoff: my eternal gratitude.

To Pantheon and all its employees: I am honored to have a seat at the table. Thank you for helping to bring Caroline into the world in this way.

To my husband, John Gregory Brown, first and last and best reader, who over the many years of my work on the novel told me no, no, no, no, no, and then, at last, yes, I dedicate this book, as I have all the others, with my enduring gratitude, admiration, and love.

ABOUT THE AUTHOR

Carrie Brown is the author of seven novels and a collection of short stories. She has won many awards for her work, including a National Endowment for the Arts fellowship, the Barnes and Noble Discover Award, the Janet Heidinger Kafka Prize, The Great Lakes Book Award, and, twice, the Library of Virginia Award for fiction. Her short fiction and essays have appeared in many literary journals. She and her husband, the novelist John Gregory Brown, live in Massachusetts, where they teach at Deerfield Academy.

A NOTE ON THE TYPE

This book was set in a modern adaptation of a type designed
by the first William Caslon (1692–1766). The Caslon face, an
artistic, easily read type, has enjoyed more than two centuries
of popularity in the English-speaking world. This version with
its even balance and honest letterforms was designed by Carol
Twombly for the Adobe Corporation and released in 1990.

Typeset by Scribe, Philadelphia, Pennsylvania
Printed and bound by Berryville Graphics, Berryville, Virginia
Designed by Jaclyn Whalen